The Human-Born Era
Book 1

The Dyslexic Friendly Edition

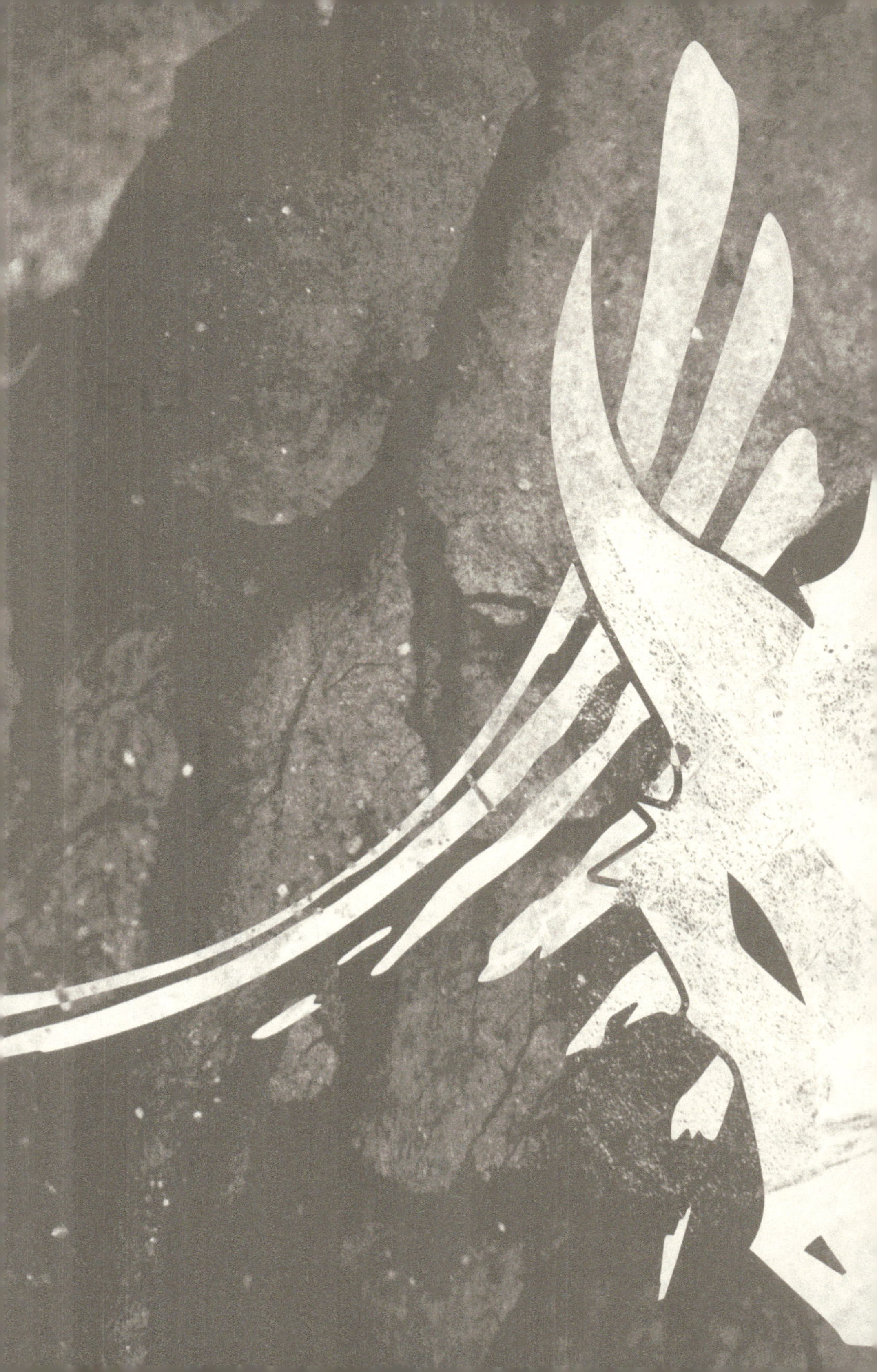

The Human-Born Era
Book 1

The RISE of The RAIDIN

The Dyslexic Friendly Edition

Text copyright © 2021 by Susan L. Markloff

Library of Congress Control Number: 2021917358

ISBN 978-1-956542-00-4 (standard edition)
ISBN 978-1-956542-01-1 (dyslexic-friendly edition)
ISBN 978-1-956542-02-8 (ebook)

Printed in the United States of America

First Paperback Edition

Book Cover Design by Gabrielle Ragusi
Character & Bestiary Designs by Michaella Barnum

www.susanlmarkloff.com

12 11 10 9 8 7 6 5 4 3

To Jon and Josh,

Without whom I never would have
been brave enough to consider
writing this story.

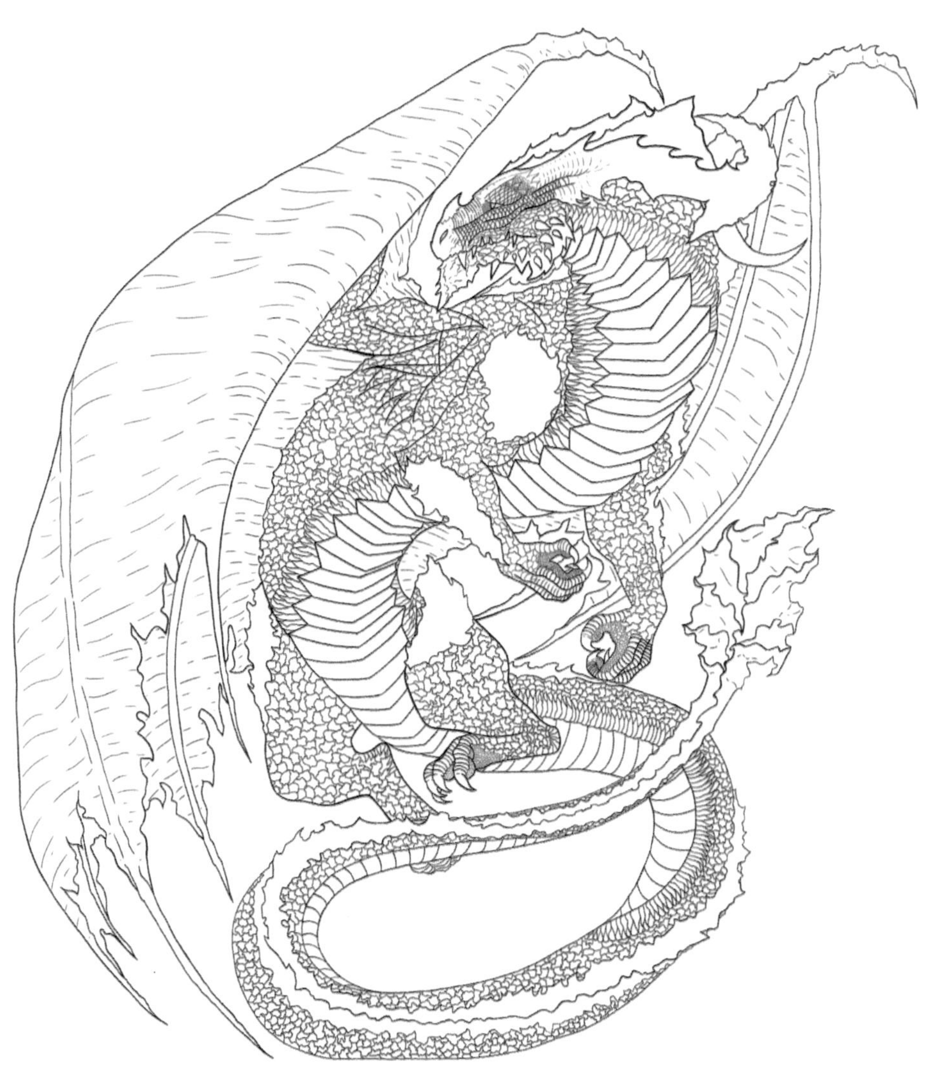

A Note on This Edition

This Dyslexic-Friendly Edition of **The Human-Born Era: The Rise of the Raidin** has been made possible by the people who developed the font you see here.

"OpenDyslexic" is a free source font that anyone may download to their computer, and freely use for personal, business, commercial, book, ebook, and website use. If you find that this font helps you (or someone you know who suffers from dyslexia), please be sure to let myself know, and let the team of developers know!

Donations to their cause, along with an avenue for questions or comments about the font can be found at https://opendyslexic.org

A special thank you to my amazing sister-in-law, Dr. Mallory Markloff, for introducing me to Open-Dyslexic, further making this edition possible for the enjoyment of my readers.

I wish you happy reading friends!

All the best,

Susan L Markloff

Pronuncation Guide

Agerius: ah-jeer-ee-us

Ar'on: are-on

Aros: air-os

Bratak'ra: brah-tak-ra

Caliga: kal-eh-ga

Cregorous: kreg-or-os

Ferveos: fer-vay-os

Kaldok: kal-dock

Krelien: krey-lin

Preliator: prey-lee-a-tor

Raidin: raid-in

Tilion: till-ee-on

Tyron: tie-ron

Zaheri: za-heer-eye

Table of Contents

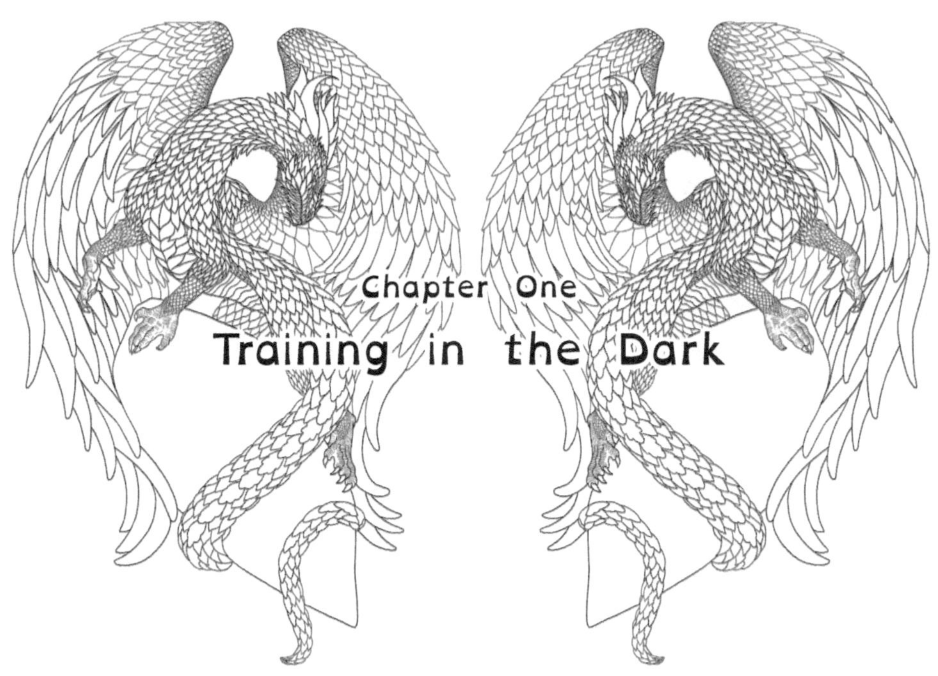

Training in the Dark

Ar'on smacked her shoulder with his wooden practice sword, and she let out a yelp, hopping a little toward the side to avoid any further hits. He frowned and rolled his eyes with a small shake of his head. An exasperated sigh left him as he let his arms fall, the sword rocking back and forth in his loose grip.

"You're still not guarding properly," Tyron said from the corner of the room, his arms crossed as he surveyed his charge's progress. He resisted the urge to remind her, again, that she was supposed to focus on her opponent's movements.

Rolling her eyes, Jennifer Monroe rubbed her wounded shoulder as she looked over at Tyron. "You're having me train with a wooden sword; what could this possibly teach me about fighting with energy?" She was only eighteen, still young in any hybrid's eyes, but picked up fighting tactics faster than he would have anticipated, especially considering she had only been aware of her abilities as a Human-Born for a little over a year.

She was short and athletically built, but never would he consider her tiny. Her medium-length brown hair framed her face, sometimes obscuring her hazel eyes when her bangs got too long. She usually had her hair hidden under a baseball cap when she trained to keep the locks from flying into her face.

Tyron's gaze hardened as he pushed himself off the wall and made his way to the middle of the room where they stood. "It's not about the weapon." He took the practice sword from Ar'on, and the elder warrior stepped aside as the Team Leader took his place. "It's about how you wield it. Your energy is a part of you, and any good swordsman will tell you that a blade is an extension of themselves. The great ones learn to treat it like a part of their bodies. You need to learn to do the same in order to keep your power in check."

"In check of what?" She shrugged. "I thought I was wielding it pretty well." To accentuate her point, she held her left hand out and twinged her fingers a bit as smokey blue tendrils flew around her digits.

Flicking the tip of his sword at her hand, Tyron smacked her and the energy dissipated.

"Hey—"

"You don't have full control of it yet. Being so lackadaisical about it will only lull you into a false sense of confidence. That's the worst thing you could do."

Jen let out a disgruntled sigh. "What harm could it possibly do?"

"That's a loaded question."

"It wasn't a question."

"It sounded like one," Tyron said as he lifted his sword.

Mirroring his stance, she was quiet for a few seconds before she said, "I really do want to know."

"You *might* hurt yourself, or someone else, or you could blow something up for all we know," he said as he jabbed forward. With a *clack, clack, clack,* the wood met in succession as he gently pushed her backward. Jen hopped with each movement fluidly, just as she had seen on shows and in movies. A simple movement. He was testing her on something, but she didn't know what.

"I can't blow things up," she said sarcastically. When Tyron didn't respond or move, she jutted her sword forward. He countered, and she pushed forward again, trying to force him backward. He kept his feet grounded, and despite her efforts to move him, he blocked each of her blows effortlessly and sent her stumbling back.

"We don't know that," he said as the wood clanked with each hit.

"You don't know anything about my energy," she retorted, getting ever angrier as he calmly and easily deflected her attacks.

He wasn't breaking a sweat, but she could feel her pulse beginning to speed up, trying to get some movement out of him. Every now and then, she might cause him to lean back slightly, but his feet never moved. She could swear not a single hair on his head shifted. Jen felt like she was dancing around, trying to find his vulnerable spot.

A smile tugged at his lips as he watched her

struggle. "We know that it's just like ours, but stronger. That being said, you should learn the basics. No one's above the basics."

Her frustration bubbling, Jen jabbed forward and let out a small yell. Tyron side-stepped and brought his blade around, smacking her in the back with little effort. He didn't hold back on the power behind his hit, though.

He wasn't going easy on her. He never did. Clearly, he had never learned to not hit girls when he was growing up.

As Jen fell to her knees and let out a hiss, he said, "No one here would doubt for a second that you're powerful, Jen. But all that means is that your energy needs to be treated with even more care than a normal hybrid."

She glared at him from over her shoulder. "Was that necessary?"

"You're not thinking through your attacks." He placed the tip of the sword on the ground and leaned against the hilt. "You're just...flailing the weapon at your enemy, hoping it'll connect. You're not actually taking in their advantages or disadvantages. It's like your mentality is that you'll wear them down."

"Maybe that method works," she said, gritting her teeth as she stood. Gently touching her back, she felt the muscles flinch at her soft inspection. It was going to bruise, and badly. She hated that he never held back. He never treated her like a fragile human.

Sure, fine, she wasn't a fragile human, but it still hurt to be whacked with the full strength of a Chief Master of the Agerian Defense.

Tyron tilted his head slightly and scrunched his face. "Mm, that's not likely."

"Look, it works in video games," she said, dead-pan.

He sniggered. "Right, because that's the best argument for why things should work in *reality*." He closed the distance between them and snatched the sword from her. Turning around, he walked to the far wall and put the swords back on the racks.

"Did you have to hit *me* so hard?" she whined.

"A little bruising never killed anyone," Ar'on said from his spot in the corner.

"Easy for you to say."

The elder hybrid grinned, an action that show-cased his wrinkles most prominently, and said, "Trust me when I say that I've had *my* fair share of sore mornings."

"Sure you have."

"We're going to keep working on this," Tyron proclaimed, walking back toward her. "These methods will help you learn how to focus what you're doing and why you're doing it. You can't just go shooting your energy around like a leaf in the wind."

Jen let out a short breath before she said, "Hypothetical question."

"Okay..."

"Let's say there are enemies around, and only enemies. And, like, you're not there. And no one's there. And it's just me."

"Jen," Tyron said with a slightly bored look.

"Let's just say I'm alone, and I get attacked. And there's no one around that could get hurt." She shrugged. "What's to say I can't just unleash some energy then?"

Tyron glanced at Ar'on before returning his gaze to her. "I'm not saying never use your energy. I'm saying you need to learn how to properly wield it so you don't hurt yourself or anyone else."

She glanced at the swords hanging on the wall and asked as she pointed at them, "And those will help with that?"

With a nod, he said, "Yes." As she opened her mouth to say something, he held up a finger and added, "With time and practice."

As though he were asking her to do a dance recital in front of the whole school, she grumbled, "Fine."

"You'll thank me for this, eventually." Glancing at his watch, he continued, "All right, it's almost two. You'd better get home and get some sleep before—"

"Tyron!"

All three of them turned toward the doorway where a five-foot tall, tan grovix, named Archer, skidded to a stop just past the threshold. Archer had a more canine structure to his face, with big ears that sat erect on his head, and large feet. Jen had never asked, but she thought it was fair to guess that Archer's weight rivaled a lion's.

"There's a Ferveos loose," Archer said.

"What?" Tyron asked, pulling his brow together.

There was a swirl of silver dust, and a lean man appeared in front of the grovix, lackadaisically holding a tablet. Called a Jumper, he had the ability to shift into and out of the third and fifth dimensions. He used it in a cavalier manner, frequently choosing to close the distance between floors rather than towns. Krelien easily could be called the most fashionable of the group and, without a doubt, the shortest.

"Hey, there's a Ferveos out in a cow field."

"Hey, dingus, I said I would get them," Archer barked.

"Obviously, not fast enough," Krelien said with a smirk. He turned back toward the others. "It's like fifteen miles from here."

The Alpha Team Leader flitted his eyes around the room for a moment before he turned to Jen, who stared at him apprehensively. A little uneasily, Tyron asked her, "You up for slaying a dragon?"

Two thirty in the morning was not an ideal time to be out and about on the back of a motorcycle, especially when it was early November in Eastern Pennsylvania. The air was bitingly chilly. Coupled with the speed in which they traveled, it would have caused a normal person to probably freeze to death.

When Tyron had decided to bring her along for the dragon slaying, something she had only ever been a spectator for in the past, Jen had thought he would choose to take something practical, like a car. Instead, when they walked out of the antique shop that was the team's headquarters, Tyron had walked over to his motorcycle.

As he had thrown a helmet to her and saw her displeased look, he'd said, "Learn how to block out the cold."

Jen had begrudgingly situated herself behind Tyron on the motorcycle and said, "We haven't seen a

Ferveos in almost a year. Why do you think there's one loose now?"

The engine had been kicked to life as Tyron responded, "For kicks and giggles?"

"That's not a serious answer."

"I didn't say it was." Without another word, he had taken off.

Their resident werewolf, Kaldok, had provided them with the coordinates for the last location that the dragon had been seen. The team had a setup of little beacons, of a nearly three-hundred-mile radius of their location, that would alert them to the presence of any enemy fighters. That distance covered almost all of Pennsylvania, New York, New Jersey, and chunks of Maryland, and Jen was pretty sure that radius was the extent of their travels in their eighteen years on Earth.

In the last year and a half that she had known them, they had never seemed to be more than a half-hour's distance from her, even when she was at school.

Though she hated to admit it, Tyron had been right. The biting cold had been treacherous on her fingers when they had taken off. She knew that she had the ability to essentially raise or lower her body temperature, and this was a prime opportunity to get better at that.

The motorcycle was slowed down, and Tyron killed the headlight as he pulled the bike off to the side of the road. He said nothing as he parked, and she took the cue to stretch her sense of hearing. It took a few seconds, but she soon heard it—leathery wings, giant feet, and ripping skin.

As she removed her helmet, Archer came up to

the two of them with another grovix at his side. The other large creature had more feline features and stood almost a foot shorter than her team member. With a pristine white coat, a picture-perfect mane, dainty paws, and vibrant red eyes, Blaze commanded attention, whether it was wanted or not, upon entering a room.

"I thought you might never sense the beast with how quickly you chose to move," Blaze said, her voice low.

"Do you...have to drive...so fast?" Archer panted out heavily, with a whine between gasps.

Tyron shushed them as he pulled his helmet off. Absentmindedly, he ruffled his hair, trying to force the short brown locks into a neater fashion than the helmet had allowed. Jen did likewise, thankful that none of her Zaheri cared what she looked like.

From the other side of the road, a loud whisper sounded, "Why'd we stop?"

Tyron rolled his eyes at the sky, and Blaze yipped in a disapproving manner, while Archer stifled a snort.

Krelien walked out from behind the tree line and said, still in a far-too-loud whisper, "I just don't get why we were practically yeeting, only to suddenly stop. I think Kaldok's in the next state by now."

"Would you be quiet?" Tyron reprimanded in a hushed anger through his gritted teeth.

Krelien leaned back a bit and held up his hands defensively. "Y'know, next time I forget the coffee, just make me go back for it."

"Yes, naturally, that is the reason for which Tyron is irate with you," Blaze whispered, glaring at Krelien.

The younger hybrid scrunched his brow a bit. "Why else would he be mad at me?"

Sometimes, Jen thought his idiocy was on purpose. This time, she wasn't entirely sure.

He took the sniper rifle that was slung across his shoulder and placed the barrel on the ground, leaning against the butt of the weapon. "For reality, why'd we stop?"

"The phrase is *for reals*," Jen corrected. "And you used yeet wrong. And we stopped because the Ferveos is over there." She pointed to the right. From what she could tell, despite the dense fog, there was a large field where some faint mooing could still be heard, presumably from cows dropped there from a nearby pasture. The smell of manure made her nose wrinkle, and Jen decided that she would focus on the scent of the frost clinging to the grass.

Straightening, Krelien glanced at Tyron then back to Jen before he said, "Good for you—hearing that far away."

"Thanks, Teach," the teenager said with a grin.

Tyron's phone buzzed and he fished it out of his pocket to read the text message that had popped up. Jen leaned around him to read it, and he glanced back at her before he put the phone away. "Ar'on's in place. We can start to move forward."

As they all began to slowly head into the field, Tyron waved the two grovix toward the right, and with the soft pad-falls, the four-legged creatures ran into the fog and disappeared. It always amazed Jen how quiet they could be, even Archer with his massive paws.

"Where do you want me?" Krelien whispered at Tyron's left.

"Rendezvous with Ar'on. Kaldok's in position exactly opposite of here. I'll keep an eye on her from this position," Tyron hushed back.

"You're the goat," Krelien said with a mock salute.

Tyron wrinkled his brow as he looked at him. When Krelien was a few feet away, Tyron then glanced to Jen and asked, "That couldn't be right. Is that right?"

Jen shrugged. "No, yeah, he's right."

"You humans and your weird sayings..."

The two of them crouched forward until they reached a stone wall that was about three feet high. Ducking behind it, Tyron took in a deep breath, and Jen stared at him with anticipation.

"All right, so here's the rules of this," he started.

"Yes!" Jen whispered victoriously.

He gave her a disapproving look, and she quieted herself.

"Kaldok is directly across the field from us. Blaze and Archer are to your right, while Ar'on and Krelien will be to your left. I'll be right here. The point of this isn't that you kill it by yourself; the point is that you begin to understand just how dangerous these guys are. I'm going to let you try to kill it by yourself. The key word is *let*. As in, I'm *letting* you try this, and if I think you don't have control of the situation—"

"Yes, yes, yes, I got it," she said impatiently.

He grabbed her jittery arm to focus her. "Jen, I'm serious. This isn't a game."

"I got it, I do. Seriously, I completely understand the danger that is happening right now."

There was silence for a couple seconds before Tyron said, "You're sure about this?"

A grin came to her face. "Definitely."

He peeked his head over the wall and glanced at the Ferveos before he returned his attention to her.

She clasped her hands and said in a pleading, whiny voice, "Please?"

He then glanced to the sky and frowned a little as he raised his hand, gesturing toward the beast.

As she began to rise from her position, he snatched her arm. "Be careful."

"Yeah, thanks for that, Sherlock," Jen quipped. She didn't wait to see his frustrated glare as she straightened.

She hopped over the fence and landed with the slightest bit of noise before she inched toward the creature. In the fog, it was hard to tell exactly how big this dragon was. She knew that Ferveos could be nearly twenty-five-feet tall with a wingspan of about twenty feet. Her spatial reasoning wasn't stellar, and it was hunched over, so determining how big it was would prove difficult.

Its bulk didn't matter. Not really. A dragon was a dragon in her book. She had to find a way to incapacitate it, immobilize it or, best option, kill it. Head, throat, heart; three main points would be her aim.

She tried to recall the diagram of the inside of a dragon. All that came to mind was a bleary exhaustion as Ar'on pointed at the various points with a muffled sort of "wah, wah" Charlie Brown level noise.

Dang, she really needed to pay better attention.

No matter. She could do this. She had seen her Zaheri take out a Ferveos before. Sure, it had been about a year since that had happened. But the memory was clear for her. At least, clearer than the classroom diagram.

She remembered being a little scared at the sound of the Ferveos' roar and slapping her hands over her ears. She remembered that it hadn't seemed to take much time. She remembered that they hadn't needed to use their guns. She could do this. Her Zaheri had taken it out with relative ease, she thought. And she was stronger than her Zaheri. That had to account for something.

The scales on the Ferveos were dark; ranges of blacks and greys all over its body. Its wings were pulled along its body, curled up against its sides. She could still hear the air rustle through them and the leathery sound of pivoting joints. Her heart pounded at the prospect of what she was about to do.

Two bone spikes slowly cracked through her skin, pushing through her shirt's self-replicating threads, and tore through familiar holes in her jacket; one at her wrist and another at her elbows. They matched the talons on her wings with their curvature and color.

That sound must have been louder than her footfalls, because the dragon suddenly lifted its head and whipped it around to stare at her. She stilled instantly and felt her muscles quake to overcompensate for tensing up.

She was thinking too much. *Just relax.* They couldn't see great in the dark and sometimes they didn't realize something was nearby until it was right on top of them.

The Ferveos shoved the dead cow aside, and its wings flapped open as it bellowed at her. She had to actively tell herself to not slap her hands over her ears, and her stomach trembled at the sound—like an inferno and a roar smashed together.

It beat its wings a couple of times, starting to lift itself into the air, and she stuttered back. Oh no, she wasn't ready for aerial combat.

In desperation, she let out a small grunt and crossed her arms like an X over her chest, and then she threw them down. The bone spikes at her wrists shot out, and she worked to cloak them in her blue energy so she could control their trajectory. One of them smacked into the dragon's wing membrane and tore a large hole into the sinew. The other, she controlled better. It soared into its main wing bone, the humerus. The bone shattered and forced its wing to fall limp.

With a cry cut short, the Ferveos landed solidly on all fours and looked to its broken wing. Snapping its fury-filled eyes at her, it let out another bellow. All the while, it kept working to move its broken wing.

"Okay, it's immobilized. Now what?" she muttered to herself, darting her gaze around the field. She found her options for a weapon limited. If the prospect of it didn't make her gag, she would just run over to the discarded cow and pry a bone loose to wield that like a sword. Maybe cloak it in her energy.

But the guts, and the brains, and the intestines, and...ew. It made bile rise in her throat that she quickly pushed back down.

Nope. Okay, bones from a cow were out.

The dragon turned and hurtled its spiked tail at her. She dove out of the way easily enough. Dodging correctly had been one of the first things she had been taught. If she braced her hands right, she could propel herself upright and land easily. That way, she wouldn't have to pick herself up off the ground. Thankfully, she had been pretty good at that.

She landed easy-ish. The ground was slick with frosty dew, and she almost flailed herself into the grass. Waving her hands outward as she landed, she let out a small, uneasy noise and got her footing.

Returning her attention to the problem at hand, she barely had time to react before the Ferveos' maw crashed down at her. She flashed her hands out, and her arms were just long enough to catch its top and bottom jaws. Sliding against the grass, she dug her heels into the ground to secure herself.

Like a dog when you try to shove a pill into its mouth, the Ferveos flailed above her, its tongue swiping this way and that. She tried not to vomit. There were chunks of bone, skin, meat, and other cow internal organs wedged into the dragon's teeth. The smell that pushed at her was nearly unbearable.

Through gagging breaths, she grunted out, "Hey, y'know, why don't you just be a good boy and leave me alone?" A trembling pressure rattled down her arms as the Ferveos worked to close its maw. "Have it your way," she muttered and screwed her face in concentration.

Gripping the jaws in her grasp, she threw the creature back with all the power she could muster. Its head snapped back, the force enough to send it back-flipping to the ground.

She fled quickly back to Tyron as the dragon tried to disentangle itself from its broken wings that flopped around unhelpfully.

At the wall, she told her Zaheri, "I immobilized it, but I need a gun."

He pulled his brow together and shrugged. "You won't always have a gun."

An infuriated roar bellowed behind her, and she turned to see the dragon flailing about. A few trees fell from its thrashing tail.

"You've already taken out its wings. It's a downed dragon," he continued.

She looked to him in desperation. "I need a weapon."

"No Jen, you *are* a weapon."

"Tyron!" She lunged for the pistol at his side, but he caught her arms and threw her back.

As she floundered backward, he said, "You said you wanted a shot at it. You won't always have a weapon on you. You need to learn to utilize your skills to take enemy fighters out. Think about what you have at your disposal."

"I am not using cow bones!" She threw a pointed finger up to accentuate her point.

He deflated and muttered, "Cow bones would break against a dragon's scales. Jen, c'mon; think."

She flailed her arms out wildly and screamed, "What am I supposed to use? My *magic ninja powers?*"

"I wouldn't call them ninja powers, but you've got *magic something.*" He snapped his head up as thudding sounded, and his snarky expression shifted to battlefield attention.

With a growl of frustration, she ran back to the dragon. It had managed to fling its broken wings to its sides and now charged at her. The deadweight limbs flanked its bulk and dragged on the ground.

"You can do this, you can do this, you can do

this." Trying to talk herself into her hastily formed plan, she leapt into the air and yelled as she aimed for the dragon's head.

"Oof!" She slammed into the dragon's snout as it slid to a frantic stop and began writhing under her. Gritting her teeth, she worked to hold on tight to one of the smaller horns on its head and shimmied up its brow. Another bone spike appeared at her wrist, and as she went to send it hurtling into the dragon's skull, it managed to throw her off. Her wayward spike flew out as she fell and smashed into the Ferveos' eye.

She hit the ground with a *thud*, her back jarring angry messages to her brain at the impact. Skittering out from under the madly pawing dragon above her, she let out an airy whine as a taloned foot nearly squashed her. She had to put some distance between her and the dragon.

With one eye blinded and the other radiating fury, the Ferveos reared back a little, and she heard the bubbling, popping sound at its throat. She didn't really think through her actions as she hurtled her hands out, and a flash of blue ghosted across the landscape, smacking into the dragon. Again, the beast hit the ground, vapors steaming from its clenched jaws.

A massive fire in the middle of a farming community wasn't okay, so she had to keep the Ferveos from spewing it. That would impact too many other people.

She had to take this thing out, pronto.

She could try another attack with brute force, using her spike again to penetrate the skull and maybe hit the brain this time. Or, she could use an energy attack against it, seeing exactly what something like that could do to a dragon. Or, she could just run up and punch it, maybe see if it would bleed to death if she hit it enough times.

Or...she could ask Tyron for help.

The last option wasn't a viable one, not yet, anyway. Neither was hoping the monster would bleed to death. It could just sit on her, and then she would be crushed, and the Ferveos would still take a while to die from its wounds. The first option probably wouldn't work, either. Controlling her spikes in midair was proving less than adequate. And getting on its head again would likely end in a similar result. That left the energy attack. Deciding this had taken less than a second.

The Ferveos let out a low snarl. The sound rumbled up its throat and sent a shockwave down Jen's spine.

She planted her left foot behind her slightly and brought her hands up in front of her, palms facing each other. Electrical zapping skittered down her arms as little blue sparks littered the air around her biceps to her fingers. A swirling blue mist pulled and gathered up around her palms. Then an orb began to take shape between her hands.

The Ferveos got back to its feet and swayed a little before it propelled itself at her.

Jen looked up at the dragon with determination. To her, it felt like time had slowed as she focused on her energy. It pooled into a vibrant blue orb in her grasp. The orb looked like a swirling blue storm, small cracks of blue lightning firing inside the confines of the sphere. All she could hear was the steady beat of her heart, the faint bellow of the Ferveos, and the storm in her hands.

Letting out a yell, she glared as she threw her hands outward, palms facing the Ferveos. Like a beam of bright blue light, her energy shot away from her, spearheaded by the orb.

For half a second, she was elated, seeing that much power come from her. Just her. She had seen her Zaheri unleash their fair share of energy attacks, letting her see how it could be used, but she had never seen so much force come from one single hit.

And she would have been so much prouder had she aimed properly.

The sheer sound and force of the blast had startled the dragon, causing it to stop in its tracks, but the hit itself was way off her mark. She hadn't focused on where the attack was supposed to go. In that moment, she had only focused on making it a powerful attack, nothing more. Too much aggression and not enough thought about where the hit was supposed to land.

Suddenly the whole learn-how-to-swing-a-sword thing made complete sense.

Her massive energy attack did surge forward, and it did hit the dragon, but it didn't collide with its chest like she had intended. Instead, it had flown toward the left of the beast, smashing into its shoulder. She saw a chunk of the shoulder disintegrate in the path of her attack. It caught a fair chunk of the Ferveos' right wing and tore it to shreds. Bone cracked and splintered, skin tore and scales were thrown asunder, flesh ripped away and was sent flying. The force of the blow sent the large dragon hurtling backward, tumbling a bit in the process.

But it wasn't enough to kill it.

As things settled slightly and the dragon struggled to its feet, Jen dropped her arms dejectedly at her sides and burst out, "Dang it!"

The Ferveos regained its footing, and despite the pain it was sure to be feeling with missing a wing and having a chunk of its shoulder torn off, it ran at her.

Getting herself back into her ready stance, she prepared another energy attack. She just had to focus. Pay attention. She could do this.

Another orb pooled quickly into her hands as she fixed her eyes on the dragon and where she needed to aim. The attack didn't feel as powerful.

Make it stronger.

No, wait. She had to make sure it went somewhere that would kill the Ferveos this time. *Focus on that.* But what if the attack wasn't strong enough to rip through its scales? No, it had to be. It could be. Should she aim for its neck and sever a blood vein? Or would it be better to hit its head? No, maybe its chest.

The energy in her palm flickered as the dragon got closer. She squared her shoulders and resolved to just pick a spot and let the attack go. She could do this. She could take it down herself.

Then a sudden, loud, quick bang filled the air and pierced the chaos in front of her. A pale blue light shot through the Ferveos' skull, right at the crest of its forehead, and out the back; its spine severed in the process.

Tumbling forward, the dead dragon fell with a low moan.

Jen watched the beast fall and took a few steps back to avoid getting crushed. Her concentration disappeared from her energy, so it evaporated from her hand. The rumble of the earth from the heavy beast's fall evaporated into small aftershocks. Steam rose from the holes in its skull.

She sighed and watched the vapor exhale from her mouth and rise into the sky. If she was going to start an argument with Tyron, she had to at least appear semi-collected. Even though it wasn't fair. She had been so close to finishing it on her own, and he had cheated. And he was such a freaking know-it-all.

Slowly, she turned and saw Tyron hand the sniper rifle back to Krelien, who in turn took the gun and stepped back a few paces.

She marched up to Tyron, fists clenched at her sides. The spikes disappeared back into her arms. Chewing her lip, she hopped up and over the stone wall and ardently kept her eyes off him. For half a second, she considered just doing the silent treatment.

But no.

Nope. She was going to speak her mind and let him know exactly what she thought.

She pursed her lips and shifted her gaze to his with a glare. Tyron returned her glare with a placid expression. Krelien flicked his eyes between them a few times as he clutched his rifle.

"Why did you do that?" she asked quietly, her jaw still tight.

"You faltered," he said simply. "I wasn't going to let—"

"I was being a weapon! Like you said!" she exploded. "Testing out my abilities and learning how to use my energy! I was even thinking about that stupid—" she motioned her arms forward as though jabbing with an invisible sword "—sword, training thing you had me doing earlier! I was learning!" She pointed to her head.

Tyron stared down at her, his face even and almost bored. "I got that."

"And then you go and, and, what? Get Krelien to come over so you can take his gun to prove I'm not ready for this?"

"Technically, he came over when you started manifesting the first attack," Tyron said nonchalantly. "I only took the rifle when he offered it."

Krelien's eyes widened as Jen looked at him in an incredulous way. He pointed to his leader and said, "He just took it; no offering involved."

Jen's face contorted, and she waved at Krelien dismissively before she looked back to Tyron. "Why would you do that? You said I wouldn't always have a gun, and then you go and pull out a freaking gun?"

"I wasn't going to let you get killed because of pride," Tyron said, a stern expression coming to his face. "I had to make a call, and I saw you falter in your second manifest."

"It was only for a second!" She flung her arms outward.

"A *second* of hesitation can cause any number of mistakes to happen on the battlefield!" He pointed behind her. "And that second of doubt can lead to someone's death. It's not only your life you're going to be protecting in these instances; there's usually other potential casualties. You will learn this in time." His tone was loud, stern, and almost cold.

"I had things—"

"No, you didn't. You think you did, but you had nothing under control, least of all your energy."

"I could've—"

"No, Jen," Tyron said with finality, "you couldn't." He held her angry gaze with his own look of determination, and when she looked to the ground, he said, "We're done for the night."

Jen snapped her head up, and in that instant, she didn't look as angry. Instead, she looked pleading. "But—"

"*Now*, Jen. Go get on the bike." He pointed back up the road where he had left the *motorcycle*.

Her expression was a mixture of frustration, disappointment, and shame as she crossed her arms and stalked off to where Tyron had pointed.

He kept himself facing toward the now empty space in front of him and closed his eyes with a short breath. Once she had been gone for a few seconds, he turned to look after her, and his features softened to a frown.

Behind him, Krelien still clutched the sniper rifle as Ar'on joined them and asked, "Why didn't you—"

"Later," Tyron cut him off.

"But it was really strong," Krelien said, relaxing his grip on the gun.

With a sigh, Tyron turned to them and asked, "How did things look from your point?"

"Krelien kept yelling at me that she was forming an orb, like that would somehow stop her," Ar'on said as he rolled his eyes and crossed his arms over his chest.

"Did not," Krelien whined.

Tyron ran a hand down his face. "That came too close."

"I think we are long overdue for Jennifer to utilize that portion of her skills," Blaze interjected as she and Archer came to stand with them. The white grovix sat down and added, "She likely would have been capable of handling the end of that confrontation on her own."

With a glance over at Blaze, Tyron said, "She's too young."

"Yeah, well, that's true," Archer said as Tyron started toward the cycle. "But you gotta admit, she's good for her age."

"She is indeed decades ahead of her peers," Blaze offered.

"What *peers*?" Krelien asked. "Other humans? They can't make energy."

Archer opened his mouth to respond, but Blaze tapped her paw against his and said, "No, it is past his bedtime, and you know how he gets with this line of questioning."

"Ah, right," Archer said with a nod.

Ar'on followed Tyron and whispered with a stern look, "You did the right thing." He raised his brow. "You should have done it sooner."

Tyron stopped and was about to answer when the horn of his motorcycle cut through the air. He turned as Jen raised her hands angrily.

"Is this an intro to parenting?" he asked as an aside.

"How would I know?" Ar'on grumbled.

"Do me a favor and get that thing moved and out of sight, quickly. The farmers nearby are bound to have heard all of that. Get Kaldok to help." He pointed toward the dead Ferveos on the ground before he hastened to his parked cycle.

"Right," Krelien said as he draped his rifle across his shoulders and leaned back lackadaisically. He grinned to Archer and asked, "Hey Arch, you hungry?"

Archer looked between Krelien and the half-masticated cow a few times. "I could eat."

"The question is, are you gonna?"

"Probably not."

"C'mon, it's fresh meat. Where's bad?"

With a roll of her eyes, Blaze said, "What Archer is neglecting to state is the fact that the Ferveos already consumed the best parts."

Krelien looked back to the dead animal and gave it a solid moment's stare. "Okay, so, how're we gonna explain the half-eaten cow? Marvins half-abducting it?"

"That sounds like a bad story, even for Earth," Kaldok said as he appeared at his side.

Krelien flinched in surprise as Kaldok walked past him. His head was wolf-like in structure, and his arms and hands were furred. He had paws more than hands with sharp claws that sat just underneath the surface of his fingers. His ears pivoted around and twitched as his dark brown eyes surveyed his team members. Kaldok stood upright, unlike most werewolves, and wore clothing.

"Don't do that!" the Jumper yelled at the werewolf.

Archer smirked. "It's about time you know how we feel when you pop up out of nowhere."

"And we should just take the cow back to the portal with the Ferveos. Problem solved," Kaldok said.

"Sound decision Kaldok," Blaze said with a nod of approval. She gave Krelien a disappointed stare. "It is not always necessary for you to concoct absurd schemes to accomplish your goals."

Wearing a look of annoyance, Krelien gestured toward the dead creatures. "Just help me with this, will ya?"

"How am I supposed to help?" Archer asked.

"He has a point," Kaldok said with a smile.

As the three walked off and continued to argue over the minutia of their assignment, Ar'on stepped up to Blaze and asked, "Any thoughts?"

The white grovix's red eyes flashed up to him before she stood and said, "Still processing. I will defer to you when I believe there is something of merit to note." With that, she walked after the other three.

Ar'on stared after the white grovix, muttering, "Gee, thanks for that insight, Blaze." He followed after the group and growled, "And would you three stop bickering?"

Chapter Two
A Day in the Life

The standard, irritatingly singular beep of an alarm clock blared at her side, startling her into a conscious state. Jen tried to focus her eyes as she smacked at the clock, looking to shut off the loud, annoying noise. As she found the off button with her fingers, silence greeted her room again.

Sitting upright, she looked at the clock through bleary eyes. 6:00 in big, red numbers stared back at her as the time changed to 6:01.

She went to stretch and felt the soreness of her muscles cry with the movement. With a wince and a groan, she allowed herself to flop back down into the comfort of her bed. *Just another minute. That's possible, right?* she thought.

Peeling her eyes open, she realized that if she did allow herself even a second to relax, she would succumb to her exhaustion. And skipping school was out of the question. The family rule was you only got out of school for legitimate things, like doctor and dentist appointments, or if you were genuinely sick. And Jen's parents didn't know she had been out most of the night. If she said she was too tired for school, they would ask why. Then it would turn into a question of what she had been doing staying up until three a.m. Then she would have to come up with a really good lie.

She had never been great at lying. It was a small miracle that she had gotten away with her training so far. She was just lucky that her family wasn't a bunch of night owls.

Rubbing her eyes to remove any remaining sleep, she thought about how it was possible she lived like this. Tyron had dropped her off two and a half hours prior. This was the third night in a row that she had gotten between two and three hours of sleep. No wonder she never remembered any of her dreams; there wasn't enough time for her to even begin a proper REM cycle.

Climbing out of bed, she walked past her forgotten homework and pulled out some clothes blindly before shuffling out of her room and down the hallway to the bathroom. The old house was chilly, the hardwood floors icy against her warm feet. She had been away for all of thirty seconds and already missed her bed.

Ten minutes later, she emerged, dragging her pajamas in her hand and running a towel through her hair. Several minutes of silence passed in the house. Jen's mom would be downstairs making coffee and her dad likely a few minutes away from heading out the door for his hour-long drive to the office.

As she was in the process of putting on her shoes, she heard banging from the hallway. With one shoe on and only halfway laced, she poked her head out as a male voice called, "Hey, Nance, when you're done, can you get me? I've gotta get to work on time today."

She looked down the hall and saw her twenty-three-year-old brother standing next to the bathroom door. He tapped his bare feet against the hard wood flooring. His apartment was still going through renovations, so he lived at home for the time being.

"Would it kill you to put a shirt on?" Jen asked him.

Groggily lifting his head up at the sound of her voice, Chip gave her a sleepy smile. His short black hair sat unevenly, sticking up in every direction from sleep. His arms were folded over his bare chest, and his fleece pants hung loosely on his hips as he grinned at her. "No, but I like to see people's reactions. I was thinking that on Friday, I'd just do this for casual day."

"I feel like you'd get fired," she said with a snort.

The bathroom door opened, and Jen's younger sister, Nancy, walked out. Her usually calm, bright blue eyes looked dark with frustration. Her long brown hair was still damp from her shower, and she had a hair dryer and straightener gripped between her elbow and side. The fluffy robe she wore was adorned with rubber duckies.

She muttered something about needing her own bathroom as she approached Jen and grabbed her by the arm with her free hand, pulling her older sister into her room. Nancy closed the door and pulled a few shirts off hangers, holding them up in front of her. "Which should I wear?" One of the tops was blue plaid, the other was a red, long-sleeved sweater.

Humming a response, Jen said, "Go blue. It makes your eyes pop. Do you even look good in red?"

"Not really, but I like the pattern," Nancy answered as she discarded the red shirt. She then straightened and asked, "Straight hair or curly?"

"Whatever you want," Jen said as she left. "I feel weird with one shoe on. You can decide. You'll look great, regardless."

It was the brief moments like these that made her pretend like everything was perfectly sane in the world.

Walking back into her room, she wiggled her foot into her other shoe and grabbed her backpack and a brown leather jacket that was draped over her computer chair.

Moo, the family cat, who was graciously cleaning herself in the middle of the hallway, padded down the stairs ahead of her owner as Jen's footfalls followed. In the old Victorian home, to a stranger, it might have sounded like she was falling down the stairs.

Before she hit the foyer, her mother called out, "Walk down those stairs, please!"

"Sorry," Jen said as she walked into the kitchen. She fell into a chair and tightened the laces on her Converse as she asked, "Do we have anymore doughnuts?"

"On the counter," her mom said absentmindedly, pouring her first mug of coffee. "Good morning to you, too," she added with a smirk.

"Morning, Mom. How'd you sleep?" Jen asked as she got up and made her way to get a sugary start to her day.

"Wonderfully. I just didn't get enough of it," her mom answered.

Jen thought, *You're telling me.*

Settling back into her chair, Jen allowed her mind to wander as she ate. The TV was on in the background, a news anchor going over the local happenings. She glanced up to the screen in time to see the meteorologist talk about the weather that evening—a balmy twenty degrees. Immediately, Jen began to wonder if there was a way to tell Tyron that she needed a night off.

The beeping of an alarm clock startled her, and she blinked a few times. Her mom kept going about her day, now making Chip's lunch.

Nancy came downstairs, and as she greeted their mom, their voices were muffled. *Great,* Jen thought as she got up.

Taking the narrow steps two at a time, she ran back upstairs and walked immediately into her parents' bedroom. Once again, her dad had forgotten to turn off his alarm, and the snooze finally gave in to alert someone to its forgotten presence. As Jen slammed the giant button on top that said *OFF,* she cursed herself. "No more wandering thoughts."

It was always in the moments that she let herself stare into space that her hearing decided that was a great time to hone in on something random, like the gross licking noise Moo made when she was cleaning herself or the panting of the neighbor's dog.

At least with this instance, she had it within her power to remove the annoying noise that would no doubt have continued to rule her hearing for several minutes. The last time it had happened, she had spent the better part of a half-hour tearing apart their attic, looking for a watch that was ticking out of rhythm. She had wound up throwing a box out the window and got grounded for a week.

Going back downstairs, she found Nancy finishing her breakfast as she read the newspaper comics. Jen glanced at the front page and saw something about the new governor of Pennsylvania and several quotes about what he promised to do now that he was in office. All she wanted him to do was lower gas costs.

In her tiny, strange reality, that was important.

Chip came down the stairs and snatched his lunch from their mom's waiting hands as he said his goodbyes. Her mom was next to leave and, shortly thereafter, the sisters made their way outside to Jen's old Volkswagen Jetta.

It was only a fifteen-minute trip, most of which consisted of sitting in traffic outside of the school because the buses were so slow at getting through traffic lights.

As they sat at the last light before entering the campus, Nancy suddenly turned to Jen. "So, how much sleep did you get last night?" the younger sister asked.

Jen furrowed her brow as she stared forward, waiting for the green arrow to finally show up so she could turn. "Um, I dunno," Jen said after a few seconds of deliberation. "Maybe six hours? Why? How much sleep did you get?"

As Jen looked over at Nancy with a smirk, she saw her younger sister giving her a skeptical look.

Jen's grin disappeared. "What?"

"I know you weren't home last night." The younger sister squinted at her.

For a second, Jen fumbled, her face blank. Recovering, she tried to say in a light tone, "What're you talking about? Of course I was home—"

"Nuh-uh," Nancy said defiantly with a shake of her head. "I went into your room a little after midnight, 'cause I couldn't figure out my stupid algebra homework and needed your help, but you weren't there."

"Well, I could have been—"

"And then I checked the bathroom, but no one was in there."

"How do you know I wasn't—"

"And Chip was passed out and snoring when I snuck into his room to see if you were talking with him."

Crap, Jen thought.

The elder sister turned forward again, and the green arrow appeared. Of course now the arrow changed. She couldn't focus on traffic and a reasonable excuse at the same time.

Following the laws of traffic, Jen pulled into the school parking lot and found her spot. Once she put the car in park, the vehicle complying with a groan, she sat there and tried to come up with something to tell her sister.

For God's sake, really? The one time I don't cover my tracks, and she asks where I was? She hit on every possible—wait.

Smugly, Jen turned to her sister and asked, "Did you check downstairs?"

The sure look Nancy had fell from her face and

changed to one of confusion. "Well, why would you be down there?"

"I couldn't sleep, so I took a book down to the family room and read in front of the fireplace till around two." The lie rolled right off her tongue easily enough.

Nancy's eyes fell to the dashboard, and she slumped against her seat.

Trying to not appear too happy at the fact that she had just somehow averted a crisis, Jen said, "Hey, I'm sorry I wasn't around to help with your homework. If you want, I can help you before homeroom and—"

"I know you're lying."

"What?"

"I know you're hiding something," Nancy said, sitting up a bit. "You waited way too long before you said you were downstairs."

Rolling her eyes, Jen looked out the front windshield. She didn't want to lie to her sister, but she also couldn't just tell Nancy what she had been up to. She wasn't supposed to tell anyone. And her sister was someone. Jen just knew that if she did tell her family what she was doing and why, Tyron would know the moment the words left her mouth.

Knowing her luck, he was somewhere nearby now and was ready to cause a scene. Or maybe a car accident. Or something.

"If you won't tell *me*, I guess it's okay," Nancy said begrudgingly.

Jen grimaced.

"You don't have to lie about it."

The older sister pinched her eyes shut. "Look,

Nance ... I ... It's ..." She looked over at her sister. "It's complicated."

"You have a secret boyfriend, don't you?" Nancy burst.

"What? No! Nance!"

"You do! And you won't tell *me* about him? I'm your sister! I'm totally reading your diary when we get home, and there's nothing you can do to stop me!"

"For crying out loud, Nance, I don't have a secret boyfriend! You would have been the first person I'd tell! Honest!" She paused momentarily, and Nancy opened her mouth to retort again, obviously not believing her elder sister. "Look, you're right; I wasn't home last night. But I wasn't with a secret boyfriend, I wasn't out doing anything illegal, and I wasn't doing anything stupid. It's just...it's something..." She had been waving her hands around emphatically, trying to talk with motions to convey to her sister what was going on without actually saying anything. At a loss for words, Jen curled her hands in anger then defeatedly dropped her shoulders with a sigh. "I'm sorry, okay? I'm really, really sorry. I wish I could tell you. I just ... I can't."

"Do Dad and Mom know?"

Treading on thin ice, Jen mused for a few seconds before she said, "No, no one knows."

"Oh ..." the younger sister trailed off, her gaze falling to the center console. She let out a huff. "You're doing something cool, aren't you?"

A small smile came to Jen's face. "That depends on who you ask." Seeing Jen's smile, Nancy decided it was okay to mirror that reaction, to which Jen said, "Here, I promise that, one day, I will tell you."

"Can that day be tomorrow?"

"No."

"Oh. When?"

With a shrug, Jen answered, "I dunno. It'll be a surprise for the both of us." She got out of the car and grabbed her backpack out of the back seat, hearing Nancy's door creak open then slam shut. As much as Jen hated to hear her car door slam, it was the only way she could be sure it actually closed.

Reaching the entrance, they were grateful for the sudden burst of warm air that hit their faces. A few feet away from the entrance, a stairwell popped up on the left, which Nancy headed down for her homeroom, while Jen continued walking straight. Then, when the hallway ended, she took a left. Walking halfway down the hall, going fairly unnoticed by her fellow classmates, she came to her locker.

From down the hall, she could hear whispers from the senior class' arch nemesis, a girl named Evelyn. She was the kind of girl every guy wanted to date, and every girl wanted to kill and worship at the same time.

"God, look at what she's wearing," Evelyn's condescending whispers met Jen's ears. A normal person probably wouldn't have heard it, but thanks to Jen's heightened hearing, she could.

Evelyn's comments might have been directed at anyone, but it was more than likely that Jen was the target of the gossip. Unlike other teenage girls, she didn't typically wear name brand clothes, almost never had on frilly, girly things, and never wore makeup. The concept of covering her acne or hiding blemishes did appeal to her, but the first few months of her trying the stuff led to a pantry full of products that either made her break out worse, were the wrong skin tone, or clumped and looked unnatural. She had spent a small fortune trying to find something to "accentuate her beauty," only to find she despised the stuff. It took too long to put on, longer to take off, and never seemed to do what she wanted.

All of that, coupled with the fact that she had never had a boyfriend, never had a date to any of the dances, and seemed to enjoy the company of the teachers more than her fellow students led to Jen being the butt of a lot of jokes. All in all, it never bothered her.

Today, though, she would have loved to show Evelyn who she was dealing with.

Setting her jaw, Jen looked into her locker and snatched the books she would need for her morning classes.

A hand rapped against the locker next to hers in a rhythmic way, and she glanced over to see her friend, Ryan, standing there, a grin on his face.

He was average height, with light brown hair that was always parted to the right and green eyes that were so dark you almost missed his pupils. He was the sort of guy who knew everyone, aced his classes without much effort, and worked as a manager for a local convenience store but somehow had boundless energy. Jen sometimes seriously wondered which of the two of them was more sleep-deprived on any given day.

Gesturing to himself, he said, "Ask me why I'm smiling."

"No," she said with a small shake of her head.

He tapped her arm. "Oh, come on; it's only fun if you ask."

With a slight roll of her eyes, she asked, "Why are you smiling, Ryan?"

"Bam!" he yelled as he produced a handful of tickets from behind his back.

Jen didn't react for a few seconds as she glanced between the tickets and his face a couple times. "Am I supposed to understand?"

"I hold in my hands, the first four tickets to the Franklin Institute's opening day of the *Star Trek* exhibit." With each word, his smile had widened more, and when he finished, he opened his mouth as if to say, "*ta-da.*"

An attempt at an excited smile came to her face as she said with mock enthusiasm, "Oh boy, when do we go?"

His shoulders slumped. "You could at least say, 'Oh Ryan, thanks for waiting forever to get the first available tickets, I'm forever indebted to you, and I'll gladly give up my Saturday to keep you safe in Philadelphia'."

"Okay, one, that was a run-on sentence."

"Touché."

"Two, of course I'll go with you. I'm just not a *Star Trek* fan."

"Ah, but you will be," he said as he pointed to her and pocketed the tickets.

"Why'd you get four? Who else is coming along?" She returned to getting her books for class.

"First, it's adorable that you assume I got you one."

"Seeing as you said I was giving up a Saturday to go, I think that's a safe assumption."

"Second, to answer your question, I thought that Grant and Aeryn would want to come."

Jen fumbled her books, and they fell to the floor.

Ryan smirked and quickly coughed when she turned to him and asked, "Why Grant? He hates *Star Trek*. And he hates Philly. And he hates trains. The only thing he hates more than Philly and trains is driving in a car in Philly, which is where the Franklin Institute is."

"All of that is true, yes," Ryan said, trying not to laugh.

A strangled word left her mouth before she asked, "Is this like some bro code thing? You trying to meddle when you shouldn't?"

Ryan held up a finger. "You never mention a bro code unless you're a bro."

"I can keep secrets, you know. Some people have called *me* a super secret keeper, yourself included."

"Look, honestly, I just thought it would be a fun trip to take."

"In winter?" she asked, not amused in the slightest.

His face scrunched. "It's not like the Franklin Institute is outside. We'll only be out in the city for, like, an hour tops."

Shaking her head slightly, Jen snatched the books on the floor and stuffed them into her backpack. As she closed her locker with a bang, she asked, "Why now?"

"C'mon, Jen; we graduate in June." Ryan's tone softened. "It only makes sense that we spend time together while we can. Everyone says it's hard to keep in touch with your high school friends when you all leave the state."

"It's not like you'll be far—off at Rutgers. I'll be at Temple. That's an easy trip."

"Yeah, but Aeryn is going to Utah, and Grant's going to that Podunk school in the middle of New York. The one I keep forgetting the name of."

"Everyone forgets the name of it. It's barely a school," Jen said dismissively as she stared at her locker. Then, returning her gaze to Ryan, who had a hopeful look in his eyes, she conceded, "I guess I see your point."

He nodded victoriously and fist-bumped the air. "Awesome! You tell Aeryn, and I'll tell Grant."

"Yeah, she'll be thrilled," Jen quipped. In truth, though, Aeryn probably would love the idea of the exhibit. She was the one who kept saying how great the old *Star Trek* TV show was.

Jen was about to walk to her homeroom when she noticed Ryan staring at her, his expression worried. A little self-conscious, she asked, "What?"

He took in a tentative breath. "Are you okay?"

"Yeah, why wouldn't I be?"

Gesturing underneath his eyes, he said, "You've got some pretty impressive black eye war paint going on."

"Oh yeah, that," she said with an awkward laugh. "It's just 'cause I haven't been sleeping well."

"Mmhmm." He narrowed his eyes and nodded. "I guess you haven't been sleeping well for a while."

"Oh gosh, Ryan," she grumbled, "can't you just let someone say they're fine and let that be that?"

"That's unlikely," a voice said from behind her.

Jen let out a small eep, and her eyes widened. She sniffled a little to recover then turned around to see Grant Connolly standing there.

Grant was tall, with a slender build, and was arguably one of the most handsome guys of the senior class. He had black hair and green eyes that seemed to hold splashes of grey in the coloring. Regardless of the time of year, he always seemed to have a slight tan, and Jen knew that was because he was almost always working outside. She had gone to the beach and the pool enough times with him to know that his farmer's tan was pretty drastic, though. He was one of the kickers for the varsity football team and definitely had his fair share of girls following him around.

And, for some reason, he was friends with Jen. Probably because they had been friends since elementary school. When he would invite her to parties, she would be the only girl playing cops and robbers with the boys, tackling people to the ground without hesitation.

Trying not to swoon like she had seen so many other girls do in Grant's presence, Jen said, "You never know; it could be a good day."

Grant tightened his hand on the strap of his messenger bag draped across his chest and grinned. "That would have to be a phenomenal day."

"Y'know, I'm standing right here," Ryan said, causing them both to turn toward him.

"Yeah, we gathered that, buddy," Grant joked.

Suddenly, Jen remembered that one of her cousins was having a bridal shower soon and said, "Ah, Ryan, when's that Saturday thing?"

Abruptly, Grant's stance switched from carefree to rigid terror. His eyes flashed from Jen's face to Ryan's as he asked tensely, "Saturday thing? What Saturday thing?"

"After Thanksgiving break. Don't worry; we've got time for you to dream about the gloriousness of it," Ryan said with glee.

"What Saturday thing?" Grant emphasized, stepping toward Ryan.

"It's some," Jen started, lifting her hand then dropping it, "*Star Trek* exhibit thing."

Ryan nodded and gave them a thumbs-up.

Grant looked at Jen, and she whispered, "He's very proud."

"It's gonna be awesome!" Ryan said exuberantly.

Grant tried not to roll his eyes but failed miserably. "Really? *Star Trek*?"

"Oh, you'll love this," Jen said, gently touching his arm as he looked at her again. "It's at the Franklin Institute."

Whipping his head to look at Ryan again, Grant practically hollered, "Philly?!"

Waving his hand to dismiss the outburst, Ryan said, "Calm yo self, homie."

"Wow, never do that again," Jen quipped. The bell rang, and she glanced toward the ceiling. "Welp, I'll see you guys at lunch."

She sighed as she started to make her way down the hall.

"Don't fall asleep in class!" Ryan yelled after her.

She turned around to throw some insult back at him, but when her eyes landed on Grant and saw his troubled expression, she found that there weren't any words in her brain. Instead, she just waved at the two boys and continued on her way.

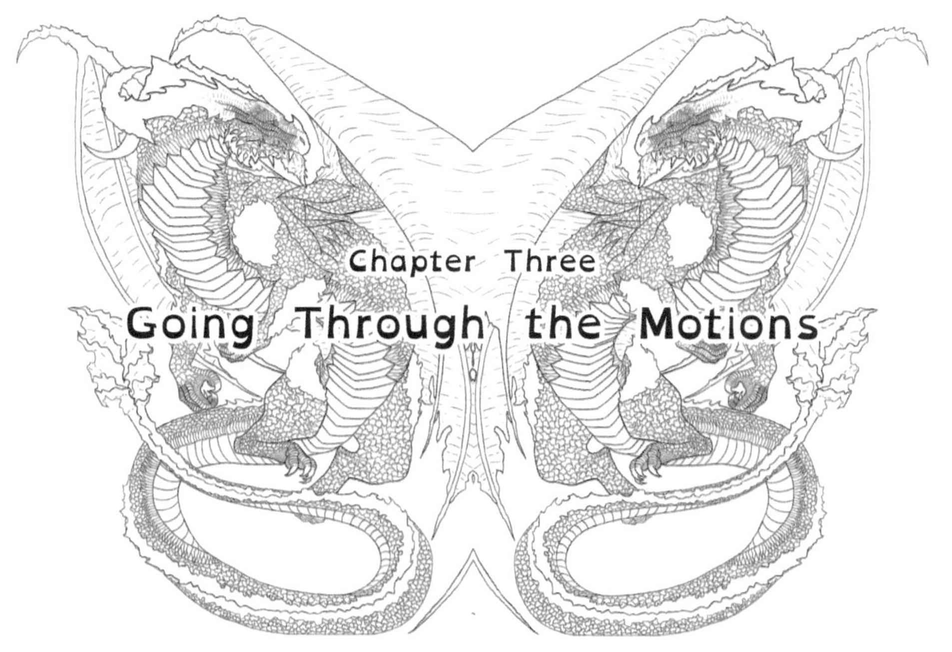

Chapter Three
Going Through the Motions

Making her way into her homeroom, Jen noticed that most of the other students were already there. As with every school, inevitably, there were those few kids in each homeroom who would walk in just as the second bell rang.

In the back right corner, a small girl sat up and started waving emphatically at Jen. "Sit down, sit down, sit down!" she squealed as Jen took the seat in front of her.

Giving her friend a suspicious look, Jen asked, "What's the word, Aer?"

"Ohmygosh, you'll never believe this," Aeryn said in a flurry as the second bell rang. She pouted a glare at the ceiling.

"That's debatable," Jen said with a grin.

Aeryn had been her best friend since the seventh grade. She was a small girl with long, dirty blonde hair and insanely bright blue eyes. She looked like the kind of girl you could knock over just by poking her and would bruise just as easily.

Dropping her voice to a whisper, Aeryn said, "James asked *me* out last night!"

"Aha! It's about time!" Jen responded in the same hushed tone.

The announcements for the day began, but they both continued their conversation.

"Yeah, it was really cute. He was talking about how he's liked me since we were sophomores, and how he wants *me* to go to the movies with him this Friday, and...Eeee!" Aeryn's ability to speak devolved into nothing but a broad smile and sustained vowel.

"That's so great," Jen told her, a wide smile on her face, as well. Aeryn's exuberence was enough to make anyone smile. "He took his sweet time, though."

"Ugh, you're telling *me*!"

A commanding shush came from the front of the classroom, and Jen rolled her eyes before she turned and faced forward.

Once their teacher took his eyes off them, Aeryn sat forward and whispered, "Can I ask you for a favor?"

"Sure, anything."

There was a pause, which caused Jen to turn and face her friend again.

Aeryn continued, "Is there any chance you could give *me* a ride in early tomorrow? I know that we usually do our whole late arrival thing, but James wanted to know if I could hang with him in the cafe and—"

Jen held up her hand. "Of course. Don't worry about it. It'll give me a chance to get work done on my grad project without staying after school."

"Thanks so *much!* You're the best!"

Beginning to turn forward to avoid being shushed by their teacher again, Jen suddenly swiveled back and said, "Oh, by the way, Ryan got us tickets to the *Star Trek* exhibit at the Franklin Institute."

"Who's us?"

"You, *me,* Ryan, and Grant," Jen said as nonchalantly as possible.

"Oooo," Aeryn said in a sing-song tone.

Rolling her eyes, Jen turned forward, trying not to let her friend put ideas into her head.

She would never deny that she liked Grant. She'd had a crush on him for a while now, but shortly after she had begun to think about boys and dating, Tyron and the gang had shown up at her house and changed her reality. Jen knew full well that if she were in a relationship with someone, they would eventually find out who she really was, and Tyron had been extremely specific about the whole not-telling-anyone thing.

Any chances of Jen being a normal girl had taken a hike to another country the day they had shown up.

In an attempt to distract herself, she half-listened to the announcements. There wasn't anything important on there, at least not pertaining to her. Everything mentioned was for people who were actually involved in the school, and Jen's various music classes didn't really count as "involved."

While Jen was at school, her **Zaheri** were at the antique shop that they used as their headquarters. It was actually where they stayed for the majority of their time. At least, to Jen's knowledge. It was located twenty minutes away from Jen's house, nestled in a quiet shopping district.

All the other buildings were empty with faded "for rent" signs in the windows. The only other building in the area that appeared to be at least occasionally inhabited was the lawyer's office next door. Jen questioned whether it was legitimate or not, because she had never noticed any signs of activity in the building, and the name of the law firm was "Son & Son." If it weren't for how her Zaheri had chosen to "advertise" the shop, the lawyer's office might have passed for weird.

The antique shop had all of three Google reviews; two of which said something along the lines of, "The guy at the counter was mean. 0/10 would not recommend." There was a hand-painted slab of wood haphazardly hammered over the doorframe that read "*Old Stuff and Rusty Things*" in a peeling white paint. Apparently, that was their attempt at a name. It had been Krelien's idea to use neon lights that said, "*Antiques*" with a big neon arrow above the store.

Needless to say, they didn't get many customers.

Jen had a part-time job at the shop after school on Tuesdays, Thursdays, and Saturdays. Her parents wouldn't let her work throughout the entire school week. On paper, her job was to pretty much sit there and be a cashier. In reality, she spent her time training, either learning how to utilize her energy, hand-to-hand combat moves, learning the weak points of a grovix, which were identical to the weak points of a bratak'ra, or learning how to fire Agerian weapons.

The first time she had seen the shop, she had laughed at the sheer insanity that the place had lasted so long with how hilarious it looked. Though, she had to admit that the selfie she had taken in front of the shop that showcased the worn sign and flashing neon lights was her most-liked photo on Instagram. Tyron had forbade her to reply to any of the questions about where the shop was located.

As the announcements ended and the halls became a bustle of noise again, Jen and Aeryn made their way to their first class of the day.

Aeryn poked Jen in the arm and asked, "So, what's this about Grant coming to the exhibit?"

With a roll of her eyes, Jen said, "Don't read into it, Aer. It's just a stupid trip. We've hung out a million times."

"C'mon, Jen; he likes you, too! Is it so bad to get excited about the possibility of something happening?"

It really could be, yes, Jen thought. However, she shrugged in response to her friend.

Shaking her head, Aeryn said, "Fine. You brood about it. I'm still gonna figure out a way to make this work."

"Yeah, no, don't do that."

Aeryn smiled in response as they continued on their way and Jen tried to stifle a yawn. This was going to be a long day.

The rest of Jen's day was fairly normal. She survived through her classes and enjoyed lunch with her few close friends. As the day came to a close, she went to the music wing of the school for her final class—choir.

Jen liked to think she didn't pride herself on many things, but one of them was her ability to sing.

Granted, she wasn't the best in the class, but she had obtained a few solos during her time in choir and felt fairly confident in what she could do.

Walking into the auditorium where the choir practiced, she dropped her backpack into a seat behind Ryan and looked over his shoulder to see what he was reading. "Hi there, creeper," he said without looking up from the paper in his grasp.

"SAT dates?" she asked.

"I'm going for a better score. Can't hurt, right?"

"Funny, I'm doing the same thing. January 18th."

He moved his head a bit to be able to look at her. "Wanna carpool?"

"Heads or tails?" she asked as she began to fish a coin from her pocket.

Ryan reached back and stopped her. "No way you're driving. I'm not leaving that to chance."

"Why not?" she asked with a shocked expression.

"Cause your car might not even start in January!" he said as he turned to face her fully.

With a shake of her head, she said, "You underestimate him."

"Oh great, now you've named it."

"Hey, studies show that when you name a car, it operates better."

He put the paper down and crossed his arms. "Oh really? What study is that?"

Jen shrugged. "I dunno. It's what you say when you want to win an argument."

"That's because I actually read studies!"

"Why is he yelling?" Aeryn asked as she walked up to them.

"He doesn't like that I named Mitchell," Jen answered.

"Aw, but I like Mitch."

Looking incredulous, Ryan said, "What is it with girls naming things?"

Gaining defiance, Jen and Aeryn draped their arms over each other's shoulders, and Jen said, "It gives us the power to control things."

"It gives you something; that's for sure," Ryan mumbled.

"Oh, stop being such a baby," Jen said as she playfully smacked him.

"Hey all, quick question," Grant said as he barged into the conversation and dumped his bag next to Ryan's seat.

Feeling jovial for the first time all day, Jen gestured to Grant and said, "Nice to see you, too."

Grant looked at her then let out a small chuckle before continuing, "I was wondering, do we want to submit *Validation* for the regional film competition?"

"Why would we want to do that?" Aeryn asked.

"Oh, because it might get us a scholarship for school," Ryan said in a bored tone. He looked at Grant. "You don't need that. You've already got a scholarship for football."

"They don't have a football team at the college I'm going to," Grant said. Then he brightened a little. "Unless you're referring to England's football. Then yes, they have football."

"What, you mean soccer?" Jen asked.

"What college doesn't have football?" Ryan asked. "Are you sure it's in America?"

Holding his hand out a little to quiet the conversation, Grant said, "For the record, lots of schools don't have football teams. They think it's too violent of a sport."

"But they have soccer?" Aeryn asked skeptically.

"Yeah, isn't that just football but with spiked feet aiming at heads?" Jen asked.

Grinning wide, Grant said, "Mock all you want, but it's true."

Ryan pinched his eyes shut. "So, you want to enter *Validation* into a contest to try to get a scholarship, because you decided to go to a school in the middle of nowhere that didn't accept the first scholarship you got."

"No, I just thought"—Grant shrugged a little, looking toward the floor—"it was a good film and might be worth something." He then lifted his head. "Fine, so it was a bad idea."

Feeling bad for teasing him, Jen said, "No, it wasn't. We could always use another scholarship, and it was a surprisingly good film."

"Surprisingly?" Ryan asked incredulously. "You helped write the damn thing!"

"Swear jar!" the other three let out almost joyfully, and Aeryn produced a small jar with some change rattling around in it.

Ryan looked at her with wide eyes. "You still carry that thing around?"

"Hey, don't mock it," Jen said, pointing at the jar. "That's gonna pay for tolls on our trip to Philly."

Grant groaned, stuffing his hands in his pockets, while Ryan glared at them and shoved a few quarters into the jar.

"Why'd you put so many quarters in there?" Aeryn asked.

Putting a finger to his head, Ryan said, "I was thinking several other obscenities and felt bad."

"Aw ..." The girls both tilted their heads slightly.

"Just, shut up," Ryan said as he gathered his music and marched toward the stage.

"Whether he admits it or not, we've made him a better person," Jen said as she pointed to the three of them.

As she stashed the jar back in her backpack, Aeryn said, "C'mon; we'd better get on stage before Mr. Mosser yells at us." She grabbed her music then made her way to her spot among the altos.

Jen was right behind her when Grant gently reached out to her, brushing her arm before quickly retracting. "Hey, uh, can I ask you something?"

Despite herself, she held her music notebook close to her chest, trying to mask whatever she might be feeling for the boy in front of her. "Uh, sure," she said, shifting her weight from one foot to the other.

Grant rubbed the back of his neck and looked around the auditorium a bit before finally looking back at her. "I know it's a little ways off, but ... I dunno. I thought I might as well—"

"Oh, Grant, *there* you are!" Evelyn called from the entrance of the auditorium. She walked up to them and linked her arm with his, using her other hand to grasp his bicep. He tried to shimmy away from her as she said, "I've been looking everywhere for you. I wanted to make sure we were still on for the winter formal."

It looked to Jen like he was biting his tongue before he said, "I never asked you, Evelyn."

"That's funny, 'cause I thought I told you I wanted to go with you," she said, still smiling, but there was a controlling, mean look in her eyes.

Grant disentangled his arm from her grip, took a

step away from her, and said, "Y'know, just 'cause you want something, doesn't mean you get it, Evelyn."

"You must have me mistaken for someone who isn't the prettiest girl in school," Evelyn said, arcing her back a little to show off her already highly visible cleavage.

Grant's gaze fell to the floor, and Jen knew why—he hated when she flounced around, trying to draw attention to her body.

Emboldened, Jen stepped up next to him and said, "Actually, Evelyn, he just asked me to the dance."

She could have punched herself in the face.

Obviously, this in no way made them a couple, but it certainly was a step in the wrong direction, especially considering Jen's life. She couldn't involve Grant in that.

Her heart pounded as she hoped to God that was what Grant had been about to ask her before they were interrupted. Otherwise, she was going to show up at the dance in a month without a date, and Evelyn was going to have ammunition for the rest of their high school career. Not like it was that long, but it was still seven months until they graduated.

That was basically an eternity.

Grant looked over at Jen, a little surprised, before he smiled.

Now she really wanted to punch herself. If she didn't get so excited seeing him happy, she might have just smacked her forehead right then and there.

Evelyn let out a scoff. "What?"

Grant whipped his head over to Evelyn and balled his fists.

The fact that Evelyn had the audacity to say

that one stupid word made Jen madder than she would have anticipated. She could feel the energy prickling down her arms, but she repressed the urge to lash out. Instead, she squinted and asked, "You need clarification? I thought it was pretty obvious."

Evelyn scoffed again, this time smiling, and tsked, "Wow, you must live in some great fantasy world, Monroe."

Jen *hated* when Evelyn called her by her last name. No one did that. Not on any sports teams, none of her teachers, none of her friends, not even friends of the family. But the way Evelyn always said it caused Jen's brain to go white.

A few claps sounded from the stage. "Come on, people; we've got a lot of music to cover!" Mr. Mosser said to the few stragglers in the audience.

Grant and Jen began to make their way to the stage, but Evelyn pushed between them and whispered to her, "It's so tragic the way you think you could possibly belong there with him." Then, in that snooty, holier-than-thou way, Evelyn practically pranced off, proud of her jab.

Jen didn't want to let it hurt her, but there was no way she would deny it.

She didn't belong at a dance. Not when she thought about the bruise she had gotten earlier on her back and the dragon she had almost killed that morning. Girls like that didn't wear dresses. They wore combat boots and leather jackets and had werewolves for friends.

She didn't want Evelyn to win, but she also knew that the other girl had a point.

As they walked up to the rest of the choir, Grant whispered, "Hey, what'd she say to you?"

Forcing herself to brush it off, Jen replied, "Just some comment meant to hurt my feelings."

They stepped away as she took her place next to Aeryn with the altos and Grant stepped up with the basses.

Singing would be a much wanted distraction from how much she wanted to scream.

Jen and Aeryn sat in the cafeteria as they waited for both Aeryn's new boyfriend, James, and Jen's sister. The sun was beginning to set as the two of them stared out the large windows, watching busses leave and hearing announcements filter through the almost empty halls.

They had been sitting there for a long while before Aeryn turned to her friend and asked, "Okay, I've waited long enough for you to start talking, so now I gotta ask; what did that witch of a girl say to you?"

Smiling at Aeryn's tenacity that she only ever showed in the quiet moments with trusted friends, Jen said, "It wasn't anything important, Aer. Just some attempt at a stinging comment. Evelyn trying to get under my skin." She looked away and found herself staring at the sunset. She wanted to fly up into the atmosphere and watch the sun eclipse the horizon. The homes nearby obstructed her view of the beautifully changing colors.

"Something's wrong though," Aeryn noted, genuine concern in her voice. "It obviously did get under your skin. You don't sound like you at all."

"Really? What would I usually say?"

Gaining an overly determined expression, Aeryn told her in a slightly different voice, "'Evelyn's just upset I stole her thunder from the last concert and sang better than her. She's too full of herself to ever let anyone else have happiness'."

"That's not what I sound like."

"Okay, so I suck at imitations, but you don't seem like you. What's wrong?"

For the third time that day, her friends and family had confronted her about something she couldn't talk about. The lies were getting tiresome, and after the day that she'd had, all Jen wanted to do was go home and take a nap, preferably in front of the fireplace after a cup of cocoa.

She figured it couldn't hurt to tell Aeryn a little bit of the truth, so she said, "Evelyn said I didn't belong at the dance, especially with Grant."

Aeryn flew her hands up to her face and gasped. Then, in a high pitched, breathless voice, she exclaimed, "Oh *my* gosh, how could you not tell *me*! You're going to the dance? With Grant?"

As her friend grasped her arm with her small hands and began tugging on her like a rope toy, Jen swatted at her. "Calm down. I only said it to bail him out of Evelyn continually badgering him about going. I doubt he took it seriously."

"But you said—"

"Right, she believed *me*." Jen turned to look at her friend. "She was harassing him about going with her, and I"—she winced—"said he had asked *me* to go to the dance, so he couldn't go with her."

Aeryn still had a hold on Jen's arm as she asked, "And Grant said ...?"

"Nothing. Evelyn started flinging her nasty comments, and then Mosser called us to the stage. After practice, well, you saw me."

"Yeah, you basically ran away," Aeryn said a little angrily. "Jen, why didn't you talk to Grant?"

"Because Evelyn's right." She suddenly found interest in her shoes. There was a new scuff on the right one. When Aeryn said nothing, she added, "I don't belong at the dance. I don't fit in with fluffy dresses and frilly skirts and slow songs."

Teetering a little back and forth, Aeryn said, "So, we'll get you a simple dress with no fluff and no frills. And I'll be the only one to dance with you during the slow songs. We can look stupid while we try to waltz."

Jen laughed a little.

Aeryn bounced in her seat. "You should go. It'll be so much fun to have you there, too."

"Aer, it's ... not just that," she said slowly.

"O-kay." Aeryn let go of her friend's arm and settled into her seat. "What is it?"

Letting out a short breath, Jen said, "In seven months, we graduate. I'll be off to Temple for their photography program, and Grant will be...seven hours away, at some school in the middle of nowhere where he gets no reception."

Aeryn scrunched her nose. "They don't even have cell towers up there? Where is he going? Amish school?"

"Apparently, there's an Amish community, like, ten minutes away." Jen flung her arm outward to emphasize the fact. She shook her head. "Say I do go to the dance with Grant, and say we do start dating. What then? We'll go off to school, and he'll probably meet some girl that prefers the middle of nowhere to some girl who wants to live in the city and take pictures."

Silence fell between them, and then Aeryn said quietly, "But what if he doesn't?"

Growing slightly stern, Jen told her, "Then I'd prefer he want to date me once he's at that school rather than us get our hopes up or whatever."

She could tell Aeryn wanted to comment about how not all relationships were doomed to failure. Aeryn's wasn't, so why would one between Grant and Jen be? But Aeryn and James were both going to the same college and had probably already talked about how many kids they were going to have after they got married. Because that's just how stupidly adorable they both were. Jen couldn't say the same for her and Grant. They had never discussed any-thing remotely like that.

After all, they were just kids. She didn't want her first relationship to be one that had such a finality to it—only seven months. And that was if they could even be in a relationship together for longer than a few days.

She had seen lots of people her age date a friend, and then, after a month or so, suddenly they couldn't even speak to one another.

Above all else, Jen didn't want that to happen to her and Grant. She truly did love their friendship and knew that they could always be friends. She didn't want to risk that because she wanted to be greedy and try to turn it into something else. Just because she got excited when she saw him, became giddy when he smiled at her, and sort of felt like staying put and running away when he hugged her didn't mean that they should be in a relationship. Things got too complicated when you went from being friends to something else.

And Jen had enough complications in her life.

Glancing over at Aeryn, she said, "Thanks."

"For what?" Aeryn asked, furrowing her brow.

"For being *my* friend." Jen smiled. "They're in short order and, well, I dunno ... I don't think I've ever actually told you that."

"Well, in that case, you're welcome." Aeryn wore an accomplished smile on her face. "And thanks"—she paused briefly—"for being *my* friend, too."

The two didn't have to wait much longer after that before James showed up to walk Aeryn home—Aeryn's family only lived a few blocks from the high school campus, and James lived a few blocks from there. They left in a fit of smiles and laughter.

Jen continued to wait for her sister as she watched the couple leave, a smile coming to her face. It was their senior year, after all. One of them should get happiness out of it, right?

The large cafeteria was a room of never-ending echoes when it was empty. In that silence, Jen sensed Evelyn's presence before she even heard the other girl's stilettos clank against the tile floor. She rolled her eyes as she thought, *Doesn't she have anything better to do?*

Evelyn didn't say anything. Instead, she just kept walking toward Jen in a calculating manner. Glaring toward the ceiling, Jen let out a frustrated sigh.

When Evelyn reached her peripheral vision, she just stood there and stared out the large windows before she looked down at Jen and said, "You know, you should just give up."

Squinting a little, Jen asked, "On what?"

"I know you're trying to find a way to overthrow me," Evelyn said with a squeak in her voice.

A snort left Jen. *That's what this was about? The ice queen of the school thought Jen was trying to take her place? That was a riot.* Then she let out a happy, almost disbelieving sigh as she turned toward the other girl. "You *must* have a really tiny worldview if that's what keeps you up at night."

"Just get one thing straight. No one will be prom queen except *me*. Not you and not your little friend. Got it?" Evelyn spat with a glare. Then she turned on her heel and began to march away.

Jen rolled her eyes.

The retreating girl turned suddenly and said, "Oh, and by the way, no one here even notices you. No one cares, especially Grant Connolly. He'll be on *my* arm at the dance, and at prom, and at graduation. You'll see. Then we'll see if you still want to laugh." Without another word, Evelyn turned and let out a high pitched *humph* as she stormed off.

While Jen knew Grant would never attend a dance with Evelyn, let alone spend any time alone with her, it still made her scowl at the thought of them together in any sense of the word.

Other footsteps caused Jen to turn, seeing Nancy step into the cafeteria. As she approached her older sister, she pointed over her shoulder and said, "The crazy girl hissed at me when I walked past her."

"She's just upset because she wasn't hugged enough as a child," Jen said as she stood.

"Why does she hate you?" Nancy asked as they made their way to the door.

"I don't know if she hates me, but she definitely doesn't like me. And I couldn't say." She shrugged. "Maybe when we were on the playground in elementary school I didn't give her, her favorite swing or something," Jen remarked offhandedly. "So, how was your day?"

With a groan, Nancy said, "You wouldn't believe how stupid my math class was today!"

Jen chuckled as they exited the building and went toward her car.

After their short trip home, the sisters went to their respective rooms and attempted to conquer their homework. Sometimes, that task was daunting, and as it was Monday, the chance of them finishing quickly was unlikely. After a short time of being in separate rooms, Nancy came over to Jen's room, and the two sat together while finishing up their homework.

As the afternoon turned into the evening, and their family members returned home, the girls finished their homework and joined everyone downstairs. The scent of dinner rolled throughout the house as homemade chicken noodle soup was prepared. Laughter filled their dining room as they congregated and enjoyed their meal and caught up on what each of them had done throughout the day.

When they all cleaned up and retreated to their separate rooms for bed around ten, Jen sat at her computer, browsing through pictures and editing them when need be. Glancing at her clock, she saw that Tyron would be around to pick her up within the hour. She still hadn't found a way out of the evening's session.

The injuries from the previous evening had certainly healed by the middle of the day, so it didn't have anything to do with that. It was simply that she needed a break. A night of proper rest sounded luxurious, and the thought of it made her want to melt into her blankets and snuggle with Moo.

As though the cat heard her thoughts, Jen heard the distinct thump of Moo jumping onto her blankets. She watched the slightly obese fluff ball knead at the comforter before nesting herself in the fabric with a yawn. A small moan of envy left Jen, and she wished she could trade places with the cat, if only for the night.

Her secondary cell buzzed to her right, nearly knocking the Bluetooth earpiece off in the process. The phone had been a gift from her Zaheri not long after she had found out about being a hybrid. It was the best way they could keep in contact without her parents wondering why strange men were calling the house, looking for their daughter.

Sighing, she prepared herself for Tyron's voice to tell her to be ready to go at midnight. She picked up the earpiece and placed it in her ear before hitting the side button. "Hey, what's up?"

"Hey kid," Tyron's voice came over the phone. "Take the night off and get some sleep. We'll pick back up tomorrow night."

"Really?" she asked, sounding happier than she had intended. She could imagine Tyron rolling his eyes at her reaction.

"Yes, really. You've been going at it pretty hard and, well, I think we could all use the night off."

"Okay, thanks, Tyron."

"Golden. See you tomorrow."

Guilt flashed into her mind as she thought about how she had reacted when he had intervened. Throughout the day, she had thought about his actions and her own, realizing that he had only done what he had thought was best. Even though she had wanted the opportunity to kill the Ferveos on her own, she didn't really have any grounds to be so *mad* at him. He had only been trying to do his job.

It wouldn't bode well for any of her Zaheri if she died because they didn't want to hurt her feelings. They treated her like an adult, so it was only fair that she tried her best to be one.

"Hey, Tyron, before you hang up," she said quickly.

"Yeah, what's wrong?"

"Nothing. It's just ... I'm sorry ... for how I acted last night. You were only trying to protect *me*, and I kind of flipped out."

There was silence for a *moment*, and Jen snatched the phone, making sure the call hadn't been dropped or something. Just as she was about to ask if he was still there, she heard him say, "Thank you, Jen. I appreciate that."

She hadn't expected him to be grateful for her apology. "Um ... you're welcome."

"Look, while we're talking about it"—he dropped his voice—"I wanted to let you know that energy attack you used..."

"What about it?" Suddenly, she was scared, worried he might tell her not to do something like that again. That it was reckless. She tried to prepare herself for a reprimand or lecture about properly wielding her energy.

"It was an extremely powerful attack. If you had aimed it right, you would have easily taken that Ferveos out on your own."

A full-faced smile cracked her lips as she asked quietly, "Really?"

"Yes. And I just wanted to caution you that, while I'm confident you can use those attacks more regularly, you have to be careful. They'll drain you if you aren't vigilant. And blacking out in the middle of a fight wouldn't be ideal."

Jen nodded a couple times and said, "Okay, noted."

"Good. Now get some sleep. I'll see you tomorrow."

"Thanks, Tyron. Night."

As the line went dead, Jen still found herself smiling. She couldn't believe that Tyron had said he was confident in her ability to fight with her energy. He had never said anything like that before, and to know that, on some level, he was proud of her really made her feel special. Like, if he approved of her, what did anything else matter?

Jen had never said it out loud, but she really admired and respected her Zaheri. Krelien calling Tyron the "greatest of all time" the night prior had been an accurate assessment to her. They were dutiful warriors with hearts of gold. She knew they always had her back and kept an eye out for her, and she knew what they were capable of.

Tyron wasn't some recreational jogger. He was a highly respected hybrid warrior who shot gold energy out of his hands and could fight effortlessly against dragons. And he was confident in her abilities.

Quickly turning to her computer, she shut it down, turned off her desk light, and then hopped into bed. Letting a sigh escape her as Moo cuddled close, she allowed herself to revel in the comfort of a good night's sleep.

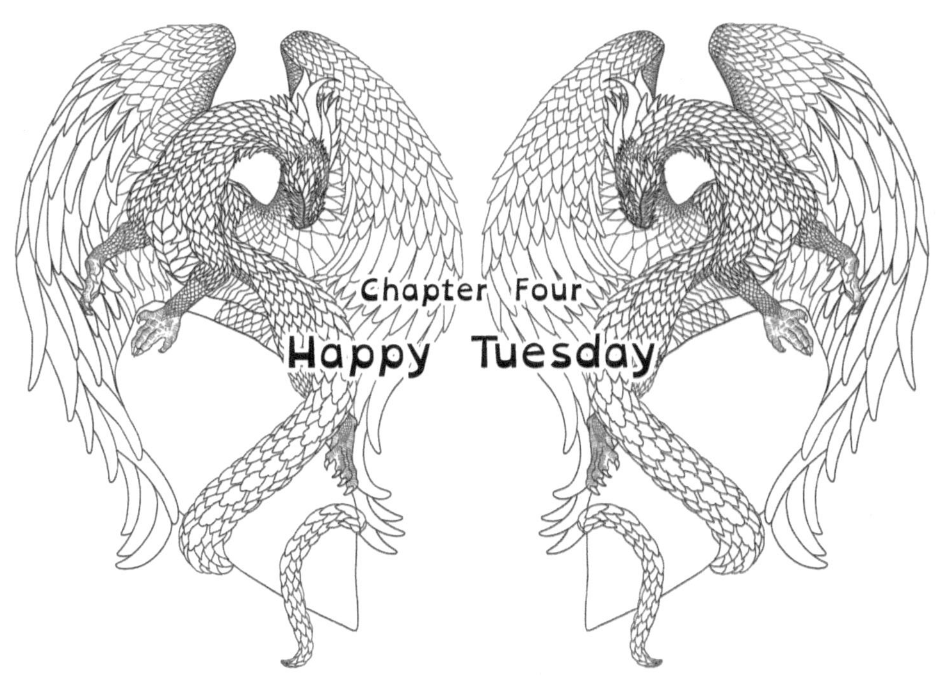

Chapter Four
Happy Tuesday

Leisurely making their way to school the following morning, Jen felt far better than she had in days. The fact that she had actually gotten eight hours of sleep the night before, combined with the knowledge that she didn't have to rush into school, made her see the day as one of those "good days." She had picked Aeryn up, and the two of them had gone off to a nearby diner to grab a small breakfast together. After some coffee and pancakes, the two made their way over to the school.

As they neared campus, Aeryn said, "You really ought to go to the dance, y'know."

Jen almost laughed. She figured that this would come up again, but she had thought she had at least until the end of the school day.

She glanced at her friend. "I really don't think I will."

Aeryn gave her an attempted stoic look. "My reasons for you going are purely selfish."

"How so?"

Bobbing her head slightly, Aeryn mused, "It's going to be my first dance with a date. And I'll need help getting ready. And what if James steps on my feet while we dance? I'll need someone trustworthy to help hobble me off the dance floor 'cause, you know, he'll just stand there, saying, 'I'm sorry' a lot."

"Okay, that's enough," Jen said with a smile.

"And not to mention the fact that there's the dress shopping and the pre-dance getting ready, and I have to have my best friend there for those things. It's just no fun if I'm the only one participating."

Rolling her eyes, Jen wondered if Aeryn had practiced this conversation. She seemed to be on a roll.

Nodding a bit, Jen agreed, "Fine, okay? I'll talk to Grant about going."

There was silence for half a second before Aeryn let out a crescendoed "Squee!" followed by, "I would totally hug you right now if you weren't driving!" As she spoke, she started hitting Jen in a light, playful manner.

Pretending the action hurt, Jen inclined her body away from Aeryn. "Just hug me when we get out of the car. There's no need for violence!"

"I'm just so excited!" Aeryn screamed in an overly dramatic way.

Jen just laughed as she parked the car, unable to think of a response.

Getting their respective backpacks, the two began to make their way to the stone stairway that would lead down to the school. Jen had to park up on one of the top tiers of the parking lot, and a walkway was designated for them to navigate down to one of the side entrances of the school.

Just before they reached the stairway though, Jen stopped and furrowed her brow. It felt like something had gone wrong and was being warped, though she wasn't sure what. The hair on her arms stood on end, and it almost felt like she was being stretched, like two opposing forces held either arm, pulling her body to its breaking point.

Blinking a few times, random flashes filled her mind—a dance club with thudding music; rolling hills and beautiful old buildings; a cave with a beautiful, blue-tinted dragon staring at her; a city awash in bright lights and a lot of bustle as rain poured; a small town with a towering mountain range in the distance; and last was a frozen landscape, the wind pushing drifts of snow across a barren horizon. Her thoughts suddenly fixated on the portal.

The portal to Tilion was something she had only ever seen activated once, behind the antique shop. Jen didn't know why, but she got the sense it was open somewhere, which was strange, because she had never felt the portal before. Heck, she had never even been through it to know what it felt like. Yet she felt it all the same.

Aeryn continued down the first few steps, but when she noticed Jen wasn't with her, she turned. "Jen? What's up?"

"Shh ..." Jen listened. Around her, other students were beginning to make their way to the school. Most of the people were seniors, although there were a few faculty members who didn't have to arrive until later.

It was similar to those times when you could hear voices through a wall but couldn't make out the words. No one had seemed to notice, but Jen could have sworn she had heard something. Something she had heard before. Something similar to ...

"Dragon wings?" she whispered to herself.

Glancing around as she gripped the railing of the stairs, Aeryn said, "Uh, okay. What about 'em?"

"No, you don't understand," Jen muttered.

Pushing her hearing past the sounds of the school, she felt like she got a flood of interference—conversations in the administrative building, a phone call across the street, a dog barking down the road, phones ringing, the shuffling of a breeze through the grass, the sound of the lake water steaming slightly in the cold November air, wind rustling through the trees on the ridge.

Dragon wings were big and leathery, and they sounded almost like a tarp flapping slowly in the wind.

"Jen, c'mon; we should get inside." Aeryn's muffled voice came from behind her.

As she opened her eyes, Jen found herself staring at the ridge just beyond the top tier of the parking lot, only a few car lengths away from them. Lifting her gaze, she looked into the overcast sky. It felt like her stomach rose in her body then plummeted to her feet.

"You're right," Jen said before she turned around. "Get inside, Aeryn."

"I meant both of us," Aeryn said sternly, her expression devoid of her usual bubbliness.

"I know you did." Jen looked her friend square in the eye. "Get inside and grab everyone you can along the way."

Aeryn snatched Jen's arm. "I'm not kidding, Jen. I'm not letting you go crazy on me!"

Jen opened her mouth to retort when a bellow filled the air. A gravely, deep roar that rumbled shockwaves down ones spine. She looked up into the thickly overcast sky and saw the faintest trace of a dragon fly by, its wing beats causing indentations in the blanket of clouds. Despite the fact she knew it was coming, the sound still made the hair on the back of her neck stand on edge as a shiver crawled up her spine. A Ferveos' cry could legitimately scare you motionless.

Looking back at Aeryn, Jen shoved her back, forcing her to move. Terror had filled her best friend's eyes, and as she fell backward, clutching the railing, the action caused Aeryn to break from her stupor of fright and look at Jen.

"Aeryn, go! Now!"

Trembling slightly, Aeryn tried to step forward but was barely able to lean in the direction that the Ferveos had come from. "B-but—"

"Now!" Jen yelled again, pointing toward the school. She couldn't spend another second getting Aeryn to move and could only hope her friend would do as she was told. If she remembered anything from all her training, it was that every millisecond spent doing the wrong thing could lead to disaster. And if a Ferveos was flying that fast in the direction of the school, that meant ground forces were likely right behind it.

As she turned on her heel, she was barely able to take two steps before she saw a bratak'ra leap onto a car ten feet from her. It smashed the fiberglass body and lunged toward her. Its massive bulk, easily four- or five-feet tall at full height, hurled at her. Its forepaws reached out, and its wide open maw revealed razor sharp teeth. Dual horns wrapped around its skull and extended past its jawline.

A dual-horned right away. This didn't help with that feeling in her stomach.

Jen had only ever encountered mono-horned bratak'ra in her training, and they were few and far between. Tyron had told her that the more horns they had, the older they were. The older they were, the more battles they had walked away from. Ergo, don't underestimate multi-horned bratak'ra.

"Noted," she had said with a nod.

Good God, she was going to die.

Quickly moving her feet, Jen skipped out of the way of the monster.

Well, while she was that close, she might as well grab it.

Despite being called a dual-horned, the beast only sported one base horn that curved around its head. Much like a ram's horn and how it wrapped around the animal's skull. But unlike horns and more like antlers, a second point broke from the central horn, running parallel to its counterpart that sat slightly lower. Both horns were long, sharp, and stretched past its snout. They flared outward slightly, almost like the tusks of an elephant.

Despite Jen's responsive actions, a horn had snagged her shirt and ripped a hole in the side.

Before the body got much farther, Jen took her right hand and braced herself for the pain that would accompany what she was about to do. Grabbing the left horn, she felt her skin tear open as she gripped onto the hard bone and yanked backward.

Her right arm wasn't strong enough, so she used her left hand too.

Swinging herself to the right, she yelled and used as much of the bratak'ra's weight and momentum to her advantage. She released the large beast halfway through the rotation and sent it flying back into a line of cars. It wasn't the brightest move ever, because she had sacrificed her hands for the action.

But she had definitely saved Aeryn, and that was worth anything.

"Go! Get everyone inside!" Jen yelled over her shoulder to a shocked Aeryn.

Her friend timidly nodded before she turned and ran down the stairs.

Knowing that Aeryn was okay, Jen took off toward her Jetta. While her Zaheri weren't prone to using her car for transportation, they had stored an Agerian pistol in the trunk in case of emergencies.

If this wasn't an emergency, she didn't want to see one.

As she ran, she felt the ground pounding just behind her. She glanced over her shoulder and saw the bratak'ra running after her. Its left horn was torn out of its skin, and probably from its skull too, from her stunt a few seconds prior. In its grotesquely yellow eyes was murder.

Deciding to forgo the keys, she leapt and reached out for the trunk. She punched the top of the trunk, and the alarm began to blare. The indent gave her something to grab onto, and she forced her body to land between her car and the one parked next to her.

The bratak'ra was right behind her and skimmed just over her. She felt one of the horns graze her shoulder and the warmth of her blood seeped through her clothes. *Well, this jacket is shot,* she thought as the neighboring car alarm began to go off. She knew the bratak'ra was on top of it.

A roar like a pig mixed with a lion, if that was possible, came from behind her, and without thinking through what she was doing, she gripped the indented area where the trunk laid on the right side of the car. With another yell, she swung the car around to her left, causing the car next to hers to fly off toward the other parked vehicles farther down the line.

Finishing her rotation, she pivoted slightly and smacked her car into the bratak'ra, sending both the monster and her Jetta careening down the hill into the second tier of the lot.

The monstrous animal yelped as it fell, the vehicle's weight crashing into it and sandwiching it between the Jetta and a set of parked cars down below.

Gasps of air left her, and after a second, she yelled, "Mitchell! Aw, dang it, you stupid beast, you made me break my car!"

Break was a bit of an understatement. She had totaled it in one movement.

Bratak'ra weighed close to five hundred pounds, and she had just whaled her car into it. Cars were totaled just by running into a tree.

She didn't want to dwell on what she had just done to her beloved vehicle. A new problem emerged as she realized she had also just effectively thrown her only weapon away from her. Not her brightest move of the day. However, her hands were healing quite nicely.

She started toward her thrown wreck of a car when another cry made her look to the sky. Going on the hunt for the pistol would only waste time. So, no weapon, and she still had a Ferveos to deal with.

Tyron's voice ran through her mind, and she whispered, "I *am* a weapon."

Throwing her arm out, the two spikes in her arm tore through her shirt and jacket. She braced herself. She was the only weapon she had, and that meant what she was about to do was going to have to count.

From the thick layer of clouds came a Ferveos, blanketing its wings against its body as it hurled itself toward the ground. It was bigger than the one she had fought two nights prior and was a swirling, speckled grey, like soot from a fireplace.

Jen brought her arm across her body then quickly threw it back down to her side. As she did, the spikes at her wrist and elbow shot away from her and toward the dragon like bullets.

Her aim was far better than it had been two nights prior. One of the spikes grazed the wing joint while the second impacted the Ferveos' skull just above the eye.

Victory rose in her, and she screamed, "Yes! I did it! I just killed that!" She pointed at the falling dragon before turning as though to rejoice with someone, only to find an empty parking lot. Glancing back to the Ferveos, she suddenly realized that her victory was poorly timed. The huge mass hurtled toward the ground and, in a few seconds, would collide with the asphalt. She turned and ran.

She didn't run fast enough. When the Ferveos

hit the ground with a low moan, its weight crashed into the cold hard ground. The asphalt tore and ripped, hurling small chunks into the air. Jen threw herself to the ground as a wayward minivan flew over her. Not ducking fast enough, one of the side mirrors clipped her side, and she felt the sudden impact of the small plastic piece and glass kick her up into the air.

Landing on her back, she sat up slightly with a groan as she gently touched her side. In spite of her gentle efforts, the pressure of her hand made her gasp out an airy breath. At least a few cracked ribs. And definite bruising.

Blood trickled into her vision from her brow. And now there was bleeding. Great.

She glanced at her hand and saw the laceration from the bratak'ra horn was gone. At least that healed.

Curse her for throwing her car. Now she couldn't even get to her duffel bag and get a change of clothes. She was stuck with what she had.

That was the least of her problems as she heard another cry from a Ferveos. Forgetting about the pain in her side, she got to her feet with a grunt and began to force herself to run toward the school. She was too outnumbered here, and unless her Zaheri showed up, there was no way she could handle this.

Reality crashed into her like a barrel of bricks. Her training two nights ago had been a cake walk compared to this.

As she hobbled toward the stairway, she tried to keep herself calm. That was the most important thing right now—staying calm. If she freaked out, she might make a mistake. Like throwing her car away.

Just before she reached the stairs, she heard the wing beats of another Ferveos, followed almost immediately by the sound of its jaws opening and a hungry, greedy growl barreling up its throat. Despite herself, she glanced over her shoulder at the sight and felt her stomach tremble. Another dragon broke through the clouds behind it.

She reached the top stairs and leapt into the air, rotating her body around. In her right hand, she concentrated an energy orb into her palm. The blue, smoky lightning storm illuminated the area briefly. As she finished the rotation to face the dragon, its mouth open wide to grab her, she gritted her teeth and threw her right arm like a sidearm pitch in baseball. The attack surged from her, ripping through the Ferveos' gullet and out through the back of its neck. Scales, leathery skin, blood, and flesh exploded from the exit wound.

Unable to control the energy any further, it evaporated shortly after doing its damage. Now she had to worry about her next immediate problem—the ground.

Jen didn't have much flight training, but she couldn't use her wings right now. She wasn't wearing a self-replicating shirt, and her wings would destroy every single article of clothing she wore on her top. And it wasn't like she was one to parade around naked. She wasn't one to parade around in a low cut top. So, wings, in that moment, were out of the question.

She had to let herself fall to the ground.

Grimacing, she braced herself and tried to curl into a ball. It didn't help much, but she was able to roll rather than bounce off the paved parking lot. Skidding to a stop, she struggled to her feet. She only had one more tier to get down before she reached the home stretch that would lead to the entrance.

Forcing herself to push past the lead filling her limbs, she kept moving. But as she turned, something hard and spiked impacted with her back and sent her flying. She didn't have time to change trajectory, so she smashed into one of the parked cars on the lower tier, landing on the hood. Her head crashed into the windshield, and she heard the glass crack, followed by the car alarm. It was muffled, and as she shook her head, she realized that there was something wet coming out of her left ear. Everything went fuzzy, and her vision swayed.

Fighting through the haze, she knew she had to gather her thoughts, but her brain felt groggy. There wasn't much time. Whatever had hit her was bound to come back to get her soon, yet she couldn't make her arms move. The only thing she could think was that she was bleeding from her ear, which didn't bode well.

Lifting her head slightly, she saw the second Ferveos land.

She tried to concentrate and do something. Attacking it wasn't completely out of the question, was it?

Grimacing, she sat up a little but not nearly fast enough. There was a stinging, coppery taste in her mouth, and her spine now ached as much as her side. The hardest part in that moment was getting herself to choose what to heal first.

The Ferveos reared up, and she tried to roll off

the car, but her *momentum* wasn't enough, and she just slapped back onto the hood.

Resigning herself to her fate, she assumed that someone might say something nice at her funeral.

Suddenly a small, yellow Corvette crashed into the side of the Ferveos' face. The dragon turned, a small trail of fire spurting out of its mouth as if it were saliva. A yell was preceded by Tyron's form flying through the air and latching onto the Ferveos' head.

The dragon thrashed about, trying to throw the hybrid off of it, but Tyron had an iron grip on a small spike on top of its head as he repeatedly punched his free fist into the beast's skull. A few seconds later, the sound of cracking bones came from the Ferveos, followed by a dull *thud.*

A hand closed around her bicep and pulled her upright. "Hi, kid, thanks for holding down the fort." Tyron's voice was slightly muffled, likely from her injured eardrums. He held her up with his strong arms as the world began to slow its spinning. She gripped his forearms for support and saw that his shirt stuck to his body and his hair was windswept and messy.

Ignoring his statement, she asked with a grimace, "Why are you all wet?"

Sounds began to come back to her left ear. It felt like she had been partially deaf and now her ear popped multiple times. It was fairly painful but wasn't that bad compared to all the other injuries she had sustained.

"Because I came charging here right after my shower. You're lucky I bothered to match my outfit today," he said, his grip tight on her elbows. "Are you okay?" He gently skimmed over the cuts on her face and tears in her jacket while he held her fast.

She wanted to fall forward and just tell him to carry her, but he wasn't making any motion toward the building, which meant something else was coming. Which meant they weren't done yet.

No naps for Jen.

"Uh, yeah," she said with a small nod as she released her hold on his arms.

He took that as a sign that she could now stand and looked around them.

"Good," he said as he wiped his hands against his jeans. Only now did she notice that his right hand was completely bloody up to his forearm.

Jen glanced down at her hand and jacket. Yep, definitely wasn't going to be salvaging that article of clothing.

"Nice job with this whole fighting thing, by the way. I'm glad you've taken to the art of running away."

Shoving him weakly, she whined, "Shut up. I took out a dual-horned bratak'ra and two other Ferveos before you even got here."

He glanced toward the upper tiers and swallowed. Nodding shakily, he said, "Wow, um, good for you." He looked back at her and cringed. "I saw the second Ferveos attack."

She straightened and realized that she had several deep gouges in her back that had torn through her clothes and skin like a Kleenex. There wasn't time to apply all her energy to healing it right now. First, she had to get her bearings.

"It was that one that got you right after you landed," Tyron continued as he pointed to the now dead Ferveos behind them. He looked to the ground and whispered, "For a second, I thought I was too late."

"Yeah, happy Tuesday," Jen muttered.

He held out a pistol to her, and she took it as she straightened. Letting out a steady breath, she said, "By the way, thanks for the rescue. Your timing was rather dramatic."

Handing her a small headset, he replied, "Drama wasn't my first priority, but thanks." As she took the headset, he tapped his own and said, "Krelien, you there?"

Krelien responded, "Yep, I'm here! Not fixing my hair or anything!"

"Krelien."

"Portal's still no go. How's Jen?"

"Safe. We have incoming Caligans. Where're Ar'on and the others?"

"Um, almost there. I think."

"Don't delay. We need backup."

"Okey dokey," Krelien said, and then the line went dead.

"Right." Tyron looked at the ground. He picked his head up and looked at her. "Okay, we need to hold them off till the others get here. Can you do that?"

Jen looked uneasy as she asked, "How long?"

"Any minute now."

He sounded so definitive. What she would give to go back in time a few hours, enjoy the shower a little more, embrace her blankets for a few minutes longer. Somehow. thinking about that helped her relax a little, and she felt the wounds on her back and side begin to patch up faster.

Jen took a deep breath. "Okay."

"You sure? You got pretty—"

"Can you do this alone?"

They shared a tense stare before he said, "Maybe. It depends on what comes over that ridge."

He was giving her an out.

If she felt she needed to be elsewhere, he wouldn't stop her. He probably would be fine. She knew he was more than capable of holding his own.

But he had a point. Depending on how many Caligans were coming and how many of them were bratak'ra, werewolves, or Ferveos, he might not be able to do this alone.

Swallowing back the taste of bile that suddenly rose in her throat, she nodded and stepped up toward him. "I'm ready."

Tyron stared down at her, and she could swear that she saw concern in his eyes. It reminded her of when Chip had seen her fall as a kid and thought she had broken her arm, and how he had taken her back to their parents, how frantic he had been. How worried he had been for her. That same expression was on Tyron's face.

It comforted her immediately. Any fear she had a second ago was gone. She didn't know why. Just that seeing Tyron that worried, and it reminding her of Chip, it made her feel safe.

Not looking away from her, Tyron touched the headset again and said, "We're on the western side of the building. Get here immediately. No excuses. We need backup." He pulled the headset from his ear and pocketed it in a fluid movement. His expression was even, stern, unwavering as he met her gaze. "It's you and me. I've got your back, you've got mine. If it's between you and me to make it, it has to be you."

"But, Tyr—"

He shook his head almost angrily. "No, you're more important. You have to live. If you have to leave me because it's getting close, you leave me. I swear by the Elders, I won't let you die here."

She didn't like this talk. She wanted him to yell at her about improper form or to concentrate more. To swat at her with a wooden sword to prove a point. To almost arrogantly tell her that he was in charge and was doing this to protect her. The dire nature to his voice, the look in his eyes ...

Jen suddenly realized what he had been to her for this last year—more of a friend than a mentor. And he was talking about her letting him die so she could live? Nothing about that seemed okay.

An image of Tyron lying on the asphalt, his eyes white and lifeless, his body mangled and torn, flashed into her mind. It made her stomach clench. She regretted that third pancake.

She did her best to give him a steady look. "Then, by the Elders, I'm not letting you die either."

He smirked. "You don't even know who the Elders are."

"Then teach me ... after this." She was trying to stay brave but could feel tears on the edge of her vision. "Now, who do we have?" she asked with a swallow, blinking away any tears to appear strong.

"We're here for you," he answered.

"No one else?" she asked, suddenly feeling defenseless. Just her Zaheri and that was it? What about the other members of the Agerian Defense?

All those fighters they kept talking about? Where were they?

Didn't they know there was a battle starting here?

Tyron opened his mouth to respond when another bellow came from over the ridge, causing them both to look toward the sound. Then he turned back to her and saw she was still staring at the tree line.

Gently placing his hand on her shoulder, he said, "Hey."

Jen looked at him.

He raised his fist to her and smirked. "You've got this."

She let out a small laugh and returned the fist bump. Not trusting her voice, Jen nodded a few times before following Tyron's lead as he took a few steps forward. Gold energy pooled into his hands and formed around his forearms like gauntlets.

She tucked the pistol into the back of her jeans, the cold metal a welcome relief to her freshly healed skin.

"Here they come," Tyron said as he looked up. He hated fighting down like this, but they didn't really have time to meet the opposition on the third tier. They would make the most of it.

Each of the tiers weren't that high between each rise, so there was a good chance they could play this to their advantage and blow up some concrete as additional projectiles.

Keeping her breathing even, she stood beside Tyron in a defensive stance, her arms loose at her sides.

From the tree line, they saw Caligan hybrids break through with a few bratak'ra surging past them in a charging line. The sound of Ferveos wings greeted their ears, but the dragons remained unseen beyond the clouds.

Blue energy manifested in her hands, reaching a central point in her palms. Simultaneously, they threw their hands outward, toward the oncoming attackers.

Up the tiers, the wave of blue and gold energy charged like a smoked lightning storm. The force of the attacks uprooted concrete, sent cars flying, and the earth rippling. Whatever forces that had broken through the tree line were instantly thrown backward, flying up into the air and crashing back into the forest.

A multitude of snapping bones and cries of pain erupted from the Caligans. Not having faced the brunt of the attack, another wave vaulted over the fallen soldiers without hesitating and began pouring down the small slopes of the ridge. Grey energy flew from them.

With a flick of Tyron's wrist, a gold shield planted between himself and Jen and the Caligans. The shield took the brunt of the energy attacks, the gold flashing to white with each impact before returning to the splendorous color. Bratak'ra continued advancing forward, undeterred by the shield's appearance.

Jen cast him a wary glance, flicking her gaze between Tyron and the approaching beasts.

It alarmed her that he didn't seem shaken, his eyes trained ahead. No part of him trembled. That steadiness helped ease her quaking gut.

The bratak'ra launched into the air, tilting their heads a little as though intending to ram the shield with their horns. The gold shield cracked and splintered like fractured glass, and a second later, it was as if tiny bombs had been laid into the shield. Shards of golden shield fragments soared into the exposed underbellies of the airborne bratak'ra.

Within seconds the rest of the horde was upon them.

As a Caligan was about to punch her, she brought her pistol around and swiped it across her body, colliding the butt of her gun with the Caligan's head.

Quickly getting herself situated, she began firing with as much accuracy as possible given the circumstances. Target practice had been the first thing she had learned in training, and Ar'on was one of the best shots around. Little blue lights shot out of the barrel of her pistol and tore through enemy fighters.

An energy attack grazed her left side, and she turned away from the attack, feeling her skin break in the process.

"Screw it," she muttered as she flung the pistol toward the enemy fighters then immediately threw a small blue orb at the gun. The gun exploded, tiny blue lights flying everywhere, like shrapnel. She ducked to miss another attack then brought her left arm swooping around her body. Blue energy, like a whip, lashed around her and sent anyone near her crashing to the ground.

Then Tyron was at her side, pulling her down. As she fell forward, Tyron kneeled and brought his fist back up, letting the small spikes in his knuckles come out and smashing his right fist into another Caligan. Then he stood and threw his arm outward. A wave of gold energy surged toward the enemy and caused the ten or so Caligans near them to fly backward. He quickly helped Jen up just in time for them both to begin to fight a few hybrids in hand-to-hand combat.

Dodging some blows and having to work with others that hit her, she moved and utilized her two spikes on her left arm.

Another Caligan ran at her, grey energy flying toward her in precedence. Out of instinct alone, she moved her left hand, and the enemy's attack flew right into the ground. She didn't think over it long as she stepped back slightly to catch the Caligan. As a Ferveos flew by, breathing a line of fire to her right, she threw the Caligan into the inferno, trying not to think too much on what she had just done.

She began to concentrate a blue orb into her right hand, and it grew past her palm when an energy attack caught her right shoulder, sending her to the ground. In a rage, she glared at the ground and drove her energy cloaked fist into the chewed asphalt as hard as she could.

For a dash of a second, the image of a shield forming around them entered her mind. As if under command from that brief message, the energy around her arm barreled into the chewed earth, and a flash of blue erupted from the spot. Expanding, the vibrant blue shield pushed and threw the enemies back a few yards, away from her and Tyron.

She stood and winced from the pain in her entire body before she stared down at where her hand had impacted the ground. A small dent in the pavement remained.

She looked over at Tyron, who stared around

at the circular blue shield around them. "How'd you ...?" Tyron started as he moved his gaze from the shield to her.

"I don't know. I just...did." She shrugged.

He had cuts along his face, a chunk of skin and shirt missing from his left shoulder, blood seeping from a laceration on his leg, and his fists were all bloody again. His shirt started to repair, and she looked to her own tattered shirt, wishing she had considered wearing her self-replicating one.

She let her gaze drift off toward where her car had last been seen. Then the two looked to the barrier and saw their opponents standing just past it.

"I don't think it's going to last forever."

"That would be a feat," Tyron said quietly. He threw her another pistol. "But it will buy us some time. Also, don't blow up your weapon."

"It worked, didn't it?" she snipped back at him.

He gave her a stern look, and she sighed.

"How much time?"

He shook his head, heaving breaths into his adrenaline riddled system. "I don't know." He went back to checking his ammo as Jen just stood there, loosely holding the gun in her hand.

"What do you mean, 'you don't know'? Aren't shields something everyone can make on Tilion?"

Wincing a little, Tyron said, "Uh ... no, it's only a fifty-fifty chance that a hybrid has the ability."

"Then how did I—"

"Jen!" He whipped around to look at her.

She stared back at him with her mouth hanging open.

Gesturing to the enemy, he told her, "We have bigger things to worry about right now. We will discuss this later. Like when we aren't trying to fight for our lives. That thing can't last too long if you don't even know how you made it." His laceration had stopped bleeding, but there was still an evident red mark on his leg.

Her shoulders drooped, and he closed his eyes before sighing.

Taking the few steps over to her, he asked, "Do you remember what I told you when we started your training?"

"I'm strong, and there are things that might happen that we won't understand, but that I do everything with meaning, whether I know it or not," she recited like a well-learned fact.

"Right, and that means you made that shield for a reason. Maybe you learned by our examples. Maybe you were being desperate. Maybe this was a total bit of favor. Right now, we really can't sit down and figure this out, okay?"

Taking a deep breath, she said, "Yeah, okay."

Her head suddenly pounded, and she felt like she had been hit on her right side. She held her hand out, and he grabbed her arm to steady her. "Whoa, okay ... I think it's breaking," she said as she held her head.

"Okay," he said with a few short nods. "You ready?" He let go of her and turned his attention back to the enemy beyond the barrier of the shield.

Just as he left her, she asked, "How do you make it do something as it breaks?"

He furrowed his brow. "You mean, shatter?"

She nodded.

He looked torn for a few seconds before he said, "Imagine it breaking like glass."

"Okay." Breaking like glass. Yeah, she could do that.

The shield popped, a low pulse accompanying it, and it did shatter like glass, tearing the shards outward and impacting most of the Caligans. The force of it even took out a few of the Ferveos in the air.

Most of the hybrids turned and ran back to the ridge, disappearing into the trees.

Another large Ferveos came out of the cloud cover and spat fire at them. A long, heavy stream of the molten attack descended toward them as a gold shield appeared and deterred the fire from hitting them.

Jen turned to Tyron but saw he stared behind them.

Up the tier ran Ar'on, who held his arm upward. He swung his arm to his right, and then again to his left swiftly. The shield in the air followed his actions, crashing into the Ferveos. The sound of cracking bones reached them as they saw its left wing crumble into its side.

"Get it!" Ar'on hollered.

Krelien ran past him before launching himself into the air. He landed on the Ferveos' back and held onto the broken wing, shoving his foot into the joint. The Ferveos flailed for a few seconds before plummeting to the ground.

The Jumper held onto the wing for support as Tyron ran up to the Ferveos.

The dragon lifted its head and inhaled to breathe a stream of fire, but Tyron kicked its snout, the force of the blow snapping its head back, and the spurt of fire shot into the air.

"Hey, watch it!" Krelien said, dodging the spurt of flame.

As its head fell back toward the ground, Tyron snatched it by two horns on its snout.

"Agerian filth," the Ferveos spat.

Jen stared at the beast in surprise. She didn't recall ever being told they could talk.

"Shut up," Tyron said, giving the Ferveos' head a harsh shake.

A guttural growl came from the dragon as it glared at Tyron's small form. Then it snickered. "The master will be pleased to hear that the Alpha Team is still willing to fight. We assumed your futile attempts at defense were crushed years ago."

Tyron scowled and jostled the beast's head again.

A growl came from the Ferveos.

"Why are you here?" Tyron asked.

The monster chuckled again, and Tyron looked at Krelien.

The Jumper forced the wing he was holding upright and jammed the broken limb into the Ferveos' shoulder bone. A grunt of pain came from the Ferveos.

"You okay?" Ar'on asked Jen as she walked over to stand next to them.

She nodded as she stared at the Ferveos, and it stared directly back at her.

Tyron looked over his shoulder at Jen before looking back at the Ferveos and shook its head again. "Why are you here?" he repeated in a dark, authoritative tone.

There was a brief pause, and then the Ferveos chuckled. "To finish what he started."

It continued to laugh, and Tyron clenched his jaw

before he took his right fist and landed a strong blow into the Ferveos' skull. The laughter ceased abruptly.

Dropping the head, Tyron stepped back. "C'mon; we need to get under cover."

Good and Bad Omens

After they walked down the row of parked cars and came to the sidewalk leading to the school entrance, Jen sat down and held her head in her hands. Tyron flopped down beside her with a long sigh.

"So, what happened?" Jen asked after a few seconds. She looked up, and it felt like she had pressure behind her eyes. It hurt to move them.

The three Zaheri were silent for a moment, looking between one another. Then Krelien opened his mouth. "Well, I personally don't have a clue," he said, putting a hand to his chest. "All I know is that I was enjoying a nice, steamy, hot shower when Ar'on here ran in and said something about a code red and that I had five minutes. Do you have any idea how annoying that is? To just be getting your muscles relaxed and then *bam!* you're torn away from even the simple act of finishing your routine."

"There are worse things to endure," Ar'on said.

"Says you. My hair will never be the same." The Jumper ran a hand through his hair, his jet black locks spraying water off the tips, leaving his hand damp. He looked down at Jen. "You don't have any hair gel with you, do ya?"

Ignoring Krelien, Ar'on said, "We don't really know what happened. We were at the shop and alarms started blaring like crazy. Then Kaldok ran in, telling me that something was happening and Ferveos were heading in the direction of the school."

"But they didn't come from your portal?" Jen asked.

Ar'on shook his head. "Not our activation, no. And that's the really weird thing. We don't have a clue what happened. The alarms sounded like the Caligans just...appeared."

"I thought the portal could only be connected to specific points on Earth?" Jen questioned, gently rubbing her forehead.

"Maybe," Ar'on offered. "We've only ever gone to the shop. There's a chance the portal works differently than we know. All we did know was that something was wrong. Caligans just showing up and all heading in one direction—"

"We could only assume they were coming for you," Tyron said.

"Lucky me," Jen muttered. "What should we do now?"

Tyron got to his feet. "Well, first we need to know who all made it here."

"No one. After you ran out the door and took off, there wasn't a portal activation at the shop," Ar'on said.

"I stayed as long as I could. Once Kal said they made it here, I figured I needed to get here, too," Krelien said.

Tyron sighed. "That's not a good sign."

Krelien stared at his damp hand; Jen had her head in her hands again, her eyes closed; and Tyron winced as he stretched his arm.

Ar'on glanced around at everyone. "You realize what this could mean, right?"

Tyron looked at his mentor but said nothing.

"Cregorous could have control of the portal."

The comment made Jen look at the eldest hybrid and ask, "What would that mean?"

Ar'on and Tyron were still staring at one another, as though they were having a silent conversation.

When neither of them said anything, Krelien looked to them and asked, "Guys, what would that mean? 'Cause if it means we're dead, then I vote we find a way to keep that from happening."

Tyron cast a quick glance to the Jumper before looking at Jen. "It would mean we're not done fighting."

Pushing her blood-matted hair out of her face, Jen sighed. "So then, what do we do?"

Rubbing the back of his neck, Tyron said, "Okay, we'll set up sniper positions on the roof and have Blaze and Archer on patrol on the ground near the entrances."

"That won't work." Jen shook her head as she stood. "There are too many entrances to the building."

Krelien grinned. "Psh, how many could there be?"

"Well, let me see." She thought about the layout of the school. "Five."

The three hybrids turned to look at one another as Krelien said, "I think we're hammered."

"Screwed," Jen corrected.

"Then we need to find a way to activate the portal now. But the closest connection I know of is back at the shop," Tyron said.

"And do what?" Ar'on asked. "If Cregorous has his army around the portal in the Expanse, then we can't hope to get to Agerius. Not with the six of us as our only option."

Groaning, Tyron shook his head. "Then what? We can't stay here."

"I could jump once we get to Tilion," Krelien offered.

Ar'on shook his head. "If he is there, you know you won't have the time for that."

"Can you activate the portal while you're jump-ing?" Tyron asked.

Krelien shrugged. "I've never had to. I've never even been near the portal when I've been in the fifth dimension."

"So, you have no clue if you can even interact with it," Ar'on deadpanned.

"Let alone see it," Tyron added quietly, rubbing his forehead.

As they talked, Jen darted her eyes between her Zaheri and realized that Ar'on probably had a point. She didn't know what the layout of Tilion was, because she had never been there. By the sounds of it, their portal wasn't as close to Agerius as she had always assumed. She would have to ask about it later. One thing she did know—they couldn't just run blindly into this, and they couldn't stay here. At least not without protection.

She sat up a bit and asked, "Why not?"

Tyron turned toward her. "Why not what?"

"Why not stay here?"

Glancing at the other two Zaheri quickly, Tyron said, a little bitingly, "Because it's suicide. We can't expect to survive trying to hold off a building this big without some form of protection, which we don't have."

"Not unless someone can make a building-sized shield," Ar'on mused.

"Well, none of us can do that, so that's out. I say we run," Krelien offered.

Ar'on looked incredulous. "Where?" he asked snidely. "Do you plan on housing everyone in another dimension? Or did you forget that he's a Jumper, too?"

Holding up his hands, Krelien said, "Anywhere's better than here."

"What if I did it?" Jen asked.

Her Zaheri were still for a few seconds as Krelien and Ar'on shared a glance. Then Tyron said, "No way. Until today, we didn't even know you could make shields."

"Jen can make shields?" Ar'on asked Krelien.

"I know nothing," Krelien said.

"That's the truth."

"But a shield could protect the entire school and leave us out of danger for the foreseeable future," Jen countered Tyron's disapproval.

"Do you have any idea how much energy that would take? Not to mention how much that's going to drain you to sustain a shield that size for an unknown amount of time." Tyron questioned, remaining steadfast. "That's a terrible idea. It's going to send you into a coma. Or worse, it could kill you."

"Coma or comma?" Krelien asked.

"Seriously, stop it." Ar'on put his hand over Krelien's mouth.

Krelien stuck his tongue out and licked Ar'on's hand.

The older hybrid ripped his hand away. "Yuck! Krelien, that's disgusting!"

"I saw it on a TV show once." He then grimaced and said, "And you definitely need to wash your hands."

"Was it on the preschool channel?" Ar'on asked with a glare as he wiped his hand on his pants.

Tyron pinched the bridge of his nose. "Once this is over, I'm removing the cable, and then I'm killing you two."

Returning to the debate, Jen said, "At the best, it'll be exactly the protection we need."

"I'm not going to let you do this."

"Can't I at least try?" She gestured toward the building.

With a sigh, Tyron said, "If you can figure out how to make another one, then yes, *maybe* we can talk about this."

"Okay," Jen said, content with the possibility of Tyron taking her seriously.

Her Zaheri rolled his eyes at her upbeat answer.

She closed her eyes and tried to think about how creating a shield would be accomplished. It was something she had seen Tyron do a few times and Ar'on had created them with ease dozens of times. But how she had made the one earlier was still a mystery. None of them had ever even mentioned how to create a shield, and she had conjured one up out of nowhere. Then she thought about how

Tyron had mentioned imagining the shield breaking like glass.

Was it all just a mental image?

Imagining a blue shield forming around the school, she felt strength well up inside of her. She opened her eyes. Behind her three Zaheri was a successful blue shield around the entire school. It wasn't solid blue and was slightly translucent in areas, while in others, large patches of blue swirled around. It was actually rather beautiful.

A smile came to her face.

"What're you smiling about?" Krelien asked.

She pointed behind them, and they turned.

Tyron's shoulders slumped. "Well, how long do you think you can hold that? Your other one only lasted a few seconds."

"This one feels stronger," Jen replied.

"Playing the enemy's side," Ar'on began.

"Please don't," Tyron said, turning to his mentor.

"If she made the first one by accident, she likely had little control over it. This one was intentional. She probably could keep this one going much longer than the first one." He leaned toward Tyron and whispered, "And she is stronger than us."

The last comment made Tyron give the elder hybrid a sideways glare.

"It feels pretty strong," Jen said again.

Tyron held his hand out. "Yes, I heard you the first time."

Her glare went completely unnoticed by him.

Krelien ruffled his hair. "She's already made it. We might as well just work with it. If it breaks, we'll try something different."

"If it breaks, it could kill her," Tyron said.

Ar'on looked doubtful. "That's been in rare cases."

"I can handle this," Jen said with conviction.

As he turned to her, she saw Tyron wore that same concerned look he had earlier. This time though, he looked both frustrated and concerned, his fists clenched at his sides, but his expression soft and worrisome.

After a few seconds, he closed his eyes and sighed. "Fine. But you tell us if, at any moment, you feel it's taxing you too much."

She nodded.

"Go grab the duffel from your car so we can get under that shield."

"Oh, um." She fidgeted with her fingers. "I kinda... wrecked my car."

"Wrecked it how?"

"I ... threw it at a bratak'ra."

The three men stared at her for a long pause, and then Krelien burst into laughter.

Tyron cast a quick glance at Ar'on. "Well ... I guess that works."

"She threw a car at a bratak'ra, Tyron. A car. That's not a good choice in the slightest. She's lucky it killed it!" Ar'on snapped.

Jen surged to her feet, and Tyron began frantically waving his hand in a dismissive manner as she said, "Hey, Tyron threw a Corvette at a dragon."

Ar'on shot the Team Leader an exasperated look, and Tyron deflated.

Jen winced. "Oh. Waving hands meant—"

"Don't say anything about the Corvette, yes," Tyron bit.

"Have you lost your senses?" Ar'on asked the younger man.

Krelien continued to laugh.

Holding his hand up, Tyron said, "I think we're forgetting that there are more Caligans on their way. We should ... shelve this topic for some other time."

"Like never?" Jen muttered.

"Never's good." He gestured toward a recently recovered Krelien. "Krelien, go get Jen's duffel out of the wreck."

Krelien straightened, and his laughter fell as he whined, "Wait a mambo, why me?"

"Mambo?" Jen chuckled.

"That's another word for minute in some"—he rolled his hand vaguely—"other language."

"Minuto. And it's Spanish."

"Krelien, just go get it," Ar'on said as he started to gently push Jen toward the doors.

Krelien pointed to himself. "Again, why me?"

Giving Krelien an incredulous look, Tyron responded, "Oh. Sorry. I just assumed you realized you move faster than the rest of us."

The Jumper begrudgingly crossed his arms and groaned, "Fine." He disappeared into silvery dust with a pulse of noise.

Ar'on pointed at Tyron and griped, "This is all your fault."

"What? The attack?" Tyron asked.

"No, him." Ar'on thumbed to the area that Krelien had been a second prior.

"I fail to see how Krelien being Krelien is my fault." He waved his hands and added, "Just ... let's get inside. I'm sure we have a whole mess of problems in there to deal with, too."

"Oh ... yeah," Jen said. Honestly, she had forgotten about the consequences of making a shield and entering the school building. Classmates and teachers and staff.

Suddenly, the Ferveos and bratak'ra weren't such a problem. She would rather stay out here and fight them some more. The stares she was sure to receive weren't something she wanted to see anytime soon.

With a deep breath, she said, "Okay, let's get this over with."

When they walked into the entrance of the school, the hallways were empty and everything was eerily quiet.

As they looked around, Jen muttered, "Oh great."

A doorway down the hall opened, and a male teacher poked his head out into the hallway. He saw them and instantly moved to shut the door as Jen screamed, "Mr. Busch! Wait! They're not—"

The sound of the door slamming shut reverberated against the empty hallway.

"Dangerous," she finished.

"Should we go in there and explain things?" Ar'on asked.

Jen shook her head. "The school's in lockdown mode. If we did that, they'd think you were trying to kill everyone and call the cops. Not that that would do anything to remedy the situation."

"So, who should we be looking for to talk to?" Tyron asked.

She turned around. "Well, where's Kaldok? And

Archer and Blaze? If they're wandering around, that might be making things worse."

Tyron hit the radio in his ear. "Kal, you there?"

"I'm here," Kaldok's voice came over the radio. "And I'm currently being held in the office of a Mr. Alderfer."

"Is he there?" Jen asked.

A muffled static came over the radio and another voice suddenly boomed, "Jennifer Monroe, where are you?"

Jen cringed at the sudden change in volume and the anger in the man's voice. Timidly, she said, "I'm down by the entrance near the cafeteria, the one that leads out to the rear parking lot."

"If you move even one foot from where you are right now, I can guarantee you no good will come of it," the man said.

"Yes, sir," Jen said in defeat and with a small nod.

After a few seconds, Ar'on asked, "Who was that?"

"My principal," she said dejectedly. Looking up at the ceiling, she said quietly, "I am so getting detention for this."

"I assume he's the man in charge," Tyron asked, and Jen nodded. "Good, because I'm going to need to talk to him."

"You'll have all the opportunity in the world in a minute. His office is on the other end of the school."

Footsteps began to reach their ears, their pace quick. Down at the end of the hall, a tall man with graying hair appeared. He usually was jolly and someone who the students actually wanted to spend time with, but now his face was flushed with anger.

Behind him walked two security guards, alongside Kaldok's intimidating form.

"Oh, that wasn't a good idea," Jen whispered. "I would lose the guards!" she hollered down the hall.

"Have you seen this thing?" Mr. Alderfer hollered back.

"What did he do to warrant an escort?" Tyron hollered as he took a few steps forward.

Ar'on did the same. "What's the meaning of this?"

"It's okay, guys. I told them it was okay!" Kaldok yelled.

"It doesn't matter! They shouldn't have done that!" Tyron answered.

Tyron and Ar'on both began to step past Jen, but she quickly reached out and grabbed their arms, pulling them back. With a shake of her head, she said, "I know what you're thinking, but it'll only make things worse." She looked over her shoulder and said to Krelien, "Don't you get any ideas."

"I'm not letting them just—"

"Yes, you are," Jen said with finality.

The Jumper begrudgingly crossed his arms over his chest as Jen released Tyron and Ar'on.

By now, Mr. Alderfer had reached them and took a deep breath before he said, "I assume you can explain yourself."

"And I assume you can let Kaldok go," Tyron retorted.

Pointing to her Zaheri, Mr. Alderfer asked, "Who are these men? What's going on here? Because I'm getting reports from my staff that *dragons* are flying about the school, and then we had this ..." He pointed over his shoulder at Kaldok.

"His *name* is Kaldok, and he's one of my Zaheri," Jen said quickly as she saw Kaldok's eyes close and ears droop.

"One of your *what*?" Her principal practically bit the last word.

Waving her hands a little, Jen said, "Basically, they're guardians, protectors of mine."

Fighting back the urge to hit the man for how he was treating Kaldok, Tyron said, "Okay, look, I'm in charge of these three and, in a sense, her." He gestured to Ar'on, Krelien, and Kaldok.

"I highly doubt that," Mr. Alderfer said with narrow eyes.

"At the moment, he's partially right," Jen said quietly.

Mr. Alderfer shot her a surprised look. "You, young lady, need to explain yourself, and explain yourself now."

"Fine! Here's your explanation: Earth is being attacked."

"By whom?" Mr. Alderfer asked.

"That's a bit of a complicated answer," Ar'on answered. "For now, we'll just say a bad guy."

His shoulders falling, the principal said with a wholly unimpressed expression, "You *must* be joking."

"No, he's being serious. He doesn't know how to joke," Krelien said.

Everyone turned to look at him.

He raised his right hand. "Does saying 'we come in peace' mean anything?" He tried to do the Vulcan salute, but it came out wrong, with his index and pinky finger separate and his middle fingers pressed together, so his hand made a W shape.

Shaking his head at Krelien, Tyron placed a hand

on his chest. "Okay, *my* name is Tyron. I'm a Chief Master in *my* world's defense."

Looking like he was choking, Mr. Alderfer started, "Your world? You've got to be—"

"The older looking one—"

"Hey!" Ar'on interjected.

"—is named Ar'on, and the young stupid one is Krelien." Tyron pointed to the two of them, respectively.

Ar'on glared at Tyron, and Krelien waved.

"And we can explain things, but first, you need to let Kaldok go. As crazy as this might sound to you, he's the most peaceful of us all."

One of the security personnel's radios went off, and from it came another voice that said, "We have a report that there are two animals on the third floor."

"That's Archer and Blaze!" Jen pointed at the radio. She then looked at Mr. Alderfer. "They're with us! Just let them be and nothing'll happen."

"That's true. Don't let them aggravate the white one," Tyron warned.

Krelien chuckled. "That's easier said than done."

Looking desperate, Kaldok said, "Krelien, now probably isn't the best time."

Mr. Alderfer held his hand out. "Enough! Everyone be quiet for a second!"

Everyone stilled, and from the radio, the other security guard said, "What are we supposed to do?"

"Okay, you,—" Mr. Alderfer pointed at Tyron "—need to explain things to me right now. The rest of you, I'm going to request head to the cafeteria so we know where you are, and you can do whatever it is that you need to."

He turned to the security guards. "Tell the other personnel to leave the animals alone and that they're friendly. Have them sent to the cafeteria."

One of the guards pointed to Kaldok, and **Mr.** Alderfer nodded. "Let him be."

"I'm going to send Ar'on with you. He'll be able to explain things better than me, and I really need to gather up my team for a meeting," Tyron said.

Looking at Jen and then at Tyron, **Mr.** Alderfer asked, "And Jen will be ... joining you?"

Jen looked over at Tyron, who just nodded to the principal.

The principal nodded. "Very well then. Ar'on, please come with me." He turned to the personnel and began to give them instructions as Kaldok walked over to the others.

"Golden," Ar'on said as he walked past Tyron, who he bumped into. "Excuse me, old person coming through."

Tyron held up his hands and opened his mouth to say something but decided against it. He turned to Jen. "Really, is there a better way to indicate which one he is next to Krelien?" As Kaldok joined them, he turned to the werewolf and asked, "You okay?"

"Well, they almost shot me," Kaldok said.

"I'm sorry, Kaldok," Jen apologized.

Shaking his head slightly, the werewolf smiled a little. "It's all right. They don't know any better."

Watching Ar'on walk down the hall with the principal, Tyron said, "Okay, c'mon; we'd better get to the cafeteria before they all freak out again."

Jen pointed behind him. "It's right behind you."

He looked over his shoulder and saw a large glass wall with glass doors encapsulating a circular room. Raising his brow a little, Tyron said, "Well, that's convenient." He waved Krelien and Kaldok in.

As Jen passed him, she stopped and whispered, "Why wasn't he mad about how they treated him?"

Tyron looked at her.

"I mean, they almost shot him. Shouldn't he be mad about not being accepted?"

Tyron's hard expression softened, and he looked toward the floor as he answered, "There are some ..." He rethought the comment and corrected himself, "Most Agerians don't accept Kaldok."

"Why?"

She didn't get it.

Kaldok was so calm and sincere. If anyone accused him of being mean, they clearly didn't know him.

Gently taking her shoulder, Tyron pushed her toward the door. "Another time."

She did as she was told, but the news that other Agerians didn't accept Kaldok made her wonder. Her werewolf Zaheri was the gentlest person she knew, and that was even taking Aeryn into account. How could anyone think he couldn't be trusted?

As Jen sat down, she stared outside and saw the blue shield gently shifting just beyond the building.

This day had gone totally off the rails. How long had it been since she and Aeryn had parked the car? Twenty minutes? It felt like an eternity had passed since then.

She found herself nervous and rethinking her choice to make the shield. Her Zaheri had made it sound like they were stuck here now. For how long? Would she be able to keep the shield up?

Trying to force her matted hair out of her face, she wondered if the cafeteria workers would be okay lending her some rags or something to clean up. Mr. Alderfer had made it clear that they weren't supposed to leave the room. So, even though she and Tyron probably could use a shower right about now, she wasn't interested in disobeying Mr. Alderfer's request.

She felt eyes on her and glanced back to the serving area, seeing the staff there, craning their necks to look at them. Quickly looking away, Jen realized that they were probably mortified by her bloody clothes and stained skin.

Digging her thumbnail under her fingernails to try to at least get the dried blood freed, she took in a deep breath and slowly released it.

It's going to be okay. We'll get through this. It's going to be okay, she thought.

Tyron and she had been able to keep a whole legion of fighters at bay a few minutes ago. And she had killed two Ferveos on her own. And a dual-horned bratak'ra. A small smile came to her face.

Krelien nudged her. "What's up?"

Glancing over at him, she caught that Tyron had spun around to look at her, panic crossing his face before he realized she was okay.

She shrugged a little. "So, I killed *my* first Ferveos. And a dual-horned bratak'ra."

Kaldok straightened, and Krelien's eyes widened a little before he looked to Tyron. The Team Leader held up his hand and gestured to Jen before saying, "All true."

"That's awesome!" Krelien said.

"Do you have any idea how high you set the bar?" Kaldok asked. "No one your age has ever taken on a Ferveos alone."

"And won!" the Jumper exclaimed. "And a dual-horned? That's ... you're awesome!"

Letting her victory pride grow from Krelien's excitement and Kaldok's astonishment, Jen looked at Tyron, hoping to see pride in his eyes. Instead, she caught him staring at her with a slight frown and a scrunched brow.

Krelien continued to boast about her, but Jen's attention had been diverted.

Tyron blinked a few times then nodded to her. "You did good, kid."

She smiled back at him a little, wishing that his affirmation had built her up more.

Chapter Six
Bad News Bears

After a half-hour of relative silence, Ar'on joined the rest of the Alpha Team in the cafeteria. During the course of his absence, Blaze and Archer had found their way to meeting up with the rest.

The two grovix had to avoid as many people as possible, because everyone wanted to pet them or hear them talk. It irritated Blaze, but Archer kept insisting they allow their species to intermingle. By the end, Blaze wound up biting Archer by the scruff of his neck and dragging him away.

Jen's silent wish for something to clean up was answered as a custodian came up to her and Tyron, offering a couple wet rags and some towels. The custodian had warily given Tyron the things, almost afraid of him.

Tyron had nodded and said, "You have my thanks, sir."

The custodian in turn had nodded before going back into the serving area.

While the rag was cold, Jen was grateful to get the worst of the blood out of her hair and off her face and hands. The towel came back smeared in blood, but she hoped she didn't look as bad as she had before.

Both she and Tyron were offered the bathroom in the back of the kitchen to change. Tyron declined, but Jen was grateful to get out of her tattered shirt. She put her torn up jacket aside, hoping that maybe it could be salvaged somehow.

When Ar'on came back, he entered the cafeteria and said, "Well, Mr. Alderfer has calmed down a bit and requested that we keep our distance from the other students. He explained a little about this 'lockdown' procedure they have. Everyone is confined to the rooms they're in until the situation is resolved." As he sat down, he pointed to Jen. "And he wants to speak to you after we're done here."

"Aw, man," Jen said as she covered her face with her hand.

"So, he understands the severity of things," Tyron said. He stood and occasionally paced near the table with his arms crossed.

"From what I could tell, yes. But he seemed a little at odds with the details. There was a point where he just told me to stop because he couldn't keep up," the elder hybrid said. With a sigh, he added, "He just wants to know what we plan to do now."

Tyron raised his brow. "Yeah, I know the feeling."

"At least things are secure here, right?" Kaldok said, scratching behind his ear.

The comment made Tyron turn to Jen. "How're you feeling."

"Brownie, you've asked her that eight times," Krelien pointed out.

"'Brownie'?" Jen asked.

"Broski?"

"Better."

"And I just want to make sure she's okay," Tyron said, shifting his gaze to a glare at Krelien.

Krelien sat back a little and held his arms at his sides. "You asked her five minutes ago!"

Before Tyron could explode, Jen sat up a little and said, "I'm fine, Tyron, really. I promise I'll let you know if I feel like I'm going to pass out."

"Y'know, most people can't tell," Kaldok whispered, and Jen shot him a look.

When Tyron looked to the werewolf, Kaldok whistled and looked away.

Ar'on looked around at the team and let his eyes linger on Blaze. The white grovix let out a short sigh and said, "We ought to assess the situation and ascertain our options."

Krelien raised his hand. "I think we should leave before things get worse and the humans expect us to save them."

He was met with a smirk from Jen and a stern look from the other Zaheri.

"What? It's an option."

"Not a viable one," Tyron chided.

"We could stay; be on the defensive until the portal becomes active or we receive backup," Archer suggested. "Or maybe we can try to get the humans out of here. Get them away from danger."

"How would we do that?" Ar'on asked. "It's not

like we can protect every one of them that walks outside of the field."

"Archer has observed a valid point. The humans are in most grave of danger here," Blaze countered.

"But they're in the safest place right now," Kaldok retorted. "Everywhere else is subject to attack, right?"

"What about putting up another shield?" Jen asked, and everyone turned to look at her.

Tilting his head, Archer asked, "One to protect the school and a second one to ... what? Trap the Caligans?"

Jen nodded. "Yeah. Then they can't harm anyone else."

"I don't think that's a good idea," Tyron said. "It's your energy that's being used to sustain the one that's out there. Adding a second could really hurt you."

"I'm with Ty; it's not a good idea," Ar'on said. "You could cause major damage to yourself."

Gesturing to him, Jen said, "But you said that was only in rare cases. What are the chances that it would actually hurt me?"

"Fairly high, actually," Tyron cut in. "Making one shield this large is a feat for a hybrid; making two the size you're suggesting is reckless."

Kaldok winced, and Ar'on looked over at him. "What is it, Kaldok."

"It's just..." the werewolf began. "Well, she isn't a normal hybrid."

As Jen pointed at Kaldok, Tyron said, "That doesn't mean anything."

Kaldok let out a small sigh. "Tyron, you know exactly what it means."

The teenager slid around the circular bench and

sidled up to Kaldok, offering up her fist for a congratulatory fist bump.

Kaldok looked at her then to Tyron without moving his furred hands.

"Really? You're gonna leave me hanging?" Jen asked.

"Just because she's stronger than us doesn't mean she should test those limits," Tyron said, ignoring Jen.

"As valiant a conversation as this is bound to be," Blaze started, "I suggest we return it to how to help the humans who are currently confined here. They undoubtedly have questions and apprehensions regarding what they have witnessed."

"You wanna go to each room and give a presentation?" Krelien asked.

Blaze cast him a wayward glance. "What I mean to say is that, regardless of what we may choose, that decision should be made with haste. We do not have time to debate the abilities or boundaries Jennifer may or may not have."

"Why?" Jen asked the group.

No one responded, and a few of them began to look anywhere but her.

Not knowing why, Jen suddenly felt dread fill her. She wanted to run away and hide somewhere, anywhere. Her heart rate shot up as though she had run a mile. It felt like the times when you could swear there was something right behind you, something that was going to scare you and make you jump out of your skin, but you were too frightened to turn and look.

The 'bad guy' as Ar'on had called him, had rarely been mentioned to Jen. Cautionary tales and quick asides, but aside from his name, Jen knew little about Cregorous. Just that he should be feared.

"He's coming, isn't he?" she asked after a few seconds.

Ar'on sighed and turned to face her. "We aren't positive yet, but there's a good chance that he is."

"The Scouts on Agerius were noticing strange movements but didn't really know the meaning behind it," Tyron said as he sat down. "We were trying to keep an eye on it, but with us here, that was difficult."

"An incursion like this has never happened before. And...there are some..." Ar'on glanced around at his fellow Agerians, "Rumors spreading."

"About?" Jen asked.

"The potentiality of an informant. It can't happen though. It's impossible," the eldest hybrid said quickly, as though dismissing the concept entirely.

"But how would he know where I am? Informant or otherwise? I thought you guys were the only ones, aside from your Council or whatever, who knew who I was and where I was," Jen said.

"Um, kind of?" Krelien said awkwardly.

Jen looked over at him with a scrunched brow.

"We're the only ones who know where you sleep, if that's what you're wondering."

"It's not."

Archer looked over at Tyron and Ar'on, but they both shook their heads.

"Why not? Now's as good a time as ever to tell her," the younger grovix said.

"Yeah, I'm with the pup on this one," Krelien said.

"Tell me what?" Jen asked.

"I do not believe we should go against the Council, Krelien," Blaze said.

"The Council isn't here," Krelien argued then turned to Jen and opened his mouth again to speak. "It's just that—"

The white grovix reared up, much like a bear. She slammed her paws onto the table, and Kaldok braced it to keep it from flipping under Blaze's weight. "I am! And as a Council member, I shall ask that you follow their wishes!" Her fur bristled along her spine, and her brow pulled into a fierce stare.

As he held his hand out toward Blaze, Kaldok said, "I respect you, Blaze, and I respect the Council the same, but I think Krelien and Archer are right about this one."

"I think we should continue with what the Council told us," Tyron said.

"And I agree with, Tyron," Ar'on said.

Scowling, Archer got to his feet. "But this changes things! The Council wouldn't want them to be kept in the dark forever, would they?"

"Certainly they would not," Blaze began. "But it is not our decision to when they should be privy to precise information."

"Them?" Jen asked.

Blaze thought back over her sentence, as did Archer, and the former glared at the latter while the latter grinned sheepishly in response.

"What're you talking about 'them'?"

Before Ar'on or Tyron could get a word in, Krelien quickly said, "You're not the only Human-Born."

"What?" Jen asked as Tyron said, "What did we just say?"

"I'm not going to sit around and let her wonder what the hey-dandily-day we're talking about," Krelien said with a glance at Tyron.

"It's hey-diddily-day, and what do you mean, I'm not the only Human-Born?" Jen asked Krelien. Quickly turning to look at Tyron, Ar'on, and Blaze, she continued, "And why can't I know? Where are the others?"

Ar'on threw Krelien a look of frustration. "Are you happy now?"

Krelien grinned and nodded.

Tyron looked over at Blaze. "What do you recommend we do now?"

"I'm right here," Jen snapped, but her frustration was ignored.

The white grovix stared her red eyes at the table under her paws before she flitted her gaze to Tyron. Letting out a slow breath but allowing herself to glare at Krelien's smug grin, she said, "There is no need for secrets when the greatest of them has been revealed." Easing herself back into a seated position, Blaze looked to Jen. "After Cregorous seized control of his armada, our Elders foresaw a right to the wrong. They informed one of our Council members that, one day, there would be hybrids born on Earth. It would be these Human-Borns that would stop Cregorous."

"Your Elders," Jen said before looking at Tyron. "You mentioned them earlier. Who are they?"

"Incredibly powerful and terribly ancient dragons," the white grovix answered. "They gave us the order and law of Agerius and will likely go on living well after this conflict is settled."

"And your Council?"

"The ones who keep order," Blaze said. "Quarrels are few in Agerius, and the Council sees to rectify them when they arise."

Jen was quiet for a second before she asked, "And ... how long ago was this 'foreseeing' told to your Council member?"

Nodding a little, Ar'on said, "Very ... very long ago."

"Ar'on was, like, twelve," Krelien interjected.

The teenager didn't think that was a long time ago. Ar'on looked like he was sixty.

She was about to ask how old Ar'on was when Kaldok said, "Agerians have revered the Elder's wisdom as prophecy ever since. But, to be honest, I'm not even sure that everyone really believed it."

"It almost was more like a legend," Tyron said offhandedly.

Looking at Jen pointedly, Blaze said, "The point being, that the Elders told us that someday, twelve Human-Borns would rise ... but among them, five would fall."

"Wait, wait, stop the train a second here," Jen said, putting her hands out. "You're telling me there are twelve Human-Born hybrids on Earth?"

"No, not twelve," Tyron said with a shake of his head. "There are only seven."

Jen was quiet for a second as she leaned back a bit. "So, when you say that five would fall, you weren't talking about...like, now. Like I could be one of the ones to fall."

The team fell silent, and Ar'on sighed. "No. They definitely fell a while ago."

Blaze's ears flattened against her head as she pinched her eyes shut. "Jennifer, you must comprehend one thing about Cregorous. While we have no proof, other than his actions, he has shown time and time again that he desires nothing more than power and lordship. He will stop at nothing to obtain what he decrees is rightfully his."

Swallowing, Jen asked, "What did he do?"

"We think he may be a Sensor," Kaldok said. Before Jen could ask, he added, "That's what we call someone who can tell the strength and abilities of a hybrid."

"They're *really* rare," Archer clarified.

"So rare that there is not a single one in all of Agerius," Blaze pressed on.

Jen crossed her arms. "That's unnerving—that he can sense us, but we can't sense him."

Eyes darting between his team members, Krelien cautiously said, "Well, I mean, that's not all he can do."

She looked over at him. "Ar'on already said he's a Jumper and a Sensor. And he's stupid powerful. What else could he do that would make him more OP?"

Tyron clenched his jaw, and Blaze whispered, "We are scaring her."

"I'm a little past scared," Jen clarified. "This madman can possibly sense people in a crowd!"

"You wanted to know," Tyron reminded her with a soft voice, giving her a stern look. "And you should be scared. He's not to be taken lightly."

Slightly shaking her head, Jen sighed. "You're right; I did want to know." Looking at Krelien, she asked, "What else?"

"We're almost positive he's a Telepath," Ar'on said.

Blinking a few times, Jen nodded then scoffed, "Of course he is." She sucked in a deep breath. "What makes you think he can do any of this?"

"Well," Ar'on started slowly, glancing to his team members, "how else would he know which babies to kill?"

Jen's eyes widened, and she felt her stomach lurch. "What?" she breathed.

Blaze looked to her. "It is the only way we can discern how he knew who the first five Human-Borns were."

Looking to the white grovix, Jen said, "So, the five that died ... they were babies?"

Kaldok looked at the table. "When we got here, we did some research to see what happened. There were two unexplained suicides, and three women who claimed their abortions weren't sanctioned, all one month apart from each other. All of them referenced some...mysterious man they thought played a part in things."

"All across the world," Archer said as he came to sit next to Jen.

The teenager instinctually reached for his neck and began to stroke his fur.

"We figured that was them."

Taking a few steadying breaths while continuing to pet Archer, Jen said, "So, he's a strong enough Telepath to convince mothers to abort their own babies and commit suicide." The terror and sorrow began to ebb away. Instead, anger filled her. "How could he?" She looked up at her Zaheri. "What gave him the right?"

"Now you understand our feelings," Tyron said, meeting her angry, confused glare. "The best we can tell, he doesn't think he has to ask for permission, or forgiveness, for that matter. He just takes."

Letting out a scoff, Jen shook her head. A part

of her wanted Cregorous to show up right now so she could punch him square in the face. Even though she knew she was fairly tired after the bout an hour ago, the rage consuming her mind was igniting energy in her.

"So, he killed five of us ... What happened to the rest?"

"They're alive," Tyron said.

"How?" Jen asked. "I mean, you just said that he can convince a mother she doesn't want her baby, for crying out loud."

Looks were exchanged, and then Krelien said, "We really don't know. All we knew was this legend."

"Prophecy," Ar'on corrected.

"So, what did the"—Jen gestured to Ar'on—"prophecy say?" The teenager looked at Blaze. She got the sense that Blaze was the only one who seemed to know anything about this legend, prophecy thing.

"That portion of the prophecy simply said that five would fall, and that the next in line could assume their burden."

Jen blinked a few times. "That's infinitely not helpful."

Krelien pointed at her. "See? Even she thinks it's stupid!"

"I didn't say it was stupid," Jen quickly defended. All eyes fell on her, and she mumbled, "Okay, it's a little stupid."

Sitting up a little, Archer said, "Most people believed that the sixth Human-Born would be powerful enough to stop Cregorous ... whatever that would look like."

"Okay," Jen said, trying to suppress her complex

questions. "So, what happened? How was the sixth born able to survive?"

The Zaheri all looked around at one another before Kaldok said, "We don't know."

Jen forced herself to not burst with anger. She was getting real sick of them saying that they didn't have answers. Pursing her lips and biting her tongue, she asked a little curtly, "What do you know?"

Ar'on held his hands up in a defensive manner. "We know what happened to the sixth Human-Born. At least, a little of what happened. Cregorous figured out how to track the Human-Borns, likely using his ability as a Sensor. We didn't know it at the time, but he must have been taking routine trips to Earth, attacking the Human-Borns one at a time."

"Then, early one morning," Blaze said, "Cregorous was shot back through the portal to Tilion, and his army amassed at the site to protect him."

Jen perked up a bit. "Wait—he was shot back?"

The white grovix was solemn as she said with a single nod of her head, "Yes."

"So, we mobilized," Tyron added.

"It was a good fight." Archer grinned. "Even some of the High Council members got in on it."

"In the end, Cregorous made his way back to Caliga." Tyron looked around at his team members then brought his gaze back on Jen. "And we were called to the Council."

"Okay." Jen felt the intense gaze of each of her Zaheri on her in that moment. She dropped her hands to her lap and began to fiddle with her fingers, trying to focus on anything but the topic at hand. "So, what happened?"

"Uh, we aren't sure," Tyron said, breaking eye

contact with her as he ran a hand through his hair. "The Council told us that the First had shown itself and had taken a stand against Cregorous. Naturally, we all thought that the Human-Born would be an adult, someone who knew what they were doing."

"Turns out, it was a baby," Ar'on said, looking at Jen as though she were suddenly precious.

"A baby?" Jen reiterated.

Archer glanced between the floor and Jen. "An unborn baby."

Blinking a few times, Jen said, "O-okay...So, then why do you think he's coming here? And what about the other six? Did he try to go after them?"

"He sent some hooligans to try to stop us but, y'know, we handled it," Krelien said.

"Hooligans?" Jen asked as she shook her head. "I have no idea how I'm supposed to correct that."

"The attacks always failed," Tyron said, pulling her attention from Krelien. "We never took our eyes off you, and I'm sure the other Zaheri didn't either."

"None of that answers *my* question of why you think he's coming *here*." Jen pointed to the table. "Why is he so interested in *me*? Am I the weakest link or something? Why aren't the others being targeted?"

"The others might be," Ar'on said.

Blaze shook her head. "That is highly unlikely."

With a sigh, Kaldok said, "He isn't like other hybrids. There have been rumors that he can control multiple exit points of the portal."

"Rumors," Blaze emphasized. "Nothing has ever been verified. Few have ever seen him and lived to tell of it, let alone engage him in battle."

Jen stared intently at Tyron. Eventually, he would

have to answer her question. She knew he would be the one to tell her what she wanted to hear, what she needed to hear, to make this itching in the back of her mind go away so she could have peace for the rest of the day that her initial thoughts were wrong. But the way he looked at her made her even more scared of what he might say.

I'm not special. I'm the weakest of the Human-Borns, and he's coming here first because, if he knocks me out, then the seven won't be complete, and that's probably significant. Somehow. Maybe.

I'm not ... I can't be ... It can't be.

The others were arguing about Cregorous' abilities, but Jen couldn't hear them. She just kept staring at Tyron, waiting for him to answer. The longer he was quiet, the more she felt this growing weight on her back and a pit gnawing at her stomach. She felt like she was going to be sick.

He finally swallowed and said quietly, "He's coming here because you're the one he wants."

Everyone went quiet as Jen stared back at Tyron.

She had to be wrong. She had to hear one of them say it; otherwise, it was going to drive her mad.

Slowly, she asked, "Why?"

Timidly, Archer said, "You're the First Human-Born."

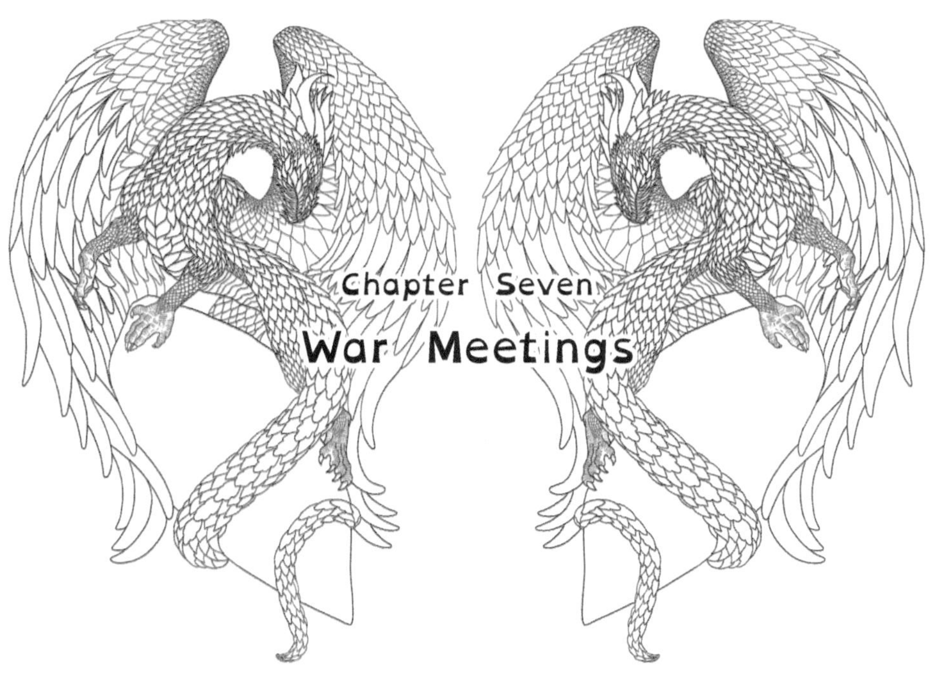

Chapter Seven
War Meetings

Jen dropped her eyes from her Zaheri as she stared at the table. This had to be a nightmare. It just had to be. There was no way that anyone would choose her to be the strongest of a group.

Oh crap. What if that *made* her the leader or something? Because if it did, these Elder prophesying things clearly didn't realize how stupid that was. She couldn't lead anyone.

And she had pushed Cregorous' attack back at him? As a baby? As an unborn, still in her *mom's* belly baby?

Looking at her fingers, she suddenly realized why she had been able to make the shield around the school, and how she had been able to take so many hits during the fight earlier. Heck, she was almost certain that she could make a second shield now, and it wouldn't do anything.

This new information was terrifying.

Why had she been chosen to be this powerful hybrid? She hadn't asked for it, and she certainly didn't want it. Her whole life, she was used to being a forgettable person, to being an outcast, to being a nobody.

Now, not only was she a somebody, but she was a really strong, potentially hero-ish figure somebody.

The word 'hero' caught her attention in her string of thoughts and made her shiver. The most heroic thing she had ever done in her life was rescue Moo from the side of the street as a kitten.

"Jen?" Tyron asked. Her Zaheri hadn't moved in the moment or so of silence that had passed. All of them were just ... staring at her.

Trying her best to keep her breathing even, Jen blinked a few times and whispered, "How did I do it?"

Tyron and Ar'on shared a look before Tyron asked, "Do what?"

"Stop Cregorous," Jen said, her gaze fixed on the table. "What made me able to keep him from ..." Great. Now she was realizing that this monster had already tried to kill her.

When she was a baby.

A pained expression came to Tyron's face. "No one knows. All we do know is that Cregorous tried once and failed. He knows that you pose the biggest threat to him." He sighed. "That's why we think he's coming here."

"So, he's going to come and kill me," Jen said. She tried to sound brave, but as the words left her mouth, a tremble accompanied them. Forcing her hands to not shake, she gripped her jeans, hoping that would somehow make her not want to crawl into herself and cry.

This was not what she thought was going to happen today. Three nights ago, she loved her life and loved that she wasn't a normal kid. Now she wanted more than anything to be some random teenager sitting in a classroom somewhere.

"Not if I have anything to say about that." Tyron scowled. The tenacity in his voice comforted her a little, but she still felt like she was floating away.

She rubbed her forehead. "So, the only thing you know is that I'm the First Human-Born, and he's probably coming here. But you don't know how I stopped him, or how we're supposed to stop him now, or if any of the others are okay." It came out like a statement weighed down with a brick.

Their inability to answer right away worried her.

They were her Zaheri. They were the people who always knew everything. They always had the answer and always brought comfort to her when things went wonky. And now, here she sat, them staring at her, telling her there was a monster in her closet and it was coming to kill her, and no one knew how she had survived against the monster the last time it had struck.

Blaze was always the bravest of them when it came to speaking. "Jennifer, there are many things that the Council does not know."

"That isn't comforting," Jen whispered.

"But what should be is what gives us comfort," Kaldok added, placing his large hand on her arm. His action caused her to look up at him. "Just because the Council doesn't know doesn't mean that no one knows. The Elders know everything."

Jen sat up a little straighter. "So, I could ask them?"

Kaldok tried to start a response, but the words just choked out of him. He looked to Blaze and Tyron.

Turning to Jen, Tyron said, "Of course you can."

"That's a little comforting," Jen said, offering a small smile to Kaldok. Then she let out a slow breath. "Okay, fine. So, I'm ..." She shook her head. "I'm whatever. Why do I pose the biggest threat to him, aside from the whole ... me being powerful thing?"

"The Elder's prophecy is common knowledge across Agerius," Blaze said. "Cregorous most certainly has heard it, and the titles each of you were given."

"Titles?" Jen asked.

"Raidin, Protector, Warrior, Healer, Shifter, Scholar, and Requisite," Archer said.

"Raidin? That's me?" Jen asked.

"It's an old title," Ar'on answered.

Jen glanced at the others before she asked, "Are you guys sure? Like, you're positive you didn't mix up who was who?"

Krelien looked to Blaze. "You wanna answer that one?"

With a sigh, Blaze said, "As a former Council member, I can assure you that this is one thing the Council knew for certain. They would not have sent us to the wrong child."

"Great," Jen mumbled. "This day just keeps getting better." Her head was starting to spin. She would give anything to just be allowed to go lie down for a few hours and pretend like all of this wasn't happening.

As the thought entered her mind, she immediately

knew that was selfish. There were over a thousand people trapped at the school. She would have to save her frustrations for later.

Squaring her shoulders, she said, "Fine. So, what do we do?"

Her Zaheri all stared at her, and Jen could tell that they were worried about how she felt. In a real way, she wanted to go on about how she did feel, but she also knew that this wasn't the time.

"Whatever we do, we *must* act before Cregorous reaches Earth," Blaze said. "Jennifer is in the gravest of danger."

"He could already be here," Tyron muttered.

Cocking his head a little to the side, Ar'on said, "We would likely already know."

"How?" Jen asked.

"For starters, your shield probably wouldn't be standing anymore."

"Wait a second," Jen said, sitting up a bit and swallowing. "If I'm some strong adversary to Cregorous, shouldn't I stay? Let him find *me*?"

"No!" they all yelled.

"If we did that, you'd be as good as dead!" Tyron continued.

"And let's face it, you're no good to anyone dead," Archer added.

"Who says I would die?" Jen asked.

Shaking his hands in emphasis, Tyron said, "This is Cregorous we're talking about. You're a target, and he won't stop until you're dead. I'm not exaggerating just to prove a point—this is reality. You have someone very powerful coming after you."

"I get that, but I stopped him once before, right? So, what's to say I can't do it again?"

"That was years ago. Elders, you were a baby," Tyron cautioned. "It was a miracle the first time. Do you really want to tempt death?"

"He's right," Krelien said as he gently touched Jen's arm. "Trust us on this one."

She looked back at Krelien and sighed. "Okay. So ...?"

Tyron let out a small sigh himself. "What're the pros and cons of our possible options?"

"The humans are in the safest place presently," Blaze said.

"Also the most dangerous," Ar'on countered.

"Releasing them would only expose them to the free-roaming Caligans."

"Unless I make another shield," Jen said.

Tyron opened his mouth to begin a retort, but she abruptly felt emboldened and cut him off.

"You just told me I was able to stop the strongest hybrid ever, and I did that when I was a fetus. I'm not feeling any strain from the shield currently out there. I could do another one just as easily."

The words tumbled out of her mouth so fast that she didn't really know what she had said. But as the sounds of the statement rang in her ears, she realized she had a point—if she was so powerful, a second shield would be easy to make. It also brought her some comfort in this uncomfortable situation.

If she could just make two shields, maybe then she would feel a little more confident about this whole the-axe-murderer-is-coming-for-you thing.

"But, if we do that, we're stuck here," Krelien said. "I like my plan more."

"Your plan was to run away," Archer said.

"Exactly. Run away and *live*," Krelien emphasized. "I'm not just being stupid. I'm on clever street here."

"Stop talking about how supposedly smart you are and tell us what you're thinking," Ar'on grumbled.

"We leave."

"There'd better be more to this brilliant plan of yours," Tyron began.

Holding up his hands, Krelien said, "And we could make them follow us. Once we're gone, they'll leave the school alone."

"That's your brilliant plan?" Ar'on asked. "Even if the group outside follows us, Cregorous will probably think we're just causing a diversion and still tear the place apart."

"You're only guessing," Krelien said with a wave of his hand. "There's always a chance it'd work."

"But so are you," Kaldok said. "Which is more likely of the outcomes?"

Krelien grumbled something and pouted.

"Cregorous has not proven to be hasty when it comes to the Human-Borns," Blaze said. "It is far more likely that he would destroy this building simply in the chance that Jennifer may be hidden within."

"We can't do that," Jen said with a forceful shake of her head. "I'm not letting my friends and family die while we run away."

"If we stay, what do we do then?" Kaldok asked. "Can we really just hold tight until reinforcements show up?"

"That's assuming that they can get through Cregorous' defenses," Ar'on said.

Nodding toward Ar'on, Blaze countered, "That is assuming that Cregorous is in control of the portal."

"Why wouldn't he be?" Krelien asked. "Why else

wouldn't we have gotten some help earlier? Or even now?"

"Krelien's right. That proves he isn't here yet," Tyron said with a few small nods. "If he were, Agerius would have control of the portal, and they'd send reinforcements."

"Then how are we supposed to get any help?" Jen asked. "If they never can get control of the portal on your end, then how can they send us reinforcements?"

Tyron shook his head. "Eventually, Cregorous will come through the portal, and he'll have to relinquish his control to do that. He can't control it while he's here."

"But that'll require us to have to hold out against whatever he throws at us," Ar'on warned.

"Maybe the Council just needs a show that we're still here," Archer mused.

Nodding, Blaze said, "Archer has raised a valid point. If the Council sees that we have done something as an effort to push back, they can know that we are safe yet in distress."

"A message," Kaldok said.

Archer nodded. "There has to be a way."

Tyron darted his eyes around the room before he stood. "There is. It's simple and crude, but it would work."

"If you're talking about shooting an orb through the portal ..." Ar'on began.

"I am," Tyron said with an assertive nod.

Sitting up, Blaze said, "Tyron, not only is that reckless, but it is also suicide in the current predicament we find ourselves in. Arriving in a proximate location of the portal now is impossible, considering you would have to fly to the shop, which would only compromise our headquarters."

Tyron shook his head. "No, I wouldn't." Everyone was still as he continued, "The numbers that we saw were just a first wave, a scouting party. Cregorous will definitely be sending more warriors through the portal sooner or later. All we have to do is be ready for when that happens and utilize the opportunity."

"Can something like that be sent through an incoming portal activation?" Kaldok asked.

"Why not?" Krelien shrugged.

"Because it's not the way the portal works. You can't just hop in it when it's been activated from Tilion and expect it to take you there. It'll just push you back," Ar'on said.

"That's us, not an energy orb," Tyron said. "It's energy; it might work."

Blaze shook her head. "It has never been accomplished."

"So, we can be the first ones to try. I'm open to alternatives."

"What good would that even do?" Jen asked.

"It would travel through the portal, hit whatever might be in its way, and then disappear."

"And how would that help us?" Archer asked.

"It would be a sign to the Council that we're here," Ar'on said reluctantly.

Nodding again, Tyron said, "Yes, it would. They'd know that, somewhere, the Zaheri are fighting. It'll let them know that we're still alive. It'll let them know they're still alive."

Kaldok's eyes were on the ground when he said, "Then I have an idea."

"What? Wait—we haven't even decided that an orb is a good idea," Ar'on said.

"I am timid to answer, but I believe that it is our best course of action," Blaze said, sighing.

Archer looked over at the werewolf. "What were you thinking, Kal?"

Looking away from Archer, Kaldok looked at Tyron. "Send us three in." He gestured to himself, Blaze, and Archer.

Blaze sat up a little bit and furrowed her brow as Archer's ears perked.

"What? Why?" Tyron asked.

"Into the thick of bratak'ra and werewolves?" Ar'on asked.

"With Blaze? What would she do? Talk them to death?" Krelien smirked.

Blaze's fur bristled, and she growled. "You would be wise to remember who it is you *mock*."

"Oh, c'mon; it's all in good fun," Krelien said, "because his plan is stupid."

"What was the phrase? 'Clever street'?" Blaze mused before she glared at the Jumper. "If you wish to continue to reside there, I suggest you shut your trap."

Krelien pouted. "You're never any fun."

Ignoring everyone else, Kaldok said, "Archer looks like an older bratak that hasn't earned its horns yet, and I am a werewolf. Blaze can play the part of captive."

"Uh, 'bratak'?" Jen asked. "Aren't they called 'bratak'ra'?"

"They get the 'ra when they get horns," Kaldok hushed as an aside.

"While this is an insane idea," Ar'on said, "it

wouldn't work. They know what Blaze looks like, and they'd know she's far too good to get captured by a werewolf."

Shrugging, Tyron said, "So, she disguises herself."

Ar'on looked over at Tyron then blinked a few times as he looked off at the wall. "That could work."

"Wait a sec—can you do that?" Jen asked Blaze.

The white-furred grovix straightened, her eyes widening. "I most certainly cannot," she said indignantly.

"Yes, you can," Krelien said.

Blaze glared at him again.

He held up his hands. "Sorry Blazer, but you can't deny what you can do."

"I refuse!" she said in an angry howl. "I was never a common Warrior, and I never shall be!"

"Ow," Archer said as he put his large paw over his chest. "You slay me, Blaze."

With a roll of her eyes, she said, "I was not referencing you, Archer."

In exasperation, Tyron threw his arms in the air. "Okay, Blaze, we'll do it your high and mighty way. You can walk on over there and, in your great diplomatic and scholarly ways, reason with Cregorous. I'm sure he'd love to chat with you."

She looked flustered, but it was hard to tell with her thick, white fur all over her body. She opened her mouth to retort then snapped shut as she glared at Tyron.

"Whoa," Krelien said. "She's speechless." He stood and walked over to Tyron, grabbing his hand. "Can I shake your hand?"

Shaking Krelien off, Tyron said, "Get off me," before he stepped up to Blaze. "Right now, defensive action isn't the right call."

Blaze sat with her mouth clamped shut and stared at no one.

Jen leaned toward her white furred Zaheri and asked quietly, "Blaze, we need you for this. Can you ... make yourself look different?"

The grovix sighed, trying to regain her composure. Screaming at Jennifer wasn't going to help. The teenager didn't know any better.

"Jennifer, I have not subjected myself to fighting for countless years."

"Even here?"

The white grovix nodded in response.

"Yeah, instead, you've let yourself go to waste sitting in that Council and talking," Krelien said, sounding bored and motioning with his hands in a talking manner. "Blazer, think about it. Ty's got a point. This is war."

"And now Krelien's got a point," Kaldok said. "The time for talk of peace has never been something Cregorous has let us have as an option. Blaze, you know that I respect you—"

"It has nothing to do about respect," she said. "It is about my pride! It took us years for anyone to consider us as proper Council members. I swore I would never don a warrior's mantle again, as I saw little need of it from a Council member's chair." The hard look on her face softened a little. "All of the work that has led to this was far more difficult than you could imagine. It is not something I wish to throw away so blithely."

"We know that, Blaze," Archer said softly. "None of us will think any less of you for it."

"And we won't think any more of you for it either," Krelien said.

Her shoulders drooped as she lost her aggressive stance. "I suppose I could look less ..."

"Pompous?"

"I will pretend I did not hear that," she replied darkly. "Conspicuous is the word I was thinking."

Running a hand through his hair, Tyron said to Kaldok, "I assume you were thinking to engage them."

"We could slip in from one of the ground entrances on the first floor of the building," Kaldok said. "When the portal activates, we can cause confusion. They'll think that a scuffle occurred or something. It'll give one of you a chance to get to the portal and send an orb through."

"There're hundreds of enemy fighters out there." Tyron pointed out the large windows around the room. "How do you propose we get there?"

Smacking Krelien, Ar'on said, "We can provide cover fire." He waved his rifle. "We didn't bring them for show."

"Ow," Krelien said in an exasperated tone as he looked over at Ar'on.

"That only leaves *me*," Tyron said.

"And *me*," Jen said.

They all stopped and stared at her.

"You can't honestly expect *me* to just stay here," she said after a few seconds.

"Yes, we can, and you will."

"What are you talking about? You can't do this alone, Tyron. And remember, you trained me," she said, emphatically pointing between the two of them.

"This is war, Jen! You can't use rationalization like that based on these stipulations!"

Blaze stood. "This will be incredibly dangerous, Jennifer."

"What exactly would you call an hour ago?" Jen shot back. "Ideal conditions?"

Blaze's eyes widened, and her ears straightened as she leaned back a little.

"The front line is no place for a teenager," Ar'on said.

Jen got to her feet, defiance and courage resounding in her stance. "An hour ago, I killed two Ferveos and a dual-horned bratak'ra *on my own*, without any sign of backup. I'm not just a teenager. You said so yourselves."

"As in, you're not just a human kid? Yeah, we know that," Krelien said. "But we don't even have Agerian warriors that are as young as you, and they've been training since they were like ... two."

"Well, I've got them beat," Jen said, looking between her Zaheri. "I'm some great warrior, right? I pushed Cregorous back, right?"

Tyron shook his head and held out his hand. "Don't. Don't start, Jen."

"Don't start what, Tyron? It's *my* fault this guy is here. He's threatening *my* world. *My* home. *My* friends and *my* family. Do you seriously think that I'm just going to sit back and let him tear through everything I know? Possibly kill you guys?

The last question caught her by surprise, and she felt a sharp pang tear through her chest.

"You're just a kid!" Tyron fired. "A year and a half ago, you didn't even know what you were, let alone what you could do! Killing two dragons and a bratak'ra doesn't mean you're battle ready!"

Blaze shut her eyes at the tone Tyron used, and Kaldok looked at her, his ears drooping.

Ar'on spoke up, using as calm a tone as he

could muster. "Jen, you're good for your age, and for your limited knowledge of what and who you are, I will give you that. But that doesn't mean that you belong on the battlefield, fighting against those monsters."

"I was there earlier. I was fighting right next to you." She pointed to Tyron.

"That was different," Tyron argued. "We didn't have any other option. The others weren't here yet."

"You trusted *me* then; why don't you trust *me* now?"

"It has nothing to do with trust!" Tyron burst. Then he took a deep breath and said sternly, "You don't belong in a battle."

"I'm going to have to someday," Jen countered.

"Who said that day was today?" Archer asked timidly, his ears uneven on his head.

"Or in this year?" Krelien added.

"Cregorous did by coming through that portal today and sending this legion to destroy *me!*" she hollered, pointing back out the window. She threw looks to her opposing Zaheri. "Is that answer not good enough?"

"No, it isn't," Tyron said definitively.

"Then what answer is?" Jen asked.

The Team Leader's face contorted between anger and sorrow. Clearly, she was aggravating him, provoking him into an argument to try to make him see things her way. He was just trying to remain calm and not chain her to a wall or something to keep her from following them. Jen wanted to punch him so badly, just to prove a point. To prove she was strong enough to handle this.

Then Tyron said with a frown, "There isn't one."

There wasn't anger behind his tone. He almost sounded broken. "I admire your tenacity, but—"

"Tyron," she said quietly, trying to rein in her anger. "Last night, you said that you were confident in my abilities. I know you only meant it in a small scale, but you said it. That's what gave me the strength to stand my ground this morning and not run away. Your training is what kept me in place when the first dragon flew overhead. Please, let me do this. Trust that I can do this. One day, you might not be here to take my place. And if what you said is true, then there's no way for you to take my place when I eventually run into Cregorous. Do you honestly plan to tell me to stay home when he comes knocking on the door and taking him on your own?"

Tyron's eyes began to lose some of their hardness as she spoke. He swallowed hard and looked like he might cry. Seeing that look in his eyes made her chest tight.

Trying to continue on her tirade, she said, "Kaldok said the Elders knew everything. Then maybe ... maybe we just have to trust that they'll protect me out there." She didn't know what made her say it. She didn't even know what these Elder dragons were. But as she said it, she felt comforted and covered, as though a blanket had just been wrapped around her shoulders.

Tyron shook his head.

All around them, the other team members were silent, staring at Jen and Tyron. They all knew what it would mean for Jen to go out and fight—she would get hurt. It wasn't even that she might get hurt. She definitely would get hurt. No one walked away from a battle unscathed.

It was hard enough for them to stare at her now, with blood all over her clothing and her wounds only just recently healed. Letting her go wasn't going to be easy, but they would have to wait for what Tyron said. He was the Team Leader, and whatever he said would have to stand, regardless of what Jen thought.

"We can't lose you Jen," Tyron said after a long pause, staring at the floor as he spoke. Before he continued, he looked up at her. "We can't. And not just because the Elders said you were the Raidin."

That comment made her stop for a few seconds before answering. There was weight to what he had just said that she hadn't anticipated. It was that title. The same title Ar'on had mentioned earlier. She still didn't even know what he meant by 'the Raidin,' but that name alone evoked some level of reverence. Even if she hadn't wanted to, Jen realized, in that singular moment, whatever name that was, it was glued to her. Like it belonged to her.

Looking between him and the floor, she said, "Then you'll just have to make sure nothing happens."

A moment passed between them all as no one said anything.

Jen thought to two nights ago; how he had intervened because he thought that was the best course of action.

The fact of the matter was that he did know better than her.

She found herself remembering who she was arguing against—Tyron, a Chief Master of the Agerian Defense, expert in hand-to-hand combat, survivor of countless battles, and he barely had a single scar to show for it.

Most importantly, he was her teacher.

"But ... you are my Zaheri," she said, letting her offensive stance fall. "And I can't force you to listen to me."

Tyron turned his head slightly to look at Ar'on, who just looked back at his old friend. This wasn't something that they had been told how to handle. It was situations like these that would shape the fate of, not only their team, but every human and hybrid's life.

He saw her logic, and it made sense.

She would have to eventually be on a battle-field against an enemy far stronger than any who were currently outside these concrete walls. She would have to face the enemy who made everyone else run away. An enemy who had decimated whole groups of warriors right before Tyron's eyes with a single attack. An enemy who he couldn't stand against. None of them could.

Jen had only been in training for a little over a year. It took decades for the Agerius Defense officials to declare someone ready for combat. Who was he to say she was ready?

As he looked at her innocent face, still marred by the effects of battle, he wanted to believe she wasn't. This fight was too much, could cost too much. They were too grossly outnumbered. They could risk it, as they'd had the training. She had not.

Yet, as he stared at her and thought about the way she had handled herself earlier, he thought that perhaps this was a situation in which she knew best when she was ready. If she was ready to get herself into what her life would have to one day be, then he would have to be okay with it, in spite of whatever the consequences might be. In spite of how he felt about it.

"You're right," he said quietly, "I do have the final say."

Jen clenched her jaw and closed her eyes. She could have sworn that her argument was sound enough that he would have listened and understood.

Blaze looked up at Tyron with questioning eyes. While she didn't wish for Jennifer to risk her life, the young woman had argued a reasonable point.

It was then that Tyron pointed to Jen. "You just have to promise me you'll be careful."

Jen snapped her head up, surprise in her eyes. "What?"

"And you two"—Tyron pointed at Ar'on and Krelien—"you're in charge of making sure no one touches her."

Ar'on nodded while Krelien timidly did the same.

Kaldok and Archer looked at one another in surprise as Blaze let a small smile fall onto her features.

Tyron looked back at Jen. "You're not afraid of what's to come, are you?"

After a few seconds, she shook her head and let a small smile come to her face. "Not at all. Not if you guys are going to be standing with me."

"Always," Tyron said with a nod.

Ar'on turned to Kaldok. "We're going to be relying on your plan."

"We'll be ready," Kaldok said as Archer looked around eagerly, to which Blaze rolled her eyes.

Tyron looked at Jen before he said, "We stay."

Jen nodded. "We fight for Earth."

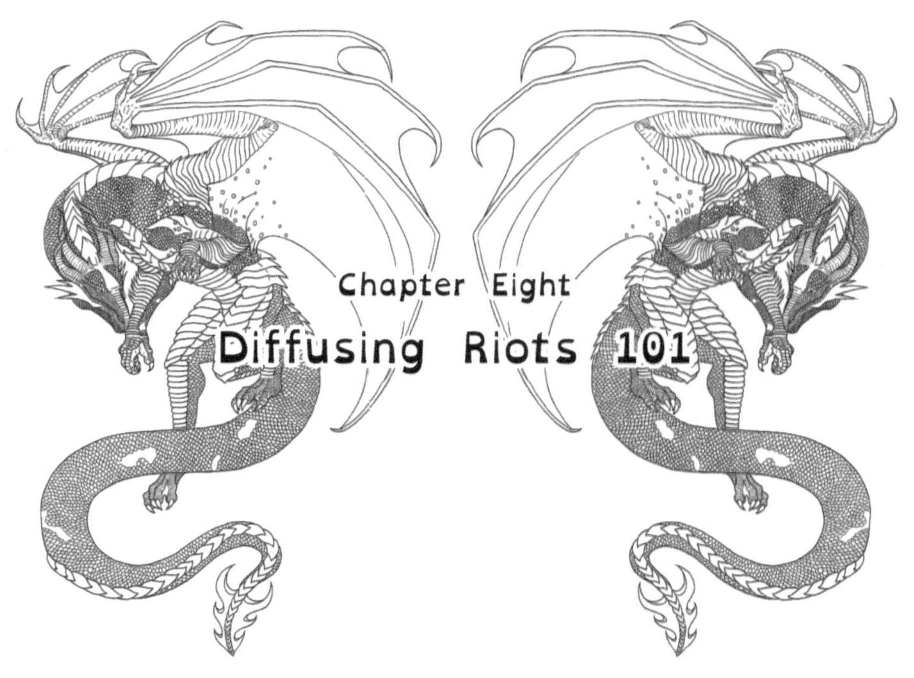

Chapter Eight
Diffusing Riots 101

Any other day, the walk from the cafeteria over to the offices would have been short. Today, however, as Jen walked down the silent hallway and could feel the occasional glance from a classroom, it felt like the long walk to the death chamber. Somewhere inside her brain, she knew that detention wasn't likely. At least, so she hoped. She had destroyed both school and personal property after all. For the greater good, but destroyed, nonetheless. There were bound to be consequences for that.

Detention wasn't very high on the list of actual, feasible punishments. Community service? That probably ranked a little higher.

Her principal probably wanted some explanations. He was due them, of course, but he didn't have to be quite so adamant about it. It wasn't like she was one of those kids who was always getting in trouble. A little compassion would go a long way for her mental well-being.

Once she reached the top floor, she made her way to the offices by one of the main entrances of the school. There were two primary entrances; one that opened to the offices and the auditorium, and the other that sat on the first floor that led directly to classrooms and the nurse's office. One of the things that set Southridge apart was the fact that it was built into the ridge, so there were all sorts of random things, like entrances that had three floors separating them.

A glass wall area revealed the offices. She had never been there outside of requesting to put up posters or to get attendance slips signed. Being a bad kid and getting sent to the principal's office wasn't part of her routine.

The door closed behind her with a gong-type noise, and the main secretary, looking frazzled, glanced to her.

"Yes, ma'am...No, ma'am, I cannot say for sure when we'll get the kids home," she said as Jen passed.

The other secretaries for each class were having similar conversations, and each of them peeked at Jen with shock or horror in their eyes.

Right, she thought, *I still look like I walked off a battlefield ... which I did.*

Her change of clothes helped ease her appearance, but she hadn't been able to get all of the blood out of her hair earlier. And she knew she'd missed spots while she was wiping her face and arms in the bathroom. She would have to see about getting properly cleaned up so she didn't cause any more panic.

She stepped behind the counter by way of a small swinging door and made her way straight back into the offices. Each grade had a separate assistant principal, a necessary action when the class sizes ranged between five to six hundred students. She passed the four offices on the right, with their secretary's offices on the left, to come to the dead end where the head principal's office sat.

A cacophony of noise came from all around her. All one-sided conversations with parents, she assumed.

Taking a short breath, she knocked against the head principal's door then heard from inside, "Enter!"

She winced at his frustrated, angry tone before opening the door. It was a fairly small office, no bigger than the other principal's. A large mahogany desk sat across from her where **Mr.** Alderfer sat in his high-backed leather chair. A tall bookcase was situated right behind him. There were two chairs angled facing his desk while, to her right, was a slightly open area where two more bookcases flanked a large window.

"You wanted to see me?" she asked.

"You think?" he retorted as he gestured to the door then the chairs across from him.

Jen closed the door then moved to take a seat but stopped herself. "Are you sure you want me to? I mean, I've still got some bloody—"

"Sit," he commanded, and she plopped herself down, instantly putting her hands in her lap. "Now, I don't even want to hear a peep out of you until you hear what I have to say. Understand?"

She nodded quickly.

"I won't say that I'm a genius. In fact, I know I'm not. But all this talk of portals and dragons and energy and other insanity is something I'm not grasping. I think it mostly has to do with the fact that you're tied to it all."

"I just—"

"Not a peep!" he reminded her, and she slumped into her chair. "Your friend, Ar'on, was nice enough to try to talk me through things. I can't say that I understand what the blazes is actually going on. I was hoping maybe you could shed some light on the situation."

He paused, and she timidly looked up. "Can I talk now?"

"I'd like you to."

"I can't shed any light on the situation."

"And why not?" Mr. Alderfer asked as he leaned over his desk.

Shrugging, she answered, "Because I only just learned about it ten minutes ago."

A scoff left him. "I find that hard to believe."

"Well, it's true."

"You're telling me that you don't know what's going on and why this is happening? Then why do you look like that? Why do you have a gun? Why are those men talking to you and holding private meetings with you?"

Jen shrank a little back into her seat. "Well, I guess I can explain some of that."

"Then explain it," he said sternly, evenly.

She looked up and saw a scowl on his face, so she fixed one on hers. "This is happening because I'm special, apparently. And not in the you're-a-snowflake way. I look like this because I killed two dragons and a bratak'ra before even thinking about what I might have for lunch. I have a gun because

I need to defend myself; otherwise, I end up bloody and bruised. Those men are talking to me and holding private meetings because we had to figure out how to handle the problem we find ourselves in without getting everyone killed. Does that answer your questions?" With each answer she offered, her tone had risen and her scowl deepened.

He rose from his chair and screamed, "Jen!"

Without thinking, she bolted out of her own chair and screamed, "Jon!"

They both fell silent as she realized that she had just called her principal by his first name, completely obliterating any lines of authority that he might have had over her. She mentally smacked herself.

Surprised at her outlet of anger, Jon's demeanor changed. He straightened and sighed. "I'll pretend I didn't hear that."

"Sorry," she whispered as she fell back into her seat. "I just really don't know what's going on, and I'm still reeling from what I've just been told."

Jon leaned forward and rested his hands against the top of the desk, staring down at his papers. "Well, I suppose that this explains your behavior."

Jen looked at him with question written on her face.

"Your dad and I ran into one another—"

"Right." She sat up. "What'd you get my dad for his birthday? I'm totally stumped this year."

He stared at her incredulously and gestured loosely. "Not really a pressing issue right now, Jen." A moment passed between the two. "I take it you haven't told them?"

Jen sighed heavily and sagged. "No."

Even if it hadn't been Jen sitting across from him, Jon would have been appalled at a student looking so mangled. It was obvious she'd tried to clean herself up, but the blood-matted hair and smeared marks of dirt, grime, and more blood across her face and arms accentuated the fact that she had looked worse.

He was doing his best to remain impartial, but he couldn't deny that his personal feelings for the young woman across from him played a factor into his reactions. This was his friend's daughter, after all; how had he even hoped to keep his emotions out of it?

"What can we do for you?" he asked quietly.

The young girl had been staring off into space. Now Jen made eye contact with him, and he realized that the little girl whom he had held in his arms eighteen years before was still inside this brave teenager. She looked terrified, and it made him want to call her father immediately to find out what he should do. But there was no way her parents could even hope to get inside the building. It looked like there were two massive circular shields protecting the school, but from his vantage point, he knew he could be wrong.

"Can you just ...? I don't know...Trust me and my Zaheri? They're good guys, they really are. A little dysfunctional, but they're good," Jen said.

He hung his head. "Why don't you go clean up?"

"But I don't have any other clothes," Jen said. "And, I mean, I tried earlier, but I know—"

Straightening, he crossed his arms. "That's just not true. Go check the lost and found; there's bound to be something in your size there."

"Jon, there isn't—"

"Go clean up. I can't bear to stare at you like this," he said with a wave of his hand.

She winced and got to her feet. Without another word, she left to go rummage through the lost and found, and then use the gym showers for the first time in her life.

Fifteen minutes later, Jen walked back into Jon's office. He was in the middle of a conversation on the phone, so she sat herself down and waited.

She had been fairly lucky and found a plain grey shirt and faded jeans that were close to her size in the lost and found.

"Yes, sir, everything is under control ... No, no, we're treating this situation as a lockdown procedure...Yes, we will keep you informed of the situation and inform you the moment we could use your help. Yes, okay, goodbye," Jon said as he hung up the phone.

"The police?" Jen asked.

He glanced over at her then eased back into his seat. "They can't reach the school. Apparently, there's some blue force field keeping anything from getting in ... or getting out," he added the last part with a knowing look.

"It was the only way to keep everyone safe."

"So, you're doing that?" he asked as he pointed out the window, and she nodded.

Jon opened his mouth to ask another question when she sat forward. "I appreciate your concern.

Really, I do. But you really don't need to be worrying about me. I've been doing this for over a year now."

"A *year*? Are you kidding me?"

"No, Jon, I'm not. And I'm not a child anymore. I haven't been for a long time now, so please stop treating me like one." Her anger flared as she spoke, but her tone stayed relatively even. "Give me some credit."

"As your dad's best friend, it's kind of hard for me to just stand by and let you do this."

"Sometimes in life, you have to do things you don't entirely want to do."

"That was rather mature of you to say," Jon said, somewhat taken aback. "Not that you aren't mature, but—"

"I know what you mean, Jon."

A rather tentative moment passed between them. Jen could tell that he wanted to say something more, but he was wary to actually say it.

Sensing the tension and wanting to move forward in her actions that needed to be taken, Jen asked, "What is it?"

"You said earlier that you were special. What did you mean by that?"

"Um ..." she began and raked a hand through her hair. Raising her hand, she quickly let it fall, her hand slapping against her thigh. "My Zaheri said that I'm the only one capable of stopping ... a really bad guy."

"What does that mean?" Jon asked with a furrowed brow.

A sad smile came to her face. "Jon, could we just drop it?"

"Do you really have to do this?"

Surprised by the question, Jen went to open her mouth to try to explain it. As she was about to justify why she had to go out there and fight the Caligans lying in wait, a knock sounded at the door. She turned slightly to see one of the secretaries gingerly opening the door.

The older woman said, "I'm sorry, Mr. Alderfer, but there's a rather insistent young man out here who wants to see you."

Jon's demeanor immediately shifted from family friend to principal in a snap, and he sat straighter as he asked, "What? How did he break the lockdown protocol?"

"Sorry about that, sir. I said I had to use the bathroom and wouldn't take no for an answer," Grant said as he gently pushed his way past the secretary and barged into the room. "I need to know if Jen came to school today. No one's seen her. and I'm worried she might be—"

"Um," Jen said as she slowly stood.

Grant looked over at her. "Oh, thank God." He stepped forward and enveloped her in a hug. "Are you okay? Aeryn sent me a text I couldn't decipher for the world. And why is your hair wet?" he asked as he pulled back and looked at her.

Jen winced. "It's a long story."

"Mr. Connolly!" Jon yelled.

Grant flinched and hopped away from Jen, turning to face his principal.

"You will remove yourself from this room before I beat you senseless. There is a crisis about, and you broke strict protocols to come check on a girl?"

"Well, sir—"

"No! No more speaking! Leaving! Now! Back to your classroom, and don't you dare tell a soul where you were, or I will have you in detention all the way to graduation!"

Grant sheepishly turned toward the door, and as he did, he whispered, "I'm glad you're okay." Then he left.

The secretary looked at Jon, and he said, "Make sure he gets to where he's supposed to be."

"Security?" the secretary asked.

Jon nodded in response. When the door shut, the principal looked at Jen and said nothing. He just pointed at the door and cocked an eyebrow.

The slightly relieved and happy feeling that Jen had at Grant's display of affection was replaced with fear of what Jon might say to her parents. Her face deadpan, she said, "Not a word. To anyone."

"Boyfriend?" Jon asked.

"Friend."

"Hmm," the principal hummed with a wince then said, "I doubt it."

"Jon ..." the teenager whined.

He held up his hands to signify defeat.

"Thank you." She sighed a little then added, "I really should get back to my Zaheri."

"Sure, but first, you should take this." He opened one of his desk drawers and pulled out a radio. "We're set to frequency two, just in case I need to correspond with you. And before you go, I have to know what your next move is."

"Well, actually ..." Jen began as she took the radio.

Another tap on the door. This time, a burly security guard poked his head into the office.

"Sir, we have a situation," the security guard said.

"What kind of situation?" Jon asked as he walked around his desk, following behind the security guard. He motioned to Jen, and she fell into step behind him.

The guard inclined his head slightly to the side. "It seems there's a riot down near the first floor's main entrance. A bunch of kids have gathered and are demanding to be sent home. Seems the cell towers came back up for a few minutes. Some kids found out what's going on."

"What did they find out? I haven't looked at a news station yet," Jon asked.

"That all hell is breaking loose. Apparently, a few ... dragons ..." he gave Jon a befuddled look, "Got free before that second barrier showed up, and the Air Force is being called in. That's all I know so far."

"It's unlikely that Cregorous is even here yet then," Jen said to herself.

Thinking she was talking to him, Jon asked, "Who's Cregorous?"

"The leader of the Caligan nation," she said absentmindedly as she looked at the floor. She wondered if there was a way to find out how much damage the loose dragons were causing. When she lifted her gaze, she found him staring at her in confusion. "The bad guy."

Turning his attention to the guard, Jon asked, "How did they ...? Never mind. I'll ask the teachers involved myself once we sort out where they came from."

The moment they stepped out of the glassed-in offices, Jen could hear the sounds of dozens of voices rising from the stairwell.

The three of them stopped before descending the staircase, and Jon said to the guard, "Head down. We'll be right there."

He turned to Jen as the guard walked down the stairs, and she asked, "What do you want *me* to do?"

"For now? Just stand there. Hopefully, word about you coming out of the wreckage earlier has spread, and everyone will recognize you as someone who has some idea of what's going on."

She nodded. "Okay. And that'll help how?"

"It wasn't like the reports were of sunshine and daisies. Hopefully, it'll remind them that it's dangerous out there."

"And if they don't realize it's dangerous out there?"

Sighing, he said, "We'll cross that bridge when we come to it." Without another word, Jon began to descend the staircase.

Jen stood there for a *moment* and tried to turn off or redirect her hearing. The yelling was overpowering, and she knew that once she reached the second floor, things were going to be much worse. From what she could tell, there was a large crowd down there, screaming any number of things. It really just sounded like a huge blast of noise.

The closer she got to the second floor, the *more* dread filled her. This wasn't going to end well; she could feel it in her bones. She knew her classmates. They would fight and kick and scream until they got what they wanted; like toddlers, angry that a parent won't let them touch fire.

Jon ran down the last bit of stairs and screamed, "Whoa! Whoa!"

Before her eyes, she saw thirty to forty kids

fighting and arguing with teachers and a few of the security personnel. While their school was big, they didn't have a massive security team.

Jon scowled then put his finger and thumb in his mouth before he let out a loud whistle that pierced through the jumble of noise. Most of the noise settled, and then he said in his authoritative way, "Now everyone remain calm!"

"Let us out of here so we can go home!" one of the bigger kids shouted.

Shaking his head, Jon called back, "I understand that you're worried, but everything is going to be fine. I wouldn't tell you that if I didn't believe it. You need to head back to your homerooms immediately."

"Our families are out there!" another kid hollered, and it was followed quickly by another rise in noise.

"I'm aware of that!" Jon screamed over the chaos. "So is mine! What you're proposing to do is far more dangerous than you could possibly realize. You might not be able to see them, but there are monsters out there that will kill you if you leave this building."

"Then what about her?" another voice sounded, a hand pointed to Jen. "She's walking around without supervision. What's made her so special?"

Jon looked up at Jen, who was still about halfway up the last stretch of stairs. "It would appear as though they don't recognize you."

"That shouldn't shock you," Jen said quickly. Of course no one recognized her. She was one of the misfits. Of all people, Jon should have known that ninety-eight percent of the school population would have no idea who she was.

Thinking for a second, Jon turned back to the students. "This is hard to understand, but Jennifer is part of the solution to this problem. We need you now to head back to your homerooms so you can remain safe. Please, we're asking for—"

It appeared as though they weren't listening anymore. Halfway through Jon's final comment a clump of students centered toward the middle of the huddle surged forward, trying to push their way to the row of glass doors.

Jon ran forward to try to help the teachers and security guards as Jen leapt down the stairs and ran for the doors. She skidded to a stop in front of them and grabbed a large boy who had broken through the defenses, throwing him back into the huddle. "You don't get it! You'll get yourself killed if you go out there!"

"Get out of my way bitch!" the boy screamed as he ran at Jen.

That made her angry. If there was anything in the world that Jen hated, it was a person calling her something that she had done nothing to deserve.

He charged at her, and she let him pass, only to grab his left arm and swing him around her as she pivoted on her right leg, hurling him back into the crowd.

A large rush of students approached her, and she had little else to do. They were going to get through unless she did something.

Tyron was going to kill her.

She turned and slapped her left hand against the door. A blue glow shot out of her hand and stretched to the walls, a shield barring the doors.

She was pushed up against the shield by the

group of students and had to kick and hit at them to get them off. They whaled against the shield, and as she got some space again, she wanted to chuckle.

If a Ferveos couldn't break her shield, what *made* them think smacking their hands against it would?

Something tugged on her pistol. Panicking, she tried to turn and grab at whoever was working to get her gun. Either she wasn't fast enough, or the person who took the pistol knew precisely what they were doing. She tried to snatch the gun back, but a body got in her way. She heard a click and a gasp, and suddenly there was room around her.

People backed away as she saw a scrawny boy holding her pistol. He pointed it straight at her.

She tried to keep her breathing calm. She had never been hit by a Tilion weapon blast and didn't know what would happen if she was shot.

Holding her hands out, she said as carefully as she could, "Okay, look, you've got a loaded weapon and—"

"I know. Let ... let *me* go," he stammered.

"Listen," Jen began.

By this point, everyone else had quieted down, and a small circle had formed around her and the boy. No one wanted to get shot. She couldn't blame them.

She didn't want to get shot either.

"No, you listen! I know you. You're a senior, right? Yeah, and—and—and—"

She flinched and gave him a confused stare. He knew her? Who was this kid?

"You can't hold us against our will!" he shouted, his hand trembling.

Jen was trying to think through who this kid was. She was fairly certain she had never met him before. He didn't look familiar. Not that she was great with the whole faces and names thing.

Whatever. That didn't matter right now. She had to calm him down and get her gun back.

"Just take a deep breath. Everything's going to be okay. You're safe here—"

"How can we trust you? You're just a kid like the rest of us!"

Out of the corner of her eye, Jen saw one of the varsity football players push his way through the crowd to the front. Rick? She couldn't remember.

He looked at the boy holding the gun then at Jen. "Just give me the gun. I don't want you or anyone else to get hurt, okay?" Her hyper-sensitive hearing could make out one of the boy's friends whispering for him to drop the gun.

"We don't want anyone to get hurt, Stephen," Jon said from behind Jen, trying to calm the teenager.

"You don't get it!" he screamed in anger. "I need to get home to my family! They could be dead! Just let me go!"

And then chaos.

Rick rushed the boy. In his heightened state of terror, the armed boy fired the gun at Rick.

Jen moved quickly to get between them, hoping maybe she could move the shield on the doors in front of her to bounce the bullet off. The shield did fly off the doors and move toward her, but not fast enough.

The bright blue light of the energy beam smacked into Jen before it bounced off her and hit the ceiling as Jen hit the ground. The shield ricocheted off the wall and disappeared up the stairwell in blue dust.

As the sound of the pistol firing began to fade away, along with an echo of screams, the boy dropped the gun as he stared at Jen's body on the ground.

Facedown, Jen braced her hands against the floor and pushed herself up with a grunt.

Both Jon and Rick ran to her aid, only to stop dead in front of her, eyes wide. Another scream swallowed the silence as Jen turned to face the scrawny boy.

Judging from the wound left behind, the blast had grazed her left temple and skimmed along her forehead, leaving exposed skin and muscle over the white bone.

The crowd stared, wide-eyed, as the wound healed in a few seconds. Wincing a bit, Jen wiped away the blood on her forehead and looked the previously armed boy in the eyes. "Don't do that. It hurts."

No one had the reaction time to catch him as he fell into a dead faint.

"Well, you did an excellent job making that riot stop," Jon told Jen, who had found herself a seat on the stairs. The students and faculty had willingly left the area shortly after Jen's bullet incident.

She sat and inspected her gun as Jon paced.

"I've gotta hand it to you, just about everything you've done today has been done with a grade-A dramatic touch."

"Oh good," Jen said without looking away from her pistol, trying to discern if it had been damaged at all. It wasn't like she was able to pick up her phone and dial a one eight hundred number to get it fixed. Something told her Ar'on would have something to say about this whole mess. "Because drama is exactly what I was looking for," she said in response to his statement.

A heavy sigh left him. "What are we gonna do, Jen?"

She looked away from the gun and focused on her principal. She felt terrible. This whole situation was nothing of his doing, and here he was, bearing the brunt of the problem. There were probably codes in the lockdown procedure he was trying to follow, but with this being only slightly similar to that pre-determined situation, it was hard to keep everything in check. There were too many variables, like cell phones being used to call home and find out dragons were attacking.

He turned to her. "Can we get them out of here?"

Jen shook her head. "There's no way to get them home safely, not without possibly killing me."

"'Possibly'."

"Yeah." She stood, putting the gun in its holster. "Those shields out there keeping the school and the rest of the world from the Caligans, it drains my energy. They're formed by my thoughts and can be destroyed if I run out of physical and mental steam. The two alone are causing a strain on my body. Nothing bad, just kinda tickles my nose a little. But if I were to try to make shields for each bus and car that left the building ..."

"You would probably die."

She shrugged. "It's what I've been told. Apparently, that outcome has the greatest success rate in the simulation."

Desperation was in his eyes as he scratched his forehead. "I can't just leave them sitting around. Too many of the students have cell phones or laptops, and they'll try to get in contact with family. If they hear bad things are happening, they'll want to run home and make sure everyone's okay. We're already stretched as it is for our security personnel."

"Why don't we call an assembly?"

"And do what?"

She raised her eyebrows momentarily. "For one, we could explain the situation."

"You could barely explain the situation to me. Do you want to try to explain it to the entire student body?"

"Can the entire student body fit in the auditorium?" Jen asked as she stared off at the wall.

"I'm taking that as a rhetorical question." Jon sighed. "It's not a terrible idea. Do you propose that you're going to make the announcement?"

Jen gave him a look of abject horror. "Heck no. I can get up and sing a stanza, but make a speech? Hard pass."

"Then you want me to explain a situation I barely understand myself?" he said, frustrated.

Gesturing to him, she said, "All we need to tell them is that dragons are attacking, and until we can get the situation under control—i.e., kill everything outside—they'll need to stay here, or die."

Closing his eyes, he said, "I can't say something like that to the student body, Jen. That has lawsuit written all over it."

"Then ... I don't know. Tell them that, until we find a viable way to get them home, they're stuck here. Maybe allow for them to wander the halls or something."

"You want *me* to allow over one thousand students to wander aimlessly about a school building? That's a bad plan."

She held up her arms. "Well then, **Mr.** Principal, you think of something to tell them."

As she began to walk away, he asked, "Where are you going?"

Turning back around to face him, she said, "I need to go get the blood off my head. I'll meet you in the auditorium."

"Fine, yes. Go clean up. And get your guardian people."

"**Zaheri,**" she corrected as she continued on her way.

Left alone in the main entrance of the school, Jon sighed. "Maybe I should write a worst-case scenario book for principals."

Jen had made a valid point. An assembly would be the best way to inform the students and staff of what was going on, even if he couldn't explain it perfectly.

As the students filed into their rows and the usual mixed noise of their conversations reached him, he thought of how he was going to do this. The lockdown procedures had long been forgotten, especially doing this. Following that course of action was still the best way to have handled the immediate problem earlier.

Now that Jen had nullified the need for panic, at least on some level, it seemed like the worst way to proceed. Too many students were getting finicky and wanted to leave. He couldn't blame them really. He wanted to leave, too. But he couldn't, and he shouldn't.

Even if they did find a way to get everyone out, something told him that Jen would stay with her ... Zaheer whatever they were. What would she do then? Probably fight, get herself bloodied some more.

The image of her walking down the hallway looking like someone coming out of a war zone flashed across his mind, and he had to force himself not to grimace.

Jen was a student, not a warrior, or a savior, or whatever these aliens viewed her as. If he was honest with himself, he would recognize that that was the thing that bugged him the most about what unfolded around him. The fact that Jen was somehow supposed to be a hero at the end of this.

She was a kid, for crying out loud! Sure, if she was twenty or so and wasn't in high school, maybe this wouldn't be as hard to swallow. But this wasn't what a senior in high school should be worrying about. They should be worrying about SAT scores, college applications, and figuring out what they wanted to do with their lives.

Jen was probably forgoing everything she had been working toward in high school right now just to try to get everyone out of this mess. Who decided this was her mess to fix?

The stage door off to his left opened, and Jen walked through, followed closely by the alien guys. Her Zahur—guardians. He'd just call them guardians.

He could handle the three men that looked entirely human. The two animals were a little harder to be okay with. The sheer size of both creatures made him feel as though he had unleashed lions in the school.

Then there was the werewolf. Even though he stood upright like the others, his pawed hands, furred arms, wolf-like head, and towering bulk made Jon remember that this wasn't a joke. This was real. He had a tail, big and puffy, like a wolf's.

When the werewolf—he thought that the one named Ar'on had called him Kaldok—had been in their custody, he had been nothing but courteous. It had surprised Jon that something so terrifying could be so calm, yet Kaldok had been the one who had moved the slowest, and his actions had seemed gentle.

If ever there was a walking oxymoron, Jon felt he stared at it right now.

Jen and Tyron walked up to him as the others stayed behind a bit.

"Tyron offered to try to explain things, if you needed," Jen said.

"I know that it can't be easy for you to do this," Tyron added.

Jon smiled. "I appreciate that. But, for now, I think I know what I'm doing."

"Okay," Jen said as she and Tyron turned to walk away.

Catching her arm, Jon said, "Um, no, you stay with me."

The other two shared a glance as Jen asked, "Why?"

"We're human, Jen; we don't believe anything without seeing."

"Jesus, Santa, and the Easter Bunny would disagree."

"You know what I mean."

Tyron flitted his gaze between them then fixed his attention on Jen. "Okay. Something tells me you wouldn't want to be alone in this."

"I kinda am," the teenager said glumly.

With a small shake of his head, the Zaheri responded, "No, you aren't."

A newfound respect filled Jon for this warrior. And a small level of trust. If this Tyron could be so in tune with Jen's needs, maybe she was in good hands, after all.

She shifted her weight. "It'll be okay, Tyron. I'd just hang back there. I'll let you know if we need you."

With a slow nod, Tyron walked back to the others.

The last of the students took their seats, and as Jen stood next to Jon, she felt a little strange being one of two people center stage. She had stood in this same position—well, in a similar position—a number of times for concerts. But even when she had been a soloist, she tended to stand off-center and there were, like, eighty people backing her up.

Now she only had her Zaheri behind her and Jon beside her. Her moral support was greatly diminished, and she wasn't entirely sure what Jon was looking for.

He clapped his hands and said, "Thank you all for your cooperation. I don't think I can express exactly how much that means to myself and the rest of the staff."

He paused and looked over at Jen before he continued, "I don't know all of the logistics of what's going on, but I can tell you what I do know. Yes, there are dragons flying around outside. Yes, real, live dragons. And from what I've been told, there are measures being taken to ensure that the few that aren't trapped here are taken care of. Furthermore, there are other monsters outside that will kill you without hesitating. That's why we can't let you leave.

"Trust me when I say that we want to let you all go home and be with your families. However, at this current moment, that's impossible.

"Now, I know that a lot of you are wondering why Jen is standing up here with me. Some of you may have witnessed what happened a few moments ago, and others may have heard about this morning. For those of you who haven't, I'd like to have Jen show you exactly why she's being set apart."

He turned to her, and she threw him a confused look as he said in a quieter tone, "You have to show them something."

To Jen, it felt like there was suddenly a spotlight on her. She scratched her arm and thought about what she could possibly do to show all these people who she was. Wings? No, that would ruin the only shirt she had. What about her bone spikes? No, they would ruin the shirt, too. All that was left, really, was her energy.

An orb.

She heard some coughing in the audience and tried to focus past the bright lights and look at the clock in the back of the auditorium. It was only ten. She had only been awake for four hours. She had only been on school property for two. Already, everything had gone haywire, and it wasn't even lunchtime yet.

Even though she knew she had to step forward and do something, her feet felt glued to the floor and her heart hammered in her chest.

Tyron walked up next to her and awkwardly nodded toward the center of the stage. She followed him as they took a few steps forward.

"Should we say something?" he mumbled out of the side of his mouth.

His awkwardness made her feel better, and she barely stifled a laugh.

"Probably not." But even with him there, next to her, she still felt terribly exposed. Time to say goodbye to whatever life might have been. "Here goes," she muttered.

Taking a deep breath, she held out her right arm slightly, and as she exhaled, a blue aura manifested around her hand. From her wrist warped blue smoke that swirled into her palm, small sparks and crackles like lightning firing between her fingers. In a few seconds, the blue smoke and lightning convened at a central point and took on an orb shape. A shimmering gold orb took form in Tyron's grasp.

Gasps and loud voices broke out as a few people sprang to their feet and pointed, as if everyone else wasn't staring at the swirling orbs in their hands.

She held onto the sphere of energy for a few seconds, momentarily enthralled by it. Somehow, it was comforting to look at. Even though it looked like she held a storm in her hand, it seemed almost peaceful the way the blues swirled around like they were caught up in a spiraling wind, the little cracks of blue-ish lightning crackling between her fingers.

Even though she knew people were saying all sorts of things, she couldn't hear them if she wanted to. For that brief moment, she was perfectly content with who she was. Because look at what she could hold in her hand.

It was beautiful.

All of a sudden, the whispers around the auditorium broke through her serenity, and she started a bit. The orb in her hand dissipated into the air like steam from a kettle.

Hundreds of faces stared at her, and despite the calm she'd had just seconds prior, she now felt self-conscious.

Tyron did a double-take and dropped his hand before he gently pushed her back.

As they passed Jon, she said, "I hope that did it, 'cause I'm not doing it again."

All of the times before when she'd had to do something requiring her energy in front of the others, it had been okay; she had been doing it because she needed to.

Right now, what she had just done, it felt like she had been put on display at a freak show for everyone to stare at. At that moment in time, she wanted nothing more than to crawl into a hole and die.

Jon clenched his jaw before he stepped back to the front of the stage. "As you can tell, Jen is ... special. You will probably see her walking around the building, and I'm sorry that I can't allow you that luxury. But your safety is my first priority. I can assure you that we are all trying our hardest to get everyone home to their families quickly."

From her position next to her Zaheri, Jen saw people looking at their friends, asking questions. She was thankful that her mind was too busy with her own questions to be able to pay attention to all their whispered wonderings.

"What I would like to do is allow all students the ability to meet up with their friends. It's the only thing I can imagine that could make this tolerable. Each student chooses a homeroom and stays there for the remainder of the day, aside from lunches. Classes are, obviously, cancelled for the day. All students are permitted to use whatever technology they have with them to entertain their time.

"Teachers, if you could go to your homeroom locations. If you don't have one, stay in the hallways to ensure all students go to a homeroom of some kind. After which, come to the front of the stage, and we'll discuss what can be done."

He turned and looked at Jen, who nodded.

To her, it was as good a plan as any. No classes and the chance to hang out with their friends? Next to the fact that they couldn't go home, she could think of nothing better to do.

"You are all dismissed. You have ten minutes to find a homeroom, so don't dawdle. Any questions, run them through your teacher, and they will contact me."

Mere seconds later, the noise in the auditorium grew as students and teachers alike stood and exited the large room.

Jen looked over the mass of people. It seemed that they, for the moment, would let her be.

No one came running up to the stage and asked for her to do the orb thing again or to read their mind or bend a spoon using her thoughts. So, she could only guess that everyone, for now, accepted her and her Zaheri as they were.

At least, she could only hope that was the case.

Chapter Nine
Friendship is Magic

While her Zaheri were given the instruction to utilize the library for the day, Jen left to seek out her friends and sister. She knew that tracking them down wouldn't be difficult. There was only one homeroom they would choose for the day.

Once the ten minutes were up and the student body had settled into their choice for homerooms, she went off to Mr. Mosser's classroom.

As she made her way out of the auditorium, she began to wonder what they might say. Would they understand? Would they still want to be friends with her? What kind of questions would they ask? Would she be able to answer them? What if she got to Mr. Mosser's homeroom, only to find it empty? What if none of them wanted to talk to her?

For a brief second, she thought of Grant and how he had lied his way into Jon's office, all to find out if she was okay. Shaking her head slightly, she realized that, at the least, Nancy would be there. And it would be shocking if Aeryn, Grant, and Ryan had all abandoned her. They had all been through a lot in the time they had known one another. Granted, this was a whole new level of hurdle for any friendship to endure.

In hindsight, Jen wished she had listened for her friends while the assembly had gone on. Maybe then she would have a better idea of what to expect from them.

When she reached the classroom, she raised her hand to knock when footsteps came from behind her. Two things happened at once. First, she saw Tyron, Krelien, and Kaldok walking up to her, and second, the door to Mr. Mosser's room opened.

"Oh *my* goodness, Jen!" Nancy screamed from the threshold, lunging at her sister to hug her tight.

"It's okay, Nance," Jen said, trying to dislodge herself from her younger sister's tight embrace.

Tyron and the others had stopped abruptly at the end of the hall when they had seen Nancy fly out of the room at Jen. Turning to them, Jen waved them down to her.

"You sure?" Tyron asked, and Jen nodded. He looked hesitant.

Krelien rolled his eyes and pushed past him to walk up to Jen.

Nancy turned as Krelien walked toward her with Tyron and Kaldok right behind him.

"Nance, this is Krelien, Tyron, and Kaldok." Jen gestured toward the three hybrids as each of them waved in turn. "They're, uh"—she paused for a second—"my Zaheri."

A stomping of feet approached them, and suddenly, Ryan, Grant, and Aeryn stood behind Nancy, just inside the room.

Jen winced as Ryan asked, "Who're they?"

Ignoring everyone else, Tyron asked Jen, "Do you need our help with anything? Like, explanations or—"

"Yes, please," Jen said as she grabbed Tyron's arm and pushed Nancy into the room with her free hand.

Once in the room, she saw Mr. Mosser sitting at his desk, reading over a book.

Her friends backed up as she shoved her way past the threshold, dragging Tyron behind her, the other two following behind them.

Stopping almost immediately after Kaldok had entered the room and shut the door, Jen said, "Everyone, this is Tyron, Krelien, and Kaldok. Guys, this is ... everyone."

"Nicely put," Krelien said.

Mr. Mosser cleared his throat and began shuffling papers as he said, "I'm just going to leave for a few minutes to give you all some privacy."

"You don't have to—"

Lifting his hand, her teacher said, "I know, but I should. I'll be back in a bit." In a few seconds, he crossed the room, politely excused himself before casting a bewildered glance at Kaldok, and then left the room.

A whiteboard sat at the front of the classroom that stretched onto the right wall, while on the left wall were posters of musicals and plays that Mr. Mosser had seen. On the back wall was a collage of the director with his choirs through the years, some candid photos, and others were professional from the school.

After a short silence, Jen said, "Is everyone okay?"

A snort left Ryan. "You're outside fighting monsters, and you're asking if *we're* okay?"

"Jen, what's going on?" Aeryn asked in a small voice.

Jen pointed at her. "Where's James?" She had assumed he would be here. It actually surprised her that he wasn't there to help Aeryn out with the sudden collapse of her knowledge of the universe. After all, her best friend had just turned out to be a super-human.

Dismissively waving her hand, Aeryn said, "He said he didn't feel like he needed to be around for this. He didn't want to intrude."

"We tried to convince him to come, but he said that he didn't think it was his place," Grant said quietly.

Letting the matter drop, Jen said, "I know I have a lot of explaining to do."

"Is this what you've been doing at night?" Nancy asked, hugging herself.

"I guess today was the day, after all," Jen told her with a half-smile. Then she turned and looked at Tyron, who stared back at her.

Krelien nudged their Team Leader. "I think she wants you to talk now."

"I know that," Tyron shot back. "I'm just trying to think through what to say."

"Oh, I can do that," Krelien said then went to raise his hand in an attempt of the Vulcan salute again.

Quickly moving, Kaldok grabbed Krelien's hand. "Don't. You did it wrong last time."

Ripping his hand away, Krelien grumbled, "I knew that."

Kaldok rolled his eyes.

"Ignore him," Tyron said, pointing at the Jumper. "And, as you could probably tell from the assembly, Jen isn't entirely human."

"Then what is she?" Grant asked, pulling his brows together.

"We're called hybrids," Kaldok said. When everyone looked at him, he sighed. "Well, they are, anyway."

"Are you a werewolf?" Ryan asked.

"Yes I am, and no I don't want to talk about it."

Before anyone could pester Kaldok, Tyron said, "We're part-human and part-dragon; you would call us dragonborn. We come from a world called Til-ion. It's linked to Earth by what we call a portal." Ryan opened his mouth to say something, and Tyron abruptly answered, "It can only be activated by a hybrid."

Confusion and concern warred on Ryan's face as he asked, "Are you a mind-reader?"

"No, it's just ..." Tyron fumbled. "I figured you'd ask why you couldn't go there."

"Have you been there?" Grant asked Jen, who shook her head.

Squinting in confusion, Nancy asked, "But what are you doing here? Why do you want Jen?" She turned to her sister and asked, "What's going on? Why is this happening?"

"That's a bit tricky. It's not that we want Jen. We're just her protectors," Kaldok said as he scratched behind his ear.

"Protectors? From what?" Grant straightened a little, balling his hands into fists.

Tyron opened his mouth, but Jen put her hand on his forearm. He looked down at her.

"Why don't you let *me* tell them?" she said.

"But you said you wanted help," her Zaheri whispered.

"Yeah, I know, but"—she cast a quick glance to her friends—"I think it's just gonna confuse them—you and *me* both trying to answer questions."

Nodding, Tyron said, "Okay, sure. Just one more thing. Where's the library?"

"Oh." Jen rested her hand against her head then pointed in the direction she had come from. "Um, head straight past Mr. Alderfer's office, and then turn right when you come to the staircase. You can't miss it."

"Okay," Krelien said as Tyron nodded slowly. "But what's a library?"

Furrowing his brow, Ryan asked, "You guys don't have libraries on your planet?"

Tyron flashed a small glare at Ryan. "If we do, we don't call them libraries."

"It's a room filled with books. It's got lots of windows as walls," Jen said.

"Oh, an archive," Tyron said. "Okay. We've got it." He gave her a thumbs-up then ushered the other two out of the room. Before he closed the door, he turned back to Jen and told her, "Call me if you need anything."

Pointing at the now closed door, Aeryn said, "Jen, why are those incredibly handsome men hanging out with you?"

"It's a good thing James isn't here," Ryan said under his breath.

Aeryn smacked *him*. "Shut up! I may be in a relationship, but that doesn't mean I'm blind."

"You guys might want to sit down," Jen said,

rubbing her forehead. "Actually, I want to sit down. You can do whatever you want." As she settled onto a desk and enjoyed the act of sitting, she took a deep breath. "I'll try to answer what I can." She turned to Nancy. "This might be a little hard to understand. In fact, it probably will be. I passed out when they told me."

"When they told you that you're a...hybrid?" Nancy asked, falling into a seat.

"Yeah. Apparently, I'm some fulfillment of a prophecy back in my Zaheri's world."

"Seriously? A prophecy?" Ryan asked with a snicker.

"Ryan."

"Just wondering if I should pull out my trope bingo card."

Grant opened his mouth then dismissively waved his hand at Ryan before he turned to Jen. "Again, why are these guys here?"

"They're here to protect me because there's... someone ... trying to hurt me."

"You mean kill you," Grant clarified, an angry edge in his tone.

"Well, yeah, if you're gonna completely forget about tact," Jen said, gesturing to him.

Nancy hugged herself again. "Why does this person want to kill you?" She winced at the question then asked, "And why aren't Chip or I hybrids?"

Shrugging, Jen said, "I don't know the answer to the second question. The person wants to kill me because, apparently, before I was born, he tried to kill me and failed. Now he wants to finish what he started. At least, that's what the Ferveos said."

"Ferveos?" Ryan asked.

"It's what they call Caligan dragons."

"Caligan?" Aeryn asked.

Jen winced. "Okay, I'm gonna try this quickly. There are two groups of hybrids; Agerians, which my Zaheri are, and Caligans; which is the enemy outside trying to kill people. The leader of the Caligans wants to kill me because he screwed up once and now he's here to try again."

The others looked between one another but didn't say anything, so Jen continued, "Now we have to figure out how to get the Caligans off Earth before anyone gets hurt. They're here because of me, so it's kinda our responsibility."

"Are you sure they're here for you?" Ryan asked.

Jen shrugged a little. "Why else would they come here? From what my Zaheri said, it's possible that the Caligans are controlling the gateway to their world. They've never done that before, so it stands to reason they aren't here just to take out my Zaheri. There's a bigger target, and I think it's safe to say that target is me."

"Well," Grant let out a breath as he stared at the ceiling, "are you sure this...evil dude isn't here for one of your Zahad whatevers?"

"It's Zaheri," Jen corrected. "And I don't think they're that valuable."

"You're sure about that?" Ryan asked.

"What does it matter?" Aeryn asked, looking between the boys. "They're here, and Jen is in danger."

Grant looked a tad hopeful. "But maybe it isn't quite as dangerous as she thinks it is."

"Okay, yes, from what I understand, Krelien being a Jumper and Kaldok being a werewolf might be something that Cregorous is after, but I think they've been on Earth since I was a baby. Wouldn't it be weird if he waited all this time just to decide now is the opportune moment to get them?" Jen said.

"Okay, devil's advocate, doesn't it seem weird he waited all this time to attack *you* when he apparently tried it when you were a baby? He's had a while to try again," Ryan posited.

"Can we please stop talking about Jen being attacked? I don't like thinking about that," Aeryn pleaded.

Jen looked between her friends and family, trying to figure out what more to say. It didn't make any sense for Cregorous to be after her Zaheri. Not after what she had been told about the others.

Rubbing her face, Jen said, "There's more about me ... I'm not the only Human-Born hybrid. There are six others out there like me, and apparently, Cregorous already killed five others before he even got to me. Apparently he's scared of us. I think that's reason enough for him to come after me."

Grant held out his hand. "Wait—what? There are more people like you?"

"Do we know any of them?" Nancy asked.

"I ... I have absolutely no idea," Jen said, starting to feel flustered. She shouldn't have sent Tyron away. This was all so far above her head that she could barely think properly.

Ryan raised his hand. "I'm sorry, I'm hung up on the fact that this dude killed some other people and somehow was stopped when he got to you."

"Yeah, a lot of people are hung up on that one."

"So what? You're like...a super-superhero?" Grant asked.

The comment made Jen suddenly self-conscious. She wasn't a hero. She wasn't a superhero. She was just Jen, the girl with the common name, the common face, and the forgettable everything. She wasn't anything special. But her friends all looked at her expectantly, sometimes almost worriedly, like they didn't know how to see her anymore. And she just wanted to go back to being a normal, boring person. She was good at that.

Shaking her head, she said, "No, I'm not a superhero. I'm just ... I'm me." Thankfully, none of her friends said anything as she sighed and let her head fall into her hands. "I don't know what I am anymore," she whispered.

She didn't see it, but her friends all looked at one another.

Nancy sat closest to her and gently reached out to touch her sister's shoulder. "Jen, are you okay?"

Jen warred with herself. She wanted to tell them that it was okay if they wanted to leave. To run away from her and scream. The more she talked, the more she realized she was some monster. For Pete's sake, she had just stood on their auditorium stage and manifested raw energy into her hand. They should be running away from her.

A selfish part of her wanted them to stay right where they were. She didn't think she would be able to survive the day, let alone the rest of her life, without her friends. They still had so much to do, and she knew that, eventually, one or all of them were going to see her bloodied and bruised. When that happened, when they saw her fight, would they run? Would it be better for them to leave now? What if they stayed and one of them got hurt?

What if they tried to help and put themselves in harm's way?

As though he was reading her mind, Grant asked, "What can we do to help?"

"Nothing," she said before she even gave herself a chance to think about a proper answer. She sat up a bit. "There's nothing any of you can do."

She needed a minute or ten alone. So, without another word, she got to her feet and walked out the door. It wasn't until she hit the threshold that she realized she was crying.

Chapter Ten
Maybe the Treasure was Friendship all Along

Her nose stung the way it always did before she was about to crumble into a sobbing mess. Fighting against herself, she blinked rapidly, trying to keep herself from breaking down. Nothing could stop it, though.

Sometimes, you just need to cry.

She walked over to one of the benches in the open area near the room, sat down, and immediately rested her head in her hands as tears began to fall.

This was a mess. Less than half an hour ago, she had been momentarily happy with who she was. But that was before she really thought about what she was.

Everything today was moving so fast. The conversation with her Zaheri hadn't been that long ago, but she had shoved a lot of her thoughts into the back of her mind, focused more on finding a solution to the problem at hand and getting Jon involved. Then the whole riot thing, and then the assembly thing, and now here she was, being called a superhero by the boy she'd had a crush on, and she couldn't take it.

Initially, when she had found out who she was or, at least, who she thought she was, Jen had been excited. Learning about her powers and seeing how she could fight, and getting to tap into a side of herself that she had never known about had been exhilarating. She had loved it.

Just last night, she had thought everything was fine. She was a Human-Born hybrid, and that meant she was special. And she was okay with that being the only explanation she had. There was training and sometimes fighting, but all in all, she was a normal kid who one day maybe would do something no one else would ever know about, except her Zaheri.

Now here she was, smack-dab in the middle of Earth, with dragons and Caligans beating against a force field that she had made to protect her school and county from destruction, and everyone knew. People she didn't even know probably were talking about her and gossiping and whispering and rumoring. Everyone suddenly knew what she was.

But she didn't even know what she was. Last night, she had been a strong hybrid. But today, she found out she was the strongest one alive? Maybe the strongest one ever? Whatever she thought she was supposed to do, whatever role she thought she was going to play for Tilion, it seemed to have gone from miniscule to title screen instantaneously.

She was just a kid. She was going to college next year.

Wait, was she going to college next year? Was she going to be in school tomorrow? Would the school still be here tomorrow? What if she failed? What if someone died? Tyron would try to claim responsibility, but if Cregorous was coming for her, wasn't it her responsibility?

And if she was so powerful, shouldn't she be able to stop all this? Shouldn't it be within her power to make this all go away so no one got hurt? What if she did? What if she didn't? What would happen if she did just hide in the school while her Zaheri did the work? Would one of them get hurt? Would one of them die?

The thought of any of her Zaheri dying made her stomach clench, and she gripped the fabric of her borrowed shirt, trying to get a hold on reality. Jen felt like she was going to be sick.

Everything was upside down.

The power she used to enjoy tickling her skin frightened her now. What if she hurt someone? She didn't know how to control this stuff. Not really. Last night, she had thought she did. Even this morning, when she had been fighting all those Caligans and taking out Ferveos, she had thought she had a handle on it.

But now she was the strongest hybrid ever.

Ever.

In all of existence, she was the strongest one.

In her tiny, little, insignificant body was the greatest energy any hybrid had ever known. And she had thrown it around like a toy this morning. Good God, what if she had used too much? What if she wasn't thinking properly with her energy and an attack was too strong, decimating the ridge? What if, when a Ferveos died, it landed on someone's car with them still inside it? What if the dragon that was loose wasn't taken care of by the Air Force and was busy destroying a building complex?

How *many* people *might* be dying right now because she had been cocky earlier?

It felt like the world went spiraling up and around, and she had to hold her head, fearing that she would fall over and collapse on the ground. She had no clue what she was doing. Not one single clue.

"Jen?" Aeryn's voice broke through her frantic thoughts.

Jen sucked in a startled gasp and sat upright.

Her eyes flashed to see Aeryn standing a few feet away from her, wringing her hands with a frown on her face. "You okay?"

Despite herself, Jen couldn't say a word. She just shook her head and looked away from her friend.

And Aeryn, oh God bless her. She didn't say anything. She just walked over and sat down next to Jen. Then she gently rested her small hand on Jen's arm and said, "It's okay. I'm not going anywhere."

That one comment felt like a spring breeze on a stifling day. Jen let out a heavy breath and looked up at the ceiling, trying to get control of her emotions.

They just sat like that for a few moments, allowing the silence to do its work in both of them. And in those few moments, Jen's heart quieted, and she felt peace.

At least she would still have one friend when all this was over.

"So, that's your plan?" Ryan asked as he looked at Jen with a less than enthused expression.

Jon had walked into the room shortly before Jen started telling her friends and sister about what the team planned to do. He stayed because he wanted to know what they had come up with. After hearing it, though, he was seriously rethinking putting their care into the guardian's hands.

"It doesn't sound like a good one," Jon said, giving Jen a wary look.

"That means you'd be going right into battle with those ... things," Nancy said, terror brimming in her voice.

"Yeah," Jen said.

"By yourself?" Jon asked. "That seems like a borderline idiotic plan."

"Or suicidal," Ryan said.

Throwing Ryan a glance, Aeryn said, "You can't go alone."

"I won't be. Tyron will be right beside me the whole time," Jen said with defiance. "And Kaldok, Archer, and Blaze will be out there, too."

"There are hundreds of those things out there; you guys can't possibly hope to take them all out," Grant said, squinting.

"We aren't. We just need to get to the portal and shoot an orb through it." She straightened and asked, "Did none of you listen to me the first time?"

"We did," Ryan answered. "We just weren't sure you heard you the first time."

She rolled her eyes. "We know what the odds are, and we're willing to take it. Krelien and Ar'on will be working sniper positions on the roof." She turned to Jon and said as a side note, "They need access to that, by the way." Jon opened his mouth to say something, but she continued, "And that leaves Tyron and me ample opportunity to get close enough to the portal's activation and send an orb through."

Ryan raised his hand. "I'm sorry, I'm confused. I thought you said there wasn't a portal activation thing near the school."

"There isn't. But we're assuming that Cregorous will be sending more warriors to the school within the field."

"That doesn't explain how you can shoot one of your orbs through it," Jon said as he gestured at her.

"We get close enough, we shoot the orb through the portal, and it reappears on the other side," Jen replied, trying not to get frustrated about going through the events of the plan for a second time.

"And what will that do?"

"It'll show the Council that we're fighting back and need assistance."

Ryan raised his hand again. "Another dumb question." He glanced to his principal and quickly added, "Mine's dumb, yours was fine Mr. Alderfer."

"Oh, thank you for that affirmation Mr. Bender," Jon said with a slight roll of his eyes.

"Don't you think they would have guessed that by now?"

"Maybe they can determine our location from that," Grant offered.

"I was told it would just let them know we're still alive and fighting," Jen said. "Right now, they might be thinking we're all dead."

"That's fair," Jon said with a nod. "They wouldn't want to risk lost lives on an endeavor that might only reveal their rescue mission was failed at the start."

"Once that's done, half the job is complete," Jen said.

"The second half being...?" Aeryn asked.

Jen squirmed slightly. "To gain control of the portal on their side."

"Right," Jon said. "Who runs this army?"

Playing with her hands, Jen murmured, "It's a defense, actually."

"Oh, well, no wonder they aren't that great at offensive thinking," Ryan jested.

The Human-Born shot Ryan a tired look as Nancy said, "Why does all of this sound like it's easy?"

"It isn't. And no one said it was going to be," Jen told her sister.

There was a slight pause, and then Grant pressed, "You're sure there's nothing we can do."

Jon raised his arm toward Grant. "Don't even entertain the thought. There's no way I'm letting students run around with loaded weapons."

Without hesitating, Ryan and Grant both pointed at Jen.

"She supersedes the standard 'student' definition."

"And just because you can shoot a gun doesn't mean you're in the army, Grant. Anyway, shooting an Earth gun and a Tilion one is completely different. These don't even use bullets," Jen said as she pulled the Agerian pistol out from its holster.

Inclining his head slightly, Ryan said, "It looks like a side arm."

"It's not a side arm."

"But it looks like one," Grant said.

Jen cast them both a glance as she continued, "But it's not. This kind of weapon uses energy collected from Tilion to fire little blue beams of energy."

"Like laser beams?" Ryan asked with a scoff.

Slumping her shoulders and giving Ryan an unamused look, she mocked, "Yes, Ryan, like laser beams. They go pew-pew and everything."

Shrugging, Grant said, "So, it's a slightly complicated side arm."

"Goodness, when do you quit?" Jen said with a groan.

Jon pointed to Jen. "When were your guardians planning on implementing this plan of yours?"

"They're called Zaheri," Jen said.

Jon shook his head and said plainly, "I'm never going to remember that. Promise."

"Look, it wasn't my plan; it was Kaldok's. Well, Kaldok's and Tyron's." She holstered the pistol. "As for timeframe, as soon as possible. There's no telling when the Caligans will activate the portal, and we need to be ready when they do."

"Okay. Just hear me out on this," he said as he held his hand out toward her. "How many weapons do your guardians happen to have? These other world ones."

"I don't know. Why?"

Grimacing slightly, he said, "If things get out of hand, we might need more hands filled with weapons."

Sitting up, Ryan pointed at the principal. "See? Even he thinks we should have guns!"

"I wasn't talking about you," Jon snapped, and Ryan shrank back into his chair. "I was talking about faculty. There are a few people who have military backgrounds, and if it gets to that, we may need them."

"I'd have to ask Tyron to see what all they can spare," Jen said.

Jon nodded then said slowly, "And I suppose, if it's absolutely necessary, having a few trustworthy students armed might not be a bad idea."

Ryan nodded. "I said it first, for the record."

"It was my idea, dinkledork," Grant said, smacking Ryan.

"There is no record, you buffoons!" Aeryn scolded.

"Okay then, I'm gonna go get ready," Jen said as she turned to head for the door.

Ryan quickly got up from his seat. "Wait a second, Jen. Just because you and Mr. Alderfer came to a conclusion doesn't mean we're okay with you risking life and limb!"

"He's right," Nancy said. "You can't go out there."

"No, he's wrong, at least partially," Jen said. "I get it, Ryan. I understand your concern. But I don't think anyone, myself included, really has any say in the matter."

"Maybe you do," Grant pressed with a defiant look.

"Fine, so maybe I do have a say," Jen said as she stepped back into the room and let the door slam behind her. "I could say that I'm staying here, sitting in the dark, waiting for my Zaheri to die for me. Or, I can take the bull by the horns and accept the road *my* life is going to take." Looking between her friends and family in the room, she continued, "I eventually have to do this. Regardless of what I want, I have to take this plunge. Why not now?"

Jon looked away and closed his eyes, his face slack but his hands clenched. Ryan let his head drop with a sigh. Aeryn looked around at everyone, trying to find support in someone's eyes.

"Jen, it's just ..." Aeryn began but faltered and eventually closed her mouth.

Grant looked at Aeryn and said softly, "Jen, I know you know where we're coming from. We don't want to see you get hurt."

"I know you don't. And you guys know that I don't want to see you get hurt. That's why I'm doing this. That's why I'm fighting so hard. Because I don't want anyone else to be hurt on *my* behalf," Jen said.

Looking around at everyone else in the room, Nancy sighed. "Then I guess it's simple. You just don't get hurt."

The sisters looked at one another, and Jen smiled. "Okay. I won't."

I've Heard if you Don't Panic, Everything Will be Fine

Jen had seen her Zaheri's various guns before. She had even recently been training using one of their assault rifles.

But seeing the arsenal splayed across tables in the library was the definition of surreal.

Blaze sat in a corner with her eyes closed while Archer stood by the massive windows, his head bobbing up and down. Tyron went through the weapons and checked the ammo, while Krelien sat across from him, dismantling a gun that looked like a sniper rifle. Another gun similar to Krelien's laid across the table, fully assembled. A small blue glow came from just under the magazine slot. Ar'on checked a scope while another one sat on his lap, and Kaldok sat next to him, surveying a map of the school.

As she walked up to them, Tyron looked up and asked, "Are your family and friends okay with this?"

Jen sighed and pulled up a chair to the table. "As okay as they'll ever be."

Krelien turned to her. "Here, gimmie your pistol and swap it out for one of the others."

"What's wrong with this one?" Jen asked as she pulled her gun out of its holster. "And how'd you get all this stuff?"

"Sent Krelien back to the shop," Tyron said. "Got you some clothes too. You'll want to change."

"A human held that pistol and may have broken it. On top of that, you need two anyway, for your two holsters," Ar'on said, not looking away from the scope in his hand.

"It's best practice to check your gun before going into battle," Tyron said as he passed Krelien two pistols in exchange for the one Jen had a moment prior.

Taking the two guns, Jen asked, "What could possibly make them faulty?"

"The same things that make human weapons faulty—malfunctions, trigger slips, things like that." Ar'on tapped the table. "Lesson: always check your-self before going into a fight."

"What if I'm not going into a fight?"

"Make time and check, anyway. You never know if the day is going to require you to use your weapon."

She stared at one of the pistols. "You know, I never asked how these worked."

Krelien picked up his head. "Nope, you didn't." Then he went back to cleaning the interworking of the gun that he was dismantling.

Giving the Jumper a bored look, Jen asked, "So, how do they work?"

Tyron and Ar'on shared a bemused grin before Tyron pushed a small button on the side of the pistol. The cartridge, no bigger than an inch tall and a third of an inch deep, fell out. Holding the cartridge, Tyron said, "You see that blue glow?"

Jen nodded.

"We call them Chora orbs. Our plant life in Agerius produces it naturally every spring."

Jen stifled a laugh and asked disbelievingly, "Flower power?"

"Sure, if you want to call it that," Tyron said with a shrug, and Jen chuckled. "What?"

Trying to keep herself from laughing hysterically, Jen said, "It's just ... nothing. Sorry, only a human would understand."

Casting her a confused look, Tyron continued, "Anyway, they last around five hundred shots or so before they die. They can't be recharged, so you have to grab another cartridge."

"Why not just get more flower power?" Jen asked, not able to contain her little fit of laughter.

Krelien slammed his gun down. "Okay, what is so funny?"

"Okay, I've got a count," Archer said as he bounded over to them. "But there's some bad news attached to it."

"That's not how it goes, Arch. 'I have bad news and worse news'."

"That's not how it goes either," Jen said through her giggling.

Ignoring Jen, Tyron asked, "What's going on, Archer?"

"They're convening on a central location," the grovix said.

Ar'on sat forward. "They're getting ready to receive a portal activation."

"Most likely," Tyron mused.

Turning away from Jen, Krelien said, "Then where's the bad news?"

"There are—at least from the quick count I just did—over one hundred and fifty Caligans out there. Maybe ten Ferveos, but I can't be sure because they were moving around a lot and all have grey-tinted scales."

"On the plus side, the grey ones are usually younger," Ar'on interjected.

"I saw maybe fifty bratak'ra and werewolves combined, but like the Ferveos, it was kind of hard to keep track," Archer continued.

Putting the pistol in his hand down, Tyron said, "Okay, everyone, this is how it's gonna play out."

Blaze walked over to them and positioned herself next to Archer. Her fur slowly changed from pure white to deep reddish-brown, and her eyes changed to yellow irises with a singular slit like the bratak'ra. Her build was adjusting too as her spine appeared to gain the hunched nature like a saber-tooth tiger.

"Kaldok, Blaze, and Archer are gonna go out there and try to integrate themselves into the crowd. Now, don't do anything crazy or outlandish," he said, looking at Archer, who rolled his eyes. "Get out there the moment Blaze is ready. Jen and I are gonna head down to the first floor main entrance, and we won't emerge until the portal activates. Once it does, you three start creating as much chaos as you can." He indicated Kaldok and the two grovix. "And Kal, I'm counting on you to keep those two safe."

"I *am* more than capable of staying safe," Blaze said in a quiet, stern tone. Her calm demeanor coming from the slowly appearing grizzly maw was a juxtaposed sight.

Tyron looked at her. "I know that Blaze. But it's been a while since you've been out there. I can't lose you here."

Blaze looked a bit frustrated but nodded.

"Krelien and Ar'on, once we're done here, make your way to the roof." He turned to Jen. "Did you get Jon's permission to get up there?"

Jen nodded. "He's waiting outside for them when they're ready. He'll take them to the stairs."

"Good," Tyron said with a nod. "Stay hidden until the portal activates. I don't need a Ferveos seeing you and trying to break the shield to get at you. Keep an eye on her at all times." He pointed to Jen.

"Just don't shoot *me*," the teenager said.

"He said to keep an eye, not target you," Krelien said.

"To-may-to, to-mah-to."

"Everyone know their part?" Tyron asked.

Sitting up a bit, Ar'on asked, "What about you, Tyron? If we're focusing so much on Jen, who's gonna look out for you?"

Offering a smile, Tyron said, "I'll be fine, old man." He then turned to Kaldok. "Kal, you'll have the most opportunity to get an orb through. If you see that chance, take it."

"But I thought we were trying to get you and Jen to the portal?" Krelien asked.

"We are, but there's always the chance that we might not be able to. If Kaldok can do it, I'm not going to risk Jen and me for pride's sake."

Kaldok shook his head. "It'll be difficult. I can't manifest an orb when I'm in werewolf form."

Sighing, Tyron said, "Understood. We'll be golden either way." He looked at Jen. "Now, I know you, and I know you're just gonna barrel right into this."

"Great way to build up *my* confidence," Jen grumbled.

"You should favor your gun more than your energy."

Sitting back a little, she asked, "Why?"

Ar'on looked at the shield outside then back to her. "Are you seriously asking that question?"

She pointed out the window. "Right, those."

"You truly don't notice them?" Kaldok asked.

Jen shrugged. "I *mean*, a little? I dunno. They kinda tickle *my* nose sometimes, but otherwise, I guess I kinda forget they're there."

Her Zaheri stared at her for a few seconds.

"What?"

Tyron shook his head a bit. "Nothing. It's just ... wow."

Knocking her knuckles against the table rhythmically, she said, "Okay, moving on from *me* and whatever you all are thinking. I really don't wanna know."

Getting to his feet, Ar'on said, "C'mon, Krelien; we need to move out."

"You three get down to the first floor, and the moment you can, slip out there and try to remain discreet," Tyron said.

Jen turned to look at Blaze as she walked off. The grovix really could change her appearance. Her coat was now a dark reddish-brown, and her entire body was now, somehow, huge. A little bigger than

Archer. And she now bore the same horns that a dual-horned bratak'ra sported.

"Hey, kid," Krelien said as Jen got up to leave. He tossed her his watch. "Keep that on you."

Jen cast him a confused look. "Why?"

A little awkwardly, Krelien got to his feet and shrugged before he made his way out of the library, Ar'on right behind him.

Despite not understanding Krelien's motives, Jen still put the watch on.

Just as she finished fastening the metal chained watch, Tyron came up to her. "Ready for this?"

Falling into step with him, she nodded. "Yeah, I think so."

"Good; you're the only backup I've got."

As they exited the library, they found Ar'on and Krelien standing with Jon, a security guard, and Grant and Ryan.

Furrowing her brow, Jen asked, "What's going on?"

"No offense, but we don't have time for this," Ar'on grumbled.

Jon glanced to the security guard. "Escort them to the roof please." He turned back to the two teenage boys and drilled a stern look at them as he answered Jen, "These two insisted on coming along."

"We just want to go with you and Tyron to the entrance," Grant said while doing a double-take at Tyron, who gave the two teenage boys harsh glares.

Crossing his finger over his chest, Ryan said, "Honest."

"Mmhmm," Tyron said gruffly before he shoved a pack at Jen. "Go change."

"Thanks," Jen said as she took the pack and walked off down the hall.

Jon and the Alpha Team Leader shared a look before Tyron said, "I can handle them until we head out, if you're okay with it."

A scoff came from Jon. "Are you kidding *me*? Their families wouldn't at all be surprised if they got hurt trying to prove something."

"Good to know."

Jon nodded down the hall. "I'll come back around to pick them up once I know the others got to the roof all right."

Leaning toward Grant, Ryan said, "Are you as scared as I am?"

Grant said nothing as he stared at Tyron, the latter making both teenagers feel tiny. Awkwardly, Grant then held his hand out. "Hi, *my* name is—"

"Grant Connolly, you're a terrible aim at a range but for some reason can master a kill shot the moment you're handed a hunting rifle. I think you think too much. Your dad's name is Hank, and your mom's name is Sharon. Nice people, but your mom's got terrible taste in curtains. Your younger sister likes ballet but can't be graceful if she tried, so they just give her good marks 'cause she's so sweet." He stared Grant dead in the eye. "And by the way, I know."

Neither boy said anything. Just stood there with mouths agape.

Barely above a whisper, Grant asked, "Who are you?"

Tyron offered a tight, toothless smile then glanced at Ryan.

The other boy stammered, "I ... I don't even want to know what, how, who ... everything you know, which I assume is everything. Is it everything? Are you seriously psychic? If you were reading my mind would you tell me?"

"Elders, you're worse than I thought," Tyron muttered and rolled his eyes.

"You could kill us and make it look like an accident, couldn't you?"

"Y'know what? I'm thinking about it."

"Oh God, he is going to kill us," Ryan whispered to Grant.

Rolling his eyes again, Tyron shook his head.

Footsteps from down the hall alerted them to Jen walking toward them. "Thank God you didn't kill them."

"Really? You think I'd kill them?" the Zaheri asked as she handed him the leather pack that he had given her. She wore a thermal, deep blue, long-sleeved shirt, her replacement jacket in her hand, which she threw into the library. "Of course not. This is far too public a place to do that."

A strangled cry left Ryan's mouth, and Grant flinched.

Jen smacked Tyron in the chest, and the hybrid grimaced as though the hit had actually hurt him. "Let's just go," she said as she walked past them, Tyron right behind her.

Falling into step with one another a few paces behind Jen and Tyron, Ryan whispered to Grant, "Okay, I'm not gonna admit this to anyone else, but damn, that guy is intimidating."

"Did you feel like you were gonna just drop to the ground in fear?" Grant asked disbelievingly.

"I almost called him sir!"

"You suck at whispering!" Tyron called from over his shoulder.

As the teenagers looked forward, they saw Jen smack him again, and Tyron laughed.

"Oh c'mon, it was funny," Tyron defended.

Ryan grabbed Grant's arm, forcing them both to stop, and the former asked, "What'd he mean by, 'he knows'?"

Grant was stoic and barely moved a muscle as he stared at his friend. Coughing slightly, he then turned and followed after Jen and Tyron.

Ryan was still for a few seconds, watching him take a few steps away. "Aw...man, really? Now? Not, like, last year?"

Grant waved toward the floor aggressively and marched off.

Ryan followed. "No, seriously, dude, this is the worst timing of all time!"

When they reached the end of the stairs, they saw Jen and Tyron staring out the large windows. They both wore sunglasses.

Giving them a confused look, Ryan asked, "What's with the glasses?"

"They come in handy," Tyron said.

"Thank you for that artful display of the descriptive process."

Tyron threw him a bored look before he went back to staring out the window.

Crossing his arms over his chest and eyeing Tyron warily, Ryan asked, "So, what all's out there?"

"Dragons, naturally," Jen said, "And creatures called bratak'ra. And a few werewolves."

"Werewolves?" Ryan asked.

"Bra-what?" Grant asked.

Rolling his eyes, Tyron said, "They brought everything with them, aside from Cregorous."

"That sounds bad." There was silence, and then Grant asked, "I'm sorry, but what's a...bratak'ra?"

"They're four-legged creatures that stand around the size of a horse with a big build and horns," Tyron rattled off.

"So, what about werewolves?" Ryan asked, a cheeky grin coming to his face. "Don't tell *me* they all look like Taylor Lautner."

Jen rolled her eyes as Tyron turned to look at him, an incredulous expression on his face. The teenage boys shrank as the Zaheri said, "I get Kaldok's frustration now."

"You've seen Kaldok," Jen said. "He's kinda stuck between a werewolf and a hybrid. From what he's told *me*, they're pretty simple beasts with a blood-lust that fuels them."

"How does the whole werewolf thing work?" Grant half-shrugged. "It's obviously not like a full moon that triggers it."

Offering a slight shrug, Jen said, "I dunno."

Keeping his eyes forward, Tyron said, "All we know is that the curse is transmitted by biting. Any Agerian that's been bitten has converted."

Shifting her eyes from the doors to Tyron, Jen asked, "But not Kaldok?"

Tyron let out a slow breath, his focus glued forward. "Not Kaldok."

"Wow," Ryan said, raising his brow. "That *makes* him pretty impressive."

"I definitely think so," Jen said with a nod.

Tyron looked over at her and a warm smile washed over his features.

After a second or two of silence, Grant said, "I still don't have a good feeling about this, Jen."

"If we were to wait until you did have a good feeling, we'd all be dead," Jen grumbled.

"Besides, it's not like you have anything to really worry about," Tyron said casually.

"We'll be *fine*, Grant. That goes for you, too." Jen pointed to Ryan. "Now knock it off before I smack you both silly."

Suddenly, a harsh white light came from outside, shining through the large windows. Shielding their eyes, the boys turned to see what was going on.

"Let's move," Tyron said before he and Jen quickly exited the building.

Both boys turned to say something to Jen but weren't fast enough, so their words just sort of died on their way to their mouths.

After a second, Ryan stuffed his hands in his pockets. "Well, at least the sunglasses make sense now."

Chapter Twelve
Take a Breath, Hold on Tight, Don't let Go

Jen and Tyron ran toward the shield, which wasn't far from the entrance of the building. As they went, they both concentrated energy into their hands and, when they broke past the barrier, they threw their hands outward. The ground rippled and tore upward from the force of the blue and gold wave of energy.

There was a massive grouping of enemy fighters around the portal, which had new warriors arriving through. All their backs were to Tyron and Jen, and when the attack started, they turned in time for a huge chunk of them to get blown away. The huddle turned and immediately began to run toward Jen and Tyron, the Ferveos taking off toward them.

However, the large dragons didn't get high or far before bullets pierced through their skulls. Five fell almost immediately from Krelien and Ar'on's shots on the roof.

Frantically, the enemy fighters began running toward whatever looked like an Agerian. A group of bratak'ra ran ahead of the Caligans toward Jen and Tyron, while a good-sized group stayed around the portal.

From Jen's vantage point, she could see something causing a commotion near the portal. She could only hope that Kaldok, Blaze, and Archer were doing a good job at confusing the Caligans.

With a yell, Tyron slid to a stop and threw his right hand over his head, shooting a gold orb toward the advancing bratak'ra.

The orb hit one bratak'ra, but the ones near it were blown backward, as well. It was as though the orb was only the main force of the attack.

Grey energy flew at Jen and Tyron and, for a moment, Jen contemplated making a shield, but she knew that wasn't a good idea. The amount of concentration it took for her to keep the two large shields up and focus on fighting the enemies around her was more than enough for her to handle.

At this rate, the Caligans were going to gain all their reinforcements before any of them could even hope to get to the portal. There were just too many of them.

Maybe this wasn't the best idea ever.

Her transformation had taken longer than Blaze would have liked. Changing her appearance had been easy, once she had concentrated on it enough. The hard part would be integrating herself with the bratak'ra.

Blaze knew she had to figure out how to carry herself without dignity and pride. While she knew the enemy well, she didn't know how to be one of them. She had never anticipated that she would need to.

Kaldok had pushed one of the horns she now appeared to have protruding from her skull, and when she did nothing, he had sheepishly said, "Blaze, you have to remember you have horns now."

Elders, this was far more difficult than she would have thought. Her head would be heavier, and she would have to compensate for the mass that her horns would add to the base of her skull.

Carry your head lower. They do not hold their heads high. They cannot. They are too heavy. You are a few steps above the muck of an inexperienced bratak'ra. You have earned your horns.

When she, Archer, and Kaldok had reached their entrance point, Archer said to her, "This may be difficult to do, but you have to make sure you don't act like yourself."

If Archer were any other grovix, she would have reprimanded him then physically abused him. But she knew he meant it in a way of attempting to help. Although he hadn't known of her prior experience on the field of battle, the younger grovix always seemed to speak to her about the warfare they had experienced as though she knew exactly what he was talking about, which she did.

He didn't know that, though.

Perhaps he had caught on to his surroundings, and those around him, better than she had given him credit for.

Archer was still a pup in many ways, but when

he wanted, he could carry himself as much older than he seemed.

The moment they were outside and had quickly snuck into the horde convening around a central location, Blaze knew she had to first bump into one of them. Not because she wanted to, but because that would be normal for a bratak'ra to do. Also, it would help get their odious scent on her and help mask who she really was. She told Archer to do the same, and they quickly integrated themselves among the disgusting animals.

There was no better way to describe bratak'ra. Blaze knew they could speak, but everything else about their nature made her believe they weren't sentient beings. On top of that, they always seemed to smell of rotting flesh and feces.

It took everything in her not to gag.

Kaldok had skulked off with the other werewolves once they had left the building. From what she could tell, he had gone unnoticed.

As she walked along, she saw other mono-horned bratak'ra giving her a look of respect, slightly bowing their heads. The smaller bratak, the ones without fully developed horns though, they cowered near her and practically ducked out of her way.

What an awful way to live, she thought.

She looked around and realized that the werewolves and bratak'ra weren't mingling; they were basically in separate groups. Sweeping her head across her surroundings, she noticed that both creatures eyed the others as though they might strike at any moment.

An idea came to her.

Glancing over toward Kaldok, they made eye contact, and she growled. "What're you looking at?"

Kaldok's eyes shifted around a little before he realized that the other werewolves around him were beginning to bristle with anger. Baring his teeth and letting his fur stand on end, he growled back, "A child, by the state of things."

A mono-horned bratak'ra surged to Blaze's side and bellowed, "How dare you, you filth!"

"You haven't survived longer than a few battles and decree yourselves greater than we?" another werewolf spat, its voice low and gravely. "Each of us here has seen lifetimes more than even your most experienced."

By now, an evident divide had formed between the bratak'ra and the werewolves.

Elders, they truly do not trust one another, Blaze thought.

The snarling and insulting continued from several members of both sides.

One of the armored Caligans walked up to them and said, "Knock it off, you mutts! We thirst for Agerian blood."

Teeth gnashing, one of the bratak'ra growled, "What would you know of it, hybrid? You're no better than an Agerian."

"And you," a werewolf howled, "are no better than a grovix."

Roaring broke out, and the two parties leapt at one another. It was impossible for Blaze to know who bit first, but staying still was out of the question. She threw herself into the thrall.

Limbs and horns and teeth were everywhere as the werewolves and bratak'ra began to tear one another apart.

Several Caligans either got in the way or were

caught up in the scuffle, and abruptly, grey energy attacks began to fire at the two groups. This only caused further chaos.

Archer soared over her and collided with a were-wolf, taking the brunt of a hit that was meant for Blaze.

For a brief second, she thought about helping Archer, but when she saw him hold his own against the monster, she turned to check on Kaldok. Her fellow Zaheri fought off two smaller bratak'ra.

"You idiots! Take out the hybrids first!" she snapped.

The two bratak'ra shared a look as Kaldok turned and rammed his paw into a Caligan, sending it fly-ing. Seeing this, the two bratak'ra turned away from Kaldok and attacked nearby Caligans. Kaldok looked to her for half a second before they both turned and continued their onslaught.

"Two shields, and she barely notices," Krelien said as they reached the roof.

"I know," Ar'on whispered as he crouched down and began to slowly make his way to the edge to stay out of sight.

Following suit, the Jumper said, "I mean, think about it. She could probably take out this whole incursion."

"But she can't," Ar'on snapped as he leaned back against the small wall at the edge of the roof. "And she shouldn't."

"But it'd be over," Krelien said with a sigh. "We

could just pack up and leave; get all of these people out of here."

Shaking his head, the elder said, "She's stretching her limits too far and too fast. Every minute that these shields stay up, she's unconsciously working toward the maximum that her energy can sustain."

Krelien's eyes darted around a little as he asked, "That's not a good thing?"

In a hush, Ar'on answered, "This isn't the right environment." He glanced over the wall to try to ascertain where the bulk of the enemy was. Squatting back down, he faced the door they had come up. "There should be boundaries, goals. Steps she should stay in."

"Why? What's so bad about her realizing how strong she could be?"

Casting a quick glance over at the Jumper, Ar'on sighed. "Absolute power can be terrifying. She's already scared. The more we point out how strong she is, the more scared she's going to be about possibly hurting someone."

They were quiet for a few seconds before Krelien said, "She's already stronger than I thought was possible."

Shaking his head, Ar'on replied, "Two shields the size of a building and both nearly opaque." He looked up at the second dome above them. "If the Protector can do half of this, then we have our hands full from here on out."

"I kinda thought we already did."

Ar'on chuckled. "Kid, I think we've still got a lot ahead of us."

The portal flashed to life, and Krelien placed his sniper rifle onto the ledge. "Ferveos."

"Yep, I see 'em," Ar'on said, and then they began to single the dragons out.

Krelien never would have thought he would be doing this. Years before he joined the Alpha Team, or rather, was forced to join, he had avoided battles on the third dimension. They were dangerous and could get him killed. He didn't want to die. The only reason he was part of the Defense was because they needed him, and he needed them for basic necessities in life, like food, water, and shelter.

But now he wanted to be here, on this roof, fighting on the third dimension. He wanted to help Jen save her school. More importantly, he wanted to help Jen save her world.

After he and Ar'on took out five Ferveos, he turned his attention to the fighters on the ground. Finding Archer, Kaldok and Blaze was difficult for him, so he stuck to firing on enemy fighters directly near the portal. He heard Ar'on's gun go off five more times as he saw through his scope other warriors exiting the portal from Tilion. They were getting their reinforcements.

The thought of Cregorous wanting to send even more troops for just six Agerians and a Human-Born made him chuckle.

Krelien flipped a switch on the side of the rifle and opened a barrage of consistent fire where the enemy fighters streamed from the portal. They dropped quickly, like sacks of potatoes, right after stepping out of the portal. A pile of bodies began to accumulate.

Through his scope, he saw Ar'on firing at the same location, so Krelien quickly looked up from his gun and looked over toward Jen and Tyron. They were still a long way away from the portal, and if Kaldok was still in werewolf form, the chances of getting an orb through were quickly diminishing.

Swinging his gun to a new position, Krelien began to lay a heavy stream of fire through a line of enemy warriors. His job was to protect Jen, after all, and that was just what he was going to do.

The Ferveos fell out of the sky quickly. Ar'on and Krelien were doing their job just as Tyron had hoped. But, for him, now he had more to worry about. While he preferred a dead Ferveos to a live one, he now had to take into account where their dead bodies would land. All the while keeping track of Jen.

A bratak'ra lunged at him, and he fell backward to duck as a blue orb smacked into the monster, sending it spiraling back where it had come from. He fell onto his back and saw one of the few dead Ferveos falling to where he and Jen needed to go. Quickly getting to his feet as Jen ran past him, he pushed her to the right as they continued to the portal.

Gold lightning surged down his left arm as he threw his arm sideways across his body. A gold, translucent wave came from his left and pushed a few enemy fighters back but didn't last long, only a few seconds. They were just clear of the Ferveos when it landed, its massive body cracking into the asphalt of the road around the school.

"Run! Run!" he hollered.

A second after that, an explosion came from behind him and blew both he and Jen off their feet. Chunks of earth, asphalt, and concrete whizzed past them and connected with his body. He felt a chunk of something imbed itself into his back as something else tore at his leg.

Aiming for a solid landing, gold energy surged around his body and splayed to the ground. The attack took out enough fighters that it made a clear area to land so they could get their footing a bit easier.

Once they landed, he had to immediately fall into combat again. He was grateful that basic melee had been first on Jen's mastery list. The knowledge that she could hold her own in this sort of situation meant he didn't have to constantly look back over his shoulder at her condition. He still checked with quick glances to ensure she was okay though.

Throwing a Caligan to his left, he felt the sting of an energy attack hit his right shoulder. He only had a moment to see that there was still too much distance between them and the portal. Dead bodies piled around the entrance of it, but still, if more warriors were coming through, they weren't going to last long.

He or Jen had to find a way to get to the portal now.

She was getting tired of being thrown into the air. At least this time she was able to control her landing a little more. The small swath that Tyron created with his attack gave her something better to aim for that wouldn't be a live enemy. Regardless, she felt a number of things graze past her and rip at her clothes before something impacted with her right leg, just around her calf. It jarred a Charlie horse sort of pang through her leg.

She dug her palms into the torn-up concrete and got to her feet. Grey energy flew all around her. She worked to dodge what she could and hit whatever got close enough to her. It was a glacial pace they moved, and the Caligans just never seemed to stop. They would clear a path and run a few feet, only to be swallowed up by the opposition again.

Her pistol was getting plenty of use, but that rinky-dink thing wasn't going to clear a route to the portal. It wouldn't be open forever, and they had no way of knowing how long it would be there. She or Tyron had to get to the portal soon, or this whole attempt would have been completely useless.

Between her bone spikes and the pistol, she did a pretty solid job of whittling through the Caligan forces. She had to admit that the occasional bratak'ra threw her off balance. One second she was punching someone, and the next, a bratak'ra's horns nearly impaled her. She could see why even a short battle could leave someone exhausted.

Tyron hit her back and forced her down. They narrowly avoided a good-sized grey blast of energy that seared over them. They pulled one another upright, and she gripped his arm for support. His knuckle spikes cut into her shirt with how he gripped the fabric in his fist.

She glanced to the portal, and then to Tyron

and thought, *He should just throw me. I can get above this, and then I can get to the portal.*

Tyron gripped her forearm, and she knew what he was going to do, even though she hadn't said anything.

Gathering all his strength, Tyron grasped Jen's arm then threw her in the air at an angle, toward the side of the school. Her shield around this section of the building was practically molded right to the side of the building.

Flying through the air, her wings tore through the back of her shirt. Bones jutted out of her back, and her skin molded to them. Dark, leathery wings took shape out of nothingness. Her shirt instantly patched itself back up, coming to end just around her wings as though the holes there were designed for it.

Beating her wings against her direction, she softened her impact with the building, which she skimmed along slightly. Her blue shield looked like she was wading through it, just reaching up past her calves as her feet beat against the windows of the library.

She ran upward, her wings taking over, and she reached the ability to fly parallel with the side of the building. All she had to do was quickly veer to her left once she gained enough speed, shoot by the portal, throw a blue orb into it, and then fly back under the shield. It wouldn't take long and, at the moment, seemed like the smart thing to do.

Suddenly, a Caligan tore through the sky, and she attempted to change her trajectory but realized she was too close to the building. Not reacting fast enough, the Caligan hit her left wing with a grey energy attack, tearing through the tendons and ripping a hole in her wing.

There were milliseconds to react, and in that time, she didn't do anything right. Her right wing grazed one of the windows, causing it to burst and shatter. The sudden change *made* her right wing break as it hit the end of the window and collided with the cinderblock of the building.

Then the Caligan tore past her, grabbed her left wing, and jerked it upward. Jen had no time to do anything before her head went straight into the side of the building.

It wasn't until the Caligan had grabbed Jen's wing that Krelien got a shot he could work with. Ar'on had tried twice and missed. This one was good, and fast. What? Was it auditioning to be one of the generals?

Not wasting the chance, Krelien pulled the trigger and sent one of his bullets straight through the Caligan's head.

One problem down.

Quickly removing his gun from a firing position, Krelien looked down and hoped to see Jen flying to the portal. He knew he wouldn't, though. He had heard the window shatter, followed by the crack of a broken bone, followed by a sickening *thud* that reverberated against the wall of the building up to his position.

As he looked over the roof, he saw that either Jen was unconscious or trying to figure out how to fly with a broken wing. It looked like she was unconscious.

Regardless of which it was, he knew she was falling, and fast. Her wings crumpled around her body, which meant she would only fall faster.

The building was four stories tall. Then, take into account that the roof was a few feet above the fourth story. Jen was somewhere near the third. That wasn't much time.

Krelien knew Ar'on had stopped firing, and so he quickly chucked his gun toward the elder hybrid before he threw himself off the building.

Ar'on caught the gun and ripped his gaze away from Krelien and Jen. He dropped Krelien's rifle and went back to covering Tyron.

Krelien got himself into a bullet position and flew toward the earth as fast as he could. Jen's body had a few second's lapse of time ahead of him, and every second to follow could mean life or death for her. She passed the second floor. He wasn't moving fast enough. He passed the second floor.

Reaching his hand out, he grasped Jen's wrist and pulled her to him. They spun for a few seconds before he finally got her body flush against his. There were maybe two seconds left before they impacted with the ground when Krelien jumped into the fifth dimension.

The instant he let go of Jen's hand, Tyron wondered what he had just done. There was no telling what his actions would cause, and he couldn't actually believe he had just thrown her away.

Not just away, but at a building.

Right after he had done that, he had to refocus his attention around him and fight off a few enemy fighters, trying to find the ability to also track what was happening to Jen.

He cleared room around him after getting hit by a bratak'ra and taking a nasty blow to his head. He refocused on Jen just as she crashed into the side of the building, and Tyron could have sworn his heart stopped.

Of all the bone-headed things to do, he had been the one to do it?

After all the times they had argued about who was in the right and who was in the wrong on a training exercise, he had been the one who got her killed?

No. No, not killed.

But definitely not okay.

The Caligan that hit her was fast, and he almost took off after it when he saw a blue bullet shoot through its head.

Sound didn't register to him. There was a ringing in his ears. It might have been caused from the fact that he wasn't worried about his own wellbeing and wasn't breathing properly. Or, it was from the nasty hit he took to his head.

Krelien went after her, and Tyron took a few tentative steps toward the building, as though that would save things.

He wasn't fast enough as a flyer; otherwise, he would have gone after her falling form. He knew he couldn't catch her. He wasn't built like that.

But Krelien was.

The Jumper was right behind her, but there was still a good gap of space between their two bodies. Tyron's heartbeat pulsed in his ears and throbbed on his neck. Then Krelien reached Jen and pulled her to him. They didn't have much room between them and the ground.

They pivoted in the air, spiraling at an odd angle for a few seconds and, with only a dozen feet to spare, Krelien jumped.

A low, pulsing sound came from the area. It was like they became silver dust, dissipating into the air. In an instant, they were gone with the breeze.

Tyron's ears popped in rapid succession, so quickly that it hurt and sent an ache to his head. Sound charged back to his system, and he heard the bratak'ra at his left just in enough time to fall to the ground and fire his pistol at it. He dodged out of the way as the monster fell, crashing to the earth.

Dimensions don't act the way one expects them to. In the third, Krelien had seconds before he would have impacted with the ground and, most assuredly, died. But as a Jumper, he supersedes laws that humans view to be true. In the fifth dimension, Krelien found himself able to slowly stop them from hitting the ground.

Normally, shifting to another dimension was as if Krelien walked from one room to another. In the new room, there was a change in perspective from how things seemed in the previous one. Up was still up and down was still down; he just had more time to do things and could, if he wanted, view things on the third dimension in both rapid and slow times. In the case of the fifth dimension, everything looked like a smeared oil painting.

This time, however, there was something wrong. It might have had something to do with Jen being a passenger on the trip, but he couldn't have been sure. All he did know was that the moment he entered the fifth dimension, his eyes burned, his ears hurt, and voices began to filter through his head. The world around him was skewed in an odd way, and it felt like a strong wind whipped around him, dousing the landscape he found himself in, in a bloody, marring way.

A screeching noise grew the longer he was there. It was a similar sound to when a ringing tone entered your ears, but it wasn't diminishing. It just kept getting worse.

Krelien pinched his eyes shut and wanted to bang his head against a rock. Tears began to fill his vision, and he blearily tried to figure out where he needed to go. They needed to get to the portal, but it was nowhere to be seen.

His breath came out in smoky, chattering vapors, and he shivered in the freezing cold.

The surging wind turned into smoke and all pulled together off to Krelien's right. At least, he thought it was his right. Nothing made sense. He felt like he was upside down but still right side up.

Suddenly, the smoke and wind swept upward, and he realized, as the wind pulled the smoke aside, there were wings and a body forming.

Despite the dry, sand-papery feeling of the air around him, Krelien's eyes widened.

A *massive* dragon pulled itself up out of the brimstone. It looked like it only had a skeleton as its physical form. The rest of its body was a mixture of fire and ash. Its teeth, jagged and uneven. Its mouth, eyes, and all throughout the cracks of its skull poured flame. All along the dragon's skeleton were bodies, charred and stuck there, as though they were part of its frame.

This dragon was unlike anything Krelien had ever seen. And he was rooted in his fear.

Wherever he was, whatever he was seeing, it was horrifying. He felt as though there was darkness all around him, and he held the only light to be found.

The dragon opened its skeletal, uneven jaw, and a horrid, unearthly sound came from its maw. Like nails on a chalkboard mixed with the feeling of something sharp stuck under your fingernail. Like a car crash mixed with a searing paper cut that sliced just under your skin. Like the first crash of thunder mixed with the dentist drilling a hole in your cavity-ridden tooth. It sounded like every terrible thing imaginable and caused the most jabbing pain beyond recognition that Krelien had ever felt. It stampeded through his body.

Just when he thought he was going to die there, in pain and torment, he felt Jen's hand tighten on his forearm and she looked up at him, but there was something different. Her eyes were a rainbow of colors, and they shined with an otherworldly brightness.

The sound stopped, and so did the burning in his body. The dragon wailed, and the brimstone covered it as it flew away. Absolute stillness filled the area, and Krelien looked away from Jen for a split-second. When he looked back at her, she was unconscious again.

A flash of noise filled his ears, and he suddenly appeared on the third dimension. His wings were wrapped around him and Jen, and he shot them outward, like he knew what he was doing. They stood next to the portal.

His head pounded, and his eyes felt strained. He had no idea how they had suddenly gotten here. After the jump, he knew they had still been far away from where the portal activation was, and he had barely moved because of the pain of whatever had happened in the fifth dimension.

Glancing down at his body, he saw abrasions ran across his skin and his shirt was repairing itself.

Had he been hurt?

There wasn't time to worry over it, though.

He was just about to turn his attention to making an orb and shooting it through the portal when Jen suddenly gasped and stood upright. Her eyes seemed more normal this time, but they kept shifting and changing in color, like when oil flowed in a stream. She gripped his forearms, and he repositioned himself, trying to hold her upright.

She shot her arm up toward the sky, and an orb a little bigger than a basketball formed almost instantly. Half a second later, the sphere of energy flew away from her and into the portal, trailing blue smoke as it went.

Both of them stared at the orb as it disappeared into the portal when Jen's eyes rolled back and she went limp. Startled, Krelien caught her as he heard a growl from behind. He had spent too much time stationary.

Without another second's hesitation, he jumped, hoping to make it through the trip unscathed.

It was strange. He entered the fifth dimension, and there was nothing wrong. The world looked inverted and painting-esque, as it always did when he jumped. But there was no wind, no pain, and there was no screeching noises or voices whirling around him.

Flying as quickly as he could and trying not to puzzle over what had happened before, he navigated and found Tyron.

Out of the corner of Tyron's eye, he saw Krelien suddenly appear behind him, holding onto Jen. A pulse accompanied their arrival, and the two of them came out of nothingness. Krelien quickly straightened and landed, using his large wings to whip around and crash into a few enemy fighters.

"That was one heck of a stunt you pulled back there!" Tyron hollered over his shoulder as he continued to fire his gun before he turned and took Krelien's arm.

Krelien gripped Jen tightly to him, her body slumped against his frame. "Hold on!" he screamed as a bratak'ra neared them. He pinched his eyes shut and tried not to think about what might happen with two passengers. Thankfully, when he jumped, nothing strange happened. The world was as he expected, and he zoomed across the landscape.

Within a few seconds, they reappeared behind Jen's blue shield, which still stood. Once they reappeared, Krelien let go of Tyron's arm and laid Jen down as gently as he could.

Tyron, who had never jumped before, staggered away from Krelien and fell down, heaving gasps of air into his suddenly quaking lungs. A coughing fit came from him as he asked, "Is she okay?"

Krelien didn't answer right away. He blinked a few times before he said, "I think so."

Staring at Jen, he saw that she had a few abrasions along her body, too. The exposed skin was already healing, but that wasn't the problem. The problem was that he had no idea what had just happened. And he couldn't even begin to find an answer.

A strange whooshing sound came from the shield as Kaldok, Archer, and Blaze ran toward them, completely unencumbered by the shield. The Alpha Team Leader got to his feet as they ran up to him and Krelien.

As Kaldok approached them, he sat back on his hind legs, and a bone-cracking sound came from him as he stood upright. He grimaced as he stood and shook out his legs.

Kneeling next to Krelien, Kaldok placed his hand on the Jumper's back and asked, "Hey, buddy, you okay?" The werewolf was missing patches of skin, had bite marks along his body, and was sporting a cut across his face and another one across his back. They were healing well and didn't appear to be too deep. He was still covered in blood, though.

With a nod, Krelien said, "I think so." He turned to Tyron. "She shot an orb through the portal. A big one."

"I saw," Tyron said as he held his sides. They burned like he had been running for miles and had side stickers. There was a gash on the side of his head, the blood matting his hair and making it stick at odd angles. Blood splatters adorned his clothes; some of the marks from his blood and others from the Caligans.

Blaze stepped up to Krelien. "How is she?" Her fur began to change to white, and her eyes lost the grotesque yellow tint and horrid slit of a bratak'ra. It was only from her changing appearance that Krelien could see blood matting her fur and that she was limping, her front left paw bleeding from what looked to be a bite mark.

Archer was worse, though. He had scratches and bite marks all over his body. Not to mention the few deep cuts from a bratak'ra's horns. However, he was standing well, his large paws keeping him balanced. Although, there did seem to be blood coming from his paw pads, making oddly interesting paw prints on the concrete of the main entrance.

The Jumper looked up at Blaze and said, "I think she's okay, but I'm not sure."

"Krelien!" Ar'on called as he exploded through the doors of the building. "Thank the Elders you caught her," the elder Hybrid said through heaving gasps. He stood up a bit straighter and winced as he tried to even his breathing. "I forgot you could have a passenger when jumping." Ar'on pointed toward Krelien as he continued to take in heavy breaths. "Is she ...?"

"We need to find someone to look at her," Tyron said before Krelien could say anything.

The Jumper was glad for that. He was getting annoyed about answering the same question over and over again.

"I can help with that," a woman called from behind them.

The Alpha Team all turned toward the entrance of the school and saw a small woman standing before them. She was petite in every sense of the word, but it was as though steel were in her bones. When she walked, people ducked out of her way, because she always had somewhere important to be. Typically because she was the one making sure a wounded Agerian lived.

Her long brown hair was swept up into a messy bun. If she hadn't been wearing blue jeans and a dressy blouse, the team would have sworn they had somehow landed in Agerius.

Blaze's eyes went wide. "Janet! Your presence is quite fortuitous."

Tyron stared at her, his mouth agape, before he asked quietly, "What are you doing here?"

"We can talk later. Right now, I need to check on her to make sure everything's okay," Janet said, holding his stare. She found herself a little unnerved and embarrassed, even though there wasn't much reason to feel either. Except that she was staring at Tyron who was, as per usual, covered in blood and wounds.

He nodded a few short times. "Right." Turning to Krelien, who looked petrified, he said, "C'mon; let's get her inside."

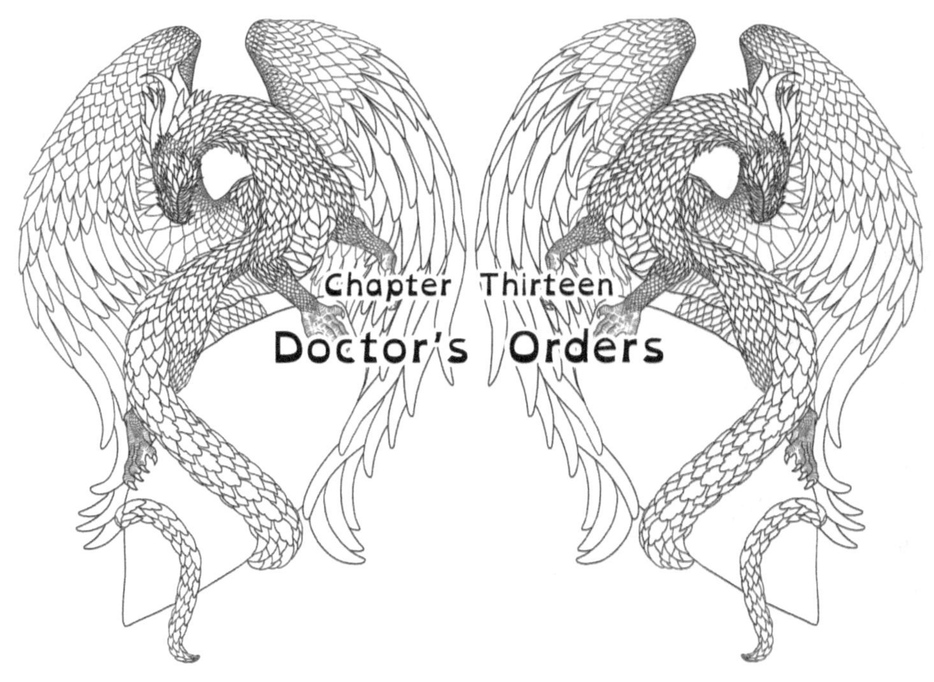

Chapter Thirteen

Doctor's Orders

"What are you doing here? When did you get here?" Tyron asked as he followed Janet to the nurse's office. Krelien was right behind him, carrying Jen in his arms. The rest of the team kept pace with Janet's hurried steps, her short legs marching forward.

"Council Member Aros sent me two days ago," Janet said as Tyron finally caught up to her.

"Aros?" Ar'on asked.

Taking a breath, Tyron asked, "Why didn't you tell me?"

"I literally started this job yesterday. If I had any idea that you were here, trust me, I would have found you," Janet said.

Looking away from her, Tyron muttered, "You shouldn't have to find me. I should be the one finding you."

Blaze perked up a little. "Aros did not inform you where you were going?"

Janet shook her head. "All he said was one of the Human-Borns was going to need a caretaker that was well-versed in human culture." She looked at Tyron and added, "The Elders told him to send me." Opening the door to the office, she ushered them in. "Krelien, place her on that bed just inside the door."

Once everyone was inside the room, Janet swiftly went to a desk and pulled out a slim tablet.

As Krelien gently set Jen down, Janet came over to the teenager. As she pressed a few points on the tablet, a scan started to run across Jen's body. "Now, Krelien, I need you to tell me everything that happened."

Tyron bit his tongue, and Janet's eyes locked with his for a moment. Then he took a step back, and she did her best to refocus on Jen.

"She hit the building." Krelien stared at Jen, a frown on his face. "I heard bones crack, and when I saw her falling, I went to catch her. I jumped and ..."

He paused and tried to determine what to say. How much detail should he go into? If he said something went wrong in the jump, he would have to explain himself. And explaining that to non-Jumpers would be like trying to explain the taste of water.

"And we got to the portal. After the blue orb shot out of her, she just fell unconscious," Krelien said as he tentatively took a step away from Jen.

Glancing to Jen then back to Janet, Tyron asked, "Any ideas?"

"I can't be certain until the scan is done, but

my guess would be that she reached mental and physical exhaustion," Janet replied as she punched a few commands into the tablet.

She swallowed back the unease that rose in her throat and tried to focus on the scanner. In all her years living in Agerius, she had never seen someone so young sustain so many injuries.

Tyron shook his head. "That can't be."

"Why not?"

"Because Jen created those shields outside. If she had completely exerted herself, they wouldn't be standing anymore," Kaldok answered.

Interjecting, the caretaker said, "That's why her body knocked her unconscious."

"I don't follow," Ar'on said.

"On some level, I would bet that Jen knew the only way to keep those shields standing was to stop using as much of her energy as possible. And seeing as she's taken on some rather...substantial damage, she has to heal. In order to save her body, her mind shut down so her body would have time to recharge and recover."

"That won't happen every time she uses her energy to make shields, will it?" Archer asked.

Blaze shook her head. "She was utilizing it without any ill effects earlier. It seems as though this is a one-time incident."

Janet looked around at the team. "Council Member Blaze is right; her body is still trying to adjust to the fact that she even has this much power. It's going to take time, and discipline, for her to be able to fully control the energy she has."

Krelien suddenly stepped forward and asked, "Is this my fault?"

Janet looked flabbergasted and was unsure how to answer. The Jumper she had always known as arrogant and irritating looked at her like he might cry. His whole demeanor made Janet want to pull him into her arms and tell him it would be all right.

Not looking away from her, Krelien asked again, "Is this my fault?"

The tablet in Janet's hands beeped a few times, allowing her to look away from the Jumper. "No, Krelien, this isn't your fault." She hated that, for all she knew, maybe it was his fault. She had no clue what had specifically sent Jen into this state.

Taking in the reading from her scanner, she kept her expression even. The warriors around her were already on edge and terribly worried about the teenager.

Across the screen, it showed the severity of Jen's wounds. While the teen's wings weren't visible, it looked as though one of them had broken, snapping in a few different spots. It wasn't ideal that the wing hadn't been set before being called into her back, but the bones were beginning to heal. Until Jen woke up, Janet wouldn't be able to inspect it properly.

As for her other injuries, she had a projectile lodged in her calf, her right shoulder had fractured, and her skull was cracked. There were small cuts along Jen's right arm, probably from the window that broke. The right side of Jen's face was bruising. It was more than the girl had likely ever gone through. And miraculously, she was healing.

Letting out a slow breath, Janet turned to the team. "She's going to be okay."

"She is?" Tyron asked as he stepped forward. He was biting his fingernails.

Wide eyed, Janet looked around. Archer was on the tips of his paws, and his ears pivoted forward. Ar'on stood there, hugging himself with his jaw clenched. Kaldok stared at her expectantly with a worried expression on his face. And Blaze practically glared at her, those red gem-eyes demanding some news.

What had happened to these tough, regimented people? Janet wasn't aware that they were capable of this kind of emotion, let alone showing it. Especially all at the same time.

Trying to ignore her questioning, she said, "She's hurt; don't get *me* wrong. I have to get something that's lodged in her leg out so it can heal. But that's the thing—she's healing, and quickly." Gesturing to Jen, she added, "This girl is amazing. Anyone else would be laid up for a few days."

A moment passed, and she could feel the tension ebb away from the room.

Thankful to feel the pressure ease up, Janet looked to Kaldok. "Can you grab the set of instruments on the panel back there?" She then turned to Tyron. "I need you to hold her leg so I can get that piece of debris out."

The two men complied and, within a moment, Janet extracted the chunk of asphalt out of Jen's calf.

Inspecting the wound, she said, "It's clean. I don't know how, but this chunk of rock hasn't left any particulates." She bandaged Jen's leg. "I can't tell you when she'll wake up. For now, it's best if we let her be."

They all nodded.

"Now," Janet said, "I need to get a look at each of you and make sure you're all okay."

"We're fine," Ar'on cut her off.

"You might be fine," Janet replied, "but the rest of you—"

"We're fine," Archer said.

She had to admit that most of them did look okay. At least, okay by "battlefield injury" standards. However, Tyron did not.

Their eyes met, and she said, "You're not fine."

Blinking a few times, Tyron let out a sigh. "Alright, you can look me over. Then I'm staying right here until she gets up."

"I've got it," Krelien said quietly.

Tyron looked over at the Jumper, who hadn't left Jen's bedside. The two shared a long look before Tyron nodded and Krelien looked down at Jen.

Janet nearly screamed in confusion.

Tyron turned to the rest of the team. "Give me a few minutes."

"We're gonna go clean up," Kaldok said as he pointed out the door.

As they left, Archer turned to Krelien. "She's gonna be okay buddy."

Krelien nodded but said nothing.

Archer's ears drooped, and he left the room, the door closing behind him. The office became quiet.

Janet waved for Tyron to follow her. She pulled the curtain back a bit to hide Jen's unconscious body, just in case any students came to her in need of assistance. Then they walked toward the back of the office where she patted one of the examination beds and said, "C'mon; just like if we were back home."

Tyron looked at her as she turned around. "If I had any idea you were here—"

"I know, Tyron." She turned back around.

He shook his head. "I don't think you do."

"Tyron, would you please just sit down?"

"I have to get this out of my head or—"

"Let *me* look at that wound or, by the Elders, I'm going to strap you to the bed *myself!*" Her hand flew to her mouth, and her eyes widened as her cheeks flamed red.

Tyron attempted to not smile, but it slowly cracked through, anyway.

"I didn't mean it like that," Janet whispered, mortified.

He laughed and sat down on the bed. "I honestly don't know how else you could have meant it."

A smile crept to her face as she stepped up to him to inspect the gash across his head. "Of course you don't. Even in nineteen years, you haven't watched a single bit of TV, have you?"

"I've had other things to spend my time on," he replied then sat a little straighter. "Nineteen years?"

"To the day," she said as she gently took his head in her hands. The action caused him to close his eyes and sigh, his shoulders falling slightly. Janet smiled at the knowledge that she could calm him with a simple touch. "Nineteen years ago, you were named a Zaheri."

He opened his eyes and looked at her. "How do you remember that?"

Inclining her head slightly, she said, "It was a pretty big day."

Sitting back a bit, he studied her. "Is that what that number was in the top left of all your letters?"

"Cheesy, isn't it?" She wrinkled her nose.

A cough of a laugh escaped him, and he shook his head. "The number of days since we last saw one another." They were quiet for a few seconds before he said, "I looked forward to every letter."

"I feel like you wrote *me* more often than I wrote you."

"I doubt that."

She took his hand, and he looked down at his lap.

"Are you all right?"

Tyron was silent and blinked a few times before letting out a few slow, steady breaths. Then he looked up at her and said, "I threw her."

"What do you *mean?*"

Gathering his thoughts, he looked away at the wall. "We were in the thick of a thrall. Bratak'ra kept coming, and Caligans were evading our attacks. I made her dodge an attack and took her arm and ... I just got this sense of urgency. I had to get her to the portal." He shook his head. "I don't know what I was thinking. I just hurled her toward the portal. And when she hit the wall ..." Tears filled his eyes, and he sniffed.

Gently, she stroked his face as he looked back at her.

"I could swear my heart stopped."

Wrapping her arms around his neck, she pulled him into an embrace. She had forgotten what it felt like to have his arms wrapped around her. The way he held her now, though, was like he was grasping for her, his strong arms pulling her up against him as he buried his face into her neck.

Running her fingers along the back of his neck,

she whispered, "She's going to be okay, Tyron. It's only a matter of time until she wakes up."

He let out a bit of a laugh. "I am so glad you're here." Pulling back from the embrace, he added, "I don't know what I would've done."

"You don't give yourself enough credit." She turned to grab a cloth and started cleaning his head. Focusing on his injury, she thought through whether she was brave enough to say what she was feeling. "I am happy, though," she started. "To be here, that is. With you."

A boyish smile came to his face.

"Things in Agerius just haven't been the same with you gone."

"You miss me that much?"

She offered a small smile. "You know I always miss you."

They shared a look as a few seconds passed.

As Janet started to step away, he said, "It's been nineteen years, and in all those letters"—she slowly turned back to him—"did I ever tell..." His courage seemed to trail off with his thought. He swallowed. "Would I be terribly forward if—"

"No, you wouldn't," she interrupted.

He got to his feet and, in one long stride, he took her in his arms and kissed her. A little more passionately than he had intended, but it was a spur of the moment kind of thing. Breaking off the kiss, he rested his forehead against hers and whispered, "I love you, Janet Fisher."

"I love you, too," she said as she reached on her tippy toes and kissed him again, both of them smiling.

In that moment, Tyron felt that whatever might

happen, so long as he had her, it was going to be okay.

"I know you were asked to come, but all the same, thank you for being here," Kaldok said to Janet as the group made their way into the seating area of the cafeteria.

The large, circular room was loud, with one of the lunch periods about halfway through as they went to find a seat. Their trays had been loaded with food for them by the grateful staff, and the food looked and smelled great. They couldn't deny, though, that their appetites were a little lackluster.

Nodding to the werewolf, Janet admitted, "It's funny, I really don't think I've done much."

"You have put our minds at rest," Blaze said.

Kaldok carried a second tray for her and Archer, the two grovix walking at his sides.

"That is invaluable at present."

As they walked into the cafeteria, a group of girls saw them searching for a table, and one of them screamed, "Uh, soldier guys! Hey! You can... you can have this table if you want."

Tyron glanced at the others then looked back at the girls. "That's kind of you. Thank you."

The teenage girls giggled and began to get their things. As they stood and the Alpha Team sat, they remained standing there for a few seconds, awkwardly staring at the team.

As Blaze took her place, and Archer began to nudge his food off the tray in front of her, she looked up at the girls and said, "Our thanks again, ladies. If you would kindly leave us."

Giving the group of girls a confused look, Tyron shifted his weight and turned to the rest of the team. "What should we do about Krelien? He probably needs something to eat, too."

From her seat next to Tyron, Janet looked at him with a smirk. "I have to admit, I'm impressed that you have concern for his wellbeing."

With a grunt, Ar'on said, "Krelien's a *member* of the team; it's only right we at least *make* sure he eats."

"Is he *prone* to forgetting?" Janet asked.

Swallowing a bite of his entree, Kaldok answered, "He's prone to eat the worst options available to him."

Archer laughed. "One time, someone forgot to hide the candy, and that's all Krelien ate for a day."

"How *much* candy did he eat?" Janet asked, fearing the worst.

Sitting back a little, Tyron said, "A bag about this big?" He held his hands out in front of him to gesture a large sack-sized bag.

"Do you realize how unhealthy that is?"

"There's a reason why we canceled the warehouse store *membership* after that," Ar'on grumbled.

Closing her eyes and shaking her head as though ridding a bad thought, Blaze said, "It was quite the unpleasant day."

Tyron tried to hide his smile by putting his hand in front of his mouth. "He burst into the kitchen around dinnertime and began to recite some dramatic break-up letter thing he found on the internet. Halfway through, he just started to hop around the room, dancing." He lost his composure and began to laugh.

Kaldok's shoulders shook as Janet asked, "Why do only some of you find this situation hilarious?"

Kaldok tried to keep his laughter under control. "Because he kicked Blaze."

"And he somehow made all of Ar'on's clothes disappear," Tyron got through his laughter as Ar'on shoved him.

"That *wasn't* funny," Ar'on snapped. "I had to go buy a whole bunch of stuff, and then, when Blaze got mad, it all got destroyed."

"For the last and final time, Ar'on, that was not *my* intention," Blaze shot as the rest of them laughed.

"Of course he would jump out of the way! You had to have known that!" Ar'on argued.

"I was not yet aware of the totality of his childish behavior. You should have known better than to immediately replace what he had sent to another dimension!"

The fits of laughter died down a little, and then Tyron let out a sigh and wiped his eyes as he said, "Elders, I needed that."

Glaring a little, Ar'on said, "Y'know what? I could use a laugh, too. Let's talk about a time Krelien did something infuriating to you so I can laugh about it."

Slapping his hand onto Ar'on's shoulder, Tyron said, "Sure thing, my friend. Choose whatever story you want."

Janet shook her head. "I can't imagine Krelien being like that."

"Yeah," Kaldok said, "I suppose all those years ago, neither did we."

Slowly, the table grew somber and everyone focused on eating.

Glancing around at them all, Janet asked, "So, Ar'on, what story would Tyron hate to hear you tell?"

Ar'on perked up. "Oh, there are so many."

"Hey, now wait a minute," Tyron started as he sat up, holding his hand out to his friend.

She hadn't realized it until now, but Janet had missed these people terribly.

Chapter Fourteen
So What're You Gonna Do?

Grant had seen the team—well, most of it, any-way—enter the cafeteria. Krelien wasn't with them, but he wasn't looking for him.

Mr. Alderfer had ushered both him and Ryan back to their homeroom after Jen and Tyron had left to enter the fight. Both of them had vehemently argued that they wanted to stay, but their principal wouldn't hear any of it.

They had just begun heading to Mr. Mosser's classroom when they had heard a window smash, followed by yelling. Against their better judgment, they had run to a window in time to see Krelien falling past the third floor window. After that? They didn't know what had happened. But the fact that the Jumper wasn't around, and neither was Jen, made Grant a little uneasy.

If everything had gone okay, Jen would be there

with everyone else. Instead, she was absent, only adding to his fear.

The last half-hour, Ryan, Aeryn, James, and Nancy had talked about everything that was going on, wondering what *might* come of Jen and whether she would be allowed to be a normal person anymore.

A part of Grant wanted to be involved in that conversation, if only to remind his friends that so long as they didn't go anywhere, Jen could stay as normal as she wanted. But his mind was elsewhere, wondering where Jen was and thinking through the worst-case scenarios.

Would it be considered normal if you thought the girl you liked was dead?

He just wanted to keep her safe, which now seemed impossible, given what Jen could do. All that kept rattling around in his mind was a moment from elementary school, when they had been playing at recess and some jerk had been picking on her. He had punched the other kid and got in a lot of trouble for it, but it had been the only way he could think to protect her in that moment. And right now, he couldn't protect her. She wouldn't let him.

Now it was as though the tables had turned, and he was the one who needed to let her do the punching. That rubbed him the wrong way. Not because he thought she wasn't capable.

Far from it.

But it wasn't wrong for him to want to be there next to her, watching her back, right? But, how could he do that if she was running into dangers that would probably kill him far faster than they could scratch her?

He thought about the monsters she fought. Did

any of them even know who she was? Did any of them care that she was just a kid? Or did they just march blindly, firing at her because they were told to do so? Grant wished he knew more about this Tilion place so he could understand things better.

A group of girls walked over toward his table and said to one of the girls at a neighboring table, "Well, we tried."

"God, how did Jen get them to like her?" one of the girls asked.

"I don't know, but I swear, I have got to figure it out. Those guys are just gorgeous."

The conversation made Grant want to be sick. All the girls were talking about the Alpha Team and how sexy they were, and it made the male population question their manhood. It must have been the blood and cuts that the hybrids had on them. Maybe his psych teacher was right; maybe signs of battle made women more attracted to guys.

It seemed stupid, but no one had ever blamed the human race for being intelligent.

He absentmindedly excused himself from the conversation the others were involved in and made for the Agerians. About halfway there, however, he was stopped.

Evelyn appeared, seemingly out of nowhere, and stepped in his way. He couldn't help it, but the more he looked at her, the more he thought that her skin looked orange. How the girl thought it was attractive was beyond him.

She put her hand out and placed it on his chest, forcibly keeping him from where he was going. "Hey there, Grant," she said in a sultry voice, gently flipping her hair.

For some reason, every time this girl came up to him, Grant wanted to scream, 'Get back, Satan' and run in the opposite direction. He didn't know why exactly, but it was always the first thing that came to mind when he saw Evelyn. However, his mother hadn't raised a disrespectful son.

Inhaling deeply, he tried to be polite. "Hi, Evelyn."

"All this otherworldly battle stuff is really scary. I feel completely unprotected," she said as she inched closer to him, not moving her hand from his chest.

Grant rolled his eyes and moved her hand as he took a step back. "You shouldn't. You've got enough of the good guys fighting for us."

"But, Grant, don't you see?" She leaned close to him and pouted. "Who will protect *me*? I need a strong man to keep the monsters away."

"Well then, good luck finding one," Grant said as he backed away, trying to give himself some personal space.

"Oh, I think I found him," Evelyn said as she stepped back into his bubble again.

Maybe in other schools, a teacher would have stepped in, but this was docile. Lots of kids were prone to making out in the hallway between classes. The staff was probably thankful this was all they had to deal with.

But this was more than enough for Grant.

He shook his head a bit and gave her an annoyed look. "Evelyn, I have absolutely no time for this. Can you play your game with someone else?"

Taken aback, Evelyn straightened. She stared at Grant, a puzzled, angry look on her face. "You're looking for that whore, aren't you?"

Grant's mind went white, and he found himself clenching his jaw. His muscles tensed in his arms, and he would have loved a punching bag that had Evelyn's face slapped on it.

"You realize she's just some freak, right? I bet she's not even human. I mean"—Evelyn laughed—"we all saw her in the auditorium. She's not normal. She's not even pretty."

He let out a heavy breath and bit his tongue. Grant glared at Evelyn as he stepped around her, intending to walk out of the cafeteria before he said something harsh.

As he passed her, Evelyn snatched his arm. "Yo, asshole, I'm talking to you. Don't you dare walk away from me."

Grant ripped his arm out of her grasp and turned to face her slowly. "I will walk away from you whenever I want, Evelyn. And that's the fact of the matter. I will *always* walk away from you. Heck, I *might* even start running."

Her face flushed for a second as she took in what he had just said to her. A deep scowl formed on her features, and she spat, "You self-righteous bastard, you can't talk to me like that."

"I just did."

He didn't wait for her slow-witted response, turning to leave.

As he walked away, he could vaguely hear Evelyn stumbling over insults to throw at him. Finally, she settled on, "You'll regret this, Grant Connolly! You'll regret ever crossing me! Tell that to your whore, too!"

Spinning around quickly, he hollered at Evelyn with his face flushed in anger, "She's not a whore!" The sheer rage in his voice boomed in the lunchroom, and it was as though every conversation ceased. His face felt hot, and he wanted nothing more than to punch Evelyn square in the face.

Evelyn's eyes popped out of their sockets and, for a split-second, Grant thought that he had finally gotten through to her. Then he heard, "Okay, Grant, we get it," from behind him.

The teenager stilled slightly and turned to see Tyron standing behind him. Taking a few steps back, Grant opened his mouth to say something, but Tyron didn't wait for his slow-witted response.

Grabbing Grant by the back of his shirt, Tyron dragged him out of the cafeteria. As he was forced away, Grant could hear some cheers and applause erupting from the room. A small smile of dignity spread across his face just in time for Tyron's stern expression to wipe it away.

The hybrid crossed his arms over his chest and asked, "What was all of that?"

Grant couldn't begin to say why he shrank in Tyron's presence. The warrior seemed to demand attention and respect everywhere he went, and Grant got the feeling that Tyron didn't actively try to make that happen. It was as though some air of seniority followed the hybrid around, and you couldn't help but step aside and almost salute him. The teenager guessed that it came from the years of fighting that Tyron had endured. He certainly felt intimidated by every one of Jen's Zaheri.

Once his eyes left Tyron's, Grant tried not to look at him again as he said, "I didn't mean to cause a scene. All I wanted to do was come over and ask you where Jen was." He lifted his gaze slightly and saw Tyron staring at him stoically. Trying to be brave, Grant added, "Is she okay?"

Tyron darted his eyes to the wall and seemed to focus on nothing at all for a moment. Then, letting out a sigh, the warrior looked down at Grant and asked, "Why haven't you told her how you feel?"

Despite himself, Grant's mouth fell open slightly. "How do you know that?"

"It's pretty obvious. Jen's just blind."

The teen shrugged slightly. "I thought I was hiding it pretty well."

"Why hide it at all? What could be so bad about telling someone how you feel?"

Grant gave him a disbelieving look. "Because she might not feel the same way."

Tyron gave him a confused look.

"I figured that was pretty obvious."

"Hmm," Tyron hummed, glancing toward the floor.

"Have you been following me?" Grant asked, and Tyron looked back at him. "I mean, you seem to know a lot about me."

"It's my business to know who Jen's been around. And you've been around for a long time."

"Wait a second—how long have you been protecting her?"

Tyron's expression softened. "All her life."

A strangled word left the teen. "Wait—so she's known who she is her entire life? Why wouldn't she—"

Holding up his hands, Tyron cut him off, "Slow down the train. She's only known for a year and a half."

"So, why have you been protecting her—"

"Kid, I don't have to answer your questions. I just want to know what your intentions are."

Grant swallowed. "My intentions?"

"Yes, your intentions. If you intend to pursue Jen, I need to know. 'Cause she'll get attached and then you'll probably get hurt, 'cause something tells me you're gonna be annoying about trying to protect her. And then I'll have to figure out how to keep her head on straight and keep you safe at the same time and still train her."

"Oh," the boy said quietly, looking away from Tyron and saying nothing further.

After an awkward pause, Tyron said, "I figured this was an easy question. It shouldn't require that much thought."

"I, uh ... I don't know what my intentions are."

Tyron was silent for a second and simply gave Grant a cross look. "I don't like that answer."

"Look, it's just ..." Grant stared past Tyron to try to gather his thoughts. "Put yourself in my position. I just found out that the girl I've liked for years is some superhuman. Meanwhile, all my time knowing her, I've tried to keep her safe, to protect her—you have to know how that feels. And then, to find out that she doesn't need my protection ... that she might not need me."

With each of Grant's comments, Tyron seemed to ease up, his shoulders slowly drooping, losing their hard edges. The hybrid looked toward the floor.

Grant mumbled, "I don't have any business being a part of her life."

"Why would you say that?"

"Because look at me," Grant said helplessly. "I'm just a normal human, right? I can't save her if she needs saving. I can't help her in any way. I'd just get in the way if I tried, even though all I want to do is help. It's like she's a star, and I'm an asteroid. I don't compare to her at all."

"You're *making* this too complicated." Tyron shook his head. "If you like the girl, you just tell her. End of story. Not everyone's a hero in the way that you're talking about. Sometimes, they're the support the hero needs to keep going."

"What if I want to be the hero ... just to say I can be for her?"

Tyron rubbed his forehead. "Look, kid, you seem like a good guy. I think you're overthinking this. Just 'cause you can't manifest energy doesn't mean you can't be her hero. We all need different people in our lives to make us the best we can be. You might be exactly what she needs."

"Really?" Grant asked, hope building in his chest.

His body deflated a little, and Tyron half-whined, "I don't know, kid. I'm not her. For Elder's sake, you might be the average Joe for her."

"That sounds like exactly the opposite of what I was hoping for," Grant muttered.

Tyron scoffed. "Kid, I would give *anything* to be the average Joe."

Grant looked at him with a furrowed brow when a voice called, "Tyron!"

They turned to see Archer bounding down the hallway toward them.

Skidding to a stop, he said, "Jen! She's awake!"

Chapter Fifteen
The Eye

Time had passed, but he didn't have any clue how long it had been since the team left. All Krelien knew was that he had been sitting there, trying to will Jen to wake up for a long time, far longer than he would have liked. Resting his head on his folded arms, he let out a sigh and closed his eyes.

His eyes burned in that way they did when it was almost a relief for them to close, if it wasn't for the pressure it seemed to create. His sinuses felt blocked, and there was a dull, rhythmic pounding in his left temple. Sitting back a little, he tried to stretch and felt his muscles protest, making him wince. He hadn't felt this exhausted since he was a kid.

He forced his neck to crack, despite the achiness in his bones. He figured whatever had happened when he had jumped was the cause for his tiredness.

He straightened and tried to rid the image of the grotesque dragon from his mind, but found it popping to the forefront of his thoughts. Whatever that thing was, it still caused him to feel terror. Even now in the safe quiet of the nurse's office. He gripped the sides of the chair and shook his head.

"Just breathe, Krelien," he whispered to try to calm himself.

Suddenly, an image of his father's dead body flashed into his mind, and he stood abruptly. Sensing that something terrible was in the room, he turned and grabbed his pistol, sweeping through the nurse's office, checking everywhere. Despite the fact that he was alone there, there was a lingering feeling of dread.

Krelien's breathing labored as he looked around, trying to figure out what he was feeling. Again, he saw the decaying dragon in his mind and could swear he heard a whisper. He glanced to his right, went to the light switch on the wall, and flicked them off then on again, just in case. The room felt dark for some reason.

Gripping his pistol, he swallowed and started back to Jen when he heard something ethereal say, *"That's where it'll end."*

Fear halted him, and he found himself too afraid to turn around.

The world around him began to warp into the strange dimension that he had landed in earlier.

When he did finally start to slowly turn, the large, decaying dragon howled, *"This is where you will die alone."* The words were drawn out, spread apart, and as each syllable stretched on, the tone of the beast grew lower.

Waking, Krelien gasped and immediately grabbed his pistol and spun around in his chair to the entrance of the nurse's office. Realizing he was alone, he let out a few deep breaths and closed his eyes. "A dream. Just a dream. Thank the Elders it was just a dream," he whispered.

He raked a hand through his hair and looked down at Jen. His shoulders slumped. "C'mon, kid; wake up." As though that would work. If only he could just undo whatever he had done to her as easily as giving a tired command.

It must have been that he did something, or that her being a passenger had done something. For half a second, he wanted to blame Tyron. It was his fault. Tyron should have known that part of her training should be to experience a jump to another dimension.

Slumping in his chair, Krelien knew that wasn't fair. Tyron hadn't ever jumped before today, so why would any of them ever think Jen would?

He had brought lots of people along for jumps before. Sure, most of them had been because he had been ordered to, but there had been others that he had jumped just because he could, as a favor to them. He had been nice. Okay, fine. So, maybe not every time he was doing it to be nice. Sure. Maybe there were times when he wanted them to owe him one.

What could he say? It was a handy thing to be the only Jumper in Agerius. It wasn't his fault the ability was valuable. So, why shouldn't he be allowed to use it however he wanted?

Glancing at the teenager in front of him, he knew she would shake her head at that. She would give him a look of annoyance and say, "Because it's not a nice thing to do! You should help people because you can!" It sounded Blaze-ish of her.

"Just do the right thing all the time and everyone will always love you. Yay, Council. Much arrogance. Such grace."

Chuckling at his caricature of Blaze in his mind, he cocked his head to the side a little.

Jen did kind of have a point. At least, fictional Jen in his head. He had a gift. He shouldn't just keep it to himself. That was what his parents would have wanted him to do, probably...maybe. If they were alive to talk with him about it.

He tapped his foot against the floor, and his brow flinched.

What was he doing?

Why was he sitting here, wasting his time? He had other things to do. He could be annoying Ar'on right now or setting up an elaborate prank against Tyron to make the shower only spray cold water, to get him back for banging against his door that morning. He could be doing anything but this.

As he flitted his eyes to Jen again, he knew there wasn't anywhere else he wanted to be. Not really. Not if he was honest with himself.

When had that happened? It really hadn't been that long ago when he had wanted nothing to do with this assignment. So, what had changed? How was it that he couldn't force himself to get up and leave this room, even for a minute? All in the hope that, when she woke up, he would be there for her?

Yes, he was convinced that it was his fault she was here, unconscious. Never mind the fact that the Caligan had hurt her and forced her face to meet cinderblock. Never mind the fact that, if he hadn't caught her, she would have hit the ground and probably died. Never mind the fact that he had saved her life. She was hurt, and it was his fault.

Guilt had never motivated him to literally do nothing but wait for a sleeping person to wake up. The teenager lying on this bed wasn't that important, was she?

Was she?

A real part of Krelien wanted to say no, that she wasn't. It was an old part of him, one that was slowly dying, and he felt that it might meet its end quickly. But it was there, nonetheless.

Just a few days prior, he had thought that maybe Jen wasn't everything they had been told she was. He liked Jen. Jen seemed to like him, too. And that simple fact only made him want to keep her around even more. Most people didn't like him right off.

And maybe, just maybe, that part of him that thought she wasn't so special was the part that wanted her to be safe from whatever it was the Elder's legend thingy was talking about.

While Krelien didn't care much for most humans, he did care for this one. And the day's events had illuminated her strengths and abilities blindingly.

Looking at her now, he knew that their chances as her Zaheri to actually protect her were diminishing. What if they really couldn't do this? Sure, he had managed to save her today, but what if, next time, they couldn't? What if, next time, Cregorous was the one attacking her? The thought made him consider fleeing for a brief moment. But he knew he wouldn't just leave her. He couldn't. Even if it meant he would die.

No. He wouldn't die. He had already avoided it several times over. He would just have to teach Jen to do the same. Then he would just have to make sure he stayed away from the "very possibly death" areas.

Though, maybe next time when he went to save her life, maybe he should just use his wings.

Wings? Wings! My wings! I could have used them! Jumping hadn't been required. He had just done that because that was what he was used to doing to avoid bad situations. Like, y'know, impacting with the ground.

Movement from Jen pulled him from his mental berating. She winced as her eyes fluttered open.

He swallowed and sat forward. "Jen?"

She pinched her eyes open and groggily asked, "Krelien? What's ...? Who's ...? Where ...?"

He smiled. "The three W's will be answered. You okay?"

Blinking a bit, she shakily sat up. Krelien moved his hand to her back to stabilize her.

"I think so? I don't know. What happened?" She rubbed her head a bit, trying to figure out where she was and to silence the throbbing in her mind.

"Well, what's the last thing you remember?" he asked as he sat next to her on the bed, keeping his hand on her back so she wouldn't fall over.

"Um ..." She closed her eyes. "Tyron throwing *me* ... *my* wings bracing *my* crash against the building ... smacking into the window ... and that's it. I think I blacked out."

He furrowed his brow. "So, that's it?"

"Yeah, I think so." She started to nod and then stopped quickly. It hurt to move, and she felt her vision sway in a stomach-tossing way. "Why? What else happened?"

"Um ..." he began. "Well, when I saw that you smacked into the side of the building, I ran off the roof to catch you. When I did, I kind of, well, took you along for the ride."

Jen looked at him with a scrunched brow.

"I jumped and brought you with *me*."

"I didn't know you could have a passenger when jumping."

With a chuckle, he said, "Well, now you know. Anyway, I landed back on the third dimension near the portal, and you"—he motioned with his hands, trying to visually show Jen what he was saying by making a sort of circle motion with his right hand then moved his left hand up toward the ceiling—"shot an orb out of you, right through the open portal. Then I jumped back to Tyron, grabbed him, and jumped us inside the shield. At that point, you were limp and unconscious. But up until the orb, you were conscious," he said matter-of-factly. "I think," he added after a second of silence.

Jen cocked an eyebrow at him. "I shot an orb out of me?"

He sat still for a moment as he thought it over. "Yeah."

"Right," Jen said as she moved a bit. "So, what happened after that?"

"Well, Janet showed up and basically told us what to do and where to take you. Because, I don't know about the other guys, but I was so worried I killed you, that I wasn't really thinking straight."

She held up her hand. "Wait—who's Janet?"

"Oh, she's a bird from Agerius."

She raised her eyebrows.

"A Caretaker. Tyron's got the sweets for her."

Jen chuckled. "First, I think you meant *chick*, and second, you probably meant to say *hots* rather than *sweets*. But none of that actually tells me who this person is."

"She's a Caretaker," he explained.

She stared back at him and waved her hand in a circular motion. "Which means ...?"

He darted his eyes around a little. "Oh! Like one of those guys, those smolder-y guys, from those shows. The ones where everyone is, like, constantly making poor life choices, and people come back to life for no apparent reason."

"Are you talking about soap operas?"

"Is that what they're called? Why are they called that? That's stupid."

"Krelien!" Jen waved her hands. "Focus! What's a Caretaker?"

Snapping his finger and pointing at her, he said with a grin, "A doctor!" He sat back with a smile on his face. "I knew I'd remember."

Nodding a little, she said, "Good for you." She stretched and felt her muscles ache at the motion. it wasn't nearly as bad as she would have thought, though. And she had to admit that she did feel a whole lot more refreshed. "So, this Janet character ... That's a human name. What's she doing on Tilion?"

Krelien did a double-take at Jen and was silent for a moment. "That's a long story. You really don't need to know." A few seconds passed before he continued, "Anyway, so we brought you here. She said she was sent by one of our Council members and used one of our scanners from Agerius to check on you."

"And that's it?"

"I mean, everyone went off to grab some lunch, maybe." He fidgeted a lot before adding, "Look, Jen, I'm sorry."

She looked at him in confusion. "You're sorry? For what?"

He let out a sigh. "For jumping when I should have used my wings. For knocking you out. For getting you into the state you're currently in."

With a disbelieving scoff, she said, "Krelien, the best I can see, you saved my life. And jumping is in your blood. I just wish I had been awake to experience it." When he still looked unconvinced, she gently placed her hand on his arm. "Really, it's not your fault. I do find your concern, however, comforting."

He chuckled. "Really now?"

"Yeah, I mean, I wouldn't have expected you to be that concerned about my wellbeing. That, and I'm surprised that you took responsibility for something that was most definitely not your fault."

"I still feel like it is."

"But it's not," she said. "Trust me; if it was, you'd be breathing through a tube right now."

"Why's that?"

"'Cause Tyron would have punched you into next week."

"That's true."

Right then, the door opened, and Archer walked in. "Hey, buddy, I figured you'd want some company," the grovix said before he looked up at her. He flinched, his legs splaying a bit in surprise, and his ears shot alert. "Jen! You're awake!"

"Yeah, Archer, I'm awake," the teenager said dismissively.

The three stared at one another for a brief second before Archer said, "I'm gonna go get everyone. Be right back!" He then turned and quickly darted out the door.

"See? You cause alarm everywhere you go," Krelien said.

Giving him a wayward glance, Jen gently smacked him. Then she glanced down at her wrist and realized she still had his watch on.

Tapping his arm, she said, "Here," as she handed him the watch.

Krelien smiled.

"I told you I'd keep it in one piece."

"Ah, I wasn't that worried about the watch staying in one piece," he said as he gently handed the watch back to her. "I was more worried about *you* staying in one piece."

"So, did the plan work?" Jen asked.

With the library missing a window from Jen's face crashing into it and the lunch hours still going on, the team met in the nurse's office.

Janet checked Jen's wing to make sure things were healing properly.

"Well, you did get an orb through the portal, so we have to assume that it did something," Tyron said.

"Does anyone know what it did?" she asked. She had been racking her brain in the hopes of remembering any of the events after hitting the side of the school, but no matter how hard she tried, her memories of any actions were obscured from her.

"We hoped that you might know," Ar'on said.

"How would I know?"

Krelien was still for a moment before he said, "'Cause you created it?"

With a roll of her eyes, Jen answered, "That doesn't mean that, while in a comatose state, I can track and follow an orb that shot out of me through the portal and into another world. Another world I've never been to."

"At the least, it will have attracted attention and alerted the Council to the fact that we are fighting back," Blaze said. She and Archer sat on either side of Jen as the teenager absentmindedly played with Archer's ear. The brown furred grovix didn't seem to be complaining as his tongue gently fell out of his mouth.

Half-shrugging, Jen asked, "So, what do we do now?"

"There isn't much else we can do," Kaldok said. "At this point, it's a matter of waiting for the Council to get through."

"I wasn't really able to keep track; did anyone see what they got for reinforcements?" Tyron asked.

"Well, I took out a number of them at the portal," Krelien said. Then he pointed toward Jen. "Until Jen got hurt."

Nodding, Ar'on said, "After that, there were only a few more, maybe a couple dozen warriors, that came through before Jen shot the orb through the portal. After that, the portal was still before it shut down. It's unlikely, but it seems like Cregorous only sent a few reinforcements."

Blaze squinted at him. "That seems most peculiar. Why would he choose to only send a meager number of warriors? Why open the portal if that was all he hoped to gain?"

"You have to remember, Krelien took out a bunch before they even got past the portal," Kaldok said. "It was hard to say, but there was a good size pile of bodies around the portal activation."

"If I had to guess, Jen and I took out maybe forty enemy fighters. I know I didn't get them all; there were too many bratak'ra for me to concentrate on," Tyron said.

"I am certain that Archer, Kaldok, and myself were capable of removing a fair number of bratak'ra and werewolves," Blaze said.

"Oh man! And you should have seen Blaze, too!" Archer said in a jolly voice, his eyes half-closed as Jen continued to stroke his ear. "Took out one after another!"

A look between satisfaction and embarrassment came to Blaze's white-furred face, but she said nothing as Archer continued to chuckle.

"For now, we'll just have to wait for reinforcements, then," Tyron said. "I know that the numbers outside are greatly less than what we had to face earlier, and that we could probably take them out, but I'm not going to risk it."

Sitting up a bit, Blaze said, "But, if we are capable of destroying them, we may be able to get the humans home and away from danger."

"But going back out there might mean losing one of us," Ar'on argued.

"We almost lost Jen last time. The numbers might be less, but that doesn't mean we're ready for another round," Kaldok said.

Tyron nodded. "On top of that, we need time to heal."

"Yes, you do," Janet said as she removed her hands from Jen's head. She had been quietly inspecting Jen's wounds as they spoke. "And she still needs to get that wing healed. It's almost there, but she still has a couple fractured ribs that need to patch up, too, so no more broken bones today." She pointed a finger at Jen.

"Really? All that?" Jen asked.

Raising her brow, Janet asked, "Why? What were you thinking?"

Jen scratched her head. "That I was healed."

Ar'on shifted his weight a little. "You're not feeling any of the remaining wounds?"

"Is that a bad thing?" Jen asked as she looked at Janet.

"No," Janet said with a shake of her head. "It's a very good thing. It means your body is probably going to be all patched up in a few minutes."

"Awesome."

"Not awesome." Tyron shook his head. "How is she healing so fast?"

Turning to him, Janet shrugged. "I'm going to go with she's the First Human-Born and very strong."

Before anyone said anything else or any more heads turned her way, Jen held out her hand and said, "Okey dokey, let's stop the 'Jen's-super-strong' train and change the subject, please."

"Course of action," Kaldok said. "What's our heading?"

Tyron glanced at Jen and sighed before straightening. "We can't handle another thrall at the moment. Jen might be healed, but I know I'm not fully there yet, and I'd bet you three aren't either." He pointed to Kaldok, Archer, and Blaze.

The three nodded their response.

"We need to rest up," he continued. "Do we have any sensors still intact we can play on as advance warning?"

Ar'on shrugged. "We can look, but it's not promising. The grounds are pretty chewed up, and it's possible they found them and destroyed them."

"What good would that do?" Krelien asked. "They can't tell when the portal is going to open. And that's what's going to happen. He'll just plop the portal right on top of us again."

"Then we should prepare ourselves as best we can," Blaze said. "Although, I disagree on the count of leaving the remaining Caligans alive."

Pointing toward the door, Tyron said, "I'll allow it only if you think you can handle them all on your own in five seconds."

Everyone looked to Blaze, who rolled her eyes. "Very well."

Archer laughed. "You hear that? Give her one chance to fight and she suddenly goes looking for a brawl."

Blaze opened her mouth then snapped it shut before she said, "There is no desire to brawl. Merely, I believe it would be the best course of action."

Now Krelien laughed. "Sure, whatever you say, Blazer."

"Okay, so we are gonna take a break?" Jen clarified.

Tyron nodded.

"Good. 'Cause I need to go get another shower, and then I need to check on my friends, and then I need some food."

With a nod, Tyron said, "Just keep that earpiece in. If something does come up, we're gonna need you ready to go."

"Uh, I don't think so," Janet said. "She was knocked into a coma, Tyron. People don't just bounce back from that immediately."

"I feel fine," Jen countered.

Krelien pointed to her. "See? If she thinks she's okay, then she probably is."

"Do you think *you're* okay?" Janet asked him.

"Well, sure," the Jumper said with a grin.

"Guys, she *might* have a point," Kaldok said before getting shoved by Krelien.

Tyron gently took Janet's arm and whispered, "If another attack does happen, we're going to need her, Janet."

"She's a child, Tyron! You can't expect her to be able to take on three battles in one day," Janet whispered back.

"Trust *me*; if I had *my* way, she would just sit in the corner and wait for us to give her the all-clear, but she won't. We can order her all she wants, but she'll still find a way out into a battle, even if we forbid her from it. In fact, if we forbid her, she'll probably be that *much* more motivated to get out there. And I'd prefer to know where she is."

With a laden sigh, she relented, "Fine. But you need to keep an eye on her."

"I always do." Tyron straightened then said to Jen, "Go enjoy your lunch, kid."

The teenager nodded then hopped off the bed and made her way to the door.

As she left, Ar'on said, "I'm surprised her friends are still standing by her."

"Yeah," Tyron said. "I really wasn't expecting anyone to still be willing to talk to her after all this."

"Her friends aren't like most humans," Kaldok said. "They seem to genuinely care about her enough to overlook her hybrid nature."

A sigh came from Blaze, and they all turned toward her.

"What?" she asked at their quizzical stares.

"What was with the sigh?" Krelien asked.

Her ears drooped slightly. "I fear this day has only just begun."

They looked between one another before Tyron asked, "What do you mean?"

"There is more going on than we can see. There must be. This whole day is about something other than what we have observed." She paused and looked at them all before saying, "We still have yet to see what is at the heart of Cregorous' actions."

Chapter Sixteen
Save the School, Save the World

After Jen's third shower of the day, an action she was getting incredibly tired of as each one passed, she radioed Jon to let him know that she was heading for the cafeteria for lunch and that her friends were joining her. He seemed less than thrilled about having the group free from supervision, and when Jen got to Mr. Mosser's classroom, she found a security guard waiting there to escort them. When the teens sat down so Jen could eat, the security guard took a seat at a neighboring table, never letting any of them out of his sight.

The five teenagers talked about things of little importance. Her friends all wanted to know what had happened, but Jen kept that to herself. She didn't need them worrying further about her safety, and she was, after all, okay. There was no reason to raise alarm when they were past the worst part.

As her friends talked about nonsense, Jen looked out the large windows and saw the wintery shadows cast in the late afternoon sunlight. Within an hour, the world would be covered in a golden hue, and then night would come.

It was hard to believe that the day was already coming to a close.

Even though the Alpha Team and Jen had succeeded in getting an orb through the portal, there was still little knowing of what might happen next.

What if they needed to stay through the night? There was nothing by means of blankets or pillows for the fifteen hundred students on campus. And they couldn't really expect all the people to be willing to sleep on the ground. If the Council didn't pull through soon, they might run into a whole new wave of problems.

Maybe the day's events would keep everyone up all night. That way, Jen wouldn't have to worry about bedding and provisions.

"Jen?" Aeryn asked, bringing her friend from her thoughts. "You okay?"

Jen slowly nodded. "I'm just thinking about what we have to do next, trying to work out what would happen if we had to spend the night here."

The group went quiet for a few seconds before Nancy said, "Well, I guess trying to get sleeping stuff would be hard."

"For probably close to eighteen hundred people? Yeah, just a tad difficult," Ryan teased.

"Ryan," Jen said in a disappointed tone as Nancy shot him a glare.

Holding up a hand, he begrudgingly apologized, "Sorry. I didn't mean to be so sarcastic."

"Should you be getting back to the others?" Grant asked.

Jen shrugged. "I guess. If I know Tyron, he's starting to think about how to make everyone okay with being stuck here past dinnertime."

As they walked back toward Mr. Mosser's classroom, Nancy suddenly asked, "What do you think the world's gonna be like after this is all over?" Everyone turned to her, and she continued, "I mean, in movies, they always try to show how governments and the public will react to a crisis. I just wonder how the real world will be."

"I hope we'll be able to find unity in it," Jen answered.

"Hasn't anyone told you?" Ryan asked.

They all stopped for a moment, and the security guard cleared his throat.

Jen held up her hand. "A minute, please." She looked back to her friends. "Told me what?"

The four friends shared a look before Aeryn said, "While you were gone, Grant and Ryan got their phones to connect to the school's Wi-Fi."

"What's wrong with the cell towers?"

"They've been down all day."

"Probably from the attacks," Jen mused. She looked at Ryan. "So, you finally cracked the password?"

Smiling at his cleverness, Ryan said, "'Huffypuffythedragon'. I told you that the staff liked our nickname."

Grant rolled his eyes. "You didn't come up with the nickname for Drake."

"I might've."

"Just because the mascot was smoking weed during one of the games, and the smoke came out the nostrils, doesn't mean it started with you saying something snarky freshman year," Grant said.

"I'm inclined to agree with Grant," Aeryn said.

"Wait—you came up with the nickname for Drake?" Nancy asked, and Ryan smiled.

"Enough about the dang mascot!" Jen yelled. "It's already ironic enough that we've had to run away from our mascot today. Can we please move on to whatever it is that I haven't heard?"

"Oh my gosh, it is!" Ryan said, pointing to her. "Holy irony, Batman!"

"Save it for the yearbook!" Jen shot. "Again, what don't I know?"

Before Ryan could try to derail the conversation once again, Aeryn said, "This isn't an isolated incident."

She flicked her eyes to each of her friends. "What do you mean?"

"You mentioned others," Grant said. "Others who are like you."

"How many were there?" Nancy asked.

"Um ..." Jen tried to keep her panic under control as a grating feeling hit her stomach. "Six. I make seven."

Ryan and Grant looked to one another before Grant said, "Okay. According to CNN and BBC, there's been attacks around the world."

"One of them was a research station in Antarctica, which makes for every continent being affected," Aeryn said.

Jen's heart suddenly plummeted into her stomach. She didn't know why, but something about Antarctica made her wish she could get there and make sure that Human-Born was okay.

Taking in a steadying breath, Jen asked, "Okay, so, has anyone said anything about, like, casualties or who's been targeted?"

"Take a breath," Aeryn said. "It's going to be okay."

"How do you know that?" Jen asked. "The other Human-Borns could be dying!" Shaking her head, she added, "I've gotta tell Tyron. We've gotta get out of here and find a way to them; make sure they're okay."

"Jen, calm down." Aeryn took her friend's hand, forcing Jen to look at her. "I'm sure they're fine. If they have protectors like you do, they're going to be okay."

Aeryn's reassurances only helped a little. Jen couldn't deny that she wanted nothing more than to be able to jump to each of the Human-Borns and help them. What if one of them was hurt? Were they all able to defend themselves? What if they weren't?

Grant looked to Nancy. "Looks like you were right."

Jen looked to her sister, and Nancy shrugged. "I dunno. Just something stupid I said."

"What?" Jen asked.

Rocking her weight between her feet, Nancy said, "Just that I thought maybe these other special humans might be your team. And maybe you're their leader."

"I certainly hope not," Jen whispered, her shoulders drooping.

"Why?" Aeryn asked.

Jen scoffed. "'Cause I'd be a terrible leader."

"I dunno," Grant said with a half-shrug. "You seem pretty concerned about them. That's gotta mean something."

Letting out a heavy sign, Jen asked, "What made you bring this up?"

Ryan fidgeted. "Oh, well, you said you hoped the world would find unity in it." He gestured to her. "I think you might be right. Remember, every continent's been affected."

Jen shook her head. "What would a teenager be doing in Antarctica?"

Shrugging, Nancy said, "Maybe you can ask them when this is over?"

"Do you think you're supposed to find them?" Aeryn asked.

"I think I might have to," Jen said. "From what I know, I'm the only one who's been able to survive against Cregorous."

"Yeah, how did you do that?" Grant asked.

"I don't know," Jen said. "I was kind of only a fetus."

Ryan smirked. "And you don't remember? What kind of super human are you?"

Jen cast him an annoyed look. "I can throw you against the wall and break every bone in your body. I'm sorry if God decided that a super amazing memory from the womb wasn't part of the package."

Grant chuckled, only to abruptly stop at Jen's glare. "Right. Not funny."

"What about this Cregorous guy? Why does he want you all dead? What do a couple of super humans mean to him?" Aeryn asked.

"Apparently, he legit just wants everyone to bow down to him," Jen said.

"How melodramatic." Ryan rolled his eyes. "Next, you'll tell me he twirls his moustache and goes 'mua-ha-ha' while petting a cat slowly."

"All I know is that, since we're basically a legend to the hybrids, they kinda have this hope that we can stop him."

"Which you can do?" Nancy asked.

Staying silent for a few seconds, Jen then said, "I don't know."

Ryan looked puzzled. "You don't know an awful lot."

"No, not really."

"Well, at least you're willing to admit it."

The sound of clapping caught their attention, and they turned to see Jon walking toward them. "Okay, you five, it's time you stopped ambling around the hallway." As he approached, he pointed to Jen. "Where did the radio that I gave you go?"

Jen glanced toward the ceiling before she shrugged. "I dunno."

"It's okay," Ryan said as Jon's shoulders fell and a sigh came from him. "She doesn't know a lot lately."

"That doesn't help," Jon said with a hint of frustration.

"Jen? You there?" Tyron's voice suddenly came over her earpiece.

Hitting the earpiece, Jen said, "Hey! Yeah, I need to talk to you."

"Of course you don't lose that," Jon grumbled as he pointed to the earpiece.

"In her defense, it's legit in her ear," Ryan said.

"Fine, talk to me when you get down here. We need to start getting a contingency plan together for if this drags into the night," Tyron said.

Nodding, Jen said, "Okay, I'll be right down." She looked up and saw everyone, including Jon, staring at her. Gesturing to the earpiece, she said, "Tyron wants to talk about what to do next."

"I'm glad he's thinking ahead," Jon said. "We're following some of the shelter-in-place guidelines, but the staff is working out other ideas. Let me go gather a few things, and then I'll meet up with you to collaborate."

With a nod, Jen said, "'Kay. We're down in the nurse's office."

"Janet told me. Get going," Jon said as he pointed over his shoulder. "And you four, get moving back to your classroom. Please make sure they get there," Jon said to the security officer.

Jen heard her friends bemoaning and could swear she heard Nancy say that she wanted to stick with Jen. The elder sister wasn't surprised that Nancy wanted to tag along, but she probably would regret that choice once she got there. Jen certainly wasn't looking forward to a meeting all about planning and logistics.

Even though she knew Tyron probably wanted her there sooner rather than later, she took her time walking down the hallway. Silence greeted her, and she turned to see that her friends and family were gone.

She took in a deep breath, just thankful for the fact that she was still breathing. Her head didn't hurt anymore, but there was an ache in her back that she could only assume came from her wing bone mending.

Everything that had happened made her wish she had been harder on herself in training and focused more on what Tyron had been trying to teach her.

Despite her mid-afternoon nap, Jen still felt

as though she could sleep for days. Granted, she wasn't aching with every movement, but there was still that low, sharp pain that occasionally spiked up her back if she twisted the wrong way.

She couldn't figure out what it was she had done to heighten her healing. If she had gone through all of this yesterday, she probably would be a walking bruise, and every motion would make her wince and groan.

Or would she? It seemed like her body just kicked into its natural abilities as they were pressed. Like the shield thing. And her healing thing.

Scratching her head, she tried not to dwell on the unexplained. There would be time to ask questions and try to figure all of this random new stuff out later. Right now, she had to keep her focus, which was a little hard to do.

The other six Human-Borns were being targeted. Her stomach clenched at the thought. She tried to remember all their titles—Archer had rattled them off so quickly.

The second one had been Protector, right? Maybe that meant they could make shields. Third was Warrior. Okay, they were probably doing well. Were they? What if they couldn't just fight their way out of it?

Crud, she couldn't remember the others. Requisite; that had been the last one. What kind of a title was that? What did it even mean? Was it like 'prerequisite'? Something needed maybe?

Taking the middle stairway, she glanced out the large windows across from her and rolled her eyes. What could it hurt?

"Okay, Elders," she muttered, "You'd better protect the other Human-Borns. I don't wanna have to do this alone."

She had only just hit the stairs that led down to the first floor when it suddenly felt like she had been run into on the right side. Her senses screamed, and her right temple throbbed. Abruptly, something shoved her aside, and she grappled for a hold on the railing and clung to it. It was as though someone had punched her in the side, and she winced when she touched her ribs and found them sore.

A pounding filled her mind. She gripped her head for a second and grimaced. *What the...?* she thought. She'd felt this before, hadn't she?

It felt similar to...

She remembered earlier that day, when she got the sense her shield was about to fall. It had felt like something had been hitting her brain, or her body, or both.

Fear rammed into her, and she looked out the windows in terror. Her shield was being attacked. And it wasn't just like it was being punched feebly; something was crashing into it.

Her shield was falling.

Pinching her eyes shut, she tried to figure out if she could make the domed one trapping the Caligans fall and convert the energy to the one against the school.

Dang it. She didn't know if it was even possible to do that. What if she did make the domed shield fall and accidentally brought the one around the school down, too?

Tapping her earpiece, she gave up and turned to head back to the second floor hallway. "Tyron!"

"Hey, kid, what's up?" Krelien responded.

"The shield is falling—"

"Archer? What's with the staring?" Krelien interrupted her.

"Krelien! We need to move quickly or something bad is gonna happen," she tried to tell him.

"Where are you?" Tyron's voice came over the earpiece.

"I'm heading for the main entrance, if you—"

She had never had a migraine before. Headaches came and went, less frequently as a hybrid, but not a migraine. Her parents had told her that it felt like having a bomb go off in your brain or a knife shoved into your spine.

If this was a migraine, then her parents had lied.

It was a full force against her senses. She was blown off her feet and crashed to the floor. Shockwaves ran along her body, and pain resounded throughout everything that she was. She tasted blood in her mouth, but there wasn't any to actually be found. Her nose burned like there was sulfur in the air, but nothing had changed in the environment. Her brain felt like it was trying to expand past her skull and squeeze out of every possible hole available.

As she hit the floor, she gasped for air as though the wind had been knocked out of her. Forcing herself onto her knees, she tried to grab at the sleek tiles and gagged, doing everything she could to force air back into her lungs.

After the tensest two seconds of her life, she felt her diaphragm allow everything to function normally and gulped heaving breaths into her lungs. Her eyes watered, and she felt like she was about to throw up.

Holding her head, she felt blood trickle down her lip and wiped a trembling hand under her nose. She tried to shake her head and get past the feeling, but it was like a constant ringing through her body, not just in her brain. Then, faintly, she heard the sound of shattering glass followed closely by a scream.

A girl was screaming.

Multiple screams joined it, and Jen pinched her eyes shut for a second before she tried to locate it. Two floors up.

Blinking a few times, she staggered to her feet. Ignoring the blood running out of her nose and the disorienting pounding of her brain, she started walking toward the stairwell. She held her hands out, trying to steady herself. It felt like the floor was wobbly, and her vision swirled with vertigo.

Heal your brain, then your nose so you can actually move, she thought then stopped for half a second to concentrate. The screaming *made* her feel rushed, and the instant the wobbly-ness of her vision began to clear, Jen bolted up the stairs.

She reached the fourth floor, moving so fast that she slammed against the lockers on the wall opposite the stairwell. A group of girls ran past her, and then she saw a bratak'ra barreling toward her. She ripped her pistol out and began firing at the beast. One of her semi-accurate shots hit its head, and it stumbled to the ground with a dying growl.

Jen turned and saw that the group of girls were all cheerleaders, some of whom Jen knew from classes.

"Are you all okay?" she asked.

They seemed too shaken to speak but nodded in response.

Nodding, she said, "Okay, c'mon; we're gonna get you to safety."

But they didn't move. Instead, they stared at the dead bratak'ra behind her.

She gestured at it. "It's okay. It's dead. It won't hurt you."

"Jen!" she heard Jon shout from behind her and turned as he ran to her. "Are you okay?"

"Jon, what're you doing here? Where are the others?" she asked, worry creeping into her bones as she realized they might have been hurt.

"I sent them with the security guard. I was on my way to the office when I heard the screams and came running." He patted her arm. "I can take things from here. You get to where you need to be."

It was then that Jen noticed Jon held a 9mm pistol in his hand. Pointing to it, she asked, "Where did you get that?"

"You don't pay any attention at your family cookouts, do you? Did you forget I'm ex-military?"

"No, I know. It's ... You ... You keep a gun at school?"

"Are you new?"

She gestured lamely at him. "So, what're you gonna do? Ward off dragons with a Glock? Have you seen anything today?"

"Jen, let's face it; I may not be the bravest man on the planet, but you're not alone in this." Jon motioned to the cheerleaders. "I can take care of these girls. I can take them over to the east end of the building. It is, after all, my building, and while they are partially your responsibility, they are mine first." He took a step closer to her. "You don't have to bear this burden alone. And yes, this gun may be completely ineffective against those monsters, but you know what? I'm willing to risk it."

Sighing, Jen said, "Well, I'm not."

"Will you stop being a teenager and let me be the adult, and obey me for once?"

As he spoke, Jen handed her Agerian pistol to him. He looked at the gun, confused.

"Don't worry; you shoot it like a regular gun. Magazine release is here, and it drops out of here. You can get close to five hundred shots out of it, so you shouldn't need to reload. Watch for the kickback; it's stronger than you're used to." She gestured to everything in order. "It'll be more effective than this dinky thing." She then put his pistol into her empty thigh holster.

He nodded. "Okay, you go to your guardians. I'll try to meet up with you once they're safe."

A little worried that he was still going to put himself in danger, she said, "Be careful."

"Godspeed," he said before ushering the girls down one of the side halls.

Jen took off down the middle stairwell, jumping down most of the stairs. Hitting the third floor, she skidded to a stop.

There were seven Caligans standing in the middle of the hallway, about to force their way into one of the classrooms. However, the squeal of her shoes against the tile floor had alerted the hybrids to her presence, and they turned their attention from the door to her.

She only allowed a second to pass before firing off a shot or two from her Agerian pistol then took off to her left at a mad dash. There was a balcony that she could use to jump down to the second floor quickly and maybe use that ability to ambush the Caligans.

Grey energy flew at her; some passing her and some grazing her as she ran in a slight angle to make it a little harder for them to hit her.

Reaching the balcony, she launched herself into the air and gripped the railing, forcing herself to swing down and into the hallway below. As she landed, she slid to a stop down the second floor before getting her footing, intending to head toward the main entrance.

It was upon turning, though, that she saw Tyron running toward her, his own little faction of Caligans at his heels.

Taking off toward him as she heard feet hit the ground behind her, she hoped he knew what she was about to do.

"Tyron!" she yelled, picking up speed. Then the two of them leapt toward one another while Jen kept a strong hold on her Agerian pistol in her left hand and made a small shield around them. She reached out with her right arm and took hold of Tyron's forearm, and he did the same.

The force of their momentums smacking into a resistance caused them to spin in a circle-like movement. As gravity brought them toward the ground, spinning, they fired at the Caligans.

Her resolve weakened slightly, and she felt the hot sting of an energy attack whiz by her chin.

They crashed to the hard ground and kept their hands clasped together. Then they got up swiftly and let go of one another. Each grabbed the second pistol in their holster and straightened, facing opposite directions. There was no resistance to be found.

They surveyed the area as their breathing came out ragged, adrenaline still pumping through their systems.

Glancing over their shoulders at one another, Tyron said, "Your aim has gotten better."

"I learned from the best," she quipped.

He took deep breaths to get his breathing even then asked, "Can you make another shield?"

"Yeah, but I don't think it'll be as strong as before."

A sigh came from him, and he shook his head. "I really don't like asking this, but you're gonna have to make one. Ar'on could, but I know yours will be stronger."

She nodded and concentrated, quickly forming another shield around the school. As she felt it complete around the building, she could already tell it wasn't as strong as her earlier one. The second shield she had made was gone. She could only assume it had been obliterated when the first shield had fallen.

If only she had focused when the shield started to fall, she could have made it shatter and maybe kill some of the Caligans, rather than just cripple her.

Hopefully, no one got hurt.

"Hey! You two okay?" Krelien called from down the hall.

As Krelien and Archer approached them, Tyron nodded. "Yeah, just had a small run-in with some Caligans."

"They moved fast," Archer said. "Something took out your shield, but I couldn't say what," he said with a nod to Jen.

"What is that?" Krelien asked as he stared at the gun in Jen's hand.

She stared down at it. "Oh, um ... it's a human weapon."

"Ooo! Can I see it?"

Tyron caught Krelien as he stepped forward and grumbled, "We can inspect it later. There are more serious issues to handle right now." He turned his attention back to Jen, who stared absentmindedly at the wall. "Hey, you okay?"

She looked at him, throwing her bangs out of the way, a little taken aback. Then, after thinking for a moment, she replied, "It's just ... I didn't think that would work. I can't believe that it worked, honestly." After a second of silence, they grinned at one another. "Really, I thought that kind of stuff only happened in movies." She looked up and down the hallway. "Man, I wish that that had been caught on camera."

"Oh!" Krelien exclaimed, handing Tyron an assault rifle. "I betcha there's a camera that caught it! Let's go break into the security office."

Catching Krelien's arm, Tyron said, "Let's not."

Krelien pouted.

"Are we secure?"

"For now," Archer answered. "But I've got a bad feeling."

"What kind of bad feeling?" Tyron asked.

"The kind when a bratak'ra is nearby—a whole bunch of 'em," Archer said. "I don't know how long our security will last."

"As long as my shield," Jen declared.

Tyron cracked his neck and winced. "Okay, let's regroup. We need to figure this out before anything else happens."

With a grin, Krelien asked, "You feelin' all right, old *man*?"

The Alpha Team Leader snapped his eyes to Krelien. "'Old *man*'? That's Ar'on, not *me*."

"One tiny fall to the ground and you're all kinds of broken," the Jumper teased with a gleeful chuckle.

A stern expression came to Tyron's face as Jen said, "You do realize he could fire you, right?"

"Oh, come on; he knows it wouldn't be as much fun without *me* around," Krelien said dismissively.

"I don't know. It would be nice to not have as many quips," Tyron said, and Krelien cast him a nervous glance. "Just don't call me old man."

Crossing his finger over his heart, Krelien said, "'Kay. Just don't fire me."

Jen smiled to Tyron. "Aw ... look, he likes you."

"No," Archer said with a shake of his head. "He likes *you*. Otherwise, he wouldn't stick around."

Shaking his head, Tyron said, "Enough. Let's regroup." He marched down the hall with Archer right next to him as Jen and Krelien stared after him for a second.

Looking over at the Jumper, Jen said, "You realize I'm hurting pretty bad from that fall, too, right?"

"Yeah, but I wouldn't dare call you 'old girl'," Krelien said.

"Why not?"

"'Cause I'm afraid of you."

Chapter Seventeen
Stick the Landing

Coming to the main entrance, Jen saw Grant, Ryan, and Nancy standing there. Outraged, she yelled, "What are you guys doing here?"

Ar'on turned to her. "We were just trying to figure that out."

"We want to help," Grant said.

"Oh, that's great! You can get killed!" Tyron said with disdain. He glared toward the boys and griped, "You can't help without getting hurt, and we're trying to not have that happen."

Looking at her sister, Jen asked, "And what are you doing here?"

"I wanted to make sure you were okay," Nancy said sheepishly.

"I'll be fine. You won't if you stay here."

Tyron ignored the teenagers and asked the other Alpha Team members, "Everything taken care of?"

Ar'on sighed. "All the warriors that got into the building have been eliminated, but that's not our problem."

"How many reinforcements did they get?" Tyron asked.

"That's just the thing—none," Kaldok said.

"None?"

"The portal didn't activate. The attack was brought on by the soldiers left over from our attack," Ar'on said.

"How'd they break the shield?" Tyron asked.

"Maybe one of Cregorous' generals was out there," Ar'on mused.

"Did you see one of them?" Kaldok asked. "I didn't sense anything, and they usually call on the werewolves."

"No, but that doesn't mean they aren't hiding."

Adjusting his assault rifle, Tyron said, "Let's just move forward on the hope that we don't have one of Cregorous' loyalists out there."

Blaze glanced toward the floor. "I am puzzled. Why would they attack so brazenly when we are closer to their numbers at present?"

Running footfalls made them turn to Jon entering the area.

"Are you all okay?" he asked as he reached them. Looking at the three students, aside from Jen, he said, "What are you all doing here?"

"We're trying to help," Ryan said.

Archer cocked his head to the side. "By risking your lives?"

"I'll let you deal with them," Tyron said with a gesture to Jon as he turned to his team. "What's the likelihood of getting reinforcements?"

"You know the answer, Ty," Ar'on replied.

Turning toward the principal just as Jon was about to reprimand the students, Tyron said, "You should call an evacuation. I don't know if we'll be able to hold this position if anything else comes our way."

"That bad?" Jon asked with worry ghosting his features.

Tyron nodded.

Letting out a sigh, Jon clicked his radio on and said, "Attention all staff: Shelter-in-place has been lifted and evacuation is to begin immediately. I repeat: evacuation is to begin immediately to the western end of the building, exit number five. Avoid the main entrance and entrance two at all costs."

Thundering paces began to echo through the halls as the students started to run for the other end of the building.

Jon stepped toward Tyron and asked, "Is there any chance you all could run?"

Shaking his head, Kaldok said, "There's nowhere we can go. Cregorous will tear this place apart then continue on a rampage until he finds Jen."

"And you're sure he's coming?" Grant asked.

The members of the Alpha Team shot him annoyed looks.

"Okay, sorry. I'm just making sure."

"This isn't helping," Ryan said. "What can we do?"

A little irritated, Tyron first looked at Jon, who sighed, and then looked back at the teenagers. "You guys aren't going to do anything. We're going to fight."

At that moment, a blinding white light flashed up the hill from the entrance.

Everyone looked toward the source and shielded their eyes. A screech hit the air, and Tyron snatched Jen as he screamed, "Everyone down!"

A flash of gold skittered across the area as the Alpha Team members sprang toward the humans.

An explosion ripped through the building, blowing glass everywhere and knocking everyone off their feet. The groaning of metal sounded as a chunk of framing from the windows twisted and fell.

It took a few seconds for the aftermath to still.

Tyron shook his head to get some of the debris off of him. He had thrown Jen to the ground and wrapped his arms and wings around her to protect her. He looked down at her. "You okay?"

"Nance?" Jen called frantically, coughing a bit, as she pushed back from Tyron. She ignored the laceration that had appeared across her face as she and Tyron got to their feet.

Whatever had caused the explosion had also torn her shield to shreds. The instant the hit had come, Jen had felt as though a sword had cut across her body.

"I'm okay," Nancy said in a small voice as Kaldok helped her up, removing his wings from around her body.

A small groan came from behind her.

Tyron let her go as she turned to find Ryan sitting up with an array of small cuts across his arm and the side of his face. She opened her mouth to say something, but he cut her off.

"Fine. I'm fine. Grant?" he asked over the mass of bodies working to get up.

Grant bore similar injuries to Ryan as he stood.

Meanwhile, Krelien ripped a chunk of metal out of

his wing. "He's fine." Krelien pointed to Grant. "I'm fine. Ar'on and Kaldok are fine. Blaze and Archer are fine." He turned to look around.

Jon sat up and nodded.

"The guy in charge is fine."

"Okay, so everyone's fine," Tyron said.

Jen hugged her sister, who stared in terrified fascination at Jen's already healing wound.

"Not for long," Grant replied.

Everyone looked out over at the main entrance of the school where cold air whipped into the building and stole the warmth.

The entrance was completely decimated.

The metal doorframes hung off-kilter; the cinderblock walls looked like they had been pushed in, chunks missing where the craftsmanship wasn't as solid; the windows were gone; and the stairwell around them looked haphazard, the railings ripped off in the blast.

The portal was open again; a large, white cylinder stretching into the sky. Warriors poured out of it, running for the school.

"Archer, Blaze, go head them off!" Tyron hollered, and the two grovix quickly turned and ran to intercept any of the enemy fighters coming toward them.

"Ar'on, you and Kaldok take Nancy and get people to the other end of the building," Tyron ordered as he turned to the others.

"Where's entrance five Jon mentioned?" Ar'on asked.

"Follow me!" Nancy said, taking off with Ar'on and Kaldok right behind her.

Jen took a few steps after them. "You two take care of her!"

"Promise!" Kaldok called from over his shoulder.

With a point at Grant, Ryan, and Jon, Tyron said, "You three are with me."

"What about—" Krelien started.

"You and Jen are sticking with me," the Alpha Team Leader told Krelien.

"Where are we going?" Jon asked.

Leaping down the stairs and reaching the first floor, Tyron sprinted toward the nurse's office. "We're getting weapons!" he hollered. "We need your help."

"Tyron!" Janet called as they neared the nurse's office. "I heard the evacuation call. One of the other staff called 911," she told Jon. "What's happened? This whole building just shook."

Taking her arm, Tyron said, "They're here. Evacuate with the others."

"But—"

"Janet, now," Tyron insisted. "I will find you when we get past this."

The Caretaker looked torn before she snatched a pistol off the table and said, "You had better." Then she kissed him with a ferocity that made Jen blush.

"Um ..." Jen started as Janet ran out of the room.

"Wow," Krelien said.

"Shut up. Gear up," Tyron spat as he threw Jon an assault rifle before forcefully shoving rifles into the teenage boys' grasps.

Looking at the rifle in his hands, Ryan said, "Uh... Jen? I don't know how to fire this."

"I know, I know," she said as she grabbed another Agerian pistol and threw the 9mm to the ground. Turning to Ryan, she continued, "It's the same as your .22 for hunting—trigger, aim, fire. The only thing that's vastly different is the kickback and the magazine. The kickback's intense—be prepared for that.

They'll shoot off roughly five hundred rounds. The extra magazines are for if you happen to run out."

"Do not engage the enemy unless they make a move toward you," Tyron interjected. "You are not to throw yourselves into battle."

"Then why are you giving us these?" Grant asked as the hybrids began to march out of the room.

As he reached the door, Tyron turned and told him, "I need you three to help with the evacuation to free up my team. Jon"—he turned toward the principal—"are you okay with them being your backup?"

"It'll have to do," Jon said as he smacked a magazine into his assault rifle. "Where do you need us?"

"Head on off to the other end of the school and take this." Tyron took out his earpiece. "Get into contact with Ar'on. He'll give you a rendezvous point, and then you can relieve him. Get the kids out of the building or, at the least, away from the battle. Are there others on your staff you know who have trained in any form of combat?"

"Yeah, there's a gym teacher and a few others around the building, but I can't guarantee I can reach them in time."

"You try to reach them and send them here for weapons. I'm not going to encumber you with more than you can carry. Now, you two, follow him." Tyron pointed at the two teenage boys. "He is your leader. If he says duck, you duck. He says run, you run. Don't come back for her." He pointed at Jen. "I'll be keeping an eye on her. And don't you dare run away unless instructed to do so, you hear me?"

Grant and Ryan looked at one another, seeming slightly off kilter.

The sounds of yelling filtered from the hallway,

and Tyron looked at the ceiling before he turned back to them. "If you aren't ready for this, that's fine. Put the gun down and run away. Otherwise, follow him and don't falter. We need you one hundred percent or not at all."

A crash rumbled the walls slightly, and Tyron looked out the door to see a dual-horned bratak'ra running for them. Without hesitating, he threw his right arm sideways across his body, and a surge of gold quickly appeared, charging down the hall. It impacted with the bratak'ra and sent it flying.

"Go now, before it's too late," Tyron ordered before he took off down the hall toward the stairwell that they had just descended.

Jen and Krelien were right behind him without a glance back at the others.

Jon turned in the opposite direction, Ryan right at his side, but Grant slid to a stop as he watched Jen disappear up the stairwell.

It felt wrong to watch her run off. He trusted Tyron, but he didn't trust Jen to stick by him. There was no telling what might happen to her out there.

"Grant, let's go!" Jon shouted from a little ways down the hall, at an elevator.

Taking a breath, he whispered, "Please be safe," before he turned and ran toward the elevator.

The stairs were overrun by Caligans, and the moment Jen turned the corner, she saw a wave of them leap down the stairwell. She planted her feet and threw her left arm across her body. A blue shield flew away from her and smacked into the line of Caligans. She held her hands up, trying to keep the shield in place.

Tyron and Krelien flanked her, both firing off round after round at the enemy fighters. As they came up to the first landing of the stairwell, Jen moved her left arm over her body, and her blue shield became a circular one, wrapping around them like an egg.

Above the noise and chaos, Tyron hollered, "Can you keep this up?"

"I think so," she said with a nod. "I can't guarantee for any specified time, but maybe a few minutes."

"How about outside?" Krelien asked.

"No problem."

They continued up the stairs with little trouble. Jen's shield did a good job of not just protecting, but also reflecting attacks. However, as they reached the second floor, she saw Caligans, bratak'ra, and werewolves running down the hallway into the building.

She was about to say something when Krelien said, "BRB," and disappeared into silvery dust.

"Now he gets it right," Jen muttered.

"Where'd he go?" Tyron hollered as he continued to focus his fire.

A Caligan threw themselves against Jen's shield, and she pushed it back, sending it colliding into a werewolf. "I don't know!" Jen yelled. "He just said 'BRB' and disappeared."

"I don't have time for this," Tyron growled as he dropped his assault rifle, letting the strap hang across his shoulder and swing down to his side. Then he took his fist and banged it against Jen's shield, a gold one slapping against it. "Use that strength and follow my lead," he said as he pulled his rifle back into his arms.

As they got to the second floor, Jen saw a line of Caligans get caught by something, their right shoulders all impacting an invisible force. For the split-second they were knocked off balance, Jen thought maybe the wind or something was the culprit. Then they disappeared into screams and dust.

Krelien. He must have been taking them out by pulling them into another dimension.

What a way to go.

Tyron's shield pushed against hers, and she glanced over to see that he was still firing his weapon while controlling his shield. She wished she could do the same.

Refocusing on what he was trying to get her to do, she caught on in a few seconds. He was pushing the Caligans backward and out of the building, using her stronger shield as a buffer that kept them from breaking past.

As they forced the Caligans out of the building, Tyron dropped the gun again and said to her, "Follow my lead. We need to clear a path."

"What're you gonna do?" Jen asked.

Krelien reappeared next to her and screamed, "I'm back!" with his hands in the air as though he had just stuck a landing in gymnastics.

"Great for you! Shield break in five," Tyron hollered.

"Oh, okay. Bye," Krelien said before disappearing.

Tyron brought his left arm across his body, and his shield cracked.

Jen did the same, doing her best to break her shield in the same way. Then she saw a Caligan about to punch her shield and panicked. She needed Tyron to be able to control her shield, too.

Not really knowing why, she slapped her hand against his side. A flash of blue skittered up his torso and flashed across his arms. He twitched at the action and had to regain his footing as she said, "It's yours!"

He looked confused for half a second before he gritted his teeth and threw his hands outward. The cracked shields both broke, and the shards all propelled forward, the blue followed along with Tyron's gold. Their combined efforts created a large enough swath to cut through the dozen or so Caligans running toward them, and the few that were already standing there.

Taking a few deep breaths, Tyron quickly surveyed their situation. His arms twitched a little and he shook them out.

They had cleared the immediate area, but it looked as though the portal just up the hill was providing an endless supply of enemy fighters.

"Still coming. Krelien!"

Krelien reappeared at Jen's side with his rifle in hand and saluted. "Present."

Tyron threw him his rifle, and the Jumper caught it before they moved.

Again, the two Zaheri flanked Jen before they ran to meet their opposition.

Jen had never imagined in her wildest dreams that there could be so many enemy fighters. It wasn't to the scale of some movies where there were just hundreds of thousands of people clashing on a field of battle, but there was no doubt that they were outnumbered. By a lot.

There had to be at least a few hundred Caligans rampaging down the hill, and she couldn't even guess how many bratak'ra and werewolves were among them. Then there were the Ferveos.

A billowing line of flame shot toward them. They avoided it easily enough, but the Ferveos kept going.

She looked at the dragons converging toward the school and almost screamed that they had to head back.

A pulse hit the air next to her, and she looked frantically to find that Krelien had disappeared from her side.

Krelien landed on the school roof and quickly took up his sniper rifle. Finding his mark in the scope, he took out a few Ferveos.

Their bodies plummeted to the ground, and one of them exploded on impact. Glass broke across the building.

He let the rifle go, catching on the strap across his shoulders, and took to the air. He landed on one of the Ferveos' heads and tapped its brow with a smirk. "You're going the wrong way!"

The Ferveos thrashed and snapped at him as he dove off its head and shot back to the others. With a roaring cry, the Ferveos turned and followed him. The others nearby did likewise. In a moment, the dragons abandoned the building.

Krelien jumped and took his spot again among Tyron and Jen.

Tyron relied solely on his energy. It looked like gold goo had slapped against his hands and fore-arms like gauntlets. He occasionally threw his arms out, and an attack would surge from him. Mean-while, Jen concentrated her fire on the bratak'ra and werewolves and did as best as she could to take care of them.

A moment later, Archer appeared, running up through a line of the opposing fighters. While doing so, he tripped, bit, and pounced on as many as he could. The bratak'ra would snap at him, but he would take out their legs, causing them to trip and take out their fellow fighters. Blaze ran alongside him a few paces away, and it was then that Jen understood her namesake.

The white-furred grovix was on fire, literally. Her fur was ignited, and fire warped and fell from her body. Everything she touched burst into flames of its own volition. The ground behind her was a line of flames, while any of the Caligans, bratak'ra, or werewolves she touched ignited, too.

The two grovix sprang over the three of them as they entered out of the ranks before them. Landing behind them, Blaze's fur became stark white again the moment she hit the ground. They both turned and flanked the three, forming a line of five. Little room remained between them and the opposing fighters.

As grey energy started to whiz at them, Jen got an idea. Taking the energy in her grasp, she pushed it out in front of them as a shield. It landed a foot or so in front of them all and hit the ground, kicking up chunks of rock, asphalt, grass, and dirt as it slammed into the cold earth and skimmed along. She kept pushing it forward as they went.

Opposing grey energy sparked against her shield like little flashes of hot lead. It was such a bombardment that her head started to thrum with pressure.

Then it hit her.

The Caligans were using energy to hit her shield. What was to say she couldn't take their power and fuel her own? It was worth trying, anyway.

Blue shot up her arm, illuminating her veins. A second later, rather than popping off her shield with sparking heat, she watched her shield envelop the grey instead. Like drops of grey falling into a stark-blue paint, the grey was absorbed into her shield. The throbbing in her head died off, and with each hit that the shield took, the stronger she felt it become.

They were nearly upon the Caligans at this point. Blaze and Archer picked up speed and ran through the shield, advancing farther and farther ahead of their Zaheri counterparts. With each bound of her feet, Blaze's fur sparked to life, crackling and flickering like a fire popping to ignite. It started at her feet and head then worked its way back to her fluffy tail.

Dual growls erupted from Archer and Blaze; Blaze's petite but commanding, and Archer's deep and furious. They harmonized in a way. And when they leapt into the thrall, Archer used his bulk to squash and rip at whatever was nearby, whereas Blaze brought with her an explosion of flame that erupted from her. Anything that got too close to her ignited almost instantly.

Just before they smacked into the first line of Caligan fighters, Jen hurtled her shield at them. The blue shattered into a million tiny pieces and tore up and out. Fragments of blue danced into the air and sliced into Ferveos wings, sending them colliding into other dragons midair. bratak'ra and werewolves stumbled to the ground with yelps and crying groans. Caligans stuttered and collapsed over each other.

And then it was just chaos.

Kicking and punching, firing a weapon, and unleashing an attack, Jen was snatched more than once by one of her Zaheri to avoid getting hit. Her Zaheri moved like a deadly dance. They would rip her out of the way, take a hit, and then nullify the problem before moving on. A moment later, another would be at her side or at her back. Archer soared over her more than once and smashed into a bratak'ra or a werewolf.

Kaldok and Ar'on exploded into the thrall after a moment. The brutality that Kaldok displayed as he dispatched werewolves shocked her a little. He was so calm and collected, but here in a battle, it was as if he held nothing back. He stayed on two legs, though, slashing his claws with savagery.

At one point, Ar'on whipped his sniper rifle around and sent the butt of the gun colliding with a Caligan's face. As though he had done it a million times before, he effortlessly swung the rifle up and shot off a few blasts with alarming accuracy. The gun barely moved as it jarred powerful kickbacks into his shoulder.

Tyron never seemed far. He would take a hit then retaliate as though he hadn't even been scratched. His knuckle spikes landed a fair number of blows into enemies with crushing force. His energy-gauntleted arms flashed into shields at a second's notice to rebuff oncoming attacks.

And Krelien bounced across the field. In pops and pulses and waves of silvery mist, he was in the air, taking down a Ferveos one moment, and the next, he was next to Jen, pulling her out of the way of an errant attack. His accuracy didn't seem as solid as Ar'on's, but he was clever and used his shots to take out more than one enemy at a time.

None of them were unscathed. Energy scorched skin and kicks fractured bones. Spikes and horns and claws left sweeping cuts and lacerations. Jen did her best to avoid any more coma-inducing injuries. She'd had her share of blood that day, and she didn't look forward to the prospect of more broken bones and lacerations and exhaustion-riddled muscles.

Only a few moments had passed since they had charged from the school, but Jen found herself relying on the adrenaline that pumped through her body more and more. Her arms raised a little slower, and her reactions were a little later. It bubbled frustration in her gut. The thought of lashing out came to mind. Explode energy outward and take them all out. She could probably do something like that.

There was this unknown something that began to thrash and pull in her core, like her brain and her heart were trying to tap into some tangible thing in her system. Apprehension rose in her, or perhaps anticipation. Or maybe it was a swelling to enact justice. A righteous anger. Frustration. The combining emotions searched for a release in this fight, right at the center of who she was. She couldn't quite describe it. There was a definite something that spiked and clawed for release.

The portal surged across the battle, startling everyone, Caligans included. As it rushed past her, a figure soared from the blinding white and kicked her.

The force of the blow barreled into her and sent

her flying back a few hundred feet. As she landed on her back, she gasped and let out a wheezing noise. She hadn't broken any bones, by some miracle. But her lungs spasmed, and her heart stuttered to her brain, *What the heck was that?*

Shakily, she gripped the ground and pushed upright. And as she lifted her head, she froze. The portal sat not far from the shattered entrance to the school. It blazed and warbled dazzlingly, and she should have squinted, but something about the figure obscured in the blinding white made her tremble instead. She could tell that it was a male, but that was all she could discern by the way he held his head and the assured edge to his shoulders.

Terror began to flood through her. For the first time, she was actually one-hundred percent afraid. It struck her heart in a jolting panic, and her hands began to shake of their own volition as she just stood there.

The figure glanced at the portal and chuckled. "Catch me if you can."

She started as he bolted for the school.

Then the portal sputtered a bit, dropping to a tiny light for half a second, before it exploded again in a cylinder of light. It slapped against the world with a heaviness that made Jen hop back. Then a large, golden-scaled dragon appeared out of the white, towering above her.

It looked down at her then lifted its head to the army behind her and bellowed as a bunch of smaller dragons shot from the portal. The smaller dragons—Scouts—dove into the battle, latched onto the Ferveos, and drug them to the ground. The larger dragon preceded other Preliators. Agerian dragons.

Large, armored grovix ran out of the portal, not sparing her a glance as they charged straight into the fight.

She glanced around at the reinforcements, and then her gaze landed on the school. Not really thinking it through, she sprinted after Cregorous.

Chapter Eighteen

The Monster's Loose

He had a good few seconds of a head start on her, but she had to at least try to get this guy back for her sufferings from the day. The only thing she could think was that he was aware of what he was up against and would try again some other time. She really didn't want to give him that opportunity.

Cregorous was fast, but she knew the school front and back. There was no way he could outrun her there. To him, the corridors would look the same, but to her, they all had a different look, and she knew the shortcuts that would lead to where she needed to go.

It was a wild guess that he would head to the roof. Even though Ar'on had mentioned that the portal wouldn't allow for a hybrid to head through an active connection from Tilion, she had a hunch that Cregorous wasn't like most hybrids.

As she reached the last few steps, she leapt up and kicked the door open. In doing so, she grabbed her pistol and, by the time she landed, she had it up and ready to fire.

She saw Cregorous, a few yards away from the edge of the roof, and screamed, "Cregorous!" Her voice seemed to echo through the empty rooftop as the door behind her slammed shut.

His back was to her as he stared at the open portal, his hands in his pockets. He turned around slowly to face her.

She had never actually heard any descriptions about his appearance, but now that she saw him, it wasn't what she had expected. She thought for sure that he would be grotesque. Maybe have horns and wear a cape and chuckle maniacally all the time. He would look evil and like someone you would want to run away from. He would look the part.

Instead, he looked ... normal.

He had short brown hair with natural highlights, like he had clearly spent his summers in the sun, his skin a perfect tan. Pool blue eyes stared at her, and she was surprised at the beauty in them. If the eyes were the windows to the soul, then she didn't understand why his were so stunningly brilliant. So full of life. His face was handsome, and he looked to be around the age of thirty. He looked striking in his attire—a tailored button-down and jeans.

She couldn't believe it, but he was attractive. So much so that she would swear he was the most handsome man she had ever seen.

He roved his gaze over her. After a second, he then smiled and let out a small laugh. He moved his hands out of his pockets and gestured in an 'ah shucks' kind of way. "Well, you caught *me*, Jennifer."

The fact that he had used her full name made her feel bitterly cold. Something about the way he had said it wasn't endearing.

He darted his gaze around the rooftop a bit and allowed a few seconds to pass before he looked back at her. "What? No backup? I would have anticipated Tyron the mighty standing right next to you to help fight me off." He sounded so conversational, mockingly flexing when he mentioned Tyron.

Jen was silent, trying to remain calm despite feeling so helter-skelter.

Cregorous tsked. "And yet you came alone." He paused and put his hands in his pockets again, his stance easy and relaxed. "Y'know, all those Agerians call you the Elder's Warrior. Their *Raidin*." He lackadaisically started to walk around, kicking up the gravel on the rooftop. His mentioning of her name, *that* name, the name Tyron had called her; how would he know what the Agerians called her? "Their little hero to stop me, the big baddie."

"Yeah, well, you know how trustworthy *they* are," she said. Despite being on edge from his intense gaze, she still held her gun steadily.

"Oh, all too well, darling," he said just above a whisper. He looked down at her gun then back at her again. A simple grin came across his face. "Really, Jennifer? A gun? Have your beloved *Zaheri* taught you nothing of *me*?"

"I know you're mortal." Her breath was visible in the frigid air, but she didn't feel cold. In fact, she felt like fire was running through every inch of her body, not just in her blood.

A coy grin came to his face, and he shrugged. "Then fire."

She furrowed her brow.

"Come on now; fire. If you're so sure of what you know, then I would die if you shot *me*, right?" He paused, waiting for her to do something. When she didn't, he said jocularly, like a young boy daring a girl to hit him, "This is the only chance you'll have. Do you really want to waste it?"

At this point, she was just so on edge from how not-evil he was being that she just needed to do something. Her arms were beginning to waver, and she knew that he was right.

This was the only chance she would get to just fire a gun at him while he stood still.

Six shots rang out of her gun, but as they flew at him, the shots stopped dead in front of him, just glowing there in the fading sunlight, like lamps hanging, illuminating whatever was closest to them.

In defeat, she lowered her pistol and let out a slow breath.

Cregorous grinned at her. "That's the thing about power, Jennifer. It defies what we think is true." He narrowed his eyes. "Now," he drew the word out, "let's see what the great Raidin is *made* of." Those insanely beautiful blue eyes suddenly flashed a bright red.

The six energy bullets shot right back at her, as if they were in rewind. Minus the fact that the blasts weren't going to go back into the gun that they had come from.

Acting on instinct, she threw her right arm in front of her. Inches away from her, the blasts suddenly diminished and fizzled out, dying with soft pops.

Cregorous narrowed his eyes again as they changed back to blue. A half-smile came to his face as he marveled, "Well now, you are something, aren't you?"

She just stood there, staring at him. There was no way of knowing what he would do next, and he just continued to stare at her with a smirk on his face.

He glanced between the rooftop and her a few times before he asked, "You do know what happened to the first Raidin, don't you?"

Jen suddenly scrunched her brow. *The first Raidin? There had been one before her?*

"Ooo..." Cregorous said with a pout. "Tsk, tsk. I can't believe they never told you about that." He took a small step forward. "Years ago, the first Raidin had their run." Pursing his lips, he hummed. "But their tale is sad and pathetic, and it bores me terribly." Pausing, he then asked, "But you"—he gave a half-smile again—"you wouldn't want to hear that story, would you?"

"No," she said without thinking. A part of her was kind of intrigued. What else might Cregorous know that her Zaheri hadn't told her?

A small chuckle rumbled from him. "Oh, Jennifer, don't lie. It's not becoming. At least not becoming for someone who's supposed to be a golden child."

She didn't say anything.

"But I will indulge your curiosity. There was a Raidin before you, and it would behoove you to ask your precious Zaheri about it. Although, they'll probably avoid telling you."

"My Zaheri tell me everything they know," she said simply.

He raised his eyebrows. "Oh, do they now? Out of curiosity, did you know, before today, that you weren't the only Human-Born?"

She clenched her jaw.

Wearing a mock look of surprise, he straightened. "No? Well, if you ever find yourself with questions, I would be happy to tell you the answers."

"If I ever want to know, I'll ask the people that I know won't lie to me," she spat back.

He shook his head and a look resembling pity filled his features. "I don't want to lie to you, Jennifer." There was something about his tone that seemed genuine. "So, I'll tell you the truth."

"Are you capable of that?" she asked coldly.

Cregorous seemed completely undeterred from her resistance. "There's no one alive in Agerius who can help you control your abilities."

She opened her mouth to shoot something back at him, but her words got lost on the way to her vocal cords. A choke left her, and she snapped her mouth shut as she looked toward the ground. Suddenly, she felt confused and terribly lost.

Shaking her head, she said, "That can't be true." She remembered Kaldok mentioning the Elders and how they knew everything. Looking up at him, she said, "The Elders. I'm going to speak with them, and they're going to tell me what I need to know."

"I wouldn't count on it," he muttered with a slight shake of his head.

She scoffed. "Of course you wouldn't."

"I say that from experience, darling," he snarked, giving her a bored look.

She straightened and took a few breaths. "How would you have experience with the Elders?"

He just smirked back at her.

She darted her eyes around in confusion. "Is this a test?"

"Life is a test," he said. "And I happen to have all the answers," he added with another smirk.

"That can't be true either."

"It can't, huh?" he asked, leaning forward a little. "How about this? I know for a fact that the first Raidin wound up having to seek the help of the Belvacor before even remotely understanding their potential, let alone how to properly control their energy."

Jen had no clue who these Belvacor were, but they sounded pretty mysterious, especially with the way Cregorous had said it.

He laughed. "And you don't even know who they are. Of course you don't. Why would you? They don't believe in them either."

She swallowed. This was all too much for her to take in.

Glancing around the roof, Jen knew Cregorous hadn't made any deliberate attempt to attack her, but in this state, she was completely defenseless.

She wished Tyron were there, even if it meant that he just stood there and yelled at Cregorous. At least then she wouldn't feel so isolated.

"You're lying," she said quietly but didn't dare to look at him.

"Well, that's your choice to believe," he said with a shrug. "But I will tell you this; I'm the only person alive, hybrid or human, who can understand your power and help you control and wield it properly. Without that control—"

She looked up at him and noticed that he had taken a step closer to her. She took a step back.

"—you could easily wind up hurting someone you don't intend to hurt."

Her thoughts from earlier in the day came rushing back to her. Pinching her eyes shut, she shook her head. She lifted her head and glared at him as she spat, "I don't need your help."

"Oh-ho-ho," he laughed. "You really do. You think I'm just saying all this to get a rise out of you?" She stared back at him as he continued, "I'm saying this because I can feel the terror in you."

Trying to keep it together, Jen took a steadying breath. "You don't know anything about *me*."

"I know what it's like to be alone, Jennifer," he said quietly. There was sadness in his tone that made her look up at him. His eyes were downcast, and there was a frown on his face. "I know what it's like to be at the top with everyone staring up at you, each of them thinking they can help, but knowing that, ultimately, they can do nothing. And I know what it's like to put your trust in something, only for them to lie to you and protect those who don't deserve protection."

Was it possible he was telling the truth? Was it possible he was the only one who could help her? What if she did hurt someone she loved?

He took another step closer. This time, she didn't step back.

"I know it's tough," he continued. "You're confused and worried you might cause more destruction than good. They don't understand that." He gestured toward the door behind her.

He was getting dangerously closer to her, but Jen found that what he said was comforting. Someone else knew how she felt. She had just had these exact thoughts earlier in the day, and here he was, offering the understanding that she was seeking.

It was true; she had seen the look on Tyron's face before. He didn't know how to help her.

Cregorous stared intently at her. "Without *me*, you're never going to know the full potential that you have." With a heavy sigh and a dark, possessive tone to his voice, he added, "And *my*, what potential you have."

She felt cold and shivered. Her brain felt like it was in a fog, with a soft voice calling out to her, telling her it was okay to trust this man who stood before her. But somewhere inside, somewhere deep inside, there was another voice screaming in outrage, begging her, pleading with her to not listen to what Cregorous was saying.

"Come with me," she heard echo in her head and looked up to see him holding out his hand to her.

"Come with me, Jennifer. I'll help you. I can help you, as no one else is able."

Her breathing was suddenly haggard, like she was hyperventilating.

"And with that, you'll find that anything—and I mean, anything—can be yours. Glory, power, wealth... it can all be yours. And I can give it to you."

That smaller voice seemed to abruptly surge in her mind, yelling, "*No!*" and breaking through the confusion in her thoughts.

"No," she finally got out as she shook her head, as if by doing so, she would be able to silence the echoing in her mind.

Blinking rapidly, she began to realize what was happening. The conversation with her Zaheri earlier, how they had said Cregorous could get into people's minds. He was doing that to her.

Sure, his words might have made sense, but that didn't mean they were true.

Glaring at him, she pushed back. "No. You can't win me. I'm not yours." She said it with tenacity, trying to appear strong, trying to gain back the ground that she had lost in his pushing. It was weird, but she could still feel him ebbing in her mind, trying to influence her to follow him.

He shook his head. "You don't really mean that."

Jen stepped back. "I do mean it," she said through gritted teeth. She felt tired, and it seemed like that other small voice was the only thing keeping her going. Shaking her head again, she told him, "I mean it. You're not getting me on your side."

"This is your only chance, Jennifer," he said as she stepped back. He swallowed and continued to hold his hand out. "I won't offer again. Do you really want to take that chance?"

She darted her eyes between his hand and his eyes a few times. A real part of her wanted to grasp his offer and cling to it. She wanted to run to him and say that she trusted him. And that part of her wasn't the echo that he had pushed into her head. However, there was one thing that kept her firmly planted.

She blinked a few times and met his gaze again. "What gave you the right?"

He cocked his head a little to the side and squinted.

The hot anger she had felt earlier flashed into her heart, and she glared at him as tears pricked her eyes. "What gave you the right to kill innocent babies?"

The question seemed to catch him off guard. He opened his mouth, but nothing came out for a second. Then, squaring his shoulders, he said, "If you come with me, you'll understand."

"That killing completely defenseless children is okay?" She shook her head. "There's no amount of rationalization you can offer that will justify that." Letting out a breath, she said, "The answer is *no*."

The soft, comforting expression on his face shifted slightly. Just enough that it seemed as though he were angry. Clenching his outstretched hand into a fist, he dropped it to his side. Then he rolled his eyes and stepped back a bit, undoing the buttons on his cuff and starting to roll his sleeves up. "Y'know," he began as he worked at his sleeves, "this could have been easy. It could have been painless. I've done my diligence and offered you an out ... twice," he spat as he met her gaze. "So, you just remember, when I bring hell on everything you love, that it could have been prevented, but you just had to be stubborn and had to die like a stupid, writhing child that claimed themselves a hero."

He finished his task of rolling up his sleeves, and she saw that he had a tattoo on his left arm. It started midway up his forearm then spiraled up and around his elbow. At the beginning, it looked like an etching, almost writing maybe, but the farther it moved up from his forearm, the more shattered and broken it became. By the time it reached his bicep, it was faded and splintered off in a haphazard manner.

In a flash, he threw his hand out toward her.

Stark red energy surged down his arm and flew toward her, his eyes mirroring the color.

Quickly reacting, she threw her hands out, intending to make a shield. Instead, blue energy flew out of her hands and collided with his.

Flinching slightly, he planted his feet on the ground and stabilized. A satisfied smirk came to his face. With a flick of his wrist, he then cut off his attack. It caught Jen off guard, as her attack had solely been in defense. Now that there was nothing to fight, her body seemed to have chosen the time to stop defending and her energy stopped fighting back.

Stumbling a little, she caught herself and stood.

Cregorous laughed. "Oh-ho-ho, this could be fun." His manner kept throwing her off. It was almost like he was playing with her. "You felt it, didn't you?" he asked, a wild grin on his face. He was enjoying this? "Imagine it again, and harness it this time. I intend to have this be enjoyable."

For a brief second, she felt like she was back in training with Tyron.

Only, the man across from her wasn't going to stop if it looked like she was getting hurt.

He threw his right hand toward her again as a blackness began to seep from the tattoo on his left arm. Darkness enveloped the area and blocked out whatever light was coming from the sunset. Red energy cloaked in black flew at her.

That strange tug in her soul came to her chest again, and she put up her right arm. As his opposing energy reached her, it divided away from her body, like she was a rock in a stream. Grimacing, she tried to keep her arm up and skidded back a little from his attack.

Her arms began to burn from her shoulders down to her fingertips. The feeling worked its way up her neck and down her back. As the energy from Cregorous' attack continued to fly at her, she pulled up her left hand and paused for a second as her palms faced each other.

A spark passed between her hands. Soon, a bright blue energy orb formed. In an instant, she took the energy orb in her right hand and threw it at Cregorous, who dodged the orb while stopping his energy attack and simultaneously sending another.

Ducking slightly, she barely missed the blast as it seared past her arm. As she turned to look at her attacker, Cregorous had already moved in front of her and punched her in the face with a strong right uppercut.

Falling slightly, she tried to use that to her advantage and kicked at his right leg, knocking him off his feet. As she landed, she got up and pulled energy into her fisted hand and moved to punch him in the back. He moved just as quickly, though, and her attack only grazed him. Though, she still tore open his skin and ripped through the muscle along his shoulder.

The simple attack made him grit his teeth, and from his kneeling position, he pulled his right arm back then landed a heavy blow to her stomach. She didn't actually fall though, as he caught the hem of her shirt and pulled her back with his left hand before he landed another blow on her face. He let her fall this time.

Breathing was difficult as she hit the ground. Her face felt like a hot iron had just shot across it, and her stomach was gurgling and convulsing. It didn't seem to know whether she should throw up or breathe.

Slowly getting her breathing back, she pushed up against the gravel of the rooftop and stood. There was a searing pain that bit at her neck, back, and arms.

A deep growl followed each of his heavy breaths. For some reason, she found it attractive.

Grimacing, she touched her face and found there was no burn. There weren't even any scratches along her face. It sure felt like there was a burn there, though.

"It hurts, doesn't it, Jennifer?" He got to his feet and gripped his right shoulder in his left hand. Blood seeped between his fingers and fell down his hand and past his wrist. Gritting his teeth, he held the wound and glared at her. "I promise you, the next time I touch you"—he took his hand away from the wound, and she saw it was still bleeding profusely and hadn't even begun to heal—"I will make you pay for this."

Confusion filled her. Even when she got hurt badly, her wounds began to heal almost instantly. It took time for them to heal fully, but his cut should have at least started to patch back up.

"You're not a hybrid?" she asked quietly.

A coy smile came to his face as a scoff left him. "Of course I am, Jennifer."

The two looked at one another.

"I'm just as intrigued about *my* injury as you are."

As he smiled broadly at her, she found herself a little off-kilter at the thought that she was able to injure him.

"As I said, I'll make you pay for that."

The jarring reminder of her strength shot through her.

He straightened then threw his right arm out at her. Red energy with a black fog swirling around it surged at her in a long, wavy line. She didn't want to give him the chance to get away, so she threw her own blue energy to combat his. The superpowers met, and sparks shot outward, like white hot lead.

The seconds ticked by, and Jen's neck, back, and arms began to burn again, a strange sensation rolling through her veins. Her brain felt like it was convulsing. There was a growing hunger in her stomach, not for food but for release and vengeance and retribution. She screwed her eyes shut and felt them sting as her arms shook from the attack.

When she opened her eyes, her vision had shifted somehow. The portal behind Cregorous warbled and waved in a white brilliance. There was a marred, messy redness that wrapped around its form, larger in some places than others, like a scarred wound. And Cregorous, he looked the same, but she saw a smattered blackness that filled his body. Like oil smeared across his being, converging around his heart and mind, clutching to a light at his core. And for a flash of a moment, she could have sworn she saw an ethereal thing flash across Cregorous' face. Something with fragmented, warped horns that screeched a jarring noise and scared her.

That something kept ebbing at her mind, again begging to be released. It made her breathe heavily as she got the overwhelming feeling that everything happening was wrong. Fear eclipsed all the other warring emotions within her, and her hands trembled.

One side of her wanted to keep fighting and kill him. Another side of her wanted to run away and hide. It was the second half that won out. She felt her control release, and her attack disappeared as Cregorous' red energy hit her.

Falling to the ground, she rolled onto her side and wrapped her arms around her waist.

It felt like something was trying to crawl its way out of her and explode through her bones. Her whole body ached.

She pinched her eyes shut as tears formed. Whatever this pain was, she tried to block it out and get up, but she couldn't find the strength. Was this Cregorous' doing? Could he control her body to send signals of pain throughout her? Could he control her nerves?

Footsteps reached her ears. It seemed like he was circling her.

"Lying down on the job, huh? This wasn't nearly as much fun as I had hoped." He scoffed a laugh. "I even gave you time."

She tried to force the pain back, but all that did was make her want to throw up.

Glancing up at him, she saw him shake his head as he kneeled down next to her. "I expected more from you. What a waste. I could have finished this years ago."

Grasping her hand and forcing her out of the fetal position, he made her look at him, taking hold of her face. "How 'bout this? I give you a minute to figure out whether you want to live or not, and then we try this again. And by then, Tyron will be here, and I can kill him in front of you."

She tugged her face out of his grasp, and he

chuckled as she rolled onto her side again, trying to get to her feet. Her shoes scattered the gravel, unable to get solid footing.

"Maybe that's all the incentive you need—that I'll kill everyone. Which, y'know, you really should know by now it's not beneath *me*."

It felt like her consciousness began to slip away. She heard him sigh angrily.

"Let's try this again later. Maybe you'll be better next time." He kneeled down over her again. "We will *meet* again, Jennifer," he whispered in her ear. His breath smelled sweet, surprisingly, and the scent of his body was intoxicating—musky and sensual and all *male*.

Her eyes fluttered open slightly and, for a second, she felt like time had kind of slowed down.

In her line of vision, she saw another teenager hit the icy ground with a *thud*, his face contorting with pain. Landing on his stomach, he reached his bloody and bruised hands toward the ground and gripped the ice, trying to force himself forward. He had several deep cuts across his face, forcing his blond hair to stick up in a haphazard direction. His grasping, bloody fingers left red marks in the snow.

She reached for him, blue energy pooling into her palm. Fear filled her at the sight of his brokenness, and she ached to help him.

Grimacing as he looked up, it was as though he saw her and reached out for her, too. Straining his fingers, green energy sparked from the digits.

Do you trust me? she heard a voice ask, but the teenage boy's lips didn't move.

Looking back at him, she responded to the voice in her head, *I do.*

Above her, Cregorous was completely unaware of what she saw, and a predatory growl echoed through her. It should have scared her but, for some reason, it didn't.

"I look forward to the day I smite the new Raidin."

With green energy cloaked fingers, the teenage boy grasped her hand and everything went white.

As though Cregorous' utterance of the word alone changed everything, the trembling in her body stopped, her eyes focused, and Jen suddenly sat up and grabbed Cregorous by the neck. He started and gasped in surprise at her iron grip.

In her hand, she exuded a blue glow up to her elbow. The blue energy swept over his body slowly. Her eyes were a rainbow of colors, shifting and changing as the milliseconds went by, as she stared into his face with a stern look.

"The seven united as one." Her voice wasn't just hers. It was loud and sounded like multiple voices in one.

"No," Cregorous strained.

"The righteous are granted redemption," the chorus sang.

"Stop." He gritted his teeth.

"The wicked will meet their demise."

Cregorous grabbed the arm holding his throat, his own red energy fighting back against hers.

Jen seemed unfazed as the chorus of voices continued, "And all shall fall for one."

His eyes were bright red as they glared at her rainbow ones.

A flash of red energy surged up Cregorous' arm, and then he wretched her hand off his neck and she was thrown backward.

Startled, Jen looked up, her hazel eyes confused as she stared up at him.

He looked down at her for a few long seconds as his chest heaved. "No, I won't fall for that again."

Jen furrowed her brow as he quickly turned and ran for the edge of the roof. His wings burst out of his back as he flew straight at the portal. Then the connection disappeared with his retreating form, and the bright white light snapped away.

She sat there for a second, her breathing even and calm, but her mind felt anything but.

What had he meant by saying he wouldn't fall for that again? What made him say that? What was it he wouldn't fall for? How was she sitting up? And why didn't her body hurt anymore? The last thing she could remember was lying on the ground in the fetal position with him hovering over her.

She got up slowly and stared at where the portal had been.

He had run ... from her.

Why?

She was obviously not prepared for an encounter with him. He probably could have killed her if he wanted. He had the chance. Instead, he had toyed with her.

The door behind her was forced open, sounding a loud bang that cut into the silence on the roof. Tyron, harried, with blood all over him and a deep gouge in his left leg, burst through the doorway. His assault rifle was up and ready to fire. As he surveyed the rooftop, he limped forward.

When he reached her, he gently touched her shoulder. "Jen?"

At first, she didn't respond, but then she slowly

turned to face him as she swallowed. They stared at one another for a few seconds, and she tried to look brave, but her jaw trembled.

After a second, he dropped his rifle and pulled her into a tight embrace, cradling her head. He let out a deep sigh of relief. She was alive. Aside from her lack of speaking and the sheer horror he had seen in her eyes, she seemed okay.

She wrapped her arms around his waist and gripped at his shirt. She barely stifled a sob that racked up her throat.

"Hey, shh ... it's okay. I've got you," he whispered. Blinking a few times to get his thoughts focused, he asked, "Are you hurt?"

She shook her head, because, physically, she was fine. Mentally, she was all sorts of not okay. Somewhere on the edge of her being, she was terrified. Not necessarily for the reason that Cregorous had been inches away from her, breathing down her neck, but because of what had happened during the fight inside of her.

She couldn't remember the last bit until he had thrown her back to the ground. The pain she had experienced made a shiver of fear ripple down her spine.

"It's okay," Tyron whispered to her. "It's over. He's gone." He rubbed her back a little, trying to find a way to help her as she buried her face into his chest, hoping that his embrace would bring her comfort.

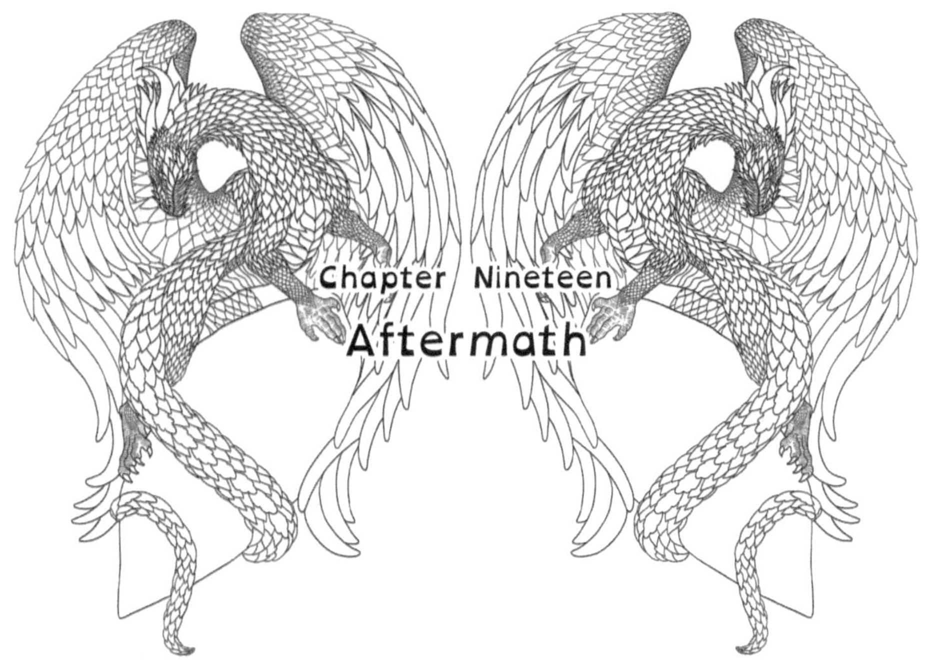

Chapter Nineteen

Aftermath

The school was a *mess*.

Because of the fighting, the entire front entrance was reduced to rubble. The concrete, asphalt, and grass around the front of the school was one giant compost heap of the three ingredients. Ferveos, Preliator, and Scouts lay everywhere among the strewn bodies of bratak'ra, grovix, werewolves, and hybrids. Agerian warriors were few among the dead, but they didn't completely evade casualties.

News vans were trying to rumble over the debris, and people poured out of the school. Even more people ran toward the school, and Jen could only assume they were family members of the students.

There were a few Agerians and grovix that Jen didn't recognize walking around, and a number of Preliators and Scouts were still there, too.

It was a strange sensation walking outside of

what had earlier been a normal-looking entrance to a normal-looking school. Seeing it as it was now, Jen almost couldn't remember what it had once been.

She glanced over at Tyron, who had a protective arm around her shoulders.

He looked over at her and said, "The Caligans retreated pretty quickly after our reinforcements arrived. I don't know where they were heading, but if I had to guess, we really got them scared. Whether or not they saw Cregorous retreat, I don't know."

Jen nodded then blankly stared forward.

Suddenly, a camera was shoved into her face, along with a microphone and a man asking her who she was and if she knew what had happened.

Tyron let go of her shoulders and forcefully shoved the camera back. "Back off," he told the man with the microphone.

Once Tyron's arm was off her shoulders, she just stood there. Shock began to overtake her system, and her hands felt like they were going numb. Her eyes were killing her, and all she wanted to do was go home, crawl into bed in the fetal position, and cry until she fell asleep.

There really wasn't any reason for crying, but somehow, it sounded like a good idea.

A hand hit her back gently, and she nearly shot a foot off the ground.

"Oh! Sorry," Krelien said from behind her, and she turned to see him recoil. "I just ... You okay?"

She wanted to say yes, but she couldn't bring herself to lie. So she just stood there, staring at him.

Pain flashed across Krelien's face, and he grimaced before he gently pulled her into a hug and rubbed her back.

None of her **Zaheri** had ever hugged her before, but she found that she liked it. It felt like a family member trying to patch you back together after a hardship had happened. And after what had just happened, it was a welcome change. To her trembling body, his warmth was comforting.

"I'm sure Ty already said this, but he's gone. It's over. Everything's gonna be fine," Krelien said as he held her.

She nodded, and then he slowly let her go.

Staring down at her, he told her, "I swear to you, it's okay."

Her mouth contorted as she tried to come up with words and eventually settled on saying in a crackling voice, "Thanks, Krelien."

He swallowed then nodded before he stepped away.

Jen took in a deep breath to try to calm herself. Adrenaline had been pumping through her system, but now she felt incredibly cold. Cold and exhausted. The shock was wearing off.

The few trees that weren't overturned or uprooted were on fire, and the firemen attempted to put them out.

She closed her eyes and let out a few slow breaths. It was over. Everything was going to be okay. Krelien and Tyron had promised it would be.

In the distance, the sun passed beyond the horizon, dipping away from sight and only leaving a splash of color across the sky.

Turning toward the school and intending to find Tyron, Jen saw Nancy running toward her.

"Jen!" her sister called and offered a flying hug, slamming into her older sister's body.

A little startled, Jen caught Nancy and stabilized them both.

"Oh *my* gosh! Are you okay? What happened? Are you hurt?" Nancy asked in a flurry.

Disentangling herself from Nancy, Jen asked, "Why would I be hurt?"

Right after the question left her mouth, she realized how stupid that had sounded. She had just been in a battle, after all. And even if Nancy wasn't aware of it, Jen was aware that she had just fought Cregorous.

"You were just in a battle, right?" Nancy asked, flabbergasted.

"Oh, yeah, right," the elder sister said absent-mindedly.

Yet again, she had blood matted in her bangs from the cut across her face when her shield had fallen. And there was dried blood all over her body from cuts that had healed. Despite the fact that she had never bathed so much in her life, she wanted to find a shower, sweatpants, and a baggy shirt.

She just wanted to go home.

Grant stepped up to her and gently eased his hold on the rifle in his grasp. "Are you okay?"

"I'm getting sick of that question." She sucked in a heavy breath and pushed her dirty bangs away.

"That's her! She's the one over there!" a girl screamed.

The teenagers turned to see a girl standing in front of a reporter, pointing at Jen.

If the reporters were seagulls and Jen was a French fry, the reaction would have been the same. A mass of bodies and cameras and microphones surged forward at her.

Jen almost screamed and created a shield around herself. Because that would help.

Thankfully, there wasn't any need for that. Her Zaheri appeared right in front of her and blocked the reporters from getting any closer.

With a glower and a stern voice, Tyron held out his hand and said, "Don't."

Kaldok didn't do anything to even hide himself. Blaze and Archer growled, and their fur bristled as they glared at the mob. They all looked awful, with various injuries adorning their appearances.

"We just wanted to ask the hero some questions. Unless you want to answer them for us?" a reporter from the middle of the crowd said.

Jen furrowed her brow. Her? A hero?

A slew of questions that melded into a slew of noise began to come from the crowd. It was just like on TV when one person was being asked a million and ten different things by different people. The voices rose up in a blast of noise and nothing really stood out.

Her ears began to burn, and she pinched her eyes shut, trying to block it out. Without even thinking what she was doing, Jen began to walk back to the school.

There wasn't any reason to go back there. There wasn't anything there she needed. All she needed was to get away from the noise and the lights and the people.

Grant caught her arm, pulled her against him as he wrapped his arm around her, and guided her back to the school. Nancy came to her other side and took her hand, trying to offer comfort, while Ryan and Aeryn quickly fell into line behind her, trying to figure out how to block Jen's view from the cameras.

Blaze and Archer saw them leave and, with a final growl and huff, turned and walked with the teenagers.

The reporters continued to shout question after question. Tyron clenched his jaw and crossed his arms over his chest. He wasn't going to tell them anything, and neither were the others, not until these humans learned to shut up. Ar'on glared at them all and didn't hide the fact that he still held a sniper rifle in his hands. Kaldok bared his teeth. Krelien did his best to look imposing.

After a moment, the humans began to catch on. They weren't going to get anything out of them that way. The noise died down and was replaced with the soft shuffling of feet and shifting of the cameras on the camera people's shoulders.

Tyron waited for a second then glanced at the others. When he got a nod from Ar'on, he turned back to the reporters. "I'm glad you learned how to shut up. Now, screaming at a scared teenage girl isn't going to get you a story. Don't make us hurt you, because we won't hesitate to do so. Your world almost ended today, and it was only by her decision and our action that it didn't. There are a lot of things you won't understand, and don't expect to. There are also a lot of questions you'll have. We don't plan to give you answers of any sort. Now, we have a lot of work to do, and I expect you to respect us and our privacy. That's all. If you follow us, I will hurt one of you to make an example."

Without another word, the remaining members

of the Alpha Team turned and began to head back to the school.

As they walked away, someone from the huddle called out in a bewildered voice, "Who are you people?"

None of them answered. They walked away, back to the building that they had protected. Back to the Human-Born they were charged to save. Back to the girl who they all were terrified they had lost somewhere in the shuffle.

The crews looked between one another and, surprisingly enough, began to pack up. No more questions were asked. It might have been because they knew Tyron was good on his threat of hurting one of them. But it was more because there was severity in the air around them, more than they were used to, and it made them understand that something important had happened, and one day they would understand what.

Once she passed what would have been the doors of the first floor's main entrance, Jen walked over to the stairs and sat down. Grant let her go, and she was grateful for it. His protective stance had been a welcome action, because at that moment, she didn't want to hear anything more from the people outside. Her friends and family let her be and kept their distance.

Blaze and Archer walked along the broken glass of the doors a second later. The white furred grovix looked at Archer for a brief moment before she walked over to Jen. "Jennifer?" she asked in a soft voice.

The teenager looked to her Zaheri. Her long, white fur was brown from dirt in some places and red from blood in others.

Blaze swallowed before she asked, "Are you all right?"

Jen blinked a few times before she said, "I don't think so, Blaze." She let out a sigh and glanced out the empty frames for what used to be the windows around the stairwell.

The remaining members of her *Zaheri* were on their way to the building, and the camera crews were packing up in the distance.

Turning to look back at Blaze, Jen said, "But I will be."

The car ride had been quiet. Jon drove, occasionally shooting his eyes to the rearview mirror. Jen huddled in his back seat next to Nancy.

After the noise of everything had died down, Jen had abruptly run to the locker room and showered. The clothes she had on now were baggy, and the jacket she wore was Krelien's. Nancy sat next to her older sister, just holding her hand.

When they pulled up to her house, Jon walked in first. Jen's parents lunged forward, asking what had happened, a barrage of concern pouring from their mouths. Jon held his hands out, keeping them at bay, and began to answer questions, telling them that Jen needed to rest and he needed to talk to them.

Her parents broke past him and hugged the sisters, saying that they loved them and they were so happy they were okay.

They didn't know.

As they stepped back from their group hug, Jen looked back at them and then focused loosely on Jon. "Can you tell them?"

Jon nodded, and her parents stared at her in question.

Without another word, Jen turned and walked up the stairs. She moved almost as though she were aimless, her steps slow and groggy. As she left the family, she could hear Jon and Nancy starting to tell her parents and brother what had happened.

She focused on her heartbeat and drowned out the world. Her shower at the school had been hasty, just to get the blood off, so she showered again. After dressing in her most comfortable pajamas, she threw the oversized clothes away, shoving them into the small trash can in the bathroom. The sleeves of the shirt overflowed, the length running down to the floor.

Thankfully, she made it back to her room before the conversation downstairs ended. She shut the door and, for the first time in her life, locked it. Then she went to her window to make sure it was shut then locked that, too. As she crawled into bed, she pulled the blankets around her like a cocoon and buried her face into the fabric. Then she cried until she fell asleep.

Her nightmare came fairly quickly. A part of her felt it was so cliché, but she was running, nonetheless. Her legs felt like they were cement, barely moving at all. As she stumbled forward, she turned and raised a shield. It might as well not have been there as he came crashing through it. Blackness cloaked his wings, and red energy sparked from his eyes.

He landed on top of her, laughing as she screamed. She didn't know how, but she knew all the same that he had already killed her Zaheri. Jen cried for them, anyway.

Cregorous held her hands in his and straddled her, grinning like a monster as she struggled against him. "What's the matter, Raidin?" he asked through his laughing. "Can't you handle this? I thought you were a hero!"

"No! Get off of me!" she cried, trying to break his hold. It sounded like the world around her was on fire. His body was heavy on top of hers, his grip unrelenting.

"Shh, shh, shh, now. C'mon," he cooed, letting his weight pin her to the ground. "This'll be fun. Just you and me, the way it's meant to be." The world went silent, and she suddenly looked right at him as he said, "Alaster will be next."

Abruptly, it felt like she got pulled away. Strong hands held her, and a protective, victorious roar filled her ears. Cregorous got blown backward, and she felt herself in a comforting embrace. Though she saw nothing, the arms holding her felt steady as a voice said, "It's okay. I've got you."

Despite the peace that flooded her with that final image, she still awoke with a start. Her heart hammered against her chest, and she found herself gasping. Her hands trembled as she suddenly felt she was suffocating, and she pulled the blankets from around her, trying to find air.

A hand came down on hers, and she looked up to see Krelien's bleary eyes staring at hers.

"Hey, hey, calm down. It's okay. It's me," he whispered.

Her breathing still ragged, Jen asked, "Krelien?"

He crouched next to her bed as she sat on the edge of the mattress. Gently, he cupped her cheek and wiped away the tears that rolled down her face. "Yeah, Ty asked me to stay the night; make sure you had someone here watching over you. The doors were locked."

Saying nothing, she fell forward and hugged him, clutching his shirt. Her trembling didn't go unnoticed by him as he rubbed her back.

"That excited to see me, huh? I didn't think I had that effect on people," he joked. "Usually when I show up out of nowhere, I get screamed at."

Smiling for the first time that night, Jen asked, "What's Ar'on usually say?"

Thankful that his joking was helping her, he answered, "I hate you. Get out of my way."

Jen disentangled herself and sat back a little, wrapping a blanket around herself. "That's not very nice of him." She sniffled back her remaining tears and wiped her eyes.

Sitting back on his haunches, Krelien replied, "He's always mean. I think he's got a stick up his nose."

She let out a small laugh. "I'm not gonna correct you on that." She took a deep breath, steadying herself. "Is everything okay?"

"You let us worry about that," Krelien said, his expression growing serious. She wasn't used to seeing that side of him. "Everything's fine. You need to sleep."

Jen wanted to ask him where Tyron was, if everyone else was okay. The whole ride home was a blur. After everything seemed to wrap up, Tyron had put her in the car and sent her off with Jon, but she couldn't really remember if she had checked to make sure all of her Zaheri were okay. Had any of them been injured badly?

"Get some sleep," Krelien said as he got up. Then, walking to the end of her bed, he sat down and rested his back against the ottoman that she had at the footboard. A blanket hit him, and he chuckled before wrapping it around himself and getting comfortable.

For a few seconds, silence passed, and then Jen whispered, "Thanks for being here, Krelien."

He smiled to himself and let out a short sigh before answering, "Anytime, kid."

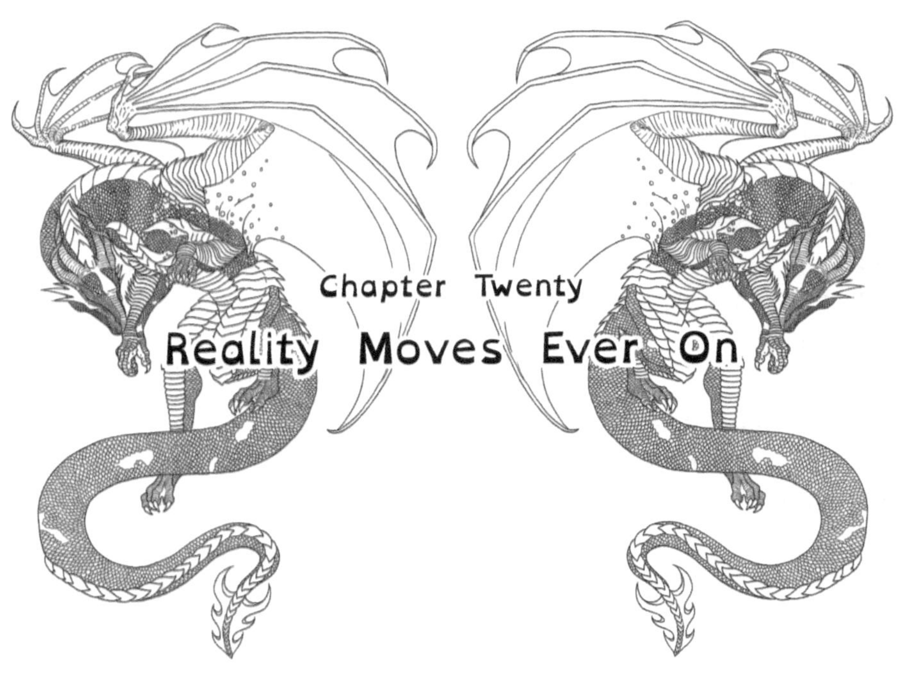

Chapter Twenty

Reality Moves Ever On

The school had been closed for three months, with several classes and activities canceled for the spring semester.

Most classes were wrapped up via online tests and assignments. Unfortunately, it took the district a couple weeks to get a functioning network up and running that could sustain the student population. The school board wound up treating the downed network as an "Early Thanksgiving Break."

That was probably the only good thing about when the attacks happened—there had already been two weeks scheduled for students and staff to be out of the building with Thanksgiving and Christmas coming up. It helped with the red tape of it all and didn't require too much remodeling of class requirements from the teachers.

Repairs to the building took much longer than

everyone had hoped. The weather snapped cold a couple days after the attack and refused to get any warmer, which meant that the concrete, window, and tile work required to get the school back to semi-functioning wasn't possible. With the building deemed unsafe, students had to start their spring semester online.

The best everyone could tell, it wasn't affecting the academics too much, so everyone just kind of crossed their fingers and prayed that they wouldn't have an influx of students flunking their classes. That didn't stop teachers from shortening their curriculums just in case.

Most of the parents were able to adapt to the change. A few "blew a gasket," as Jon had phrased it. He was able to negotiate with one of the community colleges to open up their classrooms for some of the freshman classes. They seemed to be the age group most parents were worried about leaving alone all day. Jon found it infuriating but was grateful for the help of other administrations to lend a hand.

Insurance companies were backlogged. The whole county had been labeled a "catastrophic zone." Nearly all the cars on campus that day had been crushed or destroyed in some way. There were a few houses that were impacted from the few Ferveos that had gotten loose.

Thankfully, though, the Air Force had been quick to annihilate those threats. A few F-15s were taken out in the process, and it took the military a few tries to get something strong enough to actually kill the dragons. Injuries had been reported, but no casualties. At least, no casualties that could be directly linked to the attack.

As the numbers of injuries came in over the course of her time at home, Jen became ever more thankful that she had made the second shield to lock the Caligans in place. While yes, it had caused additional damage to the school and personal property of cars in the parking lot, it had kept people safe.

Meanwhile, in Jen's world, things had been a little ... chaotic.

After a fitful night of sleep with Krelien keeping a watchful eye for any potential retaliation from the Caligans, Jen had to face her parents. Jon had come back to run interference and to talk up how well Jen had done in responsibly handling the situation.

There was no denying, though, that Krelien's presence coming out of Jen's bedroom the following morning made her parents, especially her dad, nearly assault the Jumper. And, as Krelien wasn't one to enjoy conflict, he quite legitimately ran away from the problem and left Jen on her own. Tyron nearly skinned him before showing up at the front door, requesting to explain himself.

The following day had been filled with a lengthy discussion, with Jen's parents asking her to leave on several occasions so they could discuss with Tyron and Jon some "sensitive things." Around nine o'clock at night, her parents had embraced her and said they were happy she was okay and proud of her for everything she had done.

That support wasn't the only thing she had gotten from her parents, though. A stern talking to about lying to them and not coming forward earlier had been drawn out throughout the day. Her mom must have asked ten times, "Why didn't you just come to us?"

How could I? Hey, guys, I'm part dragon for some unknown reason, and here's all the stuff I can do. And, oh yeah, I need to go save another world, okay, I love you. Bye-bye, Jen thought.

What she actually said was, "I'm sorry."

Ar'on and Tyron had gone through the details of her training that she had already been through and what they planned to teach her next. Kaldok had introduced himself and, after Nancy vouched for him, explained what sort of dangers Jen had faced and why the training was important. Blaze had been able to appeal to them with a calm, nurturing tone, while Archer had been able to regale stories to prove that Jen was not only in good hands but that she was quite capable of defending herself. Krelien had nodded off several times.

The Alpha Team had been able to bring comfort to Jen's *mom,* but her dad and brother were a different story. Both of them would ask question after question, constantly judging the loyalty the Alpha Team had to Jen and if they truly would protect her. If she hadn't been so weary, Jen might have argued with them and told them to be quiet because they didn't know what they were talking about.

In actuality, Jen had been fairly mute throughout the day's conversation, only piping in when she felt it was absolutely necessary. After everything she had been through the day prior, she hadn't really had the strength or desire to do any more talking than needed.

Once the resolution to the school's closing was announced, Jen and Nancy had set up a makeshift schoolwork area in the family living room. Meanwhile,

Ar'on and Tyron, at the behest of Jen's dad, had converted the basement into their training area.

At first, Tyron had been adamant that they already had a facility set up at the antique store. However, her dad had insisted, stating that if his daughter was going to be learning how to defend herself, he should, too.

So, about a week after the attack, Ar'on had begun training Chip and her dad as Tyron resumed her training. Things had been going well for a few weeks until Chip accidentally skewered the washing machine when he lost his grip on his practice sword. Mrs. Monroe called for all training to be suspended until further notice. Then Kaldok had shown up with fresh blueberry muffins and scones and all was suddenly forgiven.

The Alpha Team continued to monitor for any Caligan activity and were a little alarmed to find that nothing else happened. While they were grateful for the break, it made them wary of what was on the horizon. There were some reports across the world of various attacks, but it was difficult to determine the exact location of each instance. Jen helped them narrow the focus and did some research, which included watching several news broadcasts in other languages.

Eventually, they were able to get the town names where each "pillar of light" had appeared. The only problem they found was that, depending on the source, the number of locations ranged from nine to eighteen towns or cities. Two of the cities they had found were Sydney, Australia and Tokyo, Japan.

"Yeah, this won't be difficult at all. They're just massive cities with hundreds of districts and sub-urbs. No problem," Jen had muttered.

Tyron had been back to Tilion since the attack and had received confirmation that all the Human-Borns and Zaheri had survived. Some of them weren't exactly whole, and there were many reports of Defense casualties from the reinforcements. All in all, though, it sounded as though the Council had selected the right people to protect and defend the Human-Borns.

A few days after the school had been closed, phone calls and news vans had begun to arrive and bombard the family with questions. After a week or so of harassment, the team had begun to come up with ideas on how to get the news people to go away.

Ar'on had suggested shooting someone as an example. When that was politely rejected, Blaze had suggested igniting one of their vans. The two of them were then immediately dismissed from the conversation but both parties chose to ignore that. Krelien had thought ignoring them would work, and Kaldok hadn't wanted to offer an opinion, because he knew once he got on camera, someone might try to cast him for one of the many werewolf movies being produced. He was already mad enough about how Hollywood romanticized his curse. The last thing he wanted was more attention.

Tyron eventually settled on throwing someone at them. Quite literally.

Somewhere around mid-afternoon one day, a gaggle of reporters had been banging on the doors, screaming for someone to come out and answer their questions. So, Tyron had given them someone.

That someone had been Krelien.

At first, Krelien hadn't wanted to do it...until

the reporters had swarmed on him and cameras had been pointed at him and microphones had been shoved in his face. Almost instantly, Krelien had found that he loved being the center of attention, which hadn't been a shock to anyone.

They asked who had attacked, and Krelien responded with, "A bad guy."

Where did they come from? someone else asked.

"**Space?**" he replied.

Who was the girl?

"**What girl?**"

Who was he?

"I'm Krelien."

But who are you?

"I'm a Jumper."

What's that?

"It makes me special."

Why?

"I'm bored."

And so the conversation eventually devolved into the equivalent of several two-year-olds arguing over what color the sky should be. A microphone got thrown at him. He wound up throwing it back. Then someone's glasses got broken.

The important thing was that they had left and never came back.

As the day to return to school grew closer and the end of February loomed on the calendar, Jen began wishing they would just announce her as a graduate on merit's sake. She had no desire to go back to school and face her classmates. Her friends had been frequent visitors during the school closure, which had helped her remain a little grounded in the "normal" of life. That didn't mean she was ready to go back and pretend like she could just sit in classes as though nothing had ever happened. Nevertheless, that morning came, whether Jen wanted it to or not.

Her car had been transformed into a twisted pile of metal from her stunt, so she and her dad had picked out a new used car for her. Because her car had been so old, they hadn't gotten quite enough money to cover for a good used car, yet they had found one comparable, and Jen had wound up with a Toyota Camry. She promptly named it Walter.

Jen and Nancy left for school, like they always had. Things were normal up until they reached the campus. The mass of news vans that had once sat outside their house were now around the school.

Putting the car in park, Jen sighed as she looked outside.

Nancy looked over at her and asked, "Are you ready for this?"

"No." Jen grimaced as she looked at the swarm of people whom she would have to get through. If she had been thinking, she would have asked Krelien to come along and jump them into the school to avoid the chaos. However, he wasn't there, and Jen couldn't fly in either. It would be just as bad. Taking a deep breath, she took hold of the door handle and said, "C'mon; let's get this over with."

The sisters were able to make it across the parking lot with relative ease. A few people around them would stop and stare, but no one really said anything.

It wasn't until they got down to the first tier and near the news vans that things got worse. Cameras surged forward, microphones were shoved in their faces, and questions were hurtled at them. Flashes went off all around them from photographers.

Gritting her teeth, Jen grabbed Nancy by the arm. "Don't make me get my Zaheri."

There wasn't any way to know if these people were the same reporters from the day of the attacks or from the mob outside her house. Regardless, they seemed to register that threat and backed off.

The sisters pushed their way forward through the horde and made their way inside. Once they entered, though, things got weird quickly.

Jen glanced behind them and out the doors as they entered then stopped abruptly when she ran into Nancy. Turning to stare inside the building, Jen saw everyone near them stop in their tracks and look at her. Teachers, students, and staff were stilling mid-step to do nothing more than stare.

It was tense for a few seconds before Jen asked, "Well? What are you waiting for?"

No one moved or said anything.

Nancy turned to her, and Jen swallowed before she said quietly to her sister, "I'll see you later." Forcing her way past idle people and trying desperately to avoid the watchful eyes of her peers, Jen made her way to her locker. She spent no more than a few seconds there when Ryan showed up.

Homeroom was, to say the least, awkward. Jen couldn't run and hide and had to sit there. Her teacher kept staring at her and muttering how grateful he was that she had saved them, so she couldn't just turn around and ignore him.

"Shut up, shut up, shut up," Aeryn muttered behind her, over and over again, trying to will their homeroom teacher to stop.

Jen wished that was all it would take to end the misery of her situation.

The moment the bell rang, she and Aeryn practically ran to their next class, only to be met with more awkwardness.

Entertainingly, after their second class of people staring at Jen, Aeryn burst, "Would you leave her alone?"

But this was Jennifer Monroe, the girl who was part dragon and had the most gorgeous men on the planet to hang out with. She was this great warrior who had stopped some army from killing everyone.

It was a lot to live up to.

Rick had asked her to autograph his shirt. Other kids who she had never even spoken to were asking her advice on things. Girls who she didn't know would ask her for dating advice and her opinions on clothes and hair styles. It was more than she wanted ever.

Suddenly, she was a celebrity.

At lunch, when a swarm of students tried to overwhelm her, Ryan had to push his way through and said, "Yeah, yeah, I know, she's awesome. Well, guess what? I was friends with her before it was cool to be friends with her. Leave!"

Grant and Ryan were like her personal bodyguards, occasionally screaming at people to go away. In hindsight, perhaps this was funny. At the moment, however, it irritated her to no end. She hadn't asked for this after all. It had just happened. She would have loved anything to go back to being invisible to her fellow students.

At the end of lunch, she was approached by a teacher to report to the principal's office. She was thankful for it. It meant she could avoid more weirdness.

She walked into Jon's office and flopped down into the chair, letting her backpack hit the floor next to her.

Jon looked at her from across the desk. "Rough day?"

"Not the worst, but it's like I'm freaking Gandhi or something. Everyone wants to talk to *me*," she said with a dejected look.

He raised his eyebrows slightly. "Well, some of them have deals with newspapers to get a story. Others are just curious. And some are just busy-bodies. Try not to let it bother you."

Sitting up a bit, she said, "I feel like everyone's waiting for me to scream, 'Dragon'."

He inclined his head slightly. "In a way, they are. You're a hero, Jen."

She rolled her eyes.

"Granted, not everyone sees you as such, but that is what you are," he continued.

"I feel like a freak," she said as she looked at the floor. "I know it's because I *am* a freak, but I don't like everyone staring at me like I'm a freak. It just accentuates the freakiness of it."

"You aren't a freak," he said tiredly.

She threw him a doubtful look.

He darted his eyes around the room. "You're just ... different."

With a groan, she threw her head back to rest on the chair and stared at the ceiling.

"Jen, come on; you were perfectly fine three months ago when dragons were outside. What's changed?"

"What's changed?" she asked the ceiling. Then she sat up and looked back at Jon. "Everything's changed! I mean, I had an FBI guy come to my house a month back and ask me questions. He looked like David Boreanaz, so it wasn't absolutely horrible, but it was still as if he was trying to say, 'Hey, kid, you're a freakshow, and the government wouldn't mind doing experiments on you'."

"He looked like who?"

"And meanwhile, every time anyone leaves my house, they're bombarded by neighbors or reporters or nut-jobs asking them questions like we're suddenly going to tell them everything."

Furrowing his brow, he asked, "You know every-thing?"

"I know nothing!" Jen shouted. "I'm basically a glorified host of a TV show. I don't actually know anything. I just happen to possibly know people who may possibly know everything."

Jon was silent for a moment before he sighed. "I'm confused."

"That makes two of us."

"Look," he said with a slight shake of his head, "I can't say that everything's gonna be okay. I wish I could, but I can't. And you have to deal with the fact that everything has changed. Yes, people are looking at you funny now, but remember, it is high school. Give it a week, and no one's going to care."

She furrowed her brow. "Is that supposed to comfort me?"

Annoyed, he said, "Deal with it, okay? You'll be fine. You've been through worse. I've seen you go through worse. Yes, it's awkward now, but things will get better."

"That's doubtful," she said quietly. When he looked back at her, she said with a heavy sigh, "It's Cregorous. He's been like ... I don't know. Apparently, there's been nothing going on in Caliga from what the Agerians can tell. They think maybe he's gone."

"Gone?"

"Yeah. The Council said that, after he went through the portal, he shot right back to Caliga, and no one's seen or heard anything. So, he's still out there somewhere, plotting my demise."

His shoulders slumped. "He may be doing just that, but you've got three men, a werewolf, and two Grofit—"

"Grovix," Jen corrected.

"—looking out for you," he continued without worrying about the correction. "I'd be feeling relatively safe if I were you."

"And I do feel safe. It's just like there's this black cloud following me, waiting to become a thunderstorm."

"Let's try for optimism here, Jen." He tried to sound encouraging.

She plastered a fake smile on her face and said with false exuberance, "Okay!"

"Hang in there, Jen. You'll make it through this, I promise."

Dropping her mocking expression, she sighed. The two sat in silence for a few seconds before she asked, "So, what'd you call me down here for?"

"I just wanted to check up on you. You know, make sure no one's bothering you too much, see how the first day back is. That kind of stuff."

"Well, I appreciate it"—she gathered her backpack from the floor—"but I really should be going. The last thing I need is to miss something in class. Although, this has been a little nice, just being me and not worrying about a million people's eyes on me."

Jon stood, as well. "I just wanted to make sure you were doing all right. How's Nancy?"

"I don't see her throughout the day," Jen said with a shrug and a frown. "She's the one you should have called down here. She doesn't do well with people talking at her all day long, especially with the situation as crazy as it already is."

He nodded, and she began to leave the room.

When she reached the door, she turned. "Thanks, Jon. I do appreciate the checkup."

"No problem," he said with a small grin. "It was the least I could do."

Tapping the doorframe, Jen said, "Right, well, I'll see you later."

Jon continued to stand there as she left the room to head back to class, and as he stood there, he wondered whether he was right about things eventually blowing over. For most things with the American population, it seemed like people forgot stuff quickly. He hoped this would be one of those things.

Then again, it had been three months, and everyone was still hyped up about it. With a sigh, he reached down and picked up the phone. If Jen was right, Nancy might need a break from the insanity, too.

The remainder of Jen's day was similar to how it had previously gone. Choir was fairly relaxing, and Jen was glad it had been the end of her day with Mr. Mosser constantly yelling at everyone to stop staring. Still, it didn't matter that much, because regardless of where she was, she constantly felt eyes on her. She tried her best to ignore the stares and move on.

Things were quiet, and hopefully because of that, maybe Jon would be right. Things could blow over without further complications.

As the day finally came to a close, Jen gratefully picked up her backpack and walked out of the choir room with Aeryn, on their way to their lockers.

"So, how's it been today? Really?"

Jen shrugged. "As good as I could imagine, I suppose. A lot of the same. People asking questions and such. What I wasn't expecting was everyone wanting my opinion and advice."

"You make it sound like you don't give good advice," Aeryn said as they reached their lockers, which were a few apart from one another.

"It's not that I feel like I don't give good advice; it's more of that I never really saw myself as the kind of person who the vast majority of people would want to get advice from." She reached into her locker and pulled out a few books as she then removed ones she didn't need from the backpack at her feet.

The *clip clop* of heels made the two of them look over their shoulders to see Evelyn with two of her cohorts flanking her. The other two girls twirled their hair, and Evelyn stood with a hip popped out and her arms crossed over her chest.

"You must be loving this attention, huh?" Evelyn asked snidely.

Turning back to her locker, Jen slowly closed it before turning back to face Evelyn. She was about to say something when Aeryn slammed her locker door shut and said, "You should be thanking her, Evelyn. She did save your life three months ago."

"Oh, it speaks," Evelyn said.

Aeryn's face contorted in frustration.

"Leave her alone Evelyn," Jen said wearily. "She's not the one you're miffed at."

"I just hope you're happy," Evelyn said with narrow eyes. "Thanks to you and your little Tom boyish actions, you're more popular than I am."

A chuckle came from Jen. "And that's all that matters, right?"

"It won't last. Everyone will remember that you're just some freak, and you'll go back to being invisible."

"Y'know, I can't wait for that day."

Evelyn shrugged. "You can make that happen a whole lot faster if you just leave and never come back. It's not like you belong here with the rest of us normal people."

The entourage behind Evelyn laughed snidely at Jen, and Aeryn looked like she was going to pop a vein.

For half a second, Jen thought about telling Eve-lyn off. She thought about fighting back and flinging some equally stinging words at the girl in front of her. However, though she had tried to ignore it for the past few months, there was still that quiet voice in her mind. The voice that had pushed Cregorous away from her thoughts. And something in that voice told her not to be angry at Evelyn.

Jen gently grabbed Aeryn's arm as her small friend began to step forward. Then, meeting Evelyn's eyes, Jen said, "You have a choice."

With a scoff, Evelyn asked, "What?"

"You have a choice," Jen reiterated. "You can either be a product of the world you see, you can be what you think you have to be—what they tell you to be—or you can do the right thing. You can stand for the right thing. And if you don't, then I feel sorry for you. Because you'll only be hurting yourself."

There was silence as Evelyn stared at Jen incredulously before saying, "What the hell are you talking about, Monroe?"

Jen's shoulders drooped a little. "Apparently, nothing you understand." She picked up her backpack. "Goodbye, Evelyn." Without waiting another second, Jen walked away.

Aeryn quickly fell into step with her. "Where did that come from?"

"I'm not really sure," Jen said without meeting Aeryn's gaze. "I just ... I feel like there's something wrong in her life, and me fighting back won't help."

"But she's been a witch with a capital B to you for ... ever," Aeryn countered.

"Yeah, I know, but..." Jen glanced over her shoulder. She could hear Evelyn going off about how crazy Jen was, how it was only a matter of time before the government locked her up, how no one was ever going to like her. The entourage laughed. Jen shook her head. "What's it matter? It's only high school."

"We don't graduate for three more months," Aeryn replied.

Jen shrugged. "I'd rather spend that three months worrying about the things that matter."

Three months.

It would be over before she knew it.

Chapter Twenty-One
The British are Calling

The antique shop was still and quiet. Shelves of items filled the store. To the right, a small counter with a cash register sat near a large window. An open area was just past the door, and to the left was a large bookcase that sat next to a gun rack. In the back left corner, a staircase could be seen, and halfway down the right wall was a doorway. Krelien leaned over the counter, perusing a magazine.

The small bell on the door chimed as a man walked in. Seeing Krelien behind the counter, he walked up to him. "Hi there."

The Jumper didn't respond, and instead just flipped to the next page in the magazine.

A little confused, the customer asked a bit louder, "Hey, can I get some help?"

"I dunno, can you?" Krelien asked without looking up.

Thinking Krelien was joking, the man chuckled. "I'm looking for an antique pocket watch. You know, one you can wind and see the gears and all."

"We don't have any," Krelien responded without taking his eyes off the page.

Now frustrated, the man said, "Hey, are you gonna look at me?"

With a sigh, Krelien straightened. "If I have to. What'd you want?"

"A pocket watch."

"We don't have any," the Jumper repeated. He reached down to grab the magazine, but the customer snatched it away.

"How do you know? You haven't even looked."

"I know because I would never carry something so stupid as a pocket watch in this place. I sell things, like, oh, I dunno, guns." He pulled an old revolver from under the counter.

The man instantly threw his hands in the air and whelped in terror.

Looking bored, Krelien said, "It's not loaded." He put the gun down before swiping the magazine out of the customer's hand.

A little shaken, the man said, "Well, do you know where I could go to get a pocket watch?"

Krelien's shoulders slumped, surprised the man was still there. "No."

"Look, you just ignored me, didn't help me, and then you pulled a gun on me."

"I didn't pull a gun on you. I pulled a gun out," Krelien said dryly.

"The least you could do is point me in the right direction to find a pocket watch," the man said angrily.

"Oh, is that all?" Krelien pointed to the door. "There ya go. Pointing in the right direction."

The man looked dumbstruck but didn't want to deal with Krelien anymore, so the customer turned to make his way out of the building.

"That's right, buddy, keep walking. You're not nearly far enough away."

The man glared at Krelien as he exited the shop and stormed off.

The moment the customer was gone, Krelien smiled and went back to the magazine.

A second later, Ar'on walked into the room and glanced at Krelien. "Did I just hear the bells from the door?"

"No, it was a figment of your imagination. Maybe you're going senile," Krelien said as he tried to find his place in the magazine.

Ar'on walked up next to the Jumper and ripped the paper away from him.

"Hey! I was reading that!"

"Not anymore. Krelien, why are you finding it so much fun to terrorize and run our customers out of here?" Ar'on asked as he rolled the magazine up.

Krelien put his hands down on the counter. "If you must know, I'm doing a case study on the human condition."

Ar'on smacked Krelien's hand with the rolled-up magazine.

"Ow!" Krelien yelled and quickly brought his hand up and held it. "What'd you do that for?"

"You're lying, you blasted idiot. Why are you finding enjoyment in terrorizing our customers?"

"We don't need them! I mean, we don't really need money! The Council gives us everything we need." Ar'on raised his hand again to smack Krelien, and the Jumper quickly said, "Fine! Okay! I enjoy seeing their reactions! Just don't hit me again!"

Ar'on threw the magazine into a nearby trash can. "This explains why you couldn't keep your jobs."

"Look who's talking. If you think I'm weird for enjoying randomly hitting people, then you should take a look in the glass. Geeze, did you have to hit me so hard?" He held his hand and looked at it to see if it had started bleeding.

"You have to learn somehow," Ar'on said. "And I didn't hit you that hard, you runt."

Shooting his head up, Krelien pointed at the older hybrid. "I'm telling Tyron you're abusing me."

"Who's abusing who?" Tyron asked as he walked into the room, carrying an old shotgun.

"He is!" the two said simultaneously, pointing at one another.

Tyron looked between the two team members and shook his head as he placed the shotgun on a stand. "This is precisely why I can't leave you two alone."

The sound of a car rolling over gravel came from the rear of the building.

"That's Jen. Now, I want you two to knock it off. The last thing we need is her learning all of your bad habits," the Team Leader said before walking into the back room that he had just come from.

Krelien and Ar'on stared at one another before Krelien said, "You know, you continually tell me I act immature for my age, but you act the same way. Maybe there's something wrong with this photocopy."

"Or maybe I should just punch you until you can't talk for a week," Ar'on shot back as he walked off after Tyron.

"Let's not and say we did," Krelien said to himself as he followed them to greet Jen.

The back door was opened, and Jen walked in carrying two large *pizza* boxes.

As she closed the door and walked a few feet into the room, Krelien said, "Jen! Hey, so how was your first day back?"

Jen looked up from the pizza boxes and started to hand them to Tyron, to whom she said, "He's way too happy to see me. Is he in trouble?"

Tyron glanced to Krelien and shrugged. "Only as much as he normally is." He took the boxes from her. "Seriously, though, how was the day?"

She sat down as Krelien took a seat next to her and Tyron set the pizzas on the table. "Okay, I guess. I wasn't prepared for everyone suddenly wanting to be *my* friend. It's gonna take some getting used to."

Opening one of the boxes, the three hybrids grabbed a slice each as Tyron said, "Well, I guess it'll take everyone some time to get used to the way things are. But otherwise, no major problems?"

"Not really," Jen said with a shake of her head.

A loud yawn came from the shop and, a second later, Kaldok walked into the room. His ears were drooped, and his eyes half-lidded. He wore baggy pants that appeared to have been custom made, his fur sticking in all directions across his furry chest. "Morning. I smelled food. What's to eat?"

"'Morning'?" Jen asked. "It's three in the afternoon."

With a bemused smile, Kaldok said, "Werewolf, remember? I'm nocturnal."

"How's Jon doing with everything?" Tyron asked.

She shrugged. "Okay. He was handling things better than I was. I don't know why, but it just unnerves me to have everyone trying to talk at me."

"Don't you mean talk to you?" Krelien asked through a mouthful of pizza.

Jen shook her head. "No, I mean talk at you. You know, when someone's talking to you, but they don't have any reason behind it. They just want to talk for the sake of hearing their own voice. That kind of thing. Talking at you rather than with you."

Krelien thought for a second before he pointed to Ar'on. "You mean, like he does to me?"

She smiled and shook her head as no one answered.

Kaldok then asked, "Where're Archer and Blaze?"

"Agerius. Archer had to check in with the Beta, and Blaze was requested to speak with Aros," Tyron answered.

"Who's Aros?" Jen asked.

"He's one of our Council members. And she requested to speak with him, not the other way around," Ar'on corrected.

Ignoring Ar'on's comment, Tyron pointed to Jen. "Could you ask your parents if it's all right for Archer to stick with you? I'd like him to be nearby, you know, just in case."

"Sure. Can he sleep with me?" Jen asked as she perked up.

Tyron furrowed his brow. "Um ... why?"

"Well, he's basically a huge dog, right?"

"If you want to dumb it down like that," Kaldok said.

"Then he'll be a heater on these frigid nights. I could use that. My feet always get cold."

Staring at his pizza, Krelien said, "That kinda sounds weird."

"Well, so's your face," Jen retorted. Krelien looked over at her, and she said, "Sorry, it's a stupid phrase humans use as an insult. Forget I ever said it."

"Good luck with that," Kaldok said as Krelien grinned.

Tyron shot Jen a look. "You really need to stop teaching him these things."

"Oh, he knows more annoying things other than what I've taught him," Jen said with a dismissive wave of her hand.

"Not really," Ar'on grumbled.

When Jen looked to Kaldok for confirmation, the werewolf shrugged and pointed to Ar'on. "You'd have to ask him. He's the one who seems to get annoyed by it the most."

"I do not," Ar'on said as he scrunched his face.

"That's a lie. Your pants should fall off," Krelien said.

Jen started laughing.

Throwing Jen an incredulous look, Ar'on spat, "This is far more annoying than anything else I've ever had to put up with. I would take ten children over him any day."

"Until you realize they can't talk," Krelien said. "Then you'd miss me."

"I doubt that," Ar'on shot back.

Trying to ignore the present conversation, Jen asked, "Random question; have you guys heard any-thing from any of the other Zaheri?"

"Thank you for bringing that up," Tyron said as he set his pizza down and rubbed his hands together to clean them a bit. "We heard back from the Zaheri leading up the Beta Team."

"Great. So, where are they?" Jen asked, intrigued.

With a small grimace, Tyron said, "Looks like they're the ones in England. I know that right now you're in the middle of school, and technically, the other kids should be, too, but—"

"It would be best to meet sooner rather than later," Jen finished for him.

Tyron looked around at the team. "C'mon; I think it's best to talk alone right now. Ar'on, watch the front of the store. Krelien, Kaldok, head on down to the basement and apprise me of any situations."

Following everyone else's lead, Jen got to her feet and followed after Tyron. She had never seen the rest of the building, aside from the first floor and training room. So, as he walked to the stairway in the back corner, she was a little intrigued to see what else was in the shop.

Reaching the second floor, she found a long, straight hallway that nearly ran the length of the building. There were two doors to the right (both opened a little, revealing bathrooms), and they passed three doors on her left before reaching a fourth. Tyron walked in, and she entered to see a small sitting room with a set of double doors off to the left.

Her Zaheri pointed to the couch. "You have, what? Three months left of school?"

"Something like that, yeah. Why?" she asked as she sat down.

"Well, the thing of it is, we haven't been able to make contact with any of the other Zaheri."

"Since when?"

Glancing toward the ceiling, Tyron said, "Technically, since we left Tilion."

They stared at one another for a few seconds before she said, "You haven't spoken to any of them in eighteen years?"

"We weren't supposed to know where any of the other Human-Borns were. And, to be fair, we had our hands full with you."

"What's that supposed to mean?"

"Nothing. It's a point. We were all busy protecting the Human-Born we were charged to keep safe. They didn't want all of us knowing where everyone else was."

"But, why? What's the harm in that?" Jen asked. Then she sat back a little and said, "Wait a second—back on the day of the attack, Ar'on said there was talk that someone was feeding Cregorous information."

Tyron wrung his hands. "That's what he said, yes."

"So, how would this someone know where all of us were?"

He looked around and tried a few times to start his response. Then he landed on, "The rumors are... just rumors right now. The Council doesn't see any validity in it."

"But, why? I thought they were, like, super concerned about us."

He held his hand out toward her. "And they are, but ..." His gaze searched the wall before he sighed. "Jen, you have to understand; Agerians aren't ..." He grimaced. "There's no good way to put this. We aren't human. We aren't prone to lying, or cheating, or stealing, or anything that seems to run rampant here on Earth. To question the loyalty of an Agerian is ..."

"Impossible," Jen guessed, and he nodded. Her

shoulders drooped a little. "Okay, so they aren't concerned at all that Cregorous knew where we were and could target us?"

Wincing a little, he said, "Remember, there's strong evidence that he's a Sensor."

"So, they're just lumping this all into the he-can-find-them-whenever category."

"Pretty much."

She was quiet for a moment before sitting forward and saying, "But he hasn't done anything since." When Tyron said nothing, she continued, "You're worried about that, aren't you?"

"He's never sat still this long. Even after you all were born, his army still raided Agerius. It's never been this quiet. It's like ... everything's stopped."

"And ...?"

Tyron sighed. "And ... I think we need to get you connected to the Human-Borns."

Jen half-shrugged. "Okay, fine. What's that mean? We start an excursion across the world to find the others? 'Cause, remember, two of them might be in cities. Large, heavily populated cities. It's not like we can just start slapping posters around town, asking for the Human-Born to please stand up."

He nodded. "I know that."

"So ... what're you thinking?"

"Well, we do have an idea for where most of them are," Tyron said. "And, when Archer was back in Agerius a few weeks ago, he ran into the grovix from the Beta Team. Like I said, they're the ones located in England, somewhere north of London. This grovix—at least Archer thinks—let on that things aren't going well."

"Aren't going well how?"

"I'm not sure, but Archer made it sound like the second Human-Born might be in danger somehow."

It felt like Jen's stomach clenched. "What about their Zaheri? Aren't they—"

With a shake of his head, he calmed her. "I don't think it's Caligan danger the grovix was mentioning."

"What? Like danger from Earth?"

Tyron shrugged a response.

"So, what do we have to do?"

"We want to leave for England in four days," Tyron said timidly.

Shocked, Jen was silent for a second. "Uh, excuse me?"

"I know it's short notice—"

"It's not just short notice, it's incredibly inconvenient. Tyron, I only just got back to school."

"I know," he said, holding his hand out, trying to calm her down. "But Blaze is worried and wants us to go speak with the Beta Team. The only way to do that is to go to them."

"Why couldn't Archer just have this other grovix relay a message?"

"Well, they aren't Runners."

"Huh?"

He held up two fingers. "There are two different types of grovix. All the grovix that are part of the Zaheri are Warriors. They're built for fighting. The others are Runners. Think of them as messengers."

Sinking back a bit, Jen asked, "You want me to leave on Friday?" She then let out a small, sad chuckle. "When will I be back?"

"Monday," he said then quickly continued, "We'd go over there, make contact, let you two meet, and then be back on Sunday night or early Monday morning. I know, I know, we'd be ripping you away from your life, but Jen, you have to remember that this is your life. I know you didn't choose it, but..." He trailed off and stared at her.

Fidgeting with her hands in her lap, she tried hard not to bombard questions and comments at him.

He stilled and sat back, a defeated look crumbling his face. "I am so sorry," he said quietly as he stared at his hands.

"What?" she asked, surprised by the comment.

"You're eighteen; you should be running around town with your friends, having boyfriends, going to dances. Things like that."

She gave him a questioning look as he shook his head.

"I feel terrible that I have to deprive you of those basic things that most human teenage girls do."

"Oh." She sat back a little, and her shoulders slumped. "Well, technically, you aren't the one depriving me of that."

"Yeah, I am," he said with an assertive nod. "Because I'm the one asking you to leave it all behind."

"Tyron, no, you aren't."

Chuckling a little, he said, "I just asked you to fly to another continent that will require eight hours on a plane just to meet another kid."

Her gaze fell to her hands.

He looked toward the ceiling. "I'm not the brightest man in the world, but I know that, on some level, you do resent me. And you have every right to."

As she looked back at him, she found him staring at the floor, his eyes downcast. "I don't resent you."

"You really should," he replied as he looked over at her. "I'm the guy who marched into your life a year and a half ago and shook everything out of order. I'm the one who keeps asking you to make major decisions about your life based on my world's needs."

She shrugged. "You're only doing that because that's what your Council wants."

They were still for a few seconds, and then he blinked back at her. "How did you know that?"

"I—" She choked out a few consonants. "You seem pretty guilty. I just kinda figured." A sad chuckle left her. "Tyron, what other choice do I have?"

Her comment made him do a double-take. Then he let out a heavy sigh as he turned and stared at the wall. Getting to his feet, he took a few steps away and crossed his arms.

Jen watched his posture tighten then saw him scratch the back of his neck before he turned to her.

"What choice do you want to make?"

Jen stared back at him for a couple quiet seconds. "What do you mean?"

"I mean ..." He raised his hand then let it fall back to his side. "Elders, I can't believe I'm saying this," he whispered. "I mean, if you want to walk away, if you want to ... not be a part of this ..." Their eyes met, and Tyron felt like he was going to die if she walked away from them. He clenched his jaw and tried to hide the fact that he was scared to lose her. "I can't defy my Council, but I won't force you to be what you don't want a part of."

"Tyron, what are you saying?"

He swallowed. "That you have a choice."

Her mouth fell open.

"I'm giving you a choice."

She squinted a little. "But you're my Zaheri."

"That doesn't mean I'm going to forbid you from being human."

The option hadn't been something she had been given before. It never seemed like she had a choice. Could it really be that easy? Could she just walk away and be a human and never be what her Zaheri thought she was? Would that work? Would she be allowed to do that?

As she thought through what her life could be like if she was just a human, it seemed so easy. The choice was simple, wasn't it? Why put herself through frustration if she could just be human? But, as she thought it, something made her feel so wrong in thinking that.

It might have been because, even when she had been a child, she had known there was something different—a desire to be greater than normal. And now that she was offered the option, she found herself wanting to be what she was supposed to be. Maybe not what she wanted to be, but what she was destined to be.

Looking back at him, she asked, "Why?"

The true answer was one he didn't even admit to himself. Because, if he was honest about that, he would have to face the dark reality again. And the last time he had done that...things had not gone well. A half-truth was the best he could muster.

"Jen, we've watched you from the day you were born. We saw you carried into your house in your mom's arms. I know you haven't always seen us, but we've been there." He shifted his weight. "I can't say for the others, but...I would bet they would spare you whatever they could if they were able to. Because we care about you." He chuckled. "You're like a family member to us."

It had never been something she needed to hear. At least, she thought she never needed to hear it. His actions had spoken the volumes that his words never really could. Still, hearing that her Zaheri truly cared about her made her feel a level of comfort that she hadn't felt before. She felt safe, like somehow, no matter what might happen, things were going to be okay.

Her Zaheri weren't going to let her get hurt, at least not hurt enough for time to not heal the wounds.

"I know," she said.

"I know that you know. It was just something I noticed none of us had ever said before and ... and it needed to be said, I guess."

"If I were to be a hybrid and do what you guys needed, what would that mean?" she asked.

Picking his head up, Tyron looked over at her. "I don't know fully. I do understand that you would have to eventually find the other six Human-Borns. Because they're your team. Your responsibility is beyond my grasp, because it's not mine to under-stand. But the Agerians ... we do need you. Whether we know how greatly or not, we need you."

To hear Tyron say that they needed her seemed impossible. They were all so much more equipped, more prepared. How could they possibly need some scrawny little teenage girl to end a war?

This was something so much bigger than herself. Even if she wanted, her conscience wouldn't allow her to walk away. A whole world might rely on her. Who was she to deny that?

She nodded, and he stared at her, apprehension filling him.

If Jen decided to be human, what would the Council do? Would they demand that he bring her to Tilion, to be what she didn't want?

A part of him wanted her to run as far away as possible from her life as a Human-Born. The role that was set before her couldn't possibly be easy. If it were, anyone could do it. If it were easy, he would do it and spare her.

But then, what if Jen did decide she didn't want to be a hybrid? Where would that put Tilion? Where would that put Agerius?

Where would that put him?

"Say something," he said after minutes of silence passed.

She allowed herself a glance at him. "Something?"

He smiled a bit at her attempt at levity.

Jen shook her head. "I ... I know what I have to do. I know it because there's something in me that won't let me walk away."

He nodded and swallowed.

"What do I tell my family?" she asked.

Letting out a small breath, he told her, "The truth."

She grimaced.

"Jen, they'll have to be made aware of the situation, eventually. And the sooner we tell them, the better chance we have of them understanding our plight and trusting us."

"So, what? I'm supposed to go home tonight and say, 'Guess what? I'm going to England to find another kid like me so we can talk about how we're supposed to end another world's war?'"

"Well, I wouldn't say that last bit, but the first part was pretty much spot-on."

Jen sat back in her seat as she rubbed her hands together. "I'm just worried that I'm going to give my parents a heart attack."

"Don't be." He smiled. "Despite their initial reaction, they've taken to the truth of the matter pretty well. I mean, they don't even flinch anymore when Kaldok walks in."

Jen nodded absently.

Tyron's smile faded. "You're a real warrior, kid."

In a small voice, she asked, "What if I'm not ready?"

His heart began to break. The uncertainty in her eyes made his entire demeanor melt. His shoulders drooped as a small, sad frown came upon his face.

He came to sit next to her and put his arm around her shoulders. "Even when you feel the slightest bit of uncertainty, we'll be here. We'll always be here when you need us, Jen."

She turned her head to look at him.

"We're not going anywhere."

She nodded as she laid her head against his shoulder.

He normally wasn't good at touchy-feely times like this, but she was a teenage girl, and from what he could gather, there were times when she just needed a touch to let her know that he was telling the truth.

It sometimes made him uncomfortable, but ever since Cregorous almost took her away from him three months ago and he hugged her then, it didn't feel so bad anymore. The hug had been out of relief that she was still okay. Instinctually, he had reached for her, just to solidify that he was there, that it was going to be okay. That she wasn't alone.

It was times like those that made him realize that maybe he wasn't good at his job all the time.

But sometimes he got it just right.

Epilogue

When Cregorous appeared back on Tilion, he had found the Agerians assaulting his forces at the portal. Not wishing to allow them too much of a victory, he had pushed his whole army through a dimensional path back to Caliga and jumped himself back to his mansion once he knew the bulk of his forces were out of Agerian reach.

He had called his generals back to Caliga and awaited their return. When the last one had shown up much later than he would have preferred, he had nearly torn his head off as an example to the others that to delay would only cause for further pain.

He had then given them the command to rebuild the ranks of their warriors and leave him be.

Then he locked himself in his wing of the mansion and collapsed onto the floor, grasping his chest as though something were trying to claw its way out of him.

Resting his back against the door to his chamber, he had caught his breath and tried to clear his mind. Unable to do so, he had then marched to his liquor chest and drank himself into a slumber. As he had drifted off, he felt that perhaps once he awoke, he would feel better.

Within a few moments, he had realized that was wrong.

He found that, any time he allowed himself to sleep, he dreamed. Or rather, he had nightmares. Because each of those dreams centered around Jennifer.

And that was how the obsession had started.

He wouldn't classify it as an obsession, because that would imply that he had a problem.

And he didn't have problems.

At first, he had rationalized that the best way to make her crumble would be to find her weakness. The more he learned about her, the more he told himself it was so he could better understand his enemy and what made her tick.

So, he had devoted as much of his time as possible to memorizing her history. Or, at least what Caliga knew of it.

She was one of three, lived with both parents, had a pet cat that was ten years old, lived in a state called Pennsylvania, had six Zaheri; two of which were grovix. She was five-foot-three, weighed close to one hundred and twenty-five pounds, and hated the color pink.

He knew her favorite color was blue, knew she loved something called 'steak'. She cherished her camera more than anything and liked to take pictures of the sun, for some reason. She had named her vehicles and liked chipmunks—whatever those were. She sang beautifully and danced horribly.

He knew more than her father probably did. He knew more than her Zaheri probably did. Yet none of it made the dreams or the almost constant image of that annoying teenage girl go away. He could only assume one thing was happening to him, and it had taken him weeks to finally narrow it down, but the only thing that made sense was one thing.

She had touched him.

When she had, it was like an explosion had ripped through him. Emotions of all kinds had surged through his body. He had contained himself as he stood before her on that school roof, but inside, he had screamed. It was so physically shocking that he couldn't even stand there and finish her off, even though, at the moment, he had cursed himself for not having just ended things there.

Hatred, euphoria, despair, contentment, anger, jealousy, loneliness—they had surged through his brain; some of them recognized and others completely foreign to him. The most prominent was one he had never even felt before, but he knew what it was.

He knew because he had seen it in the eyes of his mistresses. He had seen it in the eyes of the human women when they looked at him.

It was a strong emotion, one that he felt might destroy him.

Lust.

Sure, the desire was one he was familiar with, but it wasn't one he had ever felt toward any one person, let alone some human.

Some ... child.

His body burned like hot coals had been thrown onto every inch of him. He looked at pictures that he found, and his mind went insane. The dreams were easily the worst, which was why he avoided sleeping. Frenzy-inducing, he would wake with a start, with nothing but an ache in the core of himself.

The first dream had been simple. It had been the night he had met her. The night she had touched him. It was as though his brain was trying to add to a story that didn't exist.

In the dream, he had won her over, and she had joined him, ready and willing to worship him. He had triumphed, and in the dream, it felt wonderful to know he had conquered her. He harbored the dreams and found himself wishing that had been the outcome.

But then it got worse.

The dreams became more elaborate and, eventually, took on a storybook feel. It would end and, the following night, pick back up where he had left off. He had never known fantasy induced from the mind, but now that he did, he hated it.

After he avoided sleep to attempt to keep himself sane, he realized that Jennifer wasn't just a formidable enemy, but possibly the only weakness he had ever encountered. Not a fact he would admit to any single soul. He barely even admitted it to himself.

When she had surveyed him on that roof—something everyone did—he had stared at her, took her in and, surprisingly enough, was happy with what he saw. She was strong, not just mentally or in the essence of her hybrid power. He had known that for years.

No, she was also physically strong. Her muscles tightened in exactly the right way to deflect attacks or initiate them. For her age, she was pretty enough... for a human. Within the next five years, he could only imagine what she would grow into.

But, as the fight had intensified, she had ripped into him.

At first, it had been shocking—the pain that had accompanied the massive laceration in his shoulder. It had been deep, and the blood had soaked into his shirt and down his side. It had taken two hours to heal.

Two. Hours.

Amazing.

It had hurt far more than he had ever experienced. Even as a child, in training lessons, he had never felt such pain. He had never been harmed in such a manner. And a mere child had done it.

Then, as though to make matters worse, she had grabbed his neck and started this whole nightmare. A stranglehold that some people might have been afraid of. But, even in the instant, he had been more alarmed at the strange plethora of emotions that had shocked through him. Ever since then, he hadn't been capable of getting her off his mind.

He wanted her ... *badly*.

And because of this overwhelming lust inside of him, he hadn't been capable of coherent thoughts. So, to avoid telling his army to do something inane, he locked himself away. His generals would ask what could be done to alleviate the pain he felt. They all thought that the wound that Jennifer had inflicted on him had caused lasting damage.

Cregorous let them continue to believe that.

He planned. He began to try to decipher the most terrible plans to strike at Jennifer. He blamed her for his condition. And the only way he could see to get out of the situation was to simply obliterate her.

His mind was so preoccupied that it took him much longer than normal to figure out how to punish someone.

"My Lord, is there anything that we can do?" one of his most trusted generals, Kelek, asked about three months after the attack.

Cregorous looked at him from over his shoulder, his eyes bloodshot from the lack of sleep and his body slumping against his desk in absolute exhaustion.

"Master, why don't you rest? Perhaps that may help you regain your strength."

Pinching his eyes shut in anger, Cregorous shot back, "My strength is fine. My mind is not."

"Is there nothing that can be done?"

Cregorous shook his head for a moment before he turned to his right hand. "You and Akeno call a meeting. I need to speak with them regarding some tentative plans."

Bowing, Kelek responded, "Yes, My Lord." He quickly stood then exited the chamber at a steady pace.

Cregorous glanced toward the door, and the huge double doors shut with a bang.

He had partially spoken the truth, but the real reason he had sent Kelek away was so he could have some quiet.

He moved around to his large glass like desk. On it were papers and pictures scattered about in no particular order. He allowed himself to sit down and pick up a picture of Jennifer closest to him.

What was it about her? She wasn't that remarkable. Yes, she was powerful, but not on the level that he was. Not in the slightest. She was too afraid of her energy, and that would be her downfall. He had known that the moment they had started fighting.

But why?

It was getting absurd to have his brain devote this much time to one person, let alone the one person who was going to try, and would fail, to destroy him.

He sat back in the chair and closed his eyes, hoping to gain concentration for a moment on what he needed to do...

He threw her backward with an energy attack as he tightened his grip on the Seventh Human-Born. Kelek had been right; the boy might be strong, but he wasn't a match for him.

As the Seventh gasped out his breaths and clawed at his arm, Cregorous smirked at Jennifer.

She glared back at him, heaving air into her tired body. "Let him go," she demanded.

With a laugh, he dangled the boy, whose fighting faltered. "Maybe a trade? Give me what I want, and I'll drop him."

The boy gritted his teeth and forced through his gasps, "Don't."

Jennifer glanced to the Seventh with a look of worry, and Cregorous glared at her.

"It's almost you and me. This child," he spat as he jostled the Seventh, who gagged out strangled noises at the action, "is all that's left. Do you really not believe that I'll kill him?"

"I swear to God!" Jen spat.

"Swear to me!" Cregorous hollered. "I am your god," he bellowed, letting his energy surge through him, scorching the boy's throat. His eyes filled with his red energy.

She yelled and pulled her arms back, forcing the boy to fly from Cregorous' grasp. Jennifer caught the Seventh and spun on her heel in time to throw a shield up to protect them as Cregorous assaulted her with his red energy.

"This fight has gone on long enough!" Cregorous yelled above the clamor of their energies.

When she pushed a blue attack at him, he dodged to miss and she snatched one of the fallen Zaheri's weapons, swinging it at him.

He pushed the blade aside and yelled, "Haven't you lost enough?"

"Not anymore!" she hollered back, landing a punch on his chest that sent him skittering backward. "I refuse to let you take everything."

He straightened and forced his ribs to heal. Then, with a grin, he warned, "Last chance."

"Never," she said.

Cregorous raised his brow. "Very well." He then snapped his fingers, and a dome of darkness swallowed the boy.

Jennifer spun around and screamed, "No!" as she ran back the short distance.

Cregorous raised his right hand and caught her, forcing her to fly backward toward him. As she landed on the ground, she tried to claw her way out of Cregorous' hold back to the Seventh.

Another few seconds passed as she struggled before the darkness lifted slowly. Then Cregorous released his telekinetic hold on her legs, and she immediately bolted for the Seventh Human-Born.

"Fitting, I think," Cregorous spat as she took the Seventh's lifeless body into her arms, "how the Elders let them die, so I've let all of you die."

She looked over at him with tears rolling down her face. "You're a monster."

"And I told you this would happen," he shot back angrily, pointing a finger at her. "I told you that if you denied me, I would bring hell. And I have." Seething, he pulled his arm toward him and brought her flying into his grasp. Pinning her against him, he growled, "Now, what will it be?"

Glaring back at him, she tried to push away, but his grip wouldn't relent. "I hate you," she said through gritted teeth.

"I hate you, too," he said simply before he moved a hand to the back of her head and let his lips crash down on hers.

He opened his eyes, his breathing ragged. Then a growl came from him as he stared down at the picture of her in his clenched hand. His eyes flashed red, and the picture burst into flames.

He angrily pushed the chair back and stood, walking over to one of the massive windows of his chamber. Glaring at the night around him, he half-heartedly punched the glass. He had no idea how to solve the problem that had presented itself to him.

For the first time in his life, he felt completely lost.

Glossary

Creatures

Creatures Listed in Alphabetical Order

BRATAK'RA

Four-legged, large creatures, normally around the size of a horse, sometimes smaller, with large horns that adorn their necks and heads. Occasionally, the more powerful bratak'ra have spikes that jut out from their joints. They usually have short ears (think cropped ears on a pitbull), though some have larger ears. Their snouts are typically tall and broad. They have massive paws and always have their claws visible. Many have teeth that jut out of their maw and are visible when they close their mouths. They look naturally horrid, with yellow eyes and small slits for an iris. They have course fur that's rough to touch. Bratak'ra can talk, and their language is limited. The older a bratak'ra is, the more horns they have. Young ones without horns are called bratak. They earn the 'ra to the end of the name once they gain horns.

Mono-horned gain horns at the crest of their head that sits behind their ears. The horns typically wrap around their skulls and reach past their jaws. Sometimes they don't wrap down and around the skull, sometimes they pull sideways from the head (kind of splay away from the sides of the face).

Dual-horned ones wind up with the equivalent of split horns. The second "set" follow along the cheekbones, while the bottom set sit around the lower jaw.

When a bratak'ra gains a new set of horns, their first set falls off, much like deer. The difference being that bratak'ra horns are very strong and durable, and only fall off when a new set is going to be formed. Bratak'ra gain new horns when the pack needs higher ranked members. It's unknown who or how the bratak'ra choose which ones among them should be given a higher rank. The point behind additional horns is that they provide more opportunities for impalements and ripping of enemies and prey.

FERVEOS

Caligan Dragons. They are compatible in height and general size to Preliators of Agerius. Ferveos, however, have darker scale colors. Their main colors are black, gray, and dark brown. These dragons are less intelligent than Preliators and Scouts. They follow blind commands and will not think for themselves while on the battlefield. They will attack anything they deem a threat to them, so they sometimes turn on their own. Ferveos don't normally speak. In fact, it's uncommon for one to know how to speak, let alone be eloquent when they do.

⅊YBRID

Part-human, part-dragon creatures. We would call them dragonborn. They resemble humans to every extent and can walk among humans undetected. Their wings can reabsorb into their body, the skeletal structure folding into their back. Every hybrid has powers similar to telekinesis and rapid cellular regeneration. Most hybrids, through their telekinetic powers, control raw energy powers that are used as their defense or offense. Each hybrid has varying degrees of strength, and there have been rare cases of hybrids born without the ability to conjure energy. Depending on its use, the energy can take forms of orbs, lightning, shields, or whips, to name a few. Due to their cellular regeneration, they live far longer than humans.

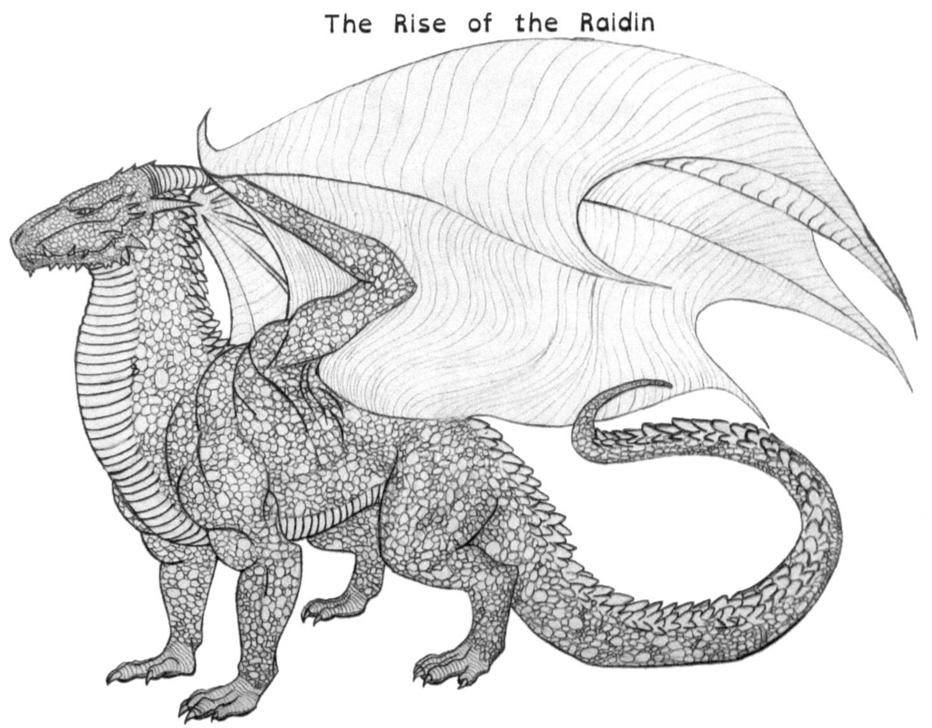

PRELIATOR

Agerian Dragons. Large dragons. Their size varies between fourteen to fifteen feet tall with their length being as long as twenty-five feet. They are four-legged, have wings, and long whipping tails. They all breathe fire. Their hides are thick; first covered in scales then a fairly substantial thick skin, followed by a thick layer of fat. The colors of Preliators are deep and rustic browns, slight greens, hushed blues, golds, bronzes, etc. A Preliators' cry is low and deep, and when they roar, the sound is like a lion's roar and an inferno as their ability to breathe fire affects how they sound. They don't normally speak, although they do have the ability. They are incredibly intelligent, so don't let their silence fool you.

WARRIOR GROVIX

The *more populated build* for common grovix. They are built with *muscle* adorning their bodies and are excellent at combat. They are good for short sprints and leaping on top of enemies, relying mostly on their weight to cause damage before using their claws and teeth. They have strong bones and even stronger jaws. Their crushing strength is immense, and they can easily take down a Bratak'ra so long as they avoid the horns. Prone to wearing armor in combat, they are easily distinguishable on a battle-field against werewolves and bratak'ra.

ℬEREWOLF

Little is known of how werewolves came to be, or what the specifics are that make their bites contagious. Werewolves on Tilion don't have the curse merely attack them during the full moon, rather all the time. Once bitten and consumed by the disease, the creatures lose all semblance of themselves and their individuality. There has only ever been one hybrid to survive the bite and retain his sense of self.

Places

TILION

Another world that is linked to Earth specifically. The two worlds share a portal that connects them, but neither place holds links to other worlds aside from the other. So far, all we know is that it's the world where Agerians and Caligans come from. There appears to be ruins of old towns throughout the world.

The portal to Tilion can only be activated by hybrids. As humans cannot manifest raw energy, neither can they produce enough strength to even view the portal in its inactive form.

AGERIUS

The nation all of the Zaheri come from. It's moreso a city than a nation by all appearances. But there's no doubt that the city would require months to explore all the little alleyways and courtyards. Its mountain acts as a natural barrier, and houses the High Council, Infirmary, Guard Quarters, and Archives. They follow the barter system, allowing citizens to haggle for reasonable prices based on what's being traded.

ALIGA

The opposing nation of Tilion, where Cregorous and his generals come from. The layout, political system, even the location of Caliga is a complete unknown for Agerius. There's no telling how far away it is, or how it functions. It's assumed that Cregorous runs the nation as a tyrant, but that's just speculation. No one in Ageirus would dare to travel in search of Caliga, as no one would be able to stand up against Cregorous on their own.

Groups

IGH OUNCIL

A group of approximately forty members of Agerius' oldest and wisest citizens. Made up of hybrids and grovix alike, they govern laws for the Agerians to follow. They are not the highest level of government in Agerius, merely the most accessible to the people.

AHERI

A grouping of thirty or so of the Agerian army's best fighters, once termed as "The Elite." But, since Jennifer Monroe's birth, they have been known otherwise as the Zaheri. They were charged with the protection and training of the Seven Human-Born hybrids.

The RISE Of The RAIDIN

Cast
of
Characters

Listed Alphabetically

Aeryn Knight

Jen's best friend since elementary school. Aeryn is quiet and calm in almost every situation. But the moment someone she cherishes is threatened or bullied, she gains a ferocity all her own. Sweet and endearing, she exudes a serenity that infects whatever room she walks into. Years of slumber parties and random car rides with Jen have awarded Aeryn the unique ability to read Jen's needs quicker than most. On very rare occasions, can work up the nerve to snap defensive comments at someone else.

Archer

Warrior grovix assigned to the Alpha Team and ensure the protection and training of Jennifer Monroe. Essentially a large dog, Archer exhibits many 'pup' qualities. Occasional hyperactiveness, rash decision making, and a bull-in-a-china-shop sort of movement. Despite this, he is a prime example of a solid Warrior grovix. His build is lean and strong. His snarl could make a bear pause in mid-charge. He's ferocious when in battle and gentle when Jen reaches out to pet him. Standing at five-feet tall at the crest of his head, Archer is intimidating upon first blush. Upon speaking with him, you will discover that 'pup' mentality isn't a fable the Alpha Team has made up. Do not threaten his team if you value your life. And do not look wrong at his Alpha unless you want him to remind you exactly how strong he is.

Ar'on

"The Grumpy One" as Krelien likes to call him. The eldest of the Alpha Team (sans Blaze). Gruff and imposing. Ar'on has all of the sunny disposition of a crotchety old neighbor that yells at the kids to get off the grass. Quick to remind anyone within earshot of the proper way to do things, Ar'on has gained a reputation for being a "stick in the river" (according to Krelien). His resting expression is on par with Grumpy Cat, and strangers quickly will divert to the other side of the street—or in some cases, other aisles in the grocery store.

Blaze

She may look like a beautiful creature that wants all the pets, but she would sooner bite your hand and snap a well articulated insult at you. Graceful and poised, Blaze demands respect and attention. If you don't offer both, you would do well to flee. Fast. Her memory is long and her gaze sees everything. If you meet her on a battlefield, something terrible has happened and you should fear for your safety. The only person she extends grace toward without question is Jen. She has great respect for Tyron, Ar'on, and Kaldok for their accolades and accomplishments. Archer has gained her favor and in many ways, her admiration. She tolerates Krelien.

Grant Connolly

One of Jennifer Monroe's dearest friends. The boy who greatly desires to be a man. Grant strives to rise to challenges, but often can be found fumbling to solutions. Because he's a handsome young man, he's automatically been considered one of the 'popular' boys in school. However, he shies away from such attention, and prefers instead to veer toward quieter individuals. He is, for all intents and purposes, the "crush" of the story for our protagonist.

Jennifer Monroe

Our protagonist, Jen is head-strong and cocky. Assured in herself and her abilities, she would eagerly engage in dangerous situations because she deems herself ready. Though she holds a fair deal of respect for her Zaheri, she wishes in many ways that they would give her more leeway in her training and allow her to test her limits. Happy to be in the background and forgotten by her fellow classmates, she sticks close to her friends. An avid photographer, she hopes to one day work for National Geographic and get to travel the world.

Jon Alderfer

The head principal of South Ridge High School. In charge of a vast student body, he knowns how to handle challenging situations. With a background in the military that saw him pursuing a teaching career once he was discharged, he feels he's seen everything. A level-headed individual and quick with a smile, Jon has earned a sparkling reputation among the student body and the faculty of South Ridge. He's among the first to participate in student-led events, and will engage with students as much as possible.

Kaldok

If you ever wanted to see the definition of calm and serene, it would be Kaldok...If not for his appearance. Kaldok is the only known survivor of the Werewolf Curse, having retained the fullness of his personality despite being bitten many years ago. He's quick with a smile and a hug, and trims his claws often to ensure he never hurts someone. Slow to speak, always thinking through his responses to situations, he's the center of the team whether he intended to be or not. The extent of his curse as a werewolf isn't fully known, and he keeps much of it hidden.

Krelien

A self-described "ray of moon-shine", Krelien brings equal doses of laughter and frustration to those around him every single day. As if he's been stuck at the age of twelve, he finds stupid things funny, and latches onto whatever sounds like it'll make people think he's cool and "with the timex". If you asked him who his best friend is, he would quickly say it's Kaldok. The werewolf may agree. Maybe.

Krelien is a Jumper, and little is known of how his ability works. Only that he is capable of traversing great distances in a seeming blink of an eye. He is very choosy with helping others and allowing them to take advantage of his gift.

Nancy Monroe

The baby of the Monroe family, Nancy is a bright-eyed sophomore at South Ridge High. She's like most younger teenage girls, and enjoys spending her days free from homework whenever possible. Fiercely loyal and loving to her elder sister, she can feel left out and left behind if not fully up to date on what Jen is doing. With Jen shying away from makeup and dresses and frills, Nancy often has to figure things out for herself when it comes to fashion. Though she routinely will still go to her sister for advice (just in case). Clever and smart, she works hard at her schoolwork and strives to do well at whatever she's tasked with.

Ryan Bender

Witty and charming, Ryan is the straight A student that can have the class understanding difficult concepts just as easily as he'll have them laughing. Universally liked by his classmates, he chooses to keep his friend circle small. Though he can be found at parties and hangouts across town, he gives a superficial friendship to all but a few. He's always had a soft spot for Jen, and low-key envies her invisibility among the student population. He's quick with a joke and quicker with support to his friends.

Tyron

Well trained and dedicated to his task, Tyron won't let anything get in his way. He's sure to stand firm against any opposition. He strikes a level of fear into others who don't know him and commands a room with relative ease. Little scares him. He fights with the knowledge that if he fails, others likely will die. And that's unacceptable to him. He's seen enough of life to know what's worth fighting for and what's not. A little unaware of social norms, he frequently has praise or adoration fly straight over his head.

Thank you so much for reading *The Rise of the Raidin!* I hope you enjoyed the first installment of *The Human-Born Era.* I would absolutely love to hear your thoughts on *Rise.* Reviews are the lifeblood of Indie Authors, and I would be absolutely honored if you would take a moment or two to hop onto Amazon or Goodreads to let people know what you thought of this book.

I truly cannot thank you enough for giving this pentalogy a chance to go "into the wild". These characters are near and dear to my heart, and I am genuinely amazed that people have embraced them and welcomed them into their hearts (and the books onto their bookshelves).

If you enjoyed *Rise,* please consider signing up for my website's newsletter, or follow me on social media (I'm most active on Instagram, but you can find me on several platforms).

And if you liked seeing a dyslexic friendly version of *The Rise of the Raidin,* let other authors and publishers know! Share this edition with friends, libraries, schools, whoever will listen! Let's work together to make Dyslexic Friendly versions of books become a norm.

Again, thank you! I look forward to hearing your thoughts on the world of Tilion!

About the Author

Susan L. Markloff was born in June of 1988. As a baby, all the neighbors would marvel as she stayed ardently on a blanket in the back yard, never straying into the vast openness of the world. They would ask her mom, "How did you get her to stay on the blanket?"

Her mom would reply that she didn't have to do anything special: Susan hated grass.

Somewhere in elementary school, Susan learned that grass wasn't so bad and quickly began to explore as far as she was allowed, culminating in a life filled with travel. From the East to West Coast, Ireland to Italy, Canada to Puerto Rico, Susan knows where her passport is and eagerly looks for her next adventure that will lead her to an unexplored corner of the world.

When she isn't writing yet another side-story or character backstory, or thinking about how people traveled in Ancient Tilion, Susan can often be found packing her car (and sometimes her dog, lodging permitting), for another excursion or visit to a friend. Or planning another trip to Disney World (yes, she is a small child). Or hiking with her trusty camera.